The Leaving of Liverpool

Maureen Lee

First published in Great Britain in 2007 by Orion,
an imprint of the Orion Publishing Group Ltd.

A CIP catalogue record for this book
is available from the British Library.

Typeset by Deltatype Ltd, Birkenhead, Merseyside

Set in Bembo

Printed and bound in the UK by
CPI Mackays, Chatham ME5 8TD

The Orion Publishing Group's policy is to use papers that
are natural, renewable and recyclable products and made
from wood grown in sustainable forests. The logging and
manufacturing processes are expected to conform to the
environmental regulations of the country of origin.

The Orion Publishing Group Ltd
Orion House
5 Upper St Martin's Lane
London WC2H 9EA

www.orionbooks.co.uk

For Liverpool, my home town.

So fare thee well, my own true love
When I return united we will be.
It's not the leaving of Liverpool that grieves me,
But my darling when I think of thee.

Author unknown

The Leaving of Liverpool

were two bottles of Digitalis in the washbag on the top of the suitcase, which was making Mollie's shoulder ache. It was stuffed with clothes, every single garment she and Annemarie possessed, all packed in the last sixty minutes so no one would see and wonder what they were up to. Clothes might cost the earth in America and it would be a shame to leave them behind.

There was a light on in Sinead Larkin's cottage. Sinead was a dressmaker and women came from as far away as Kildare to order their bridal gowns and bridesmaids' frocks, not to mention the occasional pageboy outfit. She made all Mollie and Annemarie's clothes, as well as Mammy's when she was alive. Mollie imagined the tiny dressmaker treadling away like a mad woman while she fed yards of glorious silk or satin under the flashing needle of her Singer sewing machine.

She breathed a sigh of relief and changed the suitcase to her other hand when they left the environs of the village. Ahead lay a narrow country lane with hedges on either side, the icy surface gleaming like a silver ribbon in the moonlight. About half a mile on, the land curved to the left and Mollie knew that when they rounded the curve, they would come to her brother Finn's house. Finn was an accountant, away in Dublin on business at the moment, and it was his wife, Hazel, who was helping Mollie and Annemarie escape from the horror of Duneathly.

The suitcase was getting heavier and heavier: Mollie had to resist the urge to open it and fling half the clothes into the hedge. She breathed another sigh of relief when, at last, Finn's house came into view.

'Nearly there, Annemarie,' she said encouragingly.

The garden gate creaked when it was opened and, barely a second later, Hazel flung open the front door. 'You're here! I've been listening for the gate.' She ran down the path and kissed them warmly. 'Come on in, the pair o'yis. I've tea on the brew.'

Mollie put the suitcase down with a puff. 'I'll swear both me arms are at least six inches longer.'

'And so they are.' Hazel laughed. She was tall and boisterous, brown-haired and brown-eyed, and graceful, despite the huge,

3

bulging stomach in which the Doctor's first grandchild lay. She clapped her hand to her mouth. 'I should be crying, not laughing. This is a tragedy, not a joke.'

The girls followed their sister-in-law into the cosy kitchen where the table was set with three cups and saucers, sugar and milk, and a teapot covered with the cosy Mollie had knitted as a present a year ago when Hazel and Finn married. She hadn't liked Hazel at first. She was too big, too bossy, too capable. She knew the best way of doing everything and didn't hesitate to tell people what it was. The Doctor loathed her. Perhaps it was this that had made Mollie look for Hazel's good side. It wasn't hard to find, for her brother's wife was also generous to a fault, always ready to lend a hand when it was needed, and possessed of an incredibly kind heart.

It was to Hazel that Mollie had turned when the 'thing' happened three weeks ago. 'I need to get our Annemarie away from the Doctor. I'd like us to go to America: New York,' she'd told her. 'We've an auntie there, Aunt Maggie, Mammy's sister. She's a schoolteacher and we used to see a lot of her before she went away. She still writes to us every month. Aunt Maggie will take care of us, I know she will.'

'But you'll need passports,' Hazel pointed out. 'You won't get into America without a passport.'

'We've already got them. You won't know, it happened before you met our Finn, but Mammy was planning to take me and Annemarie to see Aunt Maggie. Then she fell pregnant and didn't feel well enough to travel.' It had been disappointing at the time, but worse was to come: before the year was out, their beloved Mammy had died giving birth to her fifth child, Aidan.

'But what's this all about, Mollie, luv?' Hazel had asked, looking puzzled, as if the import of Mollie's words had only just sunk in. 'What do you mean, you have to get Annemarie away from the Doctor?'

And so Mollie was left with no choice but to explain, the words coming out haltingly with many pauses and ending in floods of tears.

4

Hazel had gone deathly pale, too shocked to speak, until she said in a horrified voice, 'You mean your father . . . ' She paused, unable to finish the sentence, then tried again. 'You mean your father raped his thirteen-year-old daughter?'

Mollie nodded. Hearing it put so bluntly, yet so truthfully, only made her cry again. 'Yes,' she whispered.

'Has he ever done it before?'

'Not to Annemarie, no.' She bit her lip. It was the wrong thing to say.

'By that,' Hazel said quietly, going even paler, 'I take it he's done it to you?'

'Every month. He goes to Kildare to meet up with his old friends from university and comes home as drunk as a lord. It started right after Mammy passed away.' Mollie shrugged. 'I just close my eyes and pretend it's not happening, but our Annemarie's different, she's not of this world.' She began to cry again. 'It's all my fault. I stayed at Noreen, my friend's house, to avoid him. I never dreamed he'd do it to Annemarie if I wasn't there.'

At this, Hazel had leapt to her feet. '*I'll* stop him,' she screamed. 'I'll give the bastard what for, and I'll tell Finn, I'll tell the whole of Duneathly and report him to the medical board, wherever that may be. Not a soul will ever go near him again.'

'*No*! There's Thaddy and little Aidan to consider. What will happen to them if he loses his job?' Once again her eyes had filled with tears at the idea of leaving her brothers behind, but she had to get Annemarie away. If the truth be known, she was anxious to escape her father herself.

'It doesn't seem right to let him get away with it,' Hazel had muttered, but she'd given in, said she'd find out when the next boat sailed from Liverpool to New York and where to buy the tickets. Mollie had enough money, for hadn't Mammy left her – left all her children apart from Aidan – a whole fifty pounds each when they reached the age of sixteen? Until last July, Finn had been the only one to see the money, but Mollie had received a letter from Mr O'Rourke, the solicitor, on her sixteenth birthday. Much against his advice, she had asked for her inheritance in cash.

She didn't want it putting in a bank where she'd have a job getting her hands on it in an emergency. It had been a wise decision, for it had seemed no time since she'd laid the fifty pound-notes beneath her gloves in the drawer when an emergency *had* arisen.

Hazel said now, 'Jimmy Mullen should be along any minute. Drink your tea quickly. It'll be a long while before you have another.' She regarded the silent, dead-eyed Annemarie tenderly. 'Come along, darlin', finish your tea.' The girl obediently picked up her cup. 'Has she lost the power of speech?' Hazel asked.

'Almost. Sister Francis came round from the convent, wanting to know if she'd taken a vow of silence: Annemarie had always been one of her best pupils. Before . . . before *it* happened, she never shut up.'

'Ah, and don't I know it. A proper little chatterbox she was, and if she wasn't talking, then she was singing – or dancing,' Hazel sighed. She turned her gaze on Mollie. 'You'll write the minute you get there, won't you, Moll? A postcard'll do, so's I know you're all right, otherwise I'll worry meself to death over the pair o'yis.'

'You're not to worry, not in your condition,' Mollie said sternly. She pulled her woolly hat over her ears, re-wound her scarf around her neck, and reached for her gloves, while Hazel helped Annemarie do the same. 'We'll be fine.'

'Will your Aunt Maggie be there to meet you?'

'Only if she gets my letter in time. If not, I'll take a taxi to her house: I've plenty of money.' By some miracle, a ship, the *Queen Maia*, was due to sail from Liverpool the day after tomorrow, arriving in New York in ten days' time. Hazel had purchased two third-class tickets through a shipping agent in Kildare. They were tucked in Mollie's bag, along with their birth certificates and the letters Aunt Maggie had sent over the years and Mollie had kept, to prove they had somewhere to stay and wouldn't be a burden on the State.

There was silence in the warm, comfortable kitchen. In the distance, Mollie could hear the sound of hooves on the icy road.

Jimmy Mullen, whom she'd never met, was taking them to Dun Laoghaire on his vegetable cart. They would catch the midday ferry to Liverpool from there. In a few hours, all hell would break loose in Dr Kenny's house when it was discovered his girls were missing, but no one was likely to guess they were on their way to America. The reason they weren't travelling to Dun Laoghaire on the bus and the train like ordinary people was so there'd be no trace of their departure. The doctor's girls would simply have disappeared into thin air. Jimmy Mullen didn't know what day it was, so there was no chance of him cracking on.

Hazel's brown eyes misted with tears. 'Look after yourselves, won't you? I'll be thinking about the pair o'yis all the while.'

'Do I need to pay Jimmy?'

'It's already been seen to, Moll.'

The gate creaked, followed by a knock on the door. She threw her arms around the ample body of her sister-in-law. ''Bye, Hazel. Thank you for everything.'

''Bye, darlin'.' Tears were streaming down Hazel's rosy cheeks. ''Bye, Annemarie.'

They all trooped outside. Jimmy Mullen, not much older than Mollie and half a head shorter, was climbing back on to a cart laden with sacks of vegetables. He acknowledged the girls with a curt nod when they joined him on the wooden seat, cracked the whip, and they set off at a brisk pace, Hazel's cries of 'tara' and 'look after yourselves now' gradually fading, until they could hear nothing except the clip-clop of the giant black horse and its occasional noisy sniff.

The moon continued to shine and the stars to twinkle. The ice became thicker and the air even colder, as Mollie and Annemarie Kenny began the first part of their journey to New York.

Mollie helped her sister on to the top bunk and tucked the bedding around her – she'd like to bet the first- and second-class cabins didn't have such coarse sheets and hard pillows. Despite this, Annemarie promptly fell asleep.

Mollie dragged off her own clothes, replacing them with a

7

thick, winceyette nightie, and climbed on to the bunk opposite her sister. Clothes had been thrown on the lower bunks, indicating they'd been taken, but there was no sign of their occupants. Anyway the tops ones were best, as you wouldn't have someone's bottom right in front of your eyes when they used the lavatory between the bunks. Her heart had sunk to her boots when she first entered the cabin and saw it. She hadn't expected to use the lavatory in front of strangers. A dim light, barely enough to see by, illuminated the dismal scene.

She was so tired she expected, like Annemarie, to fall asleep immediately. After all, they hadn't slept a wink the night before, sitting on the cart, stamping their feet to stop them from turning into blocks of ice, cuddling up to each other in a vain effort to keep warm. They'd arrived in Dun Laoghaire, more dead than alive, and had spent the next two hours in a café drinking endless cups of hot tea until they began to feel almost human again.

They had emerged to find a piercing wind had arisen, and the waters of the Irish Sea were spuming and frothing angrily when they boarded the ferry to Liverpool. Mollie had been looking forward to a restful journey, an opportunity to catch up on their sleep, but Annemarie had been sick the whole way and most of their time had been spent in the lavatory with her sister's head buried in a sink. She prayed the same thing wouldn't happen on the passage to New York.

When sleep refused to come now, she beat the pillow with her fist in an attempt to make it softer, but it had no effect. She did her best to think about nothing. When that didn't work, she tried counting sheep, but that was no good either.

She wondered what the time was. It had been just after 5 p.m. when they'd landed in Liverpool. By then it was dark and the piercing wind had become a howling gale. The *Queen Maia* was moored by the landing stage, Mollie was told: they could board whenever they pleased. They did not set sail until the next afternoon. The landing stage was a short walk along a busy road crammed with horses and carts and hundreds of people of all different colours speaking strange languages she'd never heard before. Annemarie lagged behind, as pale as a ghost, while the icy wind penetrated their thick coats, and blew up their skirts and down their necks, making their eyes water and their ears ache. Mollie allowed her imagination to stretch ahead to when they would be living with Aunt Maggie in her apartment in Greenwich Village, 'no distance from Washington Square', according to one of her letters.

The *Queen Maia*, a great white vessel with three funnels, had rows and rows of portholes like little, black eyes that stared at them balefully. Annemarie had uttered a little, fearful cry and Mollie put her arm around her thin shoulders.

'It's all right, sis. It's only a ship.' She produced their tickets and passports, surrendered the suitcase to be delivered to their cabin, and was directed towards a gangplank level with the dock.

The floodlit quayside was frantically busy. Food was being taken on to another part of the ship: bags of flour and crates of wine, sides of beef and trays of leafy vegetables. Trolleys were pushed at a demonic speed, a giant crane transferred cargo to the hold, and people rushed to and fro – aimlessly, as far as she could see. An extremely elegant lady clad in white fur was negotiating a gangplank leading to the upper part of the ship, followed by a uniformed man carrying an assortment of parcels. There seemed to be an awful lot of unnecessary screaming and shouting.

A steward showed them to their cabin along a maze of narrow corridors, the motion of the boat gentle, almost soothing, considering the fierceness of the weather. Their suitcase was waiting for them.

The first, possibly worst, part of the journey was over, thought Mollie now as she lay in the bunk, tired out of her wits, but unable to sleep, having counted so many sheep she never wanted to see another for the rest of her life. Music came from some distant part of the ship. 'I'm just wild about Harry,' a woman was singing.

She pulled the clothes over her head when one of their fellow travellers came in, undressed, and used the lavatory with a great deal of grunting followed by a horrible smell. The bunk below creaked when she got in.

The other passenger arrived in what could have been hours later or might only have been minutes: Mollie's head was swirling with clouds of tiredness and she couldn't tell. A guttural voice from down below said, 'I see you on deck with man. Is it what you do for living, get paid to go with man? Is why you go to America?'

'Mind your own business, you nosy German cow. You're only jealous 'cos no man'd go with you for a hundred quid.'

Mollie opened one eye. The light would appear to be permanently on and she saw a young woman with a pretty, heart-shaped face and bright yellow hair wearing a little cocked hat with a bent feather and a partially bald fur cape. With a series of dramatic gestures, she removed the hat and cape, kicked off her shoes, undid the buttons of her satin blouse and slipped out of a black silky skirt that was much too thin for the wintry weather, then slid into bed in her petticoat, leaving the clothes on the floor.

'Tomorrow, I report you to steward. Why you got no luggage? You not should be in cabin, you belong in steerage with immigrants.'

'Oh, shurrup, Gertie. You're keeping me awake.'

'My name is Gertrude Strauss, *Miss* Gertrude Strauss.'

'Nighty-night, *Gertie*.'

From then on, there was silence in the cabin, until Gertie began to snore, by which time Mollie had, at last, fallen asleep.

When she woke, a murky light was visible through the porthole, which was too high to see out of. Annemarie was dead to the world and the yellow-haired girl, already dressed, was sitting on the opposite lower bunk filing her stubby red nails. She smiled when she saw Mollie looking down on her. 'Oh, hello,' she said cheerily. 'You're awake. I'm Olive Raines from Deptford in London. Who are you and where are you from?'

'Mollie Kenny. I'm from County Kildare in Ireland. That's my sister, Annemarie, in the bed over yours.'

'Annemarie's a pretty name – and she looks pretty, too. Such lovely-coloured hair, sort of blue–black. What colour eyes has she got?'

'Violet, and her hair almost reaches her waist. Everyone admires it.'

'Really! Mind you,' she added, almost as an afterthought, 'you're quite pretty, too.'

'Not as much as Annemarie.' Mollie, with her ordinary brown hair, ordinary brown eyes, and a face that was often described as 'interesting', had always known that she didn't hold a candle to her beautiful sister. She lowered her head over the side of her bunk to introduce herself to Gertie, but the bed underneath was empty.

'Miss Strauss has gone for a walk before breakfast.' Olive rolled her eyes in an exaggerated fashion. 'Have you met her yet?'

'No, but I heard her come in last night. I heard you, too.'

'Did you hear what she said?'

'Yes.' Mollie had known what Gertie had meant when she accused Olive of being paid to go with men. There was a woman who lived in a cottage just outside Duneathly who made her living the same way. Her name was Eileen. None of the women would speak to her and she never went to Mass – perhaps she didn't dare. She'd often wondered why the Doctor hadn't gone to Eileen, but perhaps he was worried his reputation would suffer and he'd sooner inflict himself on his daughters.

'Oh, well.' Olive gave her an arch look. 'A girl has to earn a few bob the best way she can. What way do you earn a few bob, Mollie?'

'I've never worked, not properly. My mammy wanted me to stay at school till I was sixteen and train for a career like my brother, Finn, but she died almost two years ago and I left to look after the Doctor and Annemarie and my two little brothers.' It wasn't as arduous as it sounded. Fran Kincaid came in daily to do the heavy work and Nanny, who'd looked after all the children from Finn downwards, took care of Thaddy and Aidan. Mollie's main tasks had been to see to the meals, act as receptionist for the Doctor, and keep his records up to date.

'The Doctor?' Olive raised her arched black eyebrows, which were about an inch higher than eyebrows normally were. The roots of her blonde hair were dark brown.

'My father,' Mollie said abruptly.

'That's a strange way to refer to your pa – the Doctor. Anyway, Mollie,' she put the nail file in a worn leather handbag, 'would you mind looking the other way for a mo while I use the lavvy?'

Mollie disappeared under the clothes until Olive had finished, then requested she do the same for her. Afterwards, she got washed in the little corner sink, put on her clothes, twisted her hair into a thick plait, yanked it over her shoulder, and tied the end with a blue ribbon. 'What time's breakfast?' she asked as she laced up her boots.

'Between eight and ten.' Olive was in the process of painting her lips vivid scarlet with the aid of a hand mirror. 'Don't ask me what time it is now, because I've no idea, though there's plenty of people about so I reckon it must have gone eight.' As she spoke, there were footsteps in the corridor outside accompanied by a child's excited laughter. 'How long are you staying in New York, Mollie?'

'We're going to live there with our Aunt Maggie in Greenwich Village,' Mollie said shortly.

'What about the Doctor – your pa? Don't he mind? I mean, who'll look after him now you've gone?'

'The Doctor doesn't mind, no, and he'll soon find someone else to look after him.'

Olive's eyes narrowed. 'You're running away, aren't you? That's real spunky of you, Mollie. I've known people who've run away before, but never as far as America.'

There seemed no point in denying it, so Mollie didn't bother. 'What about you? Are you running away, too?' Last night Gertie – Miss Strauss – had said Olive should be travelling steerage with the immigrants.

'Me? No, I'm eighteen years old and off to start a new career on the stage. I can sing and dance, but haven't had much luck so far.' She stood and kicked her leg so high it was almost level with her shoulder. 'I bet you can't do that.'

'Indeed I can't,' Mollie admitted.

Olive smirked. 'I'm going to change me name to Rosalind Raines. It sounds better than Olive. Eh, what about your sister? I take it she's getting up today?'

'I'll leave her to wake up of her own accord. We had no sleep the night before last and she was sick on the ferry from Ireland. She's probably worn out.'

'And you're not, I suppose! Well, I'll love you and leave you, Mollie. It's so stuffy in here, I can hardly breathe. Tata.' She left with a cheerful wave, slamming the cabin door and waking Annemarie, who groaned, sat up, and began to retch so hard that Mollie was worried she'd crack a rib. She grabbed a towel and held it over her sister's face, but it was so long since either of them had eaten that there was no food left to bring up.

'There, there, darlin',' she said softly, and began to wonder if going to New York was turning out to be a great big mistake. In her present state, Annemarie wasn't up to the long voyage cross the Atlantic. They might be better off in Liverpool until she felt better, but the Doctor might suspect they'd come this far when he could find no trace of them in Ireland. He knew people in the city, other doctors, with whom he corresponded.

She bit her lip. Perhaps the best thing was to stay on the boat. Annemarie might improve once she got used to it and the sooner they got to New York – and dear Aunt Maggie – the better.

Her sister was asleep again, her head falling forward until it almost touched her knees. Mollie gently laid her down. It was hard to imagine this was the same, vivacious girl with whom she'd shared her life since she was born. Even Mammy's death hadn't dampened Annemarie's high spirits for long. She'd used to pretend their mother was still there; had brought her home wild flowers from the fields to put on the kitchen window-sill; had drawn pictures, sung for her, convinced that, wherever she was,

Mammy could see and hear. Her sister had lit up the Doctor's house with her bright eyes and infectious laughter. But now she lay on the bed like a corpse.

All of a sudden, Mollie felt quite overwhelmed by their situation. She was sixteen, used to coping, particularly since Mammy died, but now everything was getting beyond her. The last few weeks, since the 'thing' had happened, had been nightmarish. But she wouldn't cry. She rubbed her cheeks with her knuckles, willing away the tears that threatened to fall.

'I'll have some breakfast, a hot drink,' she said aloud. 'It'll do me the world of good.' She felt guilty for leaving her sister on her own, but if she didn't have something to eat soon, she'd become ill herself and that would never do.

It was cold on deck, but the wind had died down, the sun was out, and it was a tonic to breathe in the fresh, salty air. She swallowed great gulps of it as she took in the still busy quayside and the majestic buildings opposite. There was a clock on one: half past nine, she noted, later than she'd thought. Liverpool appeared to be a splendid city. If it hadn't been for Annemarie, she wouldn't have minded having a look around. The ship didn't sail until some time this afternoon.

There were quite a few people out for a stroll around the deck, most of the women smartly, if not richly dressed, their skirts shockingly short, ending just below their knees. It was a style that hadn't yet reached Duneathly where ankle-length skirts were still in vogue.

She made her way to the third-class dining room. It was much grander than she'd expected: wood-panelled with glass-shaded wall lights and a striped carpet on the floor. A steward took her name and cabin number and led her to a round table big enough for eight. The other six must have already eaten, as only two places were set.

'I have a Miss Annemarie Kenny on my list,' the steward remarked. 'If she doesn't come soon, we'll stop serving.'

'My sister isn't well: she won't be having breakfast this morning.'

'I hope she's better soon,' the man said sympathetically. He would have been remarkably handsome had he not had such a fearful squint. 'If it's the seasickness, you can get something for it from the ship's doctor.'

'Thank you, I'll remember that.'

A few minutes later, she was tucking into bacon, eggs, and sausages, accompanied by an entire pot of tea to herself as well as a basket of crusty rolls, jam, and butter. The jam was raspberry, her favourite.

The world seemed a much-improved place after she'd finished eating and her stomach was full – she'd almost drowned herself in tea. She returned to the cabin. Annemarie was the only one there, still asleep, breathing evenly, looking quite peaceful. Mollie decided to go back on deck for a while. It smelled nicer and she'd like to have a last look at Liverpool: she'd almost certainly never see the place again.

She was leaning on the rail, admiring the clear blue sky and a sun that was more cream than yellow, when a girl of about her own age leaned beside her. Her fair hair was a mass of ringlets and she wore a bright-red coat with a fur-lined hood. Mollie's sensible navy-blue one looked desperately old-fashioned beside it.

It turned out the girl was American. Her name was Rowena and she'd boarded the *Queen Maia* in Hamburg where dozens – it might have been hundreds – of immigrants had been herded into the steerage compartment below where it was absolutely horrid. The stench was indescribable, she'd heard, and it was apparently so crowded that there was hardly room to move.

'You should have seen them, poor things,' Rowena said in a voice thick with emotion. 'Their clothes were little more than rags and they looked so wretched. A lot of the women had babies in their arms, and the older children and the men carried all their worldly possessions in bundles on their backs. It was so sad I wanted to cry.'

'*They* probably don't feel sad and wretched,' Mollie said.

'They're setting off for a new life in a new world. They might be a bit scared, that's all.'

Rowena conceded this could well be the case. 'My grandparents were immigrants,' she said proudly. 'That's why I know so much about it. They came to America forty years ago without a cent: Papa was only two. But they started their own bakery and did really well for themselves. Papa has just taken us, my brother and me, to Hamburg, to see the place where he was born and look up some of his cousins.'

It was all extremely interesting but, after a while, Mollie felt bound to excuse herself. The big clock across the way showed half past eleven: Annemarie had been on her own for ages. 'My sister's sick, I'd better go and see if she's all right.'

'If she's OK,' Rowena said eagerly, 'perhaps we could all have a game of cards in the lounge this afternoon? That'd be neat, wouldn't it?'

Mollie agreed that it would indeed be 'neat', and they exchanged cabin numbers in case they missed each other at lunchtime.

She knew something was badly wrong when she reached the cabin and heard the screams coming from inside. She almost fell through the door and found an hysterical Annemarie sitting up in the bunk yelling, 'Mollie, Mollie, Mollie,' over and over again. A small, tubby woman with iron-grey hair was holding her by the arms, saying soothingly, 'All right, little girl, Mollie come soon.'

'I'm here, darlin',' Mollie cried. 'I'm here.' She tried to reach her sister, but before she could get near, the woman slapped Annemarie's petrified face. Annemarie stopped screaming and began to cry instead.

'You shouldn't have done that!' Mollie gasped, appalled.

'It all right, I am nurse. Your sister having nervous fit, now she better. Now she just cry, much better to just cry.' The woman, who looked in her sixties, proceeded to gently stroke the back of the sobbing girl. 'What wrong, child?' She turned to Mollie and asked in her guttural voice, 'What wrong with your sister?'

Mollie sank, trembling, on to one of the lower bunks. On reflection, a sharp slap was the best way to treat a person with hysterics. This must be Gertrude Strauss; she was being very kind. Last night, she'd got a completely different impression of the woman. 'Annemarie had a very bad shock a few weeks ago and she hasn't recovered since. Normally, she's full of the joys of spring.' At this, Miss Strauss looked bemused. 'What I meant,' Mollie explained, 'is that normally she'd an exceptionally happy person, if rather highly strung.' She'd never leave her sister alone again. Until Annemarie was back on her feet, she'd eat all her meals in the cabin.

'Her heart beat very fast, like engine. It not . . . what word I want?' Miss Strauss's round face screwed up in a frown. '*Regular*! Her heart not beat regular.'

'Oh, my God!' Mollie could feel the colour drain from her face. 'Last night, I forgot her digitalis, she has five drops on her tongue.' Until recently, Annemarie had administered the drops herself and Mollie hadn't got into the habit of remembering.

'You better get it now. Is important.'

'It's in the washbag.' Mollie leapt to her feet, her head meeting the frame of the bunk above with such force that, for a few seconds, the world went black.

'*Mein Gott!*' gasped Miss Strauss.

'I'm all right.' She reeled across the cabin to the locker where she'd put the things they'd need on the voyage. The washbag was right in front: she'd used it only that morning. She rooted through the toothbrushes, the tooth powder, soap and face flannels, but couldn't find the little brown bottles with rubber droppers that she distinctly remembered putting there before they'd left the doctor's house.

But they *must* be there. Desperate now, she emptied everything on to the bed, but there was no sign. Perhaps she'd put them somewhere else. But where? She wouldn't have left them loose in the suitcase or her handbag where the tops might become loose. Just in case, she searched both: no digitalis. Knowing it was hopeless, Mollie reached for the fat, brown envelope in which she kept the money, their passports and other papers. The bottles weren't there either.

She sat back on her heels, closed her eyes, and relived the last hour spent in the Doctor's house, packing their clothes, trying not to make a noise, Annemarie lying fully dressed on Mollie's bed, watching with her big, violet eyes. Mollie had already taken an extra bottle of digitalis from the medicine cabinet in the surgery to add to the one that was almost full. She'd put both bottles on the bedside cabinet, crept into the bathroom to collect the other items for the washbag, returned to the bedroom, picked up the digitalis . . .

No, she hadn't. When she'd looked, Annemarie had fallen asleep and she'd had to wake her, tell her they were leaving any minute, that they had a long walk ahead of them. Then she'd put the washbag in the suitcase and snapped it shut . . . leaving the digitalis on the bedside cabinet.

'I'll have to buy some,' she muttered. She rooted through the mess on the floor for a ticket to see when the boat sailed. 'Thirteen hundred hours.' Three o'clock. It was a strange way to put it. 'I've plenty of time.'

'Where you go?' Miss Strauss asked.

'To find a chemist's and buy some digitalis.' She shoved her purse into her pocket. 'Do you mind looking after Annemarie while I'm gone? I won't be long.'

'Of course I look after your sister, but—'

Mollie didn't wait for the woman to finish. She was already outside, racing along the corridor, and Miss Strauss's final words – 'Ship doctor will have digitalis' – were addressed to the empty air.

She'd forgotten her hat, and the spot where she'd banged her head felt as if someone were banging it with a hammer. There wasn't a shop of any description in the area outside the dock, let alone a chemist's, just the majestic building she'd seen from the boat and streams of traffic, including dozens of tramcars whizzing by, sparks exploding from the lines overhead. It was a sight that, normally, would have made Mollie stop and stare, entranced, had she not had more important things on her mind. She grabbed the arm of the first man she saw and asked if he knew the whereabouts of the nearest chemist.

'Let's see now.' He chewed his lips with maddening slowness. 'The nearest chemist's. Well, you won't find one around here, luv. You'll have to go into town to find a chemist's. If you cross the road and go up Chapel Street . . . no, no, Water Street, it's more direct, and turn right at Crosshall Street, you're bound to find one there. A tram would take you quicker. They start from over there, but I'm afraid I don't know what number.'

'Is it far to walk?'

'Not too far for a healthy young lady like you,' he said with a wink and a smile.

'Then I'll walk.' That way she was in control of the situation. Her legs wouldn't let her down.

Except today they did. She was half walking, half running along Water Street, when her head began to swim, the pavement began to rock, and the tall buildings looked about to topple down on her. Her legs positively refused to move in the right direction. This must be what it was like to be drunk, unable to put one foot in front of the other. People were giving her some very odd looks: a woman stopped and asked if she was all right. 'I'm fine,' Mollie insisted, although her breath was coming in little hoarse gasps. She held on to a wall and gritted her teeth so hard that her jaw hurt: the Doctor had said Annemarie's heart condition was nothing to worry about, '*As long as she uses the drops every night before she goes to bed.*' She *had* to get the digitalis for her sister or die in the attempt.

Her breathing was easier now, so she resumed her search, hanging on to railings, supporting herself along walls, more people stopped to ask if she was all right, until she arrived at Crosshall Street and saw a chemist's directly across the road. Without thinking, she stepped off the pavement and was nearly mown down by a van. It stopped, just in time, with a screech of brakes. 'D'you want to get yerself killed, you stupid bitch,' the driver yelled.

Mollie hardly heard. A bell sounded loudly when she entered the shop, hurting her ears. 'Digitalis,' she gasped. 'Two bottles, please.'

'Digitalis is a poison,' the young woman behind the counter informed her. She wore wire-rimmed spectacles and a white overall, and her brown, frizzy hair was coiled over her ears. She had a pleasant face, very friendly. 'I'm afraid I can only sell you one.'

'One will do. It's for my sister: she has a heart condition. Oh, do you mind if I sit down.' There were two chairs at the front of the shop.

'Sit down for as long as you like, luv. You look dead puffed. Would you like a glass of water?'

'Please.' Her throat was as dry as a bone and she felt desperately hot.

'Here you are, luv.' The girl came round the counter with the water. 'Crikey! There's a bump on your head as big as a football and it's bleeding. Hang on a mo, I'll get some disinfectant and bathe it. You've been in the wars, haven't you?'

'I banged it.'

'Well, you must have banged it awful hard.'

It was rather nice to just sit there, sipping the water, while the girl gently dabbed the bump with cotton wool and disinfectant.

'It's not bleeding much, but you'll need to be really careful next time you wash your hair. Don't use a scented shampoo or anything.'

'I won't,' Mollie promised.

'I'll give you a couple of Aspros. I don't know whether your head's hurting much, but it'll ache like billy-o before the day's out.' She seemed extremely knowledgeable. 'In fact, it mightn't be a bad idea if you bought a box of Aspros while you're here. Two tablets won't be of much use.'

'It's throbbing more than aching at the moment. You're being very kind,' she said gratefully.

'Oh, think nothing of it. I wanted to be a nurse, so I like

treating people, and it makes a nice change from just selling things over the counter.'

'Why didn't you take up nursing? You'd make a great nurse.'

'Ta.' The girl blushed slightly, pleased by the compliment. 'The thing is, the training takes for ever and you only get paid a pittance. When our dad was killed in the war, me, being the eldest like, had to find a job that paid a decent wage.'

'That's a pity, about your dad, and you not being able to become a nurse. Is that a clock on the wall over there?'

'Yes.' The girl regarded her worriedly. 'It's just gone half twelve. Can't you see it proper?'

'It's a bit blurred.' Everything was a bit blurred.

'You really should go to the hospital with that bump. You might have suffered brain damage.'

Mollie laughed. 'I don't think so.'

'You should at least be lying down, resting, not running like mad all over Liverpool,' the girl said sternly. 'I could tell you'd been running when you came in. Have you got far to go home?'

'I'm not going home. The truth is, my sister and I are on our way to America – New York. We were already on the ship when I found out I'd forgotten to bring her drops.'

'New York!' She looked hugely impressed. 'Flippin' heck, I'm green with envy. Shouldn't you be getting back, then? The ship might sail without you.'

'It doesn't sail for another couple of hours.' She should get back to Annemarie, but her legs still felt wobbly and her vision still wasn't right. 'You don't get many customers in this shop, do you?' Not a soul had entered since she'd come in.

'I locked the door and turned the sign over when you arrived so people'd think we were closed for dinner. I didn't want them gawping at that bump on your head.'

'Won't that get you into trouble? I'd best get out your way, I'm being a nuisance.' Mollie leapt to her feet and immediately sat down again when the floor rose up to greet her.

'I won't get into trouble, there's no need to get out me way, and you're not being a nuisance.' The girl smiled and announced she'd make them both a cup of tea. 'I'll just go and put the kettle on.' She disappeared into the back of the shop. 'Would you like a butty?' she shouted. 'It's mushy peas.'

'No, thank you,' Mollie shouted back. Even the thought of eating a mushy pea butty made her feel sick. 'I'd love a cup of tea, though. You *are* being kind. What's your name? Mine's Mollie Kenny.'

'Agatha Brophy. Most people call me Aggie, but I hate it. I'd far rather be Agatha. Have you heard of that writer, Agatha Christie? I've read all her books. I get them from the library.'

'No. Me, I like Ruby Ayres and Ethel M. Dell. They're desperately romantic.'

Agatha reappeared. 'Did you see that picture, Mollie, *The Sheik*, with Rudolph Valentino? Now *that's* romantic. He's got these dark, hypnotic eyes that make you go all funny.'

'There wasn't a picture house where I lived in Ireland,' Mollie said regretfully, 'so I've never been.'

'Well, there'll be plenty in New York.'

They smiled at each other and Mollie asked if she would remind her when it was one o'clock. 'I still can't see all that well, but it's getting better. I'll feel better all round once I've had a cup of tea, then I can make me way slowly back to the landing stage.'

At one o'clock, Mollie left the chemist's and went back the way she'd come, her legs her own again. She was sorry to leave Agatha, who'd become a good friend in the space of half an hour. 'I'll send you a card from New York as soon as I've settled in,' she promised. 'I'll address it to the shop.'

Agatha wished her all the luck in the world and said she wished she were going, too. 'Don't forget to take some more of the Aspros if your head starts to ache.'

'I won't.' They waved to each other until Mollie reached the corner of Crosshall Street and couldn't see Agatha any more. She sighed and walked steadily in the direction of the River Mersey where Annemarie and the *Queen Maia* were waiting for her return.

★

It was just a dream, the sort in which something so hideous and horrible is about to happen that you wake up before it does, heart throbbing, bathed in perspiration, terrified you'll fall back asleep and return to the dream, to be butchered in your bed or slip off the roof you'd been hanging on to with your fingertips.

But this wasn't a dream: this was real. The *Queen Maia* really was sailing away, about fifty feet from the dock on its way towards the Atlantic and New York.

Without *her*.

Mollie began to scream, to scream and scream, to continue to scream until someone grabbed her by the shoulders and shook her: a man in uniform wearing a white peaked cap. 'Calm down, miss. What on earth's the matter?'

'The ship's left early and my sister's on board,' she gabbled. 'It wasn't supposed to sail until three o'clock.'

He shook his head. 'No, miss, one o'clock.'

'But it said three o'clock on the ticket, it said thirteen hundred hours. I distinctly remember.'

'Oh, Jaysus!' He groaned. 'I'm sorry, miss, but thirteen hundred hours means one o'clock. Look, what's your sister's name? I'll get someone to telegraph the captain to say you've missed the boat.'

'Annemarie Kenny,' Mollie managed to say before she fainted dead away.

Chapter 2

Gertie had taken Annemarie to breakfast. Olive waited a few minutes before opening the suitcase. She'd wanted to do it for days, but this was the first time she'd dared. She examined the contents.

The frocks were too girlish for her taste, but the bigger ones which must be Mollie's, could stand some alteration. She wouldn't take anything yet. Gertie, who had eyes like a rat, might notice they'd gone. The underclothes were good quality; not exactly glamorous, but they'd do at a pinch. There was a small amount of jewellery in quite a nice little wooden box, nothing expensive, mainly silver: childish bracelets and medals on chains, a pearl brooch, a ring with a green stone. She closed the box and put it back in the corner where it had been neatly packed and continued to sort through the contents: shoes – none her size and too sensible anyway; stockings she wouldn't be seen dead in – they were far too thick; and two pretty crocheted hats – one white, the other pink.

'What's this?' she asked aloud, when she noticed a large brown envelope tucked in the pouched pocket beneath the case top. She emptied it on the bed: passports, birth certificates, some letters with an American stamp and 'Miss Margaret Connelly, 88 Bleecker Street, Greenwich Village, New York' written on the back – she must be the Aunt Maggie the girls were going to live with – and a leather wallet with money in. Her heart did a cartwheel when she counted it out: thirty-six pound-notes.

Thirty-six! She'd never seen so much money in her life before, not even half that much, not even a quarter. Did Gertie know about this? Had she counted it? Olive wouldn't have minded a few quid to be going on with, but it wasn't worth taking the risk. If she played her cards right, she might end up with the lot. It could be changed into dollars when she reached New York.

Picking up Mollie's passport, she wondered if she could make use of it. The photo inside was nothing like Mollie and had clearly been taken a few years ago. Her eyes were almost closed, her mouth was turned down, and she looked like a corpse. You never know, it might come in handy. It all depended on the way things turned out.

She put everything back in the suitcase, closed it, and had a quick look in the girls' locker: a washbag, two nightdresses, two more frocks, and a smart, navy-blue handbag that contained a comb, a couple of hankies, a pencil and a little notebook, but no purse. Mollie must have taken the purse with her and left the bag behind.

Olive put the bag back and lay on her bunk to think. Gertie had been right to say she should be travelling steerage. Olive had been obliged to leave London in a hurry when she'd got into some serious trouble with the Sutton brothers, gangsters really, who'd give her a good beating if they found her – that's if they didn't kill her first. It was only because she'd been doing some private business of her own and not giving them their cut. It was *her* body, she thought indignantly. She didn't see why she had to share what she made from selling it.

She'd come to Liverpool only because she happened to be near Euston Station when she'd heard the Sutton brothers were after her and the next train to leave was for Lime Street. There hadn't even been time to pack a bag. She'd hung around Liverpool for a few days until she discovered the *Queen Maia* was about to depart for New York and jumped at the chance. She'd seen New York in films: it was the sort of place where she could start a career in show business, something she'd longed to do for years. A steerage ticket didn't cost more than a few bob, easily obtained on the Dock Road where foreign sailors hung about looking for women.

It had been just as easy to persuade a friendly steward to find out if there was an empty space in third-class and get her away from the scum in steerage: dirty, smelly creatures with whinging kids and disgusting habits who couldn't even speak English.

The steward, Ashley was his name, had discovered there was an empty bunk in a third-class cabin with Gertie and the Kenny sisters. He'd brought her up through the kitchens because passengers were strictly forbidden to move from deck to deck. 'You'd better behave yourself, gal,' he advised. 'If anyone finds out, don't bring me into it. I'll swear I've never seen you before. I suggest you stick to the cabin rather than flaunt yourself on deck.'

She'd taken his advice, emerging only for an occasional breath of fresh air. The weather had been fine and, so far, the voyage had gone quite smoothly. She'd enjoyed having nothing to do for days on end apart from lie on the bunk and think about the future.

He was all right, Ashley, not bad-looking, though it was a shame about the squint. But even he, helpful though he was, couldn't manage to get her into the third-class dining room. 'The passengers' names are on a list and ticked off when they come in. There's no way I can add your name,' he said. At night, he brought her odds and ends of food: bread rolls, pieces of cheese, chocolates and bits of fruit. She repaid him in the way she was used to paying for things. It was a pity Gertie had had to see them.

At that moment, Gertie came into the cabin alone.

'Where's Annemarie?' Olive enquired.

'She gone for walk with Rowena, nice girl who came search for Mollie to play cards. Such pity about Mollie.' Her round face grew sad. 'Ship doctor have digitalis. No need for her go and miss boat.'

'Yes, it's a pity,' Olive agreed. She was genuinely sorry for Mollie who'd been really nice to her. Unlike Gertie, unlike most people, Mollie hadn't looked at her if she were a piece of dirt. Even so, it seemed as if Mollie missing the boat was going to turn out to her advantage, so it wasn't such a pity, after all.

An officer, ever such a handsome chap, had come looking for Annemarie bringing the news about her sister. She'd been too stupefied to take it in and Olive wondered if the girl was all there. Gertie had been present and had taken charge. '*I* nurse, *I* look after child. She need drops from doctor, she not have regular heart.'

Since then, Gertie had taken Annemarie under her wing, giving her the drops, taking her to see the doctor every day, urging her to eat. Today was the first time she'd had a proper meal. At least, she'd *gone* for a meal: whether she'd actually eaten it was another matter.

'Did Annemarie eat her breakfast?' she asked. It had been wrong, dangerous, to get on the wrong side of Gertie. She might remember her threat to report her. Asking after Annemarie seemed to please her.

Gertie made a face. 'Only bread and she drink some milk.'

'Oh, well, that should do her some good.'

'Only little good. Mollie say she suffer great shock. Her head all . . . ' Gertie waved her podgy hands around her own head, leaving Olive to guess what she meant. In a daze, she supposed, all woolly, round the bloody bend.

Had Annemarie been asked, had she been able to understand, she would have agreed with all three of Olive's guesses. Ever since the night her father had lain on top of her, causing her great pain, she'd been in a daze and, in the rare moments when she could think clearly, was convinced she must be going mad. Then she would retreat into the world she'd invented for herself, a world in which nothing horrid happened, a make-believe world full of smoke and clouds and thick forests in which she could hide. It was a world without danger where she was determined to stay for as long as she could.

That Annemarie was only faintly aware of another Annemarie existing outside her make-believe world, a terrified, frightened girl who hated being touched or spoken to, who blindly did what she was told, who was too confused to know who or where she was. Words had imprinted themselves on her woolly mind: New York; Aunt Maggie; Hazel. '*We're going to see Hazel,*' Mollie had said. Mollie was the girl's sister. She didn't mind when Mollie held her hand and took her to strange places. '*It's all right, sis. It's only a ship,*' Mollie had said.

But Mollie had disappeared and now another girl was holding her hand, talking to her, taking her somewhere, not knowing that Annemarie was about to retreat into her other world, hide inside one of the clouds, or bury herself in the trees where no one could see her and no one would speak. It was the only place she felt safe.

A plan was slowly hatching in Olive's sharp brain. The *Queen Maia* was more than halfway to America and, last night, Ashley had given her some bad news. 'The day we land,' he'd told her, 'you'd better get back to steerage in good time. Your name's down on the manifest: if you're missing, there'll be hell to play. The ship'll be searched and you'll be sent back to where you came from.'

'Bloody hell!' Olive swore.

'What's wrong with being an immigrant? It's what you started out as.'

'There's nothing wrong with it,' she agreed.

But the next time she was in the cabin alone, she took out Mollie's passport and studied it, then studied her own face in the mirror. If she half closed her eyes and turned down her mouth, it could have been her in the photo. In fact, it could have been almost any girl in the world. She was two years older than Mollie, but if she went without make-up she could pass for sixteen. Trouble was her hair, once the same brown as Mollie's, had been bleached almost to destruction: if she bleached it much more it was likely to fall out. Once she reached New York and became Rosalind Raines, she'd let the bleach grow out. But that was then and this was now: how could she acquire different-coloured hair in the middle of the Atlantic?

A hat! There were two in the suitcase. She'd wear the pink one, one of Mollie's frocks, and carry her fur cape inside-out –

the lining was in much better condition than the fur. She'd look the bee's knees.

Then all she had to do was find someone else to take her place in steerage and become Olive Raines. To most people, it would have seemed an impossible task, but she already had someone in mind.

Since Olive had boarded the ship, she'd been itching like mad and had a strong suspicion she'd caught something horrible – probably off one of the darkies she'd been with on the Dock Road. Once ashore, she'd buy some mercury tablets: they'd cured it the time she'd had it before. When they reached New York, immigrants were subjected to a medical examination and she didn't want anyone finding out she had a case of the clap. Then, she really would be sent home.

America, land of hope, haven of democracy, refuge of the oppressed, the country where every man had the opportunity of becoming a millionaire, was a mere two days away. The immigrants on the *Queen Maia* gathered on their deck on the chance they'd be the first to spy the Statue of Liberty holding her torch aloft, welcoming them to the place where their fortunes would be made, their children would eat three good meals a day, and there was land to spare, acres and acres of it, as much as they could farm. Or they might work in factories making cars, earning colossal wages, enough to buy a car of their own in no time. They imagined gold coins tumbling through their fingers, pockets jammed with dollars, houses full of fine furniture, tables heaped with fine food.

America! They could hardly wait to get there and sample the riches it had to offer.

Gertrude Strauss had grown very fond of Annemarie and would miss her badly when the time came for them to part. She was unable to read the letters in the suitcase, but had deduced that Miss Margaret Connelly, whose name was on the back of the envelopes, would almost certainly be waiting to meet the girls.

One of the ship's officers had come round and offered to see Annemarie off the ship, but Gertrude had assured him *she* would ensure the girl was delivered safely into Miss Connelly's hands and explain why Mollie hadn't come with her. She'd inform her that she, Gertrude, was a nurse who had looked after Annemarie throughout the voyage. Miss Connelly might not know about the drops for her heart and be unaware that the girl was in a state of deep shock.

'Mollie say normally she is happy person, but something bad happen,' she'd say. It would make Gertrude feel extremely important. Miss Connelly would thank her, perhaps even ask if she would like to come and see Annemarie when she was better. Gertrude might even make a friend in New York, and her sister, Bertha, with whom she was going to live, would be very impressed.

Since the Great War ended, Germany was no longer a good place to live. Money had become worthless and strange, unsavoury people were acquiring power; something called the Nazi Party had been formed. Bertha, who had emigrated to the United States long before the turn of the century with her husband, Hermann, was now a widow and childless, and the sisters had decided to keep each other company in their old age. America was a much better place to be than Germany.

Relating to Bertha her adventures on the *Queen Maia* would keep them occupied for days and Gertrude was very much looking forward to it.

There was a knock on the cabin door. 'Come in,' Olive called. She was lying on the bunk, itching like mad, and practising how she would speak when she became Rosalind Raines – quite soon, she hoped, if everything went to plan. The *Queen Maia* was due to berth in New York at midday. 'How do you do, darling? So pleased to meet you,' she said aloud in a dead posh voice.

Ashley entered, looking harassed, his left eye dancing all over the place. 'We'll be docking in a couple of hours and a barge will take your lot to Ellis Island. You'd better get down there quick.'

'A barge?' She hadn't the faintest idea what he was talking about. 'And what do you mean by "your lot"?'

'A barge is a boat, a flat bloody ship,' he said impatiently, 'and by your lot, I mean the immigrants. Before you ask, Ellis Island is where you're processed before you're allowed into America. I've already told you, if someone's missing, they'll search the ship. You know which way to go, don't you? Through the kitchen and down the stairs at the back, the way I brought you in the first place.'

'I know,' she said, just as impatiently. 'Just give us a minute to say tata to Annemarie and Miss Strauss.'

'Who were you talking to when I came in?' He glanced around the cabin, obviously empty apart from the two of them.

'No one. I'm rehearsing a play.' She tossed her head importantly. 'I told you I was in show business, didn't I?'

'Yeah, and I'm the King of England.' He smiled at her with unexpected warmth. 'Tata, Olive. It's been nice knowing you. I'll miss you on the voyage home.'

'Tata, Ashley.' She wouldn't miss him.

The second the door closed, she leapt to her feet, opened the suitcase, flung everything that belonged to Annemarie on to a sheet on the bunk and knotted the corners to make a bundle. Next, she took the leather handbag out of the locker, put in the thirty-six pounds and Mollie's passport, then went to look for Annemarie, praying she wouldn't be with Gertie, who'd gone to see if her sister was among the crowd waiting for the ship to dock.

The deck was already full of people, many with luggage at their feet. The ship felt as if it were merely drifting towards its final destination: New York! Olive paused and looked in wonder at the huge buildings soaring into the sky, all bunched together like candles on a plate. It was an impressive sight: frightening almost. Her heart lifted. Very soon, she would be part of this weird and wonderful place. With Mollie's money and Mollie's clothes, she could start a new life. But she wasn't there yet. There were still things to be done before she landed and became Rosalind Raines.

Most eyes were fixed on the approaching land, apart from a

solitary figure in a green coat leaning over the side of the boat, apparently studying the murky brown water.

'Annemarie!' The girl turned slowly at the sound of Olive's voice, her lovely eyes devoid of all recognition. You'd never think they'd shared the same cabin for all of ten days. 'Come with me, darlin'.' She held out her hand. The girl took it without a word and meekly allowed Olive to lead her back to the cabin.

Once there, Olive chewed her lip. She hadn't thought about it before, but she didn't want Annemarie coming to any harm. Even so, she had to put herself first. She untied the bundle, and put the girl's passport, birth certificate, and the letters from New York at the very bottom underneath the clothes, keeping back just one of the letters in case she needed it herself. It would be a while before the things were found, but at least someone would eventually discover who the girl was. She re-tied the sheet and put a piece of paper in Annemarie's hand, folding her fingers over it. 'Hold on to this, darlin',' she said. It had her own name and address written on it: 'Olive Raines, 16 Cameron Buildings, Deptford, London.' It meant no one would come searching for the real Olive Raines, least not straight away. According to Ashley, the inspection process took five or six hours. By that time, the real Olive Raines hoped to be safely ashore with Mollie's handbag and Mollie's suitcase, and wearing Mollie's clothes.

Annemarie allowed herself to be pushed and shoved on to the large flat boat. Everyone else was fighting their way on, as if worried they'd be left behind. They spoke in a language she didn't understand, but their voices were thick with excitement. It was ages before the boat took off and she wondered why they were leaving behind the great white ship they'd sailed on.

This journey didn't take long. She bore it patiently, despite being squashed against the side, a little boy clinging to her skirt, sobbing his heart out. It was all very strange. She wondered where the woman had gone who seemed to have taken Mollie's place. She missed her, and she missed Mollie. Was this a dream? Those buildings she could see, the big, ugly ones that made her shudder with revulsion, could hardly be real. Perhaps she was in hell, along with all these oddly dressed people with their thin, starved faces and haunted eyes.

Annemarie closed her own eyes and retreated to a place with no people or buildings, just clouds and trees, where she let herself drift, all alone and perfectly safe.

The barge landed at Ellis Island, the eager passengers poured off, and Annemarie was carried along with them. She left behind the bundle of clothes, having forgotten all about it. It was found later by a seaman and thrown into the baggage room where immigrants collected their belongings after they'd been processed.

'What's going to happen to her, Doctor?' the nurse enquired. She spoke with a strong Welsh accent. She and the doctor were in a small end room off the women's ward in Ellis Island hospital. Annemarie lay on the only bed, fully dressed, unmoving, her eyes wide open, but expressionless. The ribbon that Gertrude had tied on her plait only that morning had come loose, and her black, wavy hair covered her shoulders like a cape.

'They'll probably keep her for a few days in case anyone comes to claim her, then send her back to where she came from: Liverpool. The steamship line that brought her will pay the cost.' The young doctor looked troubled. 'I can't discover what's wrong with her. Physically, she's exceptionally fit, has no known diseases, and her name, Olive Raines, is down on the manifest. But how could someone who's apparently deaf and dumb have come all this way on her own without speaking to a soul?' The girl had no identification with her, just her name scribbled on a scrap of paper. Already that day, the doctor had dealt with dozens of unfortunates who'd been transferred to the hospital suspected of suffering from tuberculosis, epilepsy, trachoma, and other ailments that would prevent their entry into the United States. It was all in a day's work, but there was something about Olive Raines that disturbed him.

'She doesn't look like your usual immigrant,' the nurse

remarked. 'Those boots she's wearing cost more than a few dollars, as well as her coat.'

'Mm,' the doctor said thoughtfully. 'Look, keep her in this room tonight. I suspect she's been traumatized and it might do her more harm than good if she snaps out of it in a ward full of strange women.'

Olive had booked a room in a small hotel within walking distance of the docks. It was clean and would do for a few days until she found a place to live, preferably close to the theatre district – she suspected the theatres would be all clumped together as they were in the West End of London. Now that she had funds, there'd be no need to go back on the game if she failed an audition or two, something she'd been forced to do more times than she could count back home. Trouble was, she'd had no experience or formal training, and hadn't possessed a decent set of clothes in her life. She'd turned up for auditions looking exactly what she was: a pro, a woman of the streets, who'd just popped in hoping for a cup of tea or to get out the cold, yet she'd like to bet she could sing, dance and act as well as any girl there. She was a natural: just look at how well she'd acted today!

As soon as she'd got rid of Annemarie, she'd washed off her make-up, slipped into one of Mollie's frocks – the thick black woolly one with long sleeves and a Peter Pan collar – and pulled the pink hat down over her ears. She'd got quite a shock when she looked in the mirror and seen the prim, rather old-fashioned young woman staring back at her. But there was no time for such indulgences: she grabbed the handbag, picked up the suitcase, and left the cabin. Any minute now, Gertie would be back for Annemarie and there'd be ructions when she found the girl missing.

She mingled with the crowds on deck, waiting impatiently for what seemed like hours, her heart in her mouth, as the big ship eventually ground to a halt with a rumble and an enormous judder. Minutes later, the passengers began to pour off, Olive with them, her heart still in her mouth. She still wasn't in the clear: she had to get through Customs with Mollie's passport.

There was a queue at the barrier and she kept an eye out for Gertie, but there was no sign of her cabin mate. When it was her turn, the Customs officer looked at her closely, then back at the photo in the passport. Olive smiled at him brilliantly and said in a perfect imitation of Mollie's accent, 'It's a horrible picture, is it not? I was coming down with the 'flu the day it was taken and I look as if I'm at death's door.'

'Well, you're obviously much better now, Miss . . . ' he looked at the passport again, 'Miss Kenny. And what is your reason for visiting New York?'

'I'm on holiday. I shall be staying with my aunt, Margaret Connelly, for a few weeks. She lives in Greenwich Village: eighty-eight Bleecker Street.'

'I hope you like our city.' He gave her the passport back. 'Have a good time, miss.'

She'd done it! She went to the Bureau de Change and asked for the pounds to be changed into dollars. In return, she was given a dazzlingly thick wad of notes.

She'd actually done it!

Hours later, it had begun to go dark and she was still closeted in the room, stunned by the enormity of what she had achieved. She sat on the bed and counted the money for the fifth or sixth time: $164 and some coins. She tucked it all inside the bag: tomorrow, she'd buy a little purse for the coins. There were quite a few things she wanted to do tomorrow, apart from finding where the theatres were, buying a purse, and getting some mercury tablets for the itch that continued to plague her.

First, she intended to find a hairdresser and have her hair cut in a shingle – they were all the rage in London – and dyed back to its original dark-brown. The brassy frizz made her look like a tart. She'd like to bet she wouldn't have been treated quite so respectfully at Customs or by the man on the desk downstairs had she not been wearing Mollie's hat.

She wondered what Mollie was doing now, poor cow. She'd be worried sick for her sister and was probably planning to catch the next boat to New York, that's if she had money for the ticket. If Olive hadn't arranged for Annemarie to take her place in steerage, by now she would have been safely delivered to the aunt: Gertie would have made sure of that. The aunt could have sent Mollie enough money to buy a ticket and in a few weeks the sisters would be reunited in New York.

Olive had mucked up an awful lot of lives. 'Good never comes out of bad,' her old ma used to say. Well, Ma should know. All she'd ever known was bad, in the form of a husband who'd beat hell out of her and her kids. At thirteen, Olive had left home and had been living by her wits ever since. Even so, it was no excuse to take it out on the Kenny girls. Neither had done her any harm. Indeed, hadn't Mollie been really nice to her, spoken to her as an equal, despite knowing she was a tart?

She thought about Annemarie stranded on Ellis Island. The girl probably didn't know if she was coming or going. Did she still have the bundle with her passport inside? Anyone could have pinched it: she hadn't thought to put a label on. She remembered Ashley saying young women weren't allowed off the island unless someone came to collect them. He'd actually offered to arrange for a friend to come and vouch for her, but by then Olive had had a better plan in mind. As far as blokes went, Ashley had been quite decent and she'd probably repaid him with a dose of the itchy wriggles.

Her guilty thoughts were interrupted by gales of laughter from outside. She went over to the window. She could have been in any city in any country in the world. This part of New York was dark and barely lit, and there was no sign of the tall buildings seen from the ship. There was a rundown café across the road with a sign, 'Joe's Place', that blinked on and off. A car had stopped and four young women were making their way inside, giggling so hard they could hardly stand up. Somewhere, a clock chimed six.

Olive chewed her lip. It was a habit she must get out of: one of these days she'd have no bottom lip left. There was nothing she could do about Mollie, but she could do something about Annemarie.

She pulled on the pink hat and picked up her cape – she wouldn't put it on until she was outside so the man on the desk wouldn't see how tatty it was; she put a coat on the mental list of things to buy tomorrow – and went downstairs. The man emerged from a cubbyhole behind when she rang the bell.

'What can I do for you, miss?' He smiled at her kindly. An elderly man with a thatch of snow-white hair, he spoke English well with an accent similar to Gertie's.

'I met someone on the boat, a young girl from Ireland same as me, but she was in steerage. She was expecting her aunt to come and meet her, but worried she hadn't received her letter in time. I'd like to make sure she's been collected. If not, I'll take her to her aunt's house. Is Greenwich Village very far?' Christ, she was good at this! Her voice literally throbbed with sincerity.

'Not all that far in a cab. Cabs don't cost much,' he added when Olive's face fell at the idea of using some of the precious dollars. 'Is the girl on the island? The Isle of Tears, people call it.' Olive nodded. 'Then you'll have to catch the ferry. They run quite often, but you be careful, miss. This isn't a good area for a young girl to be out in on her own.'

'I'll be careful,' Olive promised.

She left the hotel and walked swiftly in the direction of the docks, practising what she would say when she reached the island: 'I'm Mollie Kenny. I've come for my cousin, Olive Raines. Our aunt in Greenwich Village is expecting her.' If asked, she'd produce Mollie's passport. It was a risky thing to do, but she'd got a kick out of the risks she'd taken today: the racing heart, the sweaty palms and, best of all, the glowing knowledge that she'd fooled everyone: Ashley, Gertie, the Customs' officer. She could hardly include Annemarie, poor kid but, pretty soon, she could add Ellis Island to the list.

But this would be the last risk she would take. As from tomorrow, her conscience would be clear and she wouldn't give a damn what happened to the Kenny sisters.

Bertha had prepared bratwurst with hot sauerkraut and potato salad for dinner, followed by schluender marzipan cake and Bavarian coffee. Gertrude sipped the coffee with a sigh. 'That very nice, Bertha. A long time since I have such meal. Thank you.' The sisters had decided to speak English together, so that Gertrude would improve quickly.

'There's a German butcher's on the corner,' Bertha said, 'the best in New York. Would you like more cake?'

'No, thank you, Bertha,' Gertrude replied with another sigh.

'Are you still thinking about that girl, Rosemarie?'

'*Anne*marie. I worry what happen to her. Where she disappear from?'

'Disappear *to*,' Bertha corrected, 'not from.'

Like her sister, Bertha was comfortably stout and had the same iron-grey hair. Her basement apartment, situated on Ridge Street on the Lower East Side, was dark but cosy, and filled with knick-knacks collected over a lifetime. A sepia photograph of the sisters, taken when Gertrude was fourteen and Bertha two years older, stood on the dresser beside one of Bertha and Hermann's wedding. A fire burned in the grate and the curtains had been closed on what was turning out to be a misty and not very pleasant night.

Had circumstances been different, Gertrude would have been feeling sluggishly content – her stomach full, her stays unlaced, slippers on her feet – and relieved to have left Germany for a new and better life with her sister in New York. Yet she felt on edge, unable to get Annemarie out of her mind. Where had the girl gone? She'd contacted one of the officers, told him Annemarie was missing. 'But person come to meet her, Margaret Connelly. You find, please. Make sure she got Annemarie.' But Margaret Connelly was nowhere to be found among the crowd waiting on quayside to welcome the passengers off the *Queen Maia*.

Gertrude couldn't stand it any longer. She struggled to her feet. 'I go back to ship, Bertha. Never sleep until know what happen to Annemarie.'

'I'll come with you, Gert. I'll go find a cab while you lace up your stays and put your shoes on.' Bertha regarded her sister affectionately. 'You were a worrier when you were young and it seems you haven't changed a bit in all these years.'

It was almost seven o'clock when Maggie Connelly arrived home. School had finished almost three hours ago and she'd gone for a meal with her friend and fellow teacher, Connie McGrath. She unlocked the door that led to her apartment, one of three above Ziggie's, a shop that sold sheet music. The shop was still open and Ziggie was singing a song she'd never heard before in his rusty and rather appealing voice, 'My Heart Cries, My Soul Weeps', accompanying himself on the piano. It sounded like a dirge and she suspected it was one of his own compositions.

There was mail on the little table in the hall: a letter with an Irish stamp and another posted in New York. She ran upstairs to her apartment on the first floor – Americans called it the second and counted the ground floor as the first – threw herself into a chair and opened the letter from Ireland. It was from her niece, Mollie, and contained only a single page that she read with mounting dismay.

It would appear that Mollie and Annemarie were on their way to New York with the intention of *living* with her in the tiny apartment that was hardly big enough for one person, let alone three.

Maggie loved the girls with all her heart, but she led an enjoyable and extremely busy life in New York, having made loads of friends with whom she regularly went to the theatre and the opera. She'd joined a choir, the Legion of Mary, and a bridge club. Much of this would have to stop when the girls arrived, she thought. She wouldn't be able to leave them on their own night after night.

She read the letter again, this time more worried than dismayed. Her first thoughts had been for herself, how *she* would be inconvenienced, but now she couldn't help but wonder what on earth had made Mollie, usually such a sensible girl, decide to up sticks and come all the way to New York with her sister. Did their father know? If so, why hadn't he written first to ask if it was all right for his girls to come? She'd never liked Francis Kenny and had been upset when her sister, Orla, had announced she was going to marry him. He was too arrogant, too sure of himself, though people claimed he was a good doctor. She'd felt concern for the children when dear Orla had unexpectedly passed away, but Mollie's letters made it appear as if she was coping.

She should have gone back to Ireland and made sure the children were all right. It was what Orla would have expected of her – what she would have expected of Orla had their positions been reversed – but she was having too good a time in New York even to think about it. There were some women, much nicer than her, who would have returned for good and become a mother to her sister's children. Now it would appear as if something desperately bad had happened and Mollie had turned to the only person she felt she could count on: her Aunt Maggie.

The letter was dated a fortnight ago. It said the girls would be leaving Liverpool on the *Queen Maia* in another four days and the voyage would take a further ten. She did a quick calculation and blanched: they were arriving *today*!

Jaysus, Mary and Joseph! At least it wasn't her fault that she hadn't been there to meet them. What time had the boat docked? *Had* it docked? She's better get to the landing stage straight away. She prayed the girls hadn't been waiting too long.

Everything had gone as planned. It was truly amazing the things you could do if you had the nerve, Olive thought, when she and Annemarie were on the ferry. Behind them, the lights of Ellis Island faded into the mist and the lights of New York grew ever brighter and brighter as they approached. She'd asked for her cousin, Olive Raines, been told to wait, and about twenty minutes later a grim woman in a brown overall had arrived with Annemarie.

'If she had any luggage, it can't be found,' the woman snapped. 'If you come back in a few days it might've turned up by then.'

'Thank you.' She threw her arms around Annemarie – the

woman would expect some sort of greeting. 'Hello, darlin', Aunt Maggie's waiting for you at home. It's lovely to see you again. Come on, there's a nice tea waiting.' She took the small, cold hand. The girl would have gone off with Dr Crippen had he offered to take her.

The ferry docked close to the *Queen Maia*. The quayside was as intensely lit and as full of activity as it had been in Liverpool now the ship was getting ready for its next voyage, but there was no sign of the taxis that had been there earlier in the day. She was wondering how long they would have to wait, when a black taxi drew up and deposited a man and woman only yards from the ship. The driver got out and began to unload luggage from the boot. Olive approached, holding tightly to Annemarie, just in case the girl took flight when she was about to get her off her hands and out of her mind. 'Will you take this young lady to eighty-eight Bleecker Street, please? How much will the fare be?'

'A dollar.'

She gave him a dollar and a few coins, feeling exceptionally generous. There'd been no need to pay now: Aunt Maggie could have done it when her niece arrived.

'Thank you,' the driver said courteously. In London, Olive hadn't had much to do with taxi drivers, but she'd like to bet there weren't many as distinguished-looking as this one. He was about fifty, respectably dressed in a tweed suit and cap and a collar and tie. 'What is the young lady's name?' he enquired.

'Annemarie.' She gave Annemarie a warm hug. 'I'm sorry, darlin',' she whispered, 'I've messed you up something awful, haven't I? But you'll be with your Aunt Maggie in no time and everything will be just fine and dandy.' She helped the girl into the back, the driver slid behind the wheel, and the taxi disappeared into the night. To her surprise, Olive felt two tears trickle slowly down her cheeks. She wiped them away with the back of her hand and began to run in the direction of the hotel.

The taxi had barely been gone a second when another drew up in its place and Gertrude Strauss almost fell out. 'That Annemarie,' she cried excitedly. 'That Annemarie in cab in front. I know her from so far, know green coat, long hair. Oh, Bertha, she all right! Most probable on way to Miss Margaret Connelly.'

'Are you sure it was her, Gert?' Bertha called from the back of the cab.

'Yes.' Gertrude nodded vigorously. 'It Annemarie.'

'C'mon, then.' Bertha patted the seat beside her. 'Let's go back. I'll make more coffee and we can finish off that marzipan cake.'

'I so happy, Bertha.' Gertrude climbed back in the cab. 'From now, I really endure New York.'

'Enjoy, Gert, not endure.' Bertha laughed and linked her arm while the cab took them back to Ridge Street.

'Where are you from, Anne Murray?' Levon Zarian asked his passenger. When she didn't reply, he said gently. 'I won't eat you.' She was little more than a child: thirteen possibly, fourteen at the most. 'Have you only just arrived in New York?' She still didn't answer. He stopped the cab to wait for a break in the traffic when they reached West Side Highway and took the opportunity to turn and look at his young passenger. 'Hello,' he said, but the girl just stared at her hands and didn't even raise her head.

He wondered if she were deaf. He honked the horn, her head jerked upwards, and he looked into her eyes, but they were dead and unseeing, albeit of the most beautiful colour: amethyst, clear and pure. Her white skin was like porcelain, with the same soft sheen, and her hair a wild tumble of little black waves and curls that reached her waist.

'I once had a daughter very like you,' he told her. 'Her name was Larisa and she had brown eyes. But she died.' His throat tightened at the memory of the way Larisa had been killed: raped by a dozen Turks who'd slit her white throat when they'd had enough. Within a week, he and Tamara had left Armenia, a place of old legends and bitter tears, before they too were slaughtered by the Turks, who seemed determined to annihilate the entire population of his benighted country.

Cars behind were honking their horns. Levon edged into the traffic. It was five years since they'd come to America, five years since Larisa had died, but Tamara had never stopped mourning her death. Her eyes were as dead and unseeing as those of Anne Murray.

He continued to talk to her, telling her about himself and Tamara, though he didn't mention Larisa again. 'I was a lawyer back in Armenia. Now I attend college to take the Bar exam so I can practise here. Tamara, my wife, was a singer, not professional, but she was often called upon to sing at weddings and at the homes of our friends, usually folk songs.' Tamara hadn't sung a note since they'd arrived in America. He thought about her sitting in their apartment in Grammercy Park, waiting for him to come home, her face so sad that it almost broke his heart.

Talking all the time, Levon drove through dark, empty, silent streets, and gaudily lit, noisy streets full of people, restaurants, and bars, some of which would stay open all night: New York was a city that never slept. Had circumstances been different, he suspected he would have grown to love the place by now. Each time the traffic caused him to stop, he glanced back at his silent passenger, but she could have been in another world for all the notice she took.

'Nearly there,' he remarked when he saw the sign for Washington Square. He wondered whom she was going to see in Bleecker Street. Where had she come from? Who was the young woman who'd put her in the cab? Very irresponsible, he thought on reflection. Anne Murray wasn't fit to be out on her own. What nationality was she? He had a feeling Murray was a Scottish name, but wasn't sure.

He drove into Bleecker Street and stopped outside number eighty-eight. 'We're here,' he announced. When she showed no sign of having understood, he got out and approached the building. The music shop on the first floor was closed and in darkness, and there were three bells on the door at the side. He pressed the bottom one, but no one came, so he pressed the second, then the third. Still no one came. He pressed all three at the same time and could hear them buzzing inside, but the door remained stubbornly closed. No one was in.

What was he supposed to do now? Drag Anne Murray out of the cab, sit her on the step, and hope someone came for her soon? He felt angry that such a pretty, vulnerable young girl was being treated so negligently: shoved in a cab to be taken to a place where there was no one to meet her. Two men emerged from a diner across the road embroiled in a fight. A woman tapped his shoulder: 'Are you looking for a good time, honey?'

Levon ignored her, got back into the cab, and drove away with Anne Murray still in the back.

Maggie arrived in Bleecker Street seething with fury. Her journey had been a complete waste of time. She hadn't been allowed on the *Queen Maia*. Most of the crew, she suspected, were out on the town. Nobody could give her any information. An important-looking individual in uniform had a list of passengers expected tomorrow, but not of the ones who'd arrived that day. 'Ask at the shipping office,' she was told but, by the time she'd found the shipping office, the damn place was closed. There was no sign of her nieces.

She was tramping up the stairs to her apartment when the doorbell rang. There was no one else in the building: Jim Goldberg worked nights on a newspaper and the ballerina who lived on the top floor, whose name she could never remember, was on tour. Maggie tramped down, opened the door, and scowled at the caller, a woman of about her own age wearing an old-fashioned mackintosh and a woollen hat.

'Miss Connelly, hi,' the woman gushed. 'I'm Eileen Tutty, I only live around the corner, and my daughter, Imelda, is in your class at Saint Mary's. I thought I'd better come and tell you when I saw your name on the envelopes, case it's important.'

'What envelopes?' For some reason Maggie went cold.

'Well, you know I work on Ellis Island?' Maggie didn't know, but nodded all the same. 'I'm a clerk there and tonight, just before I came home, a parcel of clothes was brought in that had been left unclaimed. There was a passport inside and some letters: they had your name and address written on the back. I would've brought them, but they wouldn't let me. They'd been sent to a Mollie Kenny in County Kildare.'

Maggie went even colder. 'Whose name was on the passport? Did you look?'

'Yes, it belonged to Annemarie Kenny. Mr Scarlatti, the supervisor, will be writing to you tomorrow. Is she a relative of yours, Miss Connelly?'

'She's my niece. Please excuse me, Mrs Tutty. It's really nice of you to have called, but I need to go upstairs and think about this.' She closed the door and stood with her back to it, breathing deeply, resisting the urge to scream at the top of her voice. First thing in the morning she'd send Francis Kenny a telegram demanding to know what was going on. In the meantime, she knew she wouldn't sleep a wink that night.

Levon Zarian opened the door of the apartment in Grammercy Park. 'Tamara,' he called softly. 'I have a surprise for you.'

'What is it, Lev?' She came out of the bedroom, her face streaked with tears. It must have been one of the bad days for she was wearing the cream lace gown she'd had on when they'd found Larisa lying in a pool of her own blood. Tamara had screamed and knelt beside the body of her daughter and her skirt still bore the stains. She refused to throw the gown away.

Levon pushed Anne Murray forward – she'd come quite willingly when he'd held out his hand. 'Tamara, my love, I have brought you another daughter.'

Chapter 3

It hadn't only been the sight of the *Queen Maia* sailing away with Annemarie on board that had made Mollie faint on that fateful afternoon. She'd been taken by ambulance to the Royal Hospital in Pembroke Place where it was discovered she was suffering from mild concussion as a result of the injury to her head.

'I'd like to keep you in for a few days so I can keep an eye on you,' the doctor said after he'd asked how many fingers he was holding up and she'd said two when there'd only been one. 'Do your relatives know you're here?'

'I haven't got any relatives in Liverpool,' she told him.

'You're a bit young to be living here all on your own, aren't you?' His name was Dr Packer and he was a rotund, cheerful-looking individual with a bright-red face and mutton-chop whiskers.

'I don't live here.' She ended up telling him the whole story, only missing out the reason she and her sister had left Ireland.

He clucked sympathetically. 'What are you going to do now?'

'Find somewhere to stay in Liverpool, then write to my aunt and ask her to send the money for another ticket.' She'd find a cheap hotel, hoping they wouldn't expect to be paid straight away and she could settle the bill when the money arrived.

Three days later, she was discharged from the hospital. Her head still ached, and she knew the terrible mistake she'd made by allowing the *Queen Maia* to leave without her would haunt her for the rest of her days. She worried constantly about Annemarie, though comforted herself with the thought that Gertrude Strauss would look after her and make sure she had her drops. Dr Packer had said the ship's doctor would have had digitalis, which only made Mollie feel stupid on top of everything else. Miss Strauss, or someone on the ship, would make sure her sister was safely delivered to Aunt Maggie, that's if Aunt Maggie wasn't there to meet her.

According to Dr Packer, there were loads of small hotels close to the centre of the city and she'd find one easily. 'Just go down London Road until you come to Lime Street, then ask someone, preferably a policeman.'

London Road was packed with pedestrians; tramcars clanked their way along, cars hooted at the slow-moving horses and carts. Mollie felt disembodied, as if her spirit were elsewhere, and the heavy traffic sounded muted in her ears. She forced herself to stop and stare into the windows of the dozens of little shops she passed, to concentrate on the fashionable clothes, the shoes with high heels that she'd always wanted, a train set that Thaddy would have loved, the jack-in-the-box that would have amused Aidan. Oh, and earrings shaped like teardrops which were similar to ones Mammy had used to wear. Her eyes pricked with teardrops of her own: since Mammy died life had become too depressing for words. Yet even though being in Liverpool on her own made her feel as miserable as sin, it was better than living in Duneathly with the Doctor. She sniffed and wiped her eyes. If everything went well, in a few weeks she would be in New York with Annemarie and Aunt Maggie and feeling herself again.

She arrived at Lime Street but, instead of asking the whereabouts of a small hotel, she stopped a woman pushing a baby in a giant pram and asked the way to Crosshall Street. She was badly in need of a friend right now.

Agatha's jaw dropped several inches when Mollie entered the chemist's. She was in the middle of serving a male customer who couldn't decide which ointment to buy. 'What on earth are you doing here?' she gasped when the man had gone. 'I thought you'd be halfway across the Atlantic by now.'

'So did I,' Mollie answered, rolling her eyes. 'At least, I did when I last saw you, but then didn't I go and miss the boat?'

'Flippin' heck,' Agatha snorted. 'I thought you left in plenty of time.'

'So did I, but it appears I got the time wrong.'

Agatha looked even more stunned. 'Where's your sister?' she enquired.

'*She's* halfway across the Atlantic.' Mollie managed to raise the glimmer of a smile.

'Jaysus! Where've you been for the last few days?'

'In hospital. I've only just been let out. It seems I had concussion.'

'Didn't I say you should go to hospital with that bump on your head?' She looked faintly smug at having been proven right.

'You did indeed,' Mollie agreed. 'I hope you don't mind me coming to see you.' She and Agatha had hardly spoken to each other for more than half an hour and it seemed a bit of a cheek to seek her out as if she were a long-lost friend.

'Mind!' Agatha snorted again. 'Of course I don't mind. If you'd let me know before, I'd have visited you in the hospital.' She came to the front of the counter. 'Sit down so I can see what the bump's like now.' Mollie sat down and Agatha gently parted her hair so she could have a good look. 'It's shrunk,' she announced. 'The bump that is, not your head.' She sat on the other chair. Behind her wire-rimmed glasses, her brown eyes shone with sympathy. 'I suppose you're feeling pretty fed up about things.'

'More than fed up,' Mollie said fervently. 'I'm devastated.'

'What are you going to do now?'

'Look for a cheap hotel where I can stay until I hear back from my aunt in New York.'

'You can stay with us,' Agatha said instantly, 'as long as you don't mind sleeping on the sofa in the parlour. It mightn't be as comfortable as a hotel, but it won't cost you a penny.'

The Brophys lived in Wavertree in a four-bedroom house with a big garden. Mrs Brophy could have moved somewhere cheaper when her husband had been killed in the Great War but, as Agatha explained, 'she's determined to hold on to the place, although it's a struggle. According to her, it's a matter of principle. She'd sooner we all went hungry than move. We get all our clothes from Paddy's Market, though don't mention that as she doesn't want people to know. The way she looks at it, once all us girls are working, she can get a job herself and there'll be plenty of money coming in and we can get rid of our creepy lodger.'

Agatha had four younger sisters: Blanche, Cathy, Dora and Ellen, who were all as thin as herself. 'I often wonder if they'd have gone through the entire alphabet if Dad had still been alive,' Agatha mused. 'I was only six when he volunteered. He and Mam had terrible rows about it – our Ellen had only just been born – but he said it was his duty to fight for his country. Not long afterwards, he was killed in the Battle of the Somme. He'd had a really good job with a shipping company and worked in an office on the Dock Road, so Mam's not used to being poor.'

Mrs Brophy was small and dainty, and welcomed Mollie into her home with a warm kiss. 'Aggie told us about you the other day. She was so envious of you going off to New York. It's such a shame what happened.'

Cathy, Dora and Ellen were still attending school. Blanche, who was fifteen and growing to be very tall, had wanted to become a mannequin and model clothes in one of the big London shops, but worked as a junior in an office down by the Pier Head.

'I'm wasting me life,' she grumbled on Mollie's first night. 'All I do is run round town with messages, do the filing, and make the tea. I'm nothing but a skivvy.'

'You're very lucky, having a nice clean job,' Mrs Brophy told her. 'If it hadn't been for your father's contacts, you could be a *real* skivvy. Then you'd have reason to complain.'

Apparently, Mr Brophy's contacts reached from beyond the grave. Agatha's job in the chemist's was also due to the manager having been a friend of her father's.

'I thought you worked there all by yourself?' Mollie commented.

'I do, but I'm not supposed to. Mr Gerard takes himself to the pub the minute it opens and doesn't come back until it closes, so I'm there by meself most of the time.'

Mrs Brophy was already in negotiation with another friend of her late husband to give thirteen-year-old Cathy a job in his restaurant in St John's Street when she left school in the summer. Dora and Ellen wondered aloud what she had in mind for them.

'We'll just have to see, girls,' their mother said enigmatically. 'We'll just have to see.'

The lodger, Mr Wainscott, occupied the big bedroom at the front of the house. He sold Bibles door to door and read aloud a passage from his wares every night before he went to bed.

'Don't be scared, Mollie, if you hear a ghostly voice quoting Leviathan or Exodus at about eleven o'clock,' Mrs Brophy warned her. 'It's just Mr Wainscott telling himself a bedtime story. He's quite harmless, really. Always pays his rent on time, never complains about the food, and is mostly very quiet.'

'He leaves a horrible smell in the lavatory, Mam,' Dora complained, 'and makes rude noises with his bottom.'

'That's because he has a problem with his bowels, love. Just ignore it; I do.'

'You can't just ignore a *smell*, Mam.'

'Then hold your nose, Dora,' her mother said sharply. 'I do that as well.'

All in all, despite her worries, Mollie quite enjoyed her stay with the Brophys, where the first thing she did was write to Aunt Maggie and Hazel. During the day, she helped with the housework and went on the occasional errand. Afternoons, she attached the buttons to gloves that Mrs Brophy had already painstakingly sewn together, a task for which she received sixpence for a dozen pairs.

'It all helps, Mollie,' she said serenely. 'They come from an old friend of Robert's. He always makes sure I receive the smallest sizes so there's less sewing to do.'

Since her husband had died, there'd been no chance of replacing the worn lino, the thinning carpets, curtains that were beginning to fray and wallpaper that had badly faded, so the house looked very shabby. Dinner consisted of the cheapest meat, which was minced in the big, cold kitchen and stewed with an enormous amount of vegetables, mostly potatoes. It tasted very watery and there was never a pudding. Yet Mollie admired Mrs Brophy for hanging on to her house. It would have been a simple matter to rent a smaller, cheaper one, but she had her standards and was determined to keep to them, even if it meant they ate like paupers and there was never a decent fire in the grate.

On Wednesday, half-day closing, she met Agatha and they went to a matinée at the Palais de Luxe, a picture house in Lime Street where they saw *Little Annie Rooney* starring Mary Pickford. Seats down at the front only cost a penny. It was the first film Mollie had ever seen.

'It was *wonderful*,' she breathed ecstatically when it was over and they were strolling back to the tram stop.

Agatha linked her arm. 'I won't half miss you when you've gone. I've got used to you living in our house.'

'I'll miss you, too,' Mollie said sincerely. 'But we can write to each other and perhaps one day you can come and see us.'

'I'd love to, but it'll be a long while before I have the opportunity,' Agatha sighed.

It would take weeks for her letter to reach Aunt Maggie and for her to answer, but Hazel's reply came within just a few days, a long letter written in big, bold writing, just like Hazel herself. 'Is your head better?' she asked. 'Oh, I bet you'd like to kick yourself, but it couldn't be helped. If I weren't nearly eight months pregnant, I'd come and see you. Finn's as mad as hell: with you, with me, but especially his father. The family you're staying with sound very nice . . . '

On the day the *Queen Maia* was due to dock in New York,

Mollie thought about her sister constantly and prayed hard she would be all right. Annemarie was only thirteen. Surely she wouldn't be left to look after herself.

A few days later, Hazel wrote again. This time the letter was short and to the point: 'Finn is coming to Liverpool on Saturday and wants you to meet him off the ferry. He should arrive at about ten o'clock.'

On Saturday, Mollie went to meet her brother, wondering why on earth he was coming to Liverpool. She hoped it wasn't to try to persuade her to go back to Duneathly. But she soon discovered that Finn was there for quite a different reason, something far more serious.

It was two weeks and four days after the *Queen Maia* had set sail for New York when Finn Kenny arrived in Liverpool on the Irish boat. In that time, the weather had miraculously improved. It was still cold, but the sun shone brilliantly in a light-blue sky, making the River Mersey shimmer. Seagulls swooped over the water, crying mournfully in their vain search for food. Finn had enjoyed two earlier visits to the city, but wished this time that the reason for his trip wasn't quite so grim.

His sister, Mollie, met him off the boat, and they went to a little café with a lofty ceiling and bare, scrubbed tables, not far from the Pier Head. The delicious smell of frying bacon wafted from the kitchen. He ignored it and ordered a pot of tea for two. Apart from a bored-looking waitress and whoever was frying the bacon, they were the only people there. Neither spoke until the tea was brought.

'Who's this friend you're staying with, Moll?' he enquired.

'Her name's Agatha Brophy,' Mollie replied. 'We met in the chemist's where I bought the digitalis for Annemarie. The family are Catholics and they're very nice.'

Finn frowned slightly, but otherwise felt satisfied with the answer. Mollie looked much thinner since he'd last seen her and he hoped the Brophys were feeding her properly, but, right how, it was his other sister he was most concerned about. 'You know,

Moll,' he said sternly, 'you should have told us about Dad the first time he . . . ' He paused, not quite knowing how to put it. 'The first time he did what he did. If you had, it would never have happened to Annemarie.'

Mollie's white cheeks went pink. 'I know that now, don't I, Finn?' she said in a small voice. 'But I didn't want to cause any trouble. The first time wasn't long after Mammy died. Everyone was already upset, and I didn't want to make matters even worse.'

'Our dad's the only one who'd've been feeling worse once I'd sorted him out,' Finn said hotly. He'd been shocked to the core when he'd discovered what had been happening in his own family and that he'd known nothing about it. He was an upright, virtuous young man and his father's behaviour sickened him. 'I'd've told him that if he touched you again I'd punch him into the middle of next week, dad or no dad.' He quivered with anger. 'The other day, I went to the house and had it out with him – Hazel told me the whole story when she got your letter saying you'd missed the boat.' They hadn't stopped rowing about it since; with him wanting to know why she hadn't told him before, and her saying she'd promised to keep it to herself. 'Until then,' he said to Mollie, 'I'd been going mad with worry, wondering where the pair o'yis had gone.'

'What did the Doctor have to say?'

'That he's sorry.' But he hadn't been all *that* sorry, not at first. He was simply surprised that it was *him* who'd driven his daughters away, though he had looked uncomfortable when his son had accused him of being a rapist and described the terrible effect it had had on Annemarie. Finn had never been all that fond of his father and his fingers had itched to punch the haughty, supercilious face. If it hadn't been for his little brothers, he'd never have gone near the house again. 'You don't have to worry, Moll. He won't dare touch you when you come home,' he said now. Should he try, he'd have Finn to deal with, not to mention Hazel, who was threatening to report him to the peelers.

'Oh, Finn, I'm not going home.' Mollie shivered at the thought. 'I never want to see Duneathly again. I want to go to

New York and be with Annemarie. I wrote to Aunt Maggie at the same time as I wrote to Hazel and asked her to send the money for the fare to Agatha's address. There's thirty-six pounds in our suitcase. It's what was left from Mammy's inheritance after the tickets had been paid for. As soon as it arrives, I'll be on the next boat to New York.'

Finn reached for her hand and squeezed it, knowing he was about to relay some really horrifying news. 'I'm sorry, Moll, but Annemarie never arrived at Aunt Maggie's,' he said gently. 'Maggie sent a telegram the next day. Since then, she's been searching for her everywhere, but hasn't had any luck so far.'

'Holy Mary, Mother of God!' Mollie crossed herself and burst into tears, causing the waitress to stare. 'Then what's happened to her?' she wailed.

'I don't know, sis.' He squeezed he hand again. 'Tomorrow, I'm sailing to New York from Southampton to help look for her. Maggie has already contacted all the hospitals and now the police are involved. Last night, I spoke to her on the telephone. I called from my office in Kildare and she answered in the shop beneath her apartment.' He still couldn't quite get over the wonders of modern technology, though dreaded to think what the call had cost.

'Can I come with you to New York, Finn?'

'No, Moll, I'm sorry,' he said firmly. 'You'll only get in the way.'

Mollie sniffed. 'There was a German woman in the cabin with us, Gertrude Strauss. I don't know why, but I thought she'd look after Annemarie. She seemed very kind.'

'Was anyone else in the cabin with you, sis?'

'There was a girl called Olive Raines. I quite liked her, but she was what Nanny would have called a "baggage". Miss Strauss accused her of all sorts of things.'

Finn nodded, but didn't speak. He didn't want his sister to know that Maggie had discovered a young woman answering to Annemarie's description had been taken to the hospital on Ellis Island where her passport had later been found. By the time

Maggie arrived, the girl had gone, collected by another young woman who'd produced Mollie's passport. The girl in the hospital had gone by the name Olive Raines. It would seem the real Olive Raines had used both his sisters for some dark, inexplicable reasons of her own.

'Have you got any money, sis?'

'No. I only had a few shillings in my purse, but I've spent it.' She hung her head. 'The rest was in the suitcase. I expect that disappeared an' all.'

'Maggie's never mentioned it, so I reckon it has. Look, take this.' He gave her five ten-shilling notes. 'I'll send more when I'm back home. I don't suppose you've got any clothes, either?'

'Only the ones I'm wearing, Finn.'

She looked so miserable it made him want to kill their father and do the same to Olive Raines should he ever get his hands on the girl. 'Hazel got Sinead Larkin to run you up a frock in a single day. Sinead had your measurements. It's in my case with a few other things.'

'Thank you, Finn,' she said gratefully. 'How is Hazel? I forgot to ask. The baby should arrive in a few weeks' time.'

'Hazel's blooming and the baby's due in the middle of April.' Finn could hardly wait to become a father. 'We're going to call it Patrick if it's a boy, but we can't decide on a girl's name.' He fancied Deirdre, but Hazel was rather taken with Geraldine, a name he loathed. They were still arguing over a compromise. Finn sighed and wished he were back in the little cottage in Duneathly with the wife he adored. He didn't feel like traipsing around a strange city on the other side of the world looking for his sister. But it had to be done. He dearly loved both his sisters and was determined to find Annemarie during the week he was about to spend in New York. He expected to be home in good time for the arrival of his first child.

She stood on the platform, waving to her brother until the train chugged out of sight in a cloud of smoke. It was even worse than watching the *Queen Maia* leave because now Annemarie was lost and it was all Mollie's fault! She'd felt miserable enough before, but it was nothing compared to how she felt now.

With a deep sigh, she trudged across to the ladies' waiting room where a bright fire burned in the grate. There were a few other women there with suitcases at their feet, and she remembered the parcel underneath her arm containing a new frock and the 'few other things'. She didn't bother to look: she couldn't care less what the frock was like or see what the 'other things' were.

What was she going to do now? It would be ages before Finn returned, but at least he'd promised to send a telegram to the Brophys when Annemarie was found – *if* she was found. A wave of horror swept over her at the thought that she might never see her sister again. She could be in a completely different part of America by now. She could have been kidnapped or even murdered – there was actually a chance that she was *dead*.

'Oh!' she groaned aloud, but was diverted from her black thoughts by a woman in a fur coat and a red cloche hat who came into the waiting room dragging a small boy by his arm. 'I shall never, *ever* take you shopping again. You've been nothing but a nuisance,' she shouted. She flung the child on to the wooden bench that surrounded the room on three sides. 'Now, sit there and don't *move*.'

The child, who only looked about two or three, immediately began to cry. The woman then slapped his face so hard that he uttered a scream of pain. There were murmurs of complaint from the other women there. 'There's no need for that,' one muttered. The woman gave her a malevolent glare and slapped the child on the other side of his face. He screamed again.

Mollie leapt to her feet. 'He's hardly more than a baby. How dare you hit him like that? You should be ashamed of yourself.'

'Should I really?' The woman did no more than stand up and slap Mollie's face. Mollie, who wouldn't normally have hurt a fly, punched her in the jaw, all the unhappiness and frustration that she'd felt over the last few weeks going into the blow. Perhaps her opponent had been suffering from similar frustrations, because she returned Mollie's punch with one of her own. Within minutes, they were in a fistfight.

'What the hell's going on in here?'

Mollie felt herself being dragged away by her collar and saw the fur-coated woman was in receipt of the same treatment. They were being held apart by the strong arms of a young policeman, splendid in his black uniform with gleaming silver buttons, a wide leather belt, and an enormous helmet. 'This is the *ladies'* waiting room,' he said sarcastically. 'If you want to fight, you'd best find a back alley somewhere and do it in private. Better still, don't do it at all and stay within the law.'

'She hit me first,' Mollie spat, 'and she was hitting her little boy so hard it made him scream.'

'She's right, officer,' one of the spectators put in – they all looked rather stunned. 'It was the other woman that started it.'

'I've a good mind to take you both to the station and book you for causing an affray,' the policeman said pompously, 'but there's the kid to consider, so I'll take your names and addresses instead. I'll have to consult with my superior officer as to whether any charges will be brought.'

'My husband will be terribly cross if the police come to the house,' Mollie's adversary said fearfully. 'I'm sorry I hit Rowley, but he's been a very naughty boy all morning. I suppose I felt at the end of my tether. And I'm sorry I hit you, too,' she said to Mollie. She looked more frightened than sorry.

Mollie ignored her. She had no intention of apologizing. She had two young brothers and knew how naughty little boys could be, but she'd never felt tempted to hit them. What's more, she'd actually been *enjoying* the fight and wished the policeman hadn't broken it up. At this moment, she didn't care if she was thrown into prison.

The policeman released their collars and produced a notebook from his pocket. Both women told him where they lived. 'If someone reports a similar incident to this, I'll know where to come,' he said, snapping the notebook shut.

★

Mollie returned to Wavertree to find Mrs Brophy sitting in the window sewing gloves. 'You look as if you've been in the wars,' she exclaimed. 'You have a bruise on your forehead and your cheeks are very red.'

'I fell over,' Mollie lied. She wasn't ashamed she'd been in a fight, but wasn't prepared to pass on the gory details to Mrs Brophy.

'What did your brother have to say?'

'That Annemarie never arrived at my aunt's. She's disappeared.'

Later that afternoon, she gave Mrs Brophy one of the ten-shilling notes. 'That's for having me all this time. Do you mind if I stay until I hear from our Finn?' If Annemarie were found, she'd go straight to New York. If she couldn't be located, Mollie had no idea what she would do.

'As far as I'm concerned, dear, you can stay for ever,' Mrs Brophy said as she gratefully accepted the ten shillings.

She was peeling a huge stack of potatoes the following morning when the doorbell rang. Mrs Brophy shouted, 'It's all right. I'll get it.' A few minutes later, she came into the kitchen and announced Mollie had a visitor. 'A rather nice young man. I've put him in the parlour.'

Mollie dried her hands, perplexed. She still had no idea who her visitor was when she went into the parlour and the young man jumped to his feet. He wore a well-pressed grey suit and clutched a dark-grey trilby close to his chest. His mackintosh had been folded neatly and placed on the back of a chair. 'Good morning, Miss Kenny,' he said respectfully.

'Good morning,' Mollie replied, as mystified as ever.

He grinned. 'You don't recognize me, do you? It was me who broke up the fight yesterday.'

'You're the policeman!' He looked very different out of uniform, much younger – about twenty-one, she reckoned – and not quite so pompous. His hair was short and brown and his eyes very blue. She supposed he was quite handsome in a way. 'What do you want?' she asked. 'Have you come to take me to prison?' She was slightly less prepared to go to prison today than she'd been the day before.

'No, I've come to ask you to the pictures one night. Do you mind if I sit down? And can I call you Mollie? I'm Tom Ryan, *Constable* Tom Ryan,' he added proudly.

'Of course you can sit down, and yes, you can call me Mollie.' She sat by the table in the window that was spread with pieces of glove for Mrs Brophy to sew. 'What do I call you – Tom, or Constable Ryan?'

'Tom.' He blushed slightly. 'What do you say about the pictures?' he asked eagerly.

'I don't know.' She was surprised he wanted anything to do with her after the fight. Another time, she would have found the situation embarrassing, but so much had happened lately, most of it bad, that she'd gone beyond the point of being embarrassed about anything. She didn't care what people thought of her or what impression she made. 'Do you make a habit of inviting criminals to the pictures?'

'You're not exactly a criminal. I know I shouldn't say this, me being a bobby, like, but I thought that woman deserved a poke for hitting her kid.' He was being pompous again and it made her want to laugh – yesterday she'd thought she'd never laugh again.

'Oh, all right, I'll come to the pictures with you.' She'd never been out with a boy before and she'd always thought the first time would be a grand occasion, but she was only going with Tom Ryan because he made her laugh and it might stop her from thinking about Annemarie, if only for a little while.

They went to a picture house in Lime Street opposite the Palais de Luxe to see *Sherlock, Jr.* with Buster Keaton, who was very famous, according to Tom. Mollie enjoyed it more than *Little Annie Rooney*, mainly due to the fact it was hilariously funny, as well as having the presence of an entire orchestra that played throughout the film.

Afterwards they had a fish supper. Over the meal, Tom told her about himself. He'd been a fully-fledged policeman for less than a year, but wanted to become a plain-clothes detective.

'What does that mean?' she asked.

His blue eyes gleamed. 'It means solving crimes – murders and robberies and stuff like that – and you wear your own clothes, not a uniform. Have you ever heard of Jack the Ripper?' he enquired. Mollie shook her head and he continued, a trifle ghoulishly, 'He murdered six women in the East End of London in a dead horrible way. He was never found, but I reckon *I'd* have caught him given half a chance. I've got a book about him at home – you can borrow it, if you like,' he said generously. 'And I've got one on Doctor Crippen, too, and loads of other murderers. I like using me brain, you see, looking for clues like Sherlock Holmes – that's why I took you to see that picture. Ordinary bobbies have got more brawn than brain.'

'I hope you don't say that to the ordinary bobbies,' Mollie remarked.

'Course not.' He wrinkled his nose. 'That's all most want to be, bobbies. Me, I intend to become a detective inspector one day.' He clearly thought very highly of himself.

'Out of interest,' Mollie said, 'why *did* you ask me out?' She felt sure she would get an honest answer because she doubted if Tom Ryan was capable of telling a lie.

'I liked your face,' he said instantly. 'It's a nice face; pretty, too. That's another thing I'm good at, reading faces. I just knew if you were fighting with that woman you had a good reason. I can tell if someone's a criminal from a mile away.'

'You're going to make a good bobby,' she told him, hiding a smile.

'I know. I was born for it. I used to tell me ma when I was little that I'd be a policeman one day.'

'And what did she say?'

'That she'd far sooner I became a priest. But I stuck to me guns, didn't I?' He grinned. 'I liked *your* ma. She seemed really nice.'

'Mrs Brophy isn't my mother,' Mollie said hastily. 'My own mother's dead and I'm just staying there temporarily.' She explained about New York and Finn and Annemarie. 'If Finn finds her, *when* he finds her,' she finished, 'I shall be off to New York on the next boat.'

'But you can't!' To her amazement, Tom Ryan's lips trembled and he looked on the verge of tears.

'Why ever not?'

'Because I'm in love with you, that's why. I told you I could read faces and the minute I saw yours I just knew I wanted you to be me wife. I wasn't going to tell you, not straight away like, case it put you off.' He threw back his shoulders and looked at her defiantly. 'So, there you are, Mollie, I've laid all me cards on the table and it's up to you whether you pick them up or not.'

Finn had come to New York prepared to dislike it at first sight. He wasn't used to cities and New York was a city and a half, a monument to Mammon where the dispossessed came from all corners of the earth to make their fortunes. But on his first day there, he'd stopped in the middle of a street where nothing could be seen except tall, magnificent buildings on all sides and a little patch of sky above. Inside him, something had stirred at the sight of this man-made wonder, as if a part of him were coming alive for the first time. His heart had raced and from then on he was caught in the vibrancy and sheer energy of the place.

He felt the same in Greenwich Village where there were no tall buildings, just houses and shops that never seemed to close, the goods displayed on the pavement outside, and every inch of wall covered with posters promoting poetry readings, plays, meetings, lectures, concerts, sporting events . . . the list was endless.

Everywhere he went he could hear music. It came from the Negro bands shuffling along the pavement in single file playing their hearts out, making Finn want to tap his feet, or from an open window where someone was practising the saxophone or the trumpet or singing at the top of their voice. It came through Maggie's floorboards from the shop below: little fat Ziggie on the piano, singing plaintively and slightly off-key. Finn had bought the music for 'Manhattan', a song from the *Ziegfeld Follies*, presently showing on 42nd Street, and asked Ziggie to sign it. He didn't own a piano or any sort of musical instrument, but he'd have it framed and hang it on the wall of the cottage where it would remain a perfect memento of New York.

Not *the* perfect memento. That would be to find Annemarie, but so far his search had proved fruitless. The truth was, Finn had already been there five days and didn't know where else to go. He hadn't realized that the island of Manhattan was quite so *big*, or so densely populated, literally teeming with people, a good proportion of them Irish. The police force seemed to be made up entirely of Irishmen who were also searching valiantly for his sister, but to no avail.

After informing the police, the next thing Maggie had done was telephone the hospitals, but they'd seen no one fitting Annemarie's description. Finn had visited the Catholic churches, though he knew the chances of finding his sister there were very slim. Between them, he and Maggie had written out dozens of cards with her name and address on to leave at the churches and all the Irish clubs he could locate. Lately, he'd taken to just wandering around, hands stuffed in his pockets, just hoping and praying for the sight of a pretty, thirteen-year-old girl with violet eyes and a smile that would light up the day.

Maggie was taking a lot of time off school. The principal fully understood her situation and the pupils said a prayer each morning at assembly that Annemarie would soon be found. Finn and his aunt usually arranged to meet up during the day: in Central Park, Times Square, or by the do'nut stall in Grand Central terminus, which was more like a cathedral than a station.

'No luck, I'm afraid,' Maggie would say when they met.

'Me, neither,' Finn would sigh. He was beginning to think they were flogging a dead horse. Trying to find his sister was like searching for a needle in a haystack.

He pressed the bell for Maggie's apartment at the end of his fifth day, feeling thoroughly disheartened. Maggie let him in. She reminded him so much of his beloved mother that the first sight of her always made his heart stop: the same black hair, blue eyes, fine nose and wide, generous mouth – Finn and Annemarie had inherited the same features – but, whereas his mother had dressed plainly and worn her hair in a severe bun, Maggie's clothes were of the latest fashion and her hair was short and elegantly waved. Mam had been forty-six when she died and Maggie two years older, yet she could have been in her thirties.

'There's some news,' she said soberly. 'I'm not sure whether you'd call it good or bad, or whether it's made me feel relieved or more worried than ever. Come upstairs and I'll show you.' Finn followed, his heart in his mouth, not knowing what to expect.

Maggie closed the door and handed him a sheet of paper. 'I found this on the mat in the hall when I came in. What do you make of it?'

It was a pencil drawing, extremely life-like, of a tiny boy wearing a nightshirt and carrying a candle in a holder. His hair was tousled and he was grinning widely, the tip of his tongue stuck mischievously out of his mouth.

'It's our Aidan!' he gasped.

'I've never seen Aidan, but I thought it might be,' Maggie said, tight-lipped. 'See what's written on the back.'

Finn turned the paper over. '*Anne is perfectly safe. She is being well looked after. You have no need to worry*,' he read. The words were written in perfect copperplate. 'He calls her Anne.'

'Why do you say "he"?' Maggie queried. 'It could have been written by a woman.'

'This is how a solicitor would write, or a clerk in a certain sort of office where a woman is unlikely to be employed. Our wedding certificate was written in copperplate. Jaysus!' He slapped his hand against his brow as the message in the note, the sheer strangeness of it, began to sink in. 'But what does this mean, Maggie? Why does he call her Anne? And how did he know to deliver it here?'

'I've no idea, unless Annemarie told him this address or he saw one of our cards. Perhaps someone else knows it – what about the woman you say was in the cabin with the girls, Gertrude Strauss?'

Maggie scowled. 'Or Olive Raines, who stole Mollie's passport and the suitcase with the money. Oh, Finn! I really don't know what to think.'

'She's happy,' Finn said thoughtfully. 'If she weren't, she'd have drawn our Aidan crying. She loved drawing: happy pictures and sad ones, depending on her mood.'

Maggie sat down with a bump. 'I suppose that's something.'

'She loved singing, too, and dancing. She was in love with life, Annemarie, but the slightest little thing – a cross word, a sick animal – could make her sink into the doldrums – the Slough of Despond, Mam used to call it – though she quickly snapped out of it. Strangely enough, she wasn't as upset as the rest of us when Mam died, because she said she could see her in heaven.'

'Your mother used to worry about her all the time. She said she was too sensitive for this world.' Maggie's face darkened. 'I can't imagine how she must have felt the night your father *raped* her,' she said savagely. 'It must have sent her out of her mind, the poor wee child.'

'Hazel said it more or less had, that she was in a sort of trance the night they left Duneathly. Yet our Mollie stood it for two whole years and didn't say a word.' Finn's voice shook. 'I actually told her off, Mollie, when we met in Liverpool, as if she'd done something wrong.'

'Mollie's a brick and Frank Kenny is a bastard. I hope and pray I never set eyes on the man again, else I'll murder him for sure.' Maggie eased herself out of the chair and went towards the kitchen. 'Me throat's crying out for a cup of tea, Finn. Once we've had it, I'll take that piece of paper round to Sergeant McCluskey at the station, see what *he* makes of it. And, instead of us sitting here all night long trying to make sense of things until we feel dizzy, we'll go for a meal and do it there instead. As you say, at least it seems Annemarie's happy, wherever she is.'

'Me, I'm aching for a pint of ale. D'you know, Maggie, I haven't seen a pub all week, though I've been keeping me eye out for one.'

'You're not likely to.' Maggie smiled for the first time since he'd met her in New York. 'Haven't you heard of Prohibition? Alcohol's banned in the United States, though there's more drunk now than when it was legal. There's a speakeasy round the corner where you can get really vile whisky at an outrageous price and there's always a chance the police will raid the joint.'

'I think I'd sooner wait until I get back to Ireland,' Finn said hastily.

He didn't have to wait quite so long. As soon as he arrived back in Liverpool, he went to the George Hotel and ordered a pint of best bitter while he waited for Mollie. He wanted to have a long talk with his sister and try to persuade her to return to Duneathly. It was too much to expect her to live in the Doctor's house, but she could live with him, Hazel and the new baby when it came. Finn hoped she still wasn't planning on going to New York. Maggie's apartment wasn't nearly big enough for two people, and weren't his legs still hurting like blazes after sleeping with his top half on one chair and the rest of him on another for seven uncomfortable days?

The boat had docked early and he had to wait a good hour and a half before his sister came, during which time he thought about Annemarie. At least she was happy – he must have said that to Maggie half a dozen times while she said the same to him. It was something, the only thing that had provided a crumb of comfort during the long futile search. He took the drawing out of his pocket and studied it yet again, visualizing Annemarie drawing it, concentrating hard, her white brow furrowed. But drawing it *where*? Somewhere in New York was the only answer. Somewhere within that busy, noisy, brightly lit, tumultuous city, Annemarie had sat and drawn a picture of their little brother.

'That's our Aidan,' said a voice, and he looked up and saw Mollie staring at the picture. 'I can't remember Annemarie doing that.'

He leapt to his feet, took her in his arms, and held her tightly for a good minute, wanting to cry for some reason. 'It's good to see you, Moll,' he said, kissing both her cheeks before letting her go.

'You didn't find her, did you?' she said sadly. 'Else you'd've sent a telegram like you promised.'

'No, Moll,' he said gently. 'But Annemarie's all right.' He signalled to a waiter to fetch the tea he knew she'd want, then told her about his useless search for their sister – the visits to the churches, the Irish clubs, the cards he and Maggie had written out together – and, finally, the delivery of Aidan's picture through the front door of Maggie's apartment house. 'Read what's on the back, sis.'

'"*Anne is perfectly safe. She is being well looked after. You have no need to worry*,"' Mollie read aloud. 'Why do they call her Anne and not Annemarie?'

Finn shrugged. 'Who knows?'

Mollie continued to ask the same questions that he and Maggie had asked each other without coming up with a single answer that made sense. 'Well, at least she's happy,' she said at last.

'Maggie's determined to keep on searching and the police haven't given up. She'll be found one day, Moll, you'll see.'

Mollie smiled sweetly and Finn was struck by how lovely she was. She didn't have Annemarie's flamboyant beauty, the sort that made your head turn, but a quiet, serene loveliness that grew on you. He noticed a well-dressed young man seated a few tables away who seemed unable to keep his eyes off her.

'What are you going to do with yourself now, Moll?' he asked. If she wanted, he told her, she could come back with him to Duneathly today.

'I'm going to stay in Liverpool, Finn,' she said quietly.

'But it's not your home, sis. You hardly know a soul here except the Brophys. You'd have to get a job and a proper place to live.'

'I've already done both. I arranged it as soon as I realized you hadn't found Annemarie. If you had, then I'd've gone to New York and come back to Liverpool as soon as she was herself again.'

'But *why*?'

She looked at him shyly. 'Because I'm getting married in July on my birthday, that's why.'

'Jaysus!' Finn nearly dropped his beer. 'Who to?'

'To Tom Ryan, he's a policeman.'

'He sounds much too old for you.' It was all he could think of to say.

'He's twenty-one, same as you. Would you like to meet him? That's him over there. Today's his day off, that's why he's not in uniform.' She signalled to the young man who'd been watching her so avidly. He jumped to his feet and came over. 'Tom, this is my brother, Finn. I've just told him we're getting married.'

Finn arrived in Kildare feeling limp and dejected. He'd had nearly four weeks off work – his boss was just as understanding as Maggie's. He hadn't liked Tom Ryan; he was too full of himself for words. What's more, he wasn't sure if he'd ever feel content again in Ireland after the hustle and bustle of New York. He caught the bus to Duneathly and stared gloomily at the scenery, the rolling fields, the trees just bursting into bud, the little cottages, like his own, nestling at the foot of the hills. It was all too damned quiet and dull.

The bus stopped outside his cottage, he opened the creaking gate that he kept meaning to fix, and went in the front door, to be met by a strange cry from upstairs. He dropped his suitcase, mounted the stairs two at a time, and burst into the bedroom.

Hazel was lying on the bed, looking as if she'd just climbed Mount Everest with lead in her boots, and Carmel O'Flaherty, the midwife, was holding a tiny baby covered in blood, who was yelling loud enough to bring down the roof.

'You're just in time to say hello to our son, Finn,' Hazel said with an exhausted smile.

'Is there something wrong with him?' Had his son cut himself already?

'It's your wife's blood, Mr Kenny. I'll wash it off him in a minute. As for the crying, that's quite normal. *You'd* cry if you'd just come out of a lovely warm place into the cold of the big wide world.' Carmel gave him a severe look. 'You shouldn't really be here. Most husbands take themselves off to the pub, leaving their wives to have their babies in peace. But,' she relented, 'seeing as you are here, would you like to hold the baby while I tidy your wife up?'

'Yes, please,' Finn croaked. The baby was wrapped in a towel, still screaming, and placed in his arms.

'Would you mind looking the other way for a wee while, Mr Kenny?'

He did as he was told, but not before glancing at Hazel, seeing the love in her eyes that he knew was reflected in his own. He stood in front of the window holding his baby. In the space of only a few minutes, he had forgotten all about New York and his sisters. Now he was just thankful that he was back in Ireland with his wife and his new son.

'Hello, Patrick,' he whispered.

Chapter 4

He opened the door and she came dancing towards him, her black hair flaring out.

'We bought pizza from Lombardi's, Lev, your favourite,' she sang, 'with cheese and tomatoes and Italian sausage and olives.' She threw her arms around his neck. 'I'm starving,' she announced. He watched, fascinated, as her hair settled in a tumble of little curls and waves around her shoulder.

'Then we shall eat immediately.' Levon Zarian removed his cap and jacket and put them in the lobby cupboard. His own hair was just as black and lustrous, if considerably shorter. 'Where's Tamara?'

'In the kitchen, getting things ready. I've been helping. We're having wine, red, and there's coffee ice cream in the ice box.'

He smiled – Anne always made him smile. 'Is there a reason for this feast? Or are we just celebrating the fact it's Tuesday, the sun is out, and the trees in Central Park are in full bloom? I passed today and it looked lovely. We must go there for a walk one day soon.'

'I don't think we're celebrating anything, Lev.' She hung on to his arm when he went into the kitchen where Tamara was preparing a salad.

'Hello, my love.' He rubbed his cheek against her smooth one and she kissed his nose. Tall and queenly, with plaits wound around her well-shaped head, to him she always seemed out of place in a kitchen. In Armenia, servants had done everything for them. 'Are you all right?' She looked rather strained, he thought.

'Something's happened, I'll tell you later.' Her eyes flickered towards Anne, who was attempting to uncork the wine.

Levon's stomach lurched. 'Does it mean we might lose her?' he enquired in their old language.

'No, and please speak English, Lev,' Tamara whispered, 'otherwise you'll frighten her.'

Neither could understand why Anne's face froze and she ran from the room when sometimes, inadvertently, they addressed each other in a foreign tongue. Perhaps she felt shut out or scared by something she didn't understand.

'Lev will see to the wine, darling,' she said. He saw that Anne's efforts were taking pieces out of the cork. 'You set the table. I've nearly finished the salad.'

They ate in the small dining room, the sinking sun illuminating the room like a stage set. It was a cheerful meal, gay and full of laughter, so different from the meals eaten in the same room before Anne had arrived to bless their lives with her vivid smile and delightful presence.

It was three months since he'd found her and he found it unbelievable how quickly she'd settled in. Within the space of a day or two, she had begun to talk in a strong Irish accent, not about the past, but the present. She seemed to accept him and Tamara without question, calling them by their first names, as if she'd known them all her life. Levon realized that her brain wasn't wholly sound: no normal girl would behave the way she did.

Tamara thought she was hiding from something. 'What?' Levon had asked.

'How should I know, Lev? She shows no sign of being homesick: she isn't missing anybody. She never talks about her past, yet she must have one. I think she feels safe with us: she knows we'll never harm her.'

Tamara was a new woman nowadays. She taught Anne the songs she'd sung at weddings back in Armenia, translating the words, bought her clothes, ornaments, ribbons for her long hair, purses, and pretty shoes. And she bought clothes for herself: lacy blouses and skirts, not as short as the latest fashion — Tamara wouldn't dream of showing her knees — a hat made entirely of pink velvet petals to frame the aristocratic face that now seemed miraculously free of careworn lines.

Anne had been there barely a fortnight when she'd asked for a drawing pad and pencil. Tamara, always willing to indulge her every whim, rushed out and bought them. When he came home, she showed him the drawing Anne had done: a small grinning boy in a nightshirt with a candleholder in his hand.

'She said his name is Aidan.' They had studied the drawing, not speaking. 'It might be her brother,' Tamara had said eventually.

'I wonder if he's missing his sister?' For the first time, Levon felt a sense of guilt. It had been rash and utterly irresponsible to virtually kidnap the girl off the streets. He'd told himself he was rescuing her from the people who'd been careless enough to put her in a taxi to be delivered like a parcel to an address where no one was in. He couldn't have just *left* her there to wait for someone who might never come. *That* would have been even more irresponsible.

The day after the drawing, he'd said nothing to Tamara, but had taken it with him when he went to collect the taxi from the depot, written a message on the back, and put it through the letterbox of 88 Bleecker Street. If someone were worried, it would reassure them that Anne was safe.

Since then, she'd drawn more pictures: another boy older than the first whose name was Thaddy; a sad-eyed girl called Mollie; a young man named Finn; a woman of about Tamara's age who appeared to be seated on a cloud. Tamara, who seemed attuned to the girl's every mood, deduced that this was her mother and she was dead. 'The cloud means she's in heaven,' she explained.

One morning, she'd taken Anne to Mulberry Street market on the Lower East Side where there was a stall that sold Italian lace. The minute they got off the bus, they'd come across a man savagely whipping an old, ailing horse that was attempting to pull a cart heaped with sacks. Anne had been so distressed that they had returned straight home. That afternoon, she'd drawn the face of a black-eyed man with heavy eyebrows and lips twisted in a sneer. 'She even drew horns on his head,' Tamara had told Levon, shocked. 'At the bottom, she wrote "The Doctor".'

'Where is the picture?' Levon had asked.

'She ripped it to pieces, very slowly and deliberately, then threw it in the trash. Something bad has happened to her, Lev. I'm convinced of it.'

The meal over, Tamara and Anne cleared the table and went into the sitting room to play records on the phonograph, while Levon stayed at the table to study for the Bar exam. He would be relieved when he was able to practise law in America and no longer had to drive a taxi, something he did more to pass the time than for the money. He was already a moderately wealthy man, and had managed to bring his small fortune with him, if not the rich contents of his house in Armenia. Not that *things*, however beautiful and finely crafted, mattered after they'd lost their beloved Larisa.

The strains of Tchaikovsky's *Nutcracker Suite* drifted into the room. He bent his head over his work until, a few minutes later, Tamara came in and sat at the table with him. He laid down his pen, remembering she had something to tell him.

'Anne is dancing,' she said. 'She makes up the steps as she goes along. She gets quite lost in it.'

'Perhaps we should send her to a stage school,' Levon suggested, 'where she can learn to sing and dance professionally?'

'That's a good idea, Lev, but not just yet.' She played with the earring in her left ear, a sign she had something important to say. 'I took Anne to the doctor's this morning,' she said in her mother tongue. 'She needed more drops for her heart.' It was Tamara who'd noticed the girl's heart beat unevenly on occasions. The doctor had prescribed a drug called digitalis. 'It's nothing serious, but it's best to be safe than sorry. Just give her five drops a day on her tongue,' he'd said.

'Is she all right?' Levon asked now, alarmed.

'Fine, Lev, but there's just one thing: I thought Anne had yet to start having periods, but that's not the case at all. She doesn't have them because she's pregnant.' She laid her hand on his arm. 'Lev, darling, Anne is expecting a child.'

There'd been poor people in Duneathly, farm workers mostly, who lived in shacks on the farmers' land. They weren't seen all that often in the village. They had no need of solicitors, banks, or dress shops. Occasionally, they might call out the doctor, but doctors didn't work for free and it had to be a real emergency. The women sometimes went to the butcher's just before it closed to buy bones for a stew that would last all week, and the men packed into O'Reilly's pub on Friday night after they'd been paid. Mollie had been woken from her sleep many times by the sound of a desperate row going on outside. A woman would be dragging her husband out of the pub screaming, 'Before you spend every penny of your wages on the ale and leave your kids to starve, you flamin' eejit!'

In Liverpool, there was Mrs Brophy, in her fine four-bedroom house with a big garden, struggling to keep her head above water until she and all her girls were at work and the money would come pouring in. At least Mrs Brophy was in a position to have dreams. For some people, life was truly hopeless.

Mollie realized this for the first time when Tom Ryan took her home to meet his mother. Irene Ryan's house was spotless, the windows shone, the step was scrubbed, and there was food in the larder. The house stood out from its dreary, filthy neighbours in Turnpike Street off Scotland Road where Tom and his three brothers had been born and where scores of sickly, half-starved children played in the cobbled street dressed in little more than rags. Most were barefoot. Mollie couldn't believe such poverty existed in a big, vigorous city like Liverpool.

The reason for Mrs Ryan's affluence was due entirely to the generosity of her four sons, who had all passed the scholarship and had good, well-paying jobs. Mike, the eldest, worked as a supervisor in the post office in Moorfields, Brian was traffic manager for the Liverpool Tool Company, and Enoch had served his apprenticeship as a carpenter and now had his own little furniture business, which was doing extremely well. Mrs Ryan showed Mollie two chairs he'd made with lovely carved backs and curved arms. And then there was Tom, a policeman, though Mrs Ryan had wanted him to become a priest.

'I always fancied having a priest in the family,' she sighed when she and Mollie first met.

Tom had winked at Mollie from behind his mother's back. 'I'd've made a hopeless priest, Ma, and I'd never have learned the Latin.'

'You can do anything if you try hard enough,' his mother said severely.

Tom told Mollie later that this phrase had been drummed into him for as long as he could remember. 'She said the same to all of us: "You can do anything if you try." She used to get books out the library and help us with our schoolwork so we were always top of the class in everything,' he said proudly. 'Ma was determined we'd all get good jobs, not go on the parish like the rest of the lads in Turnpike Street. After our dad died not long after I was born, she used to take me cleaning with her, and she took in washing an' all. Night-times, she worked in a pub on Scottie Road and our Mike looked after me.'

Irene Ryan was a small, knobbly woman who walked with a slight limp. Her hands were red and swollen and her back was hunched as a result of a lifetime of hard work. It was hard to believe she'd given birth to four strapping lads. A photograph of them stood on the sideboard, taken the day Tom had become a fully-fledged policeman, their little tough mother in the centre, wearing the beaver lamb fur coat that was her pride and joy. The lads had clubbed together and presented it to her on her fiftieth birthday.

They thought the world of their mam, who had encouraged them to dream and impressed on them they could do anything they wanted if they tried hard enough. They took turns sending money every week because it only seemed fair. If it hadn't been for Mam, they wouldn't be where they were today, but standing on street corners playing pitch and toss or hanging around the Docks or St John's Market in the hope of getting a few hours' work, while their wives and kids had to rely on charity for food.

Tom was the only son still single, but only until Mollie's birthday came along in July when she would become seventeen and a married woman, both on the same day. She was looking forward to it because she liked Tom very much and he made her laugh – there hadn't been much to laugh at in Duneathly over the last few years. And Tom loved her so wholeheartedly that it would be a shame to throw it back in his face because she doubted if a love like his came along twice in a woman's life.

She'd left the Brophys months ago and now lived with Tom's mother in the little house in Turnpike Street, sleeping in the same feather bed where Tom had slept when he was little – she could have sworn she could smell the fresh, tingling soap he used whenever her head touched the pillow. He was in a hostel where all the young, single policemen lived until they found themselves a wife. Once they were married, they would be given a police house. Tom didn't know yet where it would be.

Mollie couldn't wait.

'Morning, luv,' Mrs Ryan grunted when she limped into Mollie's room with a cup of tea, as she did every morning.

'Morning, Irene.' Mollie struggled to a sitting position. She'd been told to call her future mother-in-law by her first name, as it sounded friendlier.

'It's a lovely day outside,' Irene remarked, pulling back the curtains and allowing the golden sunshine to come pouring in. It was May and unseasonably warm for the time of year.

'I wish you wouldn't do this, you know,' Mollie said uncomfortably. 'I mean, it should be *me* bringing *you* tea, not the other way around.'

'No, it shouldn't, luv. Me, I'm a lady of leisure these days and I don't have much to do with me time.' Her prematurely wizened face split into a grin. 'Anyroad, you're a doctor's girl: you're probably used to being waited on.'

'Indeed I'm not. No one got cups of tea in bed back in Ireland.'

'Are you quite sure your father won't be coming to the wedding, luv?'

'No, he won't,' Mollie said quickly. 'He'll be too busy, and I think I told you he gets seasick easily, so he can never leave Ireland. There's just my brother, his wife, and baby coming, Aunt Maggie from New York, and of course the Brophys, all six of them, including Agatha, who's my bridesmaid.'

Aunt Maggie wasn't crossing the Atlantic just for the wedding, but to meet Hazel, Patrick and Aidan for the first time, not to mention Thaddy, who'd only been a baby when she left for America. She would be staying in Finn's cottage for two weeks after the wedding.

It was going to be quite a big wedding. Tom's brothers, their wives and seven children would be there, plus half a dozen policemen and Irene's best friend, Ethel, with whom she went every Saturday to the music hall in the Rotunda Theatre on Scotland Road.

Finn had sent five pounds, which meant everything had to be done as cheaply as possible, but Irene was good at doing things on the cheap. 'Look after the pennies, and the pounds'll look after themselves,' she said wisely. She'd taken Mollie to Paddy's Market where she'd bought a wedding dress with its own silky petticoat for one and sixpence — it needed taking up an inch or two, but otherwise fitted just fine — and a pair of stiff silk shoes, only slightly worn. The dress was made of slipper satin with a lace yoke and long tight sleeves, and smelt just a little bit of mothballs.

Mrs Brophy was letting Mollie borrow her veil and a wreath that was a mixture of pearls and little wax flowers. Ethel was making the cake. Pauline, Lily and Gladys, Irene's daughters-in-law, with whom Mollie got on exceptionally well, had promised to make loads of sandwiches for the reception, which would be held in a room over the Throstles' Nest, a local pub.

'That way,' Irene had said with a chuckle, 'you only have to provide a drink for the toast. Afterwards, everyone can buy their own and it means you get the room free of charge.'

'Anyroad, girl,' Irene said now, 'I'll go and start on the brekky. I suppose you only want toast again?'

'Yes, please. I'll never get into that wedding dress if I have any more of your big fried breakfasts.'

'You could do with more fat on you, Mollie.'

'And so could you,' Mollie retorted. She doubted if Irene weighed more than six stones.

'Don't be cheeky,' Irene said good-humouredly. 'The toast'll be ready in five minutes.'

Mollie drained the tea, poured water into a bowl from the jug she'd brought up the night before, and quickly got washed. There was no bathroom in the house and she bathed in a tin bath in front of the fire on Saturday nights after Irene and Ethel left for the Rotunda and before Tom arrived to take her to the pictures. She put on the dress that Sinead Larkin had run up in a single day: pale-grey and dark-grey stripes with three-quarter-length sleeves and a plain, round neck. It was a trifle shorter than she was used to. Every time she put it on she thought about Annemarie.

She caught her hair in a bunch, pulled it over her shoulder, and began to twist it into a plait. Annemarie had used to do the same, and Mollie recalled the way she'd squinted at it the longer the plait became.

'Don't do that, darlin',' Mammy used to say. 'One of these days the wind will change and your eyes will stay that way.'

'Don't care,' Annemarie would cry. 'Don't care, Mammy, don't care.'

The toast was ready: she could smell it. She wished Irene would use butter instead of margarine. At home, they'd only had butter, as one of the farmers used to deliver a huge pat every Friday morning, along with two dozen eggs and a jug of cream. Nowadays, Irene could easily have afforded butter, but old habits died hard and it probably didn't cross her mind to buy anything but the cheapest margarine that tasted of petrol – at least, so Mollie thought.

She went downstairs to the little living room where Irene was holding a slice of bread as thick as a doorstep on a fork in front of the fire. There was no need of a fire today, but it was the only way of acquiring hot water.

'It's nearly done, luv. Pour yourself another cuppa, the pot's on the table. You can pour me one while you're at it.' She said the same thing every day.

Mollie sat at the table that overlooked a small, white-washed yard where the tin bath hung from a hook on the wall. There was a lavatory at the end which was full of spiders and very inconvenient to use if it was raining, even more so when it was dark and it was necessary to take a candle that was likely to go out before you got as far as the door.

Irene fussed around, piling toast on to Mollie's plate. She protested she couldn't possibly eat it all. One slice would have been sufficient.

'Never mind, girl,' Irene said, 'I'll give what's over to the lads next door.'

The lads belonged to Tossie Quigley, who could be heard through the thin walls screaming at them at the top of her voice. Barely twenty, her two tiny boys looked more like toddlers than three- and four-year-olds. Tossie's husband had just walked out one day and never come back, and she'd been left to cope on her own. Irene helped as much as she could, but Turnpike Street was full of people like Tossie and her stunted kids, and she couldn't possibly feed them all. 'Much as I'd like to,' she often said sadly.

Mollie ate most of the toast, though it was an effort, collected her small white hat with a turned-down brim, white gloves, and black patent leather handbag from the parlour, and shouted, 'I'm off now, Irene.'

'Tara, luv,' Irene shouted back. 'What time will I see yis tonight?'

'Not until late. Tom's on early shift this week: he's collecting me at half past five and we're going to the pictures.'

'Have a nice time, then, girl.'

Before opening the door, Mollie steeled herself. She hated stepping out into the street dolled up to the nines and coming face to face with women who'd probably never had a new frock in their lives, who wore tatty black shawls over their heads, and never seemed to comb their hair from one week to the next. The looks she got were full of envy or contempt, even hatred for this smartly dressed stranger who was about to marry a man with a decent job and a regular wage coming in. She waved at an elderly woman who was sitting on her doorstep enjoying the glory of the early-morning sunshine. 'Good morning,' she cried.

'Morning,' the woman replied sullenly.

A little girl was skipping with a rope that didn't have any handles. Mollie patted her head. 'Hello, darlin'.'

'Hello.' The girl stopped skipping and gave her a lovely smile. 'I like your hat, miss.'

'It used to have a feather on, but I took it off.' She returned the girl's smile. 'What's your name?'

'Betsy. I'm going to have a hat like that when I grow up.'

'I hope you have ten hats like this, Betsy.'

The street negotiated, she gave a sigh of relief when she reached Scotland Road where she caught the tram into town. Mollie had managed to get a job all on her own without the intervention of the long-dead Mr Brophy. She worked in Roberta's Milliners in Clayton Square, but only until she married Tom. By then, Roberta's daughter, Erica, who normally helped her mother in the shop, would have returned from Milan where she was taking a millinery course.

Roberta – whose real name was Doris – sold posh hats to posh women and was a dreadful snob. Mollie was convinced she'd only got the job because her father was a doctor. She suspected Roberta would like to have had the fact tattooed on her forehead for her posh customers to see.

She arrived at the shop and paused in front of the window where Roberta was changing the display, something she did regularly with enormous enjoyment: she was a widow and the shop was her life.

'That's nice,' Mollie mouthed, pointing to the hat Roberta was fitting on to a faceless bald head. It was pink organdie with a wired brim and a floppy rose on the side, perfect for a wedding.

She opened the door and Roberta said, 'It's a copy of a Worth model.' She mainly stocked copies of famous brands – Chanel, Jeanne Lanvin, Callot Soeurs – some of which she made herself. Her customers passed them off as the real thing. Now that it was summer, most of the hats were straw: lacquered straw, wild straw, plain straw, and a few pastel-coloured felts. The in-style this year was the cloche, though there were a few with wide brims for women who had no taste or didn't give a fig whether or not they wore the latest fashion. Mollie's own hat was a last year's model that Roberta had let her have for quarter-price. Originally, it had sported a giant ostrich feather, which she'd removed and given to Irene.

She made the first cup of tea of the day and stood behind the counter to wait for the customers to arrive. Roberta seated herself on one of the padded chairs in front of a long mirror, complaining that her feet were giving her gyp. From time to time, she glanced admiringly at her reflection. She was beautifully, if plentifully, made up, her lips painted bright red and hair dyed much the same colour. Her navy-blue costume with huge white buttons would have looked better on a woman twenty years her junior, but she was attractive in a showy sort of way.

She'd wanted to go on the stage when she was young, she'd told Mollie. 'But my mother was dead set against it. She said it was a terribly common profession, and encouraged me to become a milliner instead. Then I met Stewart and we fell in love and got married.' She sighed. 'But I still wish Mother had let me go on the stage. I mean, there's nothing common about Gertrude Lawrence or Beatrice Lillie, is there? And Sybil Thorndike is very highly thought of.'

'There's nothing at all common about them,' Mollie agreed, though she'd never heard of any of the women.

Now Roberta was admiring her long, red nails, and Mollie immediately remembered waking up on the *Queen Maia* to see Olive Raines painting hers the same colour, Annemarie still fast asleep in the top bunk. She must have thought about her sister a hundred times a day. In her heart, she had the strongest feeling that Annemarie was safe and almost certainly happy – the drawing of Aidan was proof of that. By now, she would be fourteen. It was her birthday on April Fool's Day. Had she remembered? Mollie wondered.

She recalled the night she'd gone to stay with her friend, Noreen, in order to avoid the attentions of the Doctor, and the next morning finding her sister lying like a corpse in her bed, her nightie stained with blood. Since that terrible day, Annemarie had barely spoken, let alone drawn a picture. But it appeared as if the spell she was under had been broken and all Mollie could hope and pray for was that one day she'd find her sister again – or that Annemarie would find her.

The door opened and a woman came in dressed entirely in fawn crêpe: her frock, loose coat, and toque hat were all made from the same material.

'Mrs Ashton!' Roberta leapt to her feet. 'How lovely to see you. You're looking well, I must say.'

'We're not long back from Bermuda,' Mrs Ashton boasted. 'We spent the winter there.'

Mollie rushed forward and grabbed a chair, holding it invitingly for the woman to take. According to Roberta, once a customer was seated, they were far more likely to make a purchase.

'You are *so* lucky,' Roberta gushed. 'My daughter is in Milan at this very minute. I'm *so* envious. Would you like a glass of sherry, Mrs Ashton, while you make your choice?' Customers were even more likely to buy a hat once they'd had a glass of sherry.

'Well, I wouldn't say no: sweet, if you don't mind.' She seated herself on the chair, allowing Mollie a glassy smile.

Roberta waved a majestic hand – she *would* have been good on the stage. 'Mollie, fetch Mrs Ashton a sweet sherry, there's a dear.'

'Has your daughter left the shop for good, or is this girl just filling in, as it were?'

'Oh, Mollie's just filling in. Her father's a doctor,' Roberta hissed. 'Now, Mrs Ashton, do you want a hat for a special occasion? Or is it because it's spring and you feel like something new?'

'Both, I suppose,' Mrs Ashton conceded. 'I feel like something new and my first grandson is getting christened the Sunday after next.'

Roberta gasped. 'I can't believe you're old enough to have grandchildren.'

'Actually, he's my third. I already have two granddaughters.'

'That's quite incredible. Don't you think it's incredible, Mollie?'

'Incredible,' Mollie concurred, though Mrs Ashton looked a good fifty.

After it was established that she wanted a white hat, 'preferably straw', Mollie was commanded to fetch a series of white hats from the stock room at the back. 'The cloche with the red silk flower, and the one with the lace insets — blue lace, Mrs Ashton. It's terribly pretty. Oh, and bring that little boater with the petersham ribbon, dear.'

The shop quickly became a jumble of hats and round, candy-striped boxes. Mrs Ashton tried on all of them, had another glass of sherry, and eventually bought the pink organdie hat with a wired brim and a floppy rose on the side that Roberta had not long put in the window.

She departed, saying she would now have to buy an entirely new outfit to go with it, and Roberta collapsed in a chair. 'It looked ghastly on her, but I couldn't very well tell her that, could I?' she said, looking pious.

'Not really.' The pink hat, Roberta had insisted, made Mrs Ashton look just like Lady Elizabeth Bowes-Lyon who, not long ago, had married the Duke of York in Westminster Abbey. It was as big a lie as Ena Gerraghty claiming she stocked the latest Paris fashions in her shop in Duneathly.

The same performance was repeated four more times that morning, with only one woman managing to resist Roberta's flowery compliments and leaving the shop hatless.

At one o'clock, dinner-time, Mollie made her way to Blackler's, a big department store no distance from Clayton Square, where the hats were only a fraction of Roberta's prices, not that it was a hat she was after. The weather was becoming increasingly warmer and she badly needed a couple of summer frocks: the one she was wearing was made of thick material and made her feel sticky and hot. She wondered what had happened to the ones in the suitcase that she'd been taking with her to New York. More importantly, what had happened to the money, the thirty-six pounds that Mammy had left her? It had seemed an enormous amount and to some people it was a small fortune, more than they would expect to earn in an entire year – if they had a job, that is. With thirty-six pounds, she could have had a really splendid wedding, but it wouldn't have been so much fun. She'd enjoyed wandering around Paddy's Market searching for a wedding dress and shoes, and it was lovely to know lots of people were contributing the food for the reception.

She looked through the frocks, trying to make up her mind which to buy – not easy for someone who'd always had every stitch of clothing made by an expert dressmaker. All she'd had to do at Sinead Larkin's was look through a pattern book and pick whatever she fancied. Some frocks weren't grand enough for Roberta's, and others were too ostentatious for Turnpike Street but would do as a going-away outfit. The honeymoon was a long weekend in Blackpool.

'I'll think about it tonight and come back tomorrow,' she said to herself, as she left Blackler's and made her way to Crosshall Street to see Agatha.

The chemist's was closed, so she knocked on the window and Agatha appeared from the back munching a sandwich. 'Would you like one?' she asked after she'd let Mollie in.

'No, thanks, it looks horrible.' She regarded the sandwich with distaste. 'Why is the bread all pink?'

'Because it's got beetroot on, that's why,' Agatha replied, munching away. 'It's good for you, beetroot.'

'Irene's already made me sandwiches. I don't know what's on them, but the bread'll be three times too thick. I have them when Roberta goes for her dinner, save wasting my own dinner-time eating.'

'What happens if someone comes in to buy a hat?'

'Then I stop eating, don't I?' Unlike Roberta, she didn't shower the customers with false compliments, but still managed to sell quite a few hats.

They went into the back of the shop, where Agatha, who'd been expecting her, poured tea. 'About me bridesmaid's frock,' Agatha began.

Mollie groaned. 'I told you, you can wear anything you want: any colour, any style, I don't care.'

'What about plum?'

'Plum's fine.'

'Plum with sequins?'

'That's fine, too.'

'I was going to take the sequins off, but I removed one and it left a little mark, so I had to stick it back on.'

'That's still fine.'

'I wish you'd express an opinion,' Agatha said sulkily.

'I've just expressed three opinions: fine, fine, and fine again.'

'I don't want to turn up looking a sight.'

'Do you like plum, Aggie?' Mollie raised her eyebrows questioningly.

'It's me favourite colour – and don't call me Aggie, you know I hate it.'

'I only called you Aggie because you're getting on my nerves.' She gave her friend a stern look. 'Do you like sequins?'

'I *love* them.' Agatha clasped her hands together under her chin. 'I've always wanted a frock with sequins, preferably plum.'

'Then I shall be highly offended if you don't wear your new frock to my wedding. Where did you buy it?'

'Where d'you think? Paddy's Market. The place where you got your wedding dress, where everyone buys their clothes if they want to look fashionable but haven't got the money. I bought a tiara at the same time. It's got two diamonds missing, but I don't think anyone'll notice.'

The girls grinned at each other, then began to laugh until their sides ached. When they'd finished, Agatha said, 'I know

I shouldn't say this, Moll, but I'm not half glad you missed the boat to New York and stayed in Liverpool. I've never had a friend like you before.'

'And I've never had one like you, either.'

'We'll still see each other when you're married to Tom, won't we?' Agatha said anxiously.

'Of course,' Mollie assured her. 'We'll go the pictures once a week, like always, and you can come and visit when Tom's working nights, so we can have a natter.'

'That's all right, then.' Agatha gave a happy sigh.

She'd been desperately lucky, Mollie thought as she made her way back to Roberta's. Her first few days in Liverpool had been truly horrible, but the Brophys had taken her to their hearts and made her feel one of the family. They would always be friends. Then she'd met Tom, and the Ryans had done the same. Tom made her feel very special in a way no one had since Mammy died. She wondered if God had had a hand in making her miss the boat, because Liverpool was the place where He had intended her to be and New York was the place for Annemarie.

At half past five, Roberta's door opened and Tom came in, smartly dressed, hat in hand, looking well scrubbed and extremely handsome. Mollie's heart gave a little leap – it had been happening a lot lately, the way her heart jumped whenever she saw him.

'You look nice, luv,' he remarked. He said the same thing every time they met.

Mollie replied, as she always did, 'So do you.' The shop seemed to have acquired a rosy glow since Tom had entered.

Roberta cried, 'And where are you two lovebirds off to?'

'To the Majestic to see *Orphans of the Storm* with Dorothy and Lillian Gish,' Tom informed her. 'It's directed by D.W. Griffith, who's a genius, in my humble opinion.' It was also Tom's humble opinion that, had he not become a policeman, he would have made an excellent film director, though not, he conceded with rare modesty, of quite the same calibre as D.W. Griffith.

'Did you catch any criminals today?' Mollie asked when they were outside.

'Not *exactly*. Most criminals only come out of doors when it's dark. There was this chap who was knocked down and killed by a motor car in Renshaw Street and I had to go and inform his missus.'

'Oh, that must have been awful for you!'

'It was even worse for his missus.' Tom shuddered. Despite his brash, confident manner, inside he was an extremely sensitive young man. 'She didn't half cry, poor woman. Then I had words with some lad who was riding his bike on the pavement. He told me – well, I won't repeat what he told me, but I had to march him to the station where Sarge gave him a good telling-off. Otherwise, I just plodded around, telling people the time or showing them the way to places. I keep hoping I'll come across a villain holding up a bank. I always glance inside the doors, just in case, but no luck so far.'

'Never mind,' Mollie soothed, hiding a smile. 'One of these days it might happen.'

'I love being a copper, Moll.'

'I know you do, Tom.'

'And I love you an' all.' He paused in the middle of the street and kissed her on the lips. 'I've been wanting to do that all day.'

'And I've been wanting you to.' Had she actually said that? Did she mean it? 'I love you, Tom Ryan,' she said, just to see how the words sounded.

'I know, luv, I know.' He put his arm around her shoulders and squeezed them. Mollie had no idea how he could have known: she hadn't known herself until that very minute.

Levon's thoughts were very dark as he drove the cab in the direction of Wall Street, the financial district of New York, where the skyscrapers blocked out the sun, leaving some of the streets in permanent shadow. It made him feel as if he were a tiny insect crawling along at the very bottom of the world.

His passenger, a young fellow wearing a business suit and a straw boater, was determined to talk. He'd already asked Levon where he was from, and confided his own folks had come from Russia almost a quarter of a century ago. 'Our surname was unpronounceable: even I can't remember how it was spelt. The Ellis Island inspectors changed it to Dymitrik, so Pop decided to keep it that way.'

'What do you do?' Levon enquired, just to be polite. Not all his passengers were as friendly as this young chap, who'd insisted on sitting next to him rather than in the back.

'I'm a loans manager with Morgan's Bank. Just think,' he chuckled, 'when Pop was my age, he was picking vegetables on a farm back in Vologda. Now, he's got his own little place in Buffalo. I came to New York in the hope of making a few dollars, and I'm doing just fine. I've just been to Macy's to buy my wife a new purse for her birthday, and I could actually afford to pay for a cab there and back.' His homely face shone with pride and the sheer joy of being alive. 'America's the greatest place on earth and New York's the greatest city. I bet you never dreamed you'd end up driving a cab here one day.'

'That's true,' Levon conceded.

'I can see a hold-up straight ahead. Drop me off here and I'll walk the rest of the way. How much do I owe you, my friend?'

'A dollar.'

'Here's two. I'm feeling lucky today and I'd like to share it.' He doffed his hat and leapt out of the cab. Levon watched him walk jauntily away, hands in pockets. Had he been within earshot, he suspected he'd be whistling something: 'Yankee Doodle Dandy' or 'Alexander's Ragtime Band'.

There was a hot dog stand on the corner of the street. He parked, got out, and bought a black coffee in a cardboard cup. He leaned against the cab and sipped it slowly as his dark thoughts returned, though not perhaps quite as dark as before. His young

87

passenger had reassured him that life had a lighter side, that it wasn't all doom and gloom.

Some fiend had raped his darling Anne, but that was the past. Pretty soon a new baby would begin its life in the apartment in Grammercy Park. Tamara was excited about it, but Levon didn't know what to feel. Anne had been present when the doctor had announced she was expecting a child, but either she hadn't taken it in, or she'd rejected the idea altogether and refused to consider it. She turned away when Tamara tried to bring up the subject, flatly refusing to listen.

'We'll just have to play it by ear,' Levon had said. It was an expression unknown in Armenia, but it made perfect sense. They would have to take things day by day and see what happened. Tamara was all of a flutter buying baby clothes, learning to knit, and translating old lullabies into English to sing to the baby.

He wished he could think and act as positively. America was the greatest country on earth, as his recent fare had so confidently asserted, and New York the greatest city. He was lucky to be here, lucky to have a wife like Tamara, lucky to have replaced their dear, dead Larisa with another daughter, just as pretty, just as enchanting.

As Anne herself would have said, he was desperately lucky. 'Desperately' was a word she used frequently, entirely out of context, in his opinion. He tucked one of the dollars he'd just been given in his breast pocket. From now on, he would regard it as his lucky dollar and it would never be spent.

Chapter 5

It had rained during the night and the cobbled surface of Turnpike Street was still wet when Mollie drew back the curtains on the morning of her wedding. The sky was a mass of grey clouds and there wasn't even a gleam of sunshine.

In a few hours, at exactly eleven o'clock, she would marry Tom Ryan. The reality, the fact that she would shortly become a married woman, hadn't properly sunk in until last night when she'd met her family in the George Hotel. Aunt Maggie was already there, having come straight to Liverpool from New York. At first, she hadn't recognized her aunt with her shingled hair, smart green costume and high-heeled shoes, so different from the dowdy schoolteacher she remembered.

They embraced warmly, both close to tears, and sat, hand in hand, on a sofa, talking about old times and new times, Duneathly and New York, and, of course, Annemarie. 'Sergeant McCluskey comes regularly to see me, but the police haven't found a trace of her,' Aunt Maggie said, blushing slightly for some reason. 'They sent her description to other states, but no luck so far, I'm afraid.'

Barely an hour later, Finn, Hazel and Patrick had arrived from Ireland. It had been an emotional reunion. Hazel reminded her that the last time she'd set eyes on Mollie was when she'd waved goodbye as she and Annemarie set off for America on Jimmy Mullen's cart.

'And who in the whole wide world would've thought things would turn out the way they have?' she cried.

Finn said Thaddy and Aidan were missing their big sisters

dreadfully and Nanny sent her love. Fran Kincaid, who did the cleaning, had left and Nanny was doing her best, but the house was getting in a bit of a state. Nobody mentioned the Doctor.

Mollie nursed her first nephew, Patrick, a big pudding of a baby with a winsome smile that threatened to break hundreds of female hearts in what she prayed would be a long and happy life.

It was then that it dawned on her: *these people had come all this way for her wedding.* Aunt Maggie had bought a new outfit in New York. Sinead Larkin had made Hazel a lovely cream voile frock and a sailor suit for Patrick. It really was happening. Tomorrow, she would stand in front of the altar in the church of Our Lady of Reconciliation and become Mrs Thomas George Ryan. Never again would she be Mollie Kenny. Was she making an awful mistake? She hardly knew Tom – he hardly knew her. Was it too late to back out?

Hazel had nudged her. 'You're wondering what you're about to let yourself in for, aren't you, Moll? I can tell by your face. I felt the same before I married Finn. I'd like to bet most women do – and most men an' all. It's like taking a big leap into the dark, but it has to be done. If you don't take a big leap now'n again, you'll get nowhere in life.'

Later, they'd sat down to a big dinner, but Mollie couldn't eat a thing and the mouthful of wine she'd drunk had made her feel nauseous. Even when Finn proposed a toast to her and Tom, it was an effort to smile when she felt like being sick.

She'd still felt sick on the tramcar home while nursing the velvet box containing a lovely pearl necklace and earring set that Aunt Maggie had given her for her birthday and, in her bag, two pounds for her and Tom to buy a wedding present. 'You'll know best what you'll want for your new home,' her aunt had said. Tom had been allocated a police house in Allerton.

Finn and Hazel were giving them a canteen of cutlery that Finn would bring tomorrow when he came in a taxi to take her to the church, and a bottle of scent called 'La Vie en Rose' for her birthday.

Somewhere in town, Tom had gone for a drink with his mates.

She only hoped he wouldn't end up feeling as sick as she did, or their marriage would get off to a really bad start.

Irene came into the bedroom the next morning with a cup of tea. 'Ah, you're up, girl. It's not much of a day, is it? Still, there's still plenty of time for the sun to show.'

Mollie got back into bed and accepted the tea, the last she would have in bed as a single woman. 'I feel desperately odd, Irene,' she confessed.

'And what girl doesn't feel odd on the morning of her wedding?' Irene scoffed. 'It'd be even odder if you didn't. Oh, and Happy Birthday, luv.' She'd already had Irene's present: a pair of white gloves to wear with her going-away outfit, which was a blue and white polka-dotted frock and her white hat.

'Ta. I never dreamed I'd be married when I was only seventeen. I hadn't even had a boyfriend before I met your Tom.'

'Well, he's never had a girlfriend, so you'll be learning things together.' Irene sat on the edge of the bed. She wore a voluminous flannel nightdress that made her look like a child with an old woman's face, a face that suddenly turned red with embarrassment. 'You know about "things", don't you, luv? Like the things people do together once they're married. Did your mammy tell you before she died?'

'No, but I worked for the Doctor, didn't I?' Mollie felt equally embarrassed. 'I know how babies are made.'

'That's good.' Irene squeezed her foot through the bedclothes, clearly relieved to know Mollie was already fully aware of the facts of life. 'It can come as a bit of a shock to a girl if she doesn't know what to expect. Well, I'll love you and leave you, Moll. The girls'll be along in a minute to help you get dressed.' By 'girls', she meant her daughters-in-law, although Mollie couldn't understand why she should need three grown women to help her put on her wedding gown and do her hair.

She discovered the reason later when she found all her fingers had turned to thumbs and she couldn't fasten her new brassiere. Lily had to do the hooks for her before she put on the long white petticoat that made a hissing noise as it fell to her feet. Gladys helped roll on the silk stockings Roberta had given her along with an extra week's wages when she'd left the shop for good the day before, and Pauline folded her brown hair into something called a French pleat. 'It's a bit more sophisticated than a plait for your wedding day,' she said. Mollie couldn't have plaited her hair to save her life.

Agatha arrived with the plum, sequinned frock in a parcel under her arm. The girls looked a trifle shocked when she unfolded it.

'It's not exactly a bridesmaid's frock, is it, luv?' Lily remarked with a disapproving sniff.

'I said she could wear whatever she liked,' Mollie put in, 'on condition I can do the same when *she* gets married.'

Pauline, who had a knack with hair, piled Agatha's frizzy mop into a pile on top of her head and secured it with hairpins, then arranged the tiara so the missing diamonds wouldn't show.

Every now and then, everything would stop, Irene would make yet another pot of tea, and Pauline and Lily would have a ciggie before they started work again. Mollie's nails were painted with clear varnish that made them shine; 'La Vie en Rose' was dabbed behind her ears and sprinkled on a new white hankie; the pearl necklace from Aunt Maggie was clasped around her neck and the earrings clipped to her ears.

There was a knock on the door: the woman from the florist's had arrived on her bike with the bridal bouquet – six white roses surrounded by a frill of fern – a little posy of forget-me-nots for Agatha, and a dozen buttonholes.

It was all very unreal. Mollie was beginning to feel rather like a tailor's dummy as she stood in the middle of the parlour, allowing people to turn her round, do things to her hair, her ears, her nails, sit her down, make her stand. The girls worked mainly in silence, issuing occasional commands. They looked extremely serious and hardly smiled at all, not even red-haired Gladys who was a terrible giggler. Irene said they didn't get on all that well together, but today they worked in perfect harmony.

'Sit down a minute, Moll, while I put your shoes on,' Lily said, or it might have been Pauline or Gladys. The girls' faces were beginning to merge into one.

Mollie obediently sat down and stuck out a foot.

Irene said, 'I gave them shoes a good scrubbing with a soft brush and they've come up a treat.'

Mollie stuck out her other foot.

'The soles and heels hardly look worn,' Irene continued. 'I bet someone only wore them the once.'

'Stand up, Moll, and we'll put your dress on.'

Apparently, it required all three girls to hold the frock and ease it gingerly over Mollie's head, put her arms into the sleeves, pull it gently so it lay smoothly on her hips and fell until the hem rested on the toes of her shoes. 'It feels like a glove,' Mollie said.

Mrs Brophy's veil fell over her like a cloud and the girls circled around, tugging it a bit this way, then the other, until they judged it was perfectly even. Then the wreath was placed on her head, the bouquet put in her hands, and someone said, 'Fetch the mirror out the hall so she can see what she looks like.'

Mollie looked in the mirror, but the young woman who looked back couldn't possibly be her. She was too tall, too slim, too beautiful. 'It's not me,' she said, shaking her head, at exactly the same time as the young woman in the mirror shook hers. 'It's someone else altogether.'

'Of course it's you, Moll,' Agatha assured her with a catch in her voice. 'You look really lovely.'

'I think I'm going to cry,' Mollie sniffed.

'You *can't*!' several voices said at once.

'Your eyes'll turn all red and you'll get spots all over your frock,' Irene warned.

Mollie took a deep breath. 'All right, I won't.' She took a final look in the mirror and turned to the girls, who were admiring their handiwork. 'Thank you, I don't know what I'd've done without you.' Preparing the bride for the ceremony was almost as big an occasion for them as it was for her.

There was another knock on the door. This time it was Finn

with the taxi that would take her to a place where her life would be changed for all time. There were tears in his eyes as he lifted the veil and kissed her softly on both cheeks. 'You look marvellous, Moll. If only Mam were here to see you now.'

'And Annemarie,' Mollie whispered.

Finn nodded. 'And Annemarie.'

There was a gasp of admiration followed by a cheer when she stepped outside to discover the sun had come out and half the street had gathered to see her off.

'Ooh! Doesn't she look lovely,' the women sighed.

'Good luck, girl!' cried the men.

Mollie, who had thought no one liked her, was stunned. She shook a few hands and patted a few small heads, until Finn helped her into the taxi, followed by Irene and Agatha, who raised a few cheers of her own in her sequinned dress and diamond tiara. The girls were making their own way to the church: it was only a few minutes' walk away.

It seemed no time before she was inside the church, holding Finn's arm, floating up the aisle, seeing Tom waiting for her and watching her with an expression of such adoration that it made her want to weep. Then Finn stopped, removed his arm, and there was only her, Tom and old Father Fitzgerald, who was about to make them man and wife.

'Well,' Tom said after they'd boarded the Blackpool train, and he'd put their suitcase on the rack overhead, and sat beside her, 'that was a reception and a half, that was.'

'It was indeed,' Mollie agreed. 'It was wonderful. Your family and mine really got on well together.' The reception would continue for hours yet and probably end up even rowdier than it had been when she and Tom had left.

'Your Aunt Maggie's the gear. I really liked her, and Hazel, too. Patrick's a proper little charmer. Me mam was really taken with him. But,' he said, frowning slightly, 'I don't think your Finn likes me all that much.'

It was hard for Tom to accept that he wasn't universally liked by everyone he met. 'He's probably just worried about me, that's all,' she assured him. 'I mean, he hasn't had the opportunity to get to know you properly, has he?'

The frown disappeared. 'That's probably the reason.'

'Aunt Maggie's going to stay at the George the night before she goes back to New York, so I'm going to see her. We didn't have much time to talk. You can come with me if you're not on duty.'

'That'd be nice, luv.' He glanced at the other occupants of the compartment, a man and a woman both staring vacantly out of the window at the other end, and gave her a quick kiss. 'I love you, Mrs Ryan,' he whispered.

'And I love you, Mr Ryan.' She removed a glove and stared at the plain gold ring on the third finger of her left hand. 'I can hardly believe I'm a married woman.'

'I've got a certificate in me pocket to prove it.' He picked up her hand and kissed that, too.

She nestled her head against his shoulder. 'I know you have.'

'This is going to be the best marriage that ever was, Moll.'

'I know that an' all.'

But only a matter of hours later, it seemed as if their marriage was already over.

They arrived at the boarding house just in time for dinner. The sharp-faced landlady looked at them suspiciously when they signed in. 'You don't look old enough to be married,' she snapped at Mollie, and Tom had to produce their wedding certificate to prove they were man and wife.

'We're on our honeymoon,' he said importantly. 'We only got married this morning.'

The woman softened slightly at the news. 'You're on the second floor, room eight. If you'd like to take your things upstairs, I'll set a place in the dining room. What sort of soup would you like? There's oxtail or tomato.'

'Oxtail,' said Tom. Mollie chose tomato, but it turned out to be very watery and she wished she'd asked for oxtail.

The roast beef that followed was as tough as old leather, the roast potatoes looked nice enough but were underdone, as were the carrots and the peas. But Mollie and Tom were on their honeymoon and didn't give a damn.

Afterwards, they went for a walk along Blackpool Pier, arm in arm, aware only of each other and hardly noticing the jangling music and crowds of holidaymakers with their strange accents and funny hats. It was a magical evening, the sun still warm in the sky, the sands scattered with courting couples lying in each other's arms, children paddling in the silvery water, the girls with skirts tucked in their knickers, men with their trousers rolled up and a hanky with the four corners knotted shielding their heads. The women were packing away buckets and spades, empty lemonade bottles, dirty clothes and towels. A man was leisurely collecting deck chairs and putting them on a cart.

After a while, Tom announced he was hungry. 'That dinner wasn't up to much, was it, Moll?'

'I don't think it was, no,' Mollie agreed. 'Do you fancy some fish and chips? There's a stall over there.'

The fish and chips bought – it was Tom's favourite meal – they sat on a bench and listened to the water swirling against the iron supports underneath. Mollie couldn't tell if the tide was coming in or going out, and Tom said he couldn't tell either and, what's more, he didn't care.

By now, the sun had disappeared and dusk fell upon them. Only the courting couples remained on the sands. The moon appeared, almost full, the lights were turned on, and the entire waterfront glittered like a million stars. The big wheel was spinning like a top and the music on the pier was getting louder, the crowds more raucous, the air a little colder.

'I think it's likely to get a bit rough here any time soon.' Tom stood and reached for her hand. 'We'd best be getting back. Shall we stop and have a cup of cocoa on the way?'

'Yes, please.' She took his arm with a slight feeling of trepidation. Very soon, she and Tom would become as close as a man and woman could possibly be. She wasn't dreading it, but nor was she exactly looking forward to it. She was more impatient for it to be over so that tomorrow they could make love in an entirely natural way, all the awkwardness and embarrassment of the first time behind them.

They were soon back in their room where the moon provided just enough illumination to see by.

Tom said casually, 'I won't bother lighting the gas mantel, luv. There's no real need.'

'I can see perfectly well without it,' she said, relieved they were undressing in the near dark. She removed her clothes, put on her new nightie, which cost two and elevenpence in Blackler's and was far inferior to the pretty, handmade ones in the suitcase she'd been taking to America, and slid into bed. A few minutes later, Tom joined her. They lay in silence for a while, until he tentatively slid his hand around her waist.

'Can I kiss you, Moll?'

'Of course, Tom.' She turned to face him and suddenly they were kissing each other with an eagerness that quickly turned to passion and Tom's hands were touching her breasts through the nightdress, then underneath the nightdress. Just as suddenly, Mollie had nothing on and neither had Tom, though she had no idea where the clothes had gone. And now they were making love. It wasn't quite as thrilling as she'd expected, but gave her a lovely, satisfied feeling that she and Tom were joined together as one.

Finally Tom gave an almighty groan, collapsed on top of her, then rolled on his side so that he had his back to her. There was another silence that went on for much longer than the first.

Eventually, Mollie spoke. 'What's the matter?' she whispered.

'You've done this before, haven't you, Moll?' His voice was hoarse and full of hurt. 'It was the very last thing I expected from a girl like you.'

Mollie could feel her blood turning to ice. It was silly of her, unimaginably stupid, but she'd still considered herself a virgin. She'd thought of Tom as the first man she would sleep with, the first man with whom she'd make love. The times with the Doctor had been put to the back of her mind because they were too painful, too cruel and unwanted to occupy a fraction of her brain.

How could she explain all that to Tom? She felt so ashamed. He'd want to know why she hadn't pushed the Doctor away or locked her door, yet Mollie didn't know the answer to those questions. She'd actually thought it was her duty, that it was what all fathers did when they'd lost their wives. It was just something she had to put up with. It wasn't until he'd touched Annemarie that it had seemed a sin of such enormous proportions as to be unforgivable.

'I'm still waiting for an answer,' Tom said gruffly.

'*You* must have done it before to have known.' It was the very worst thing to have said, but all she could think of at the moment.

He sat up in the bed and she could sense the anger emanating from him like sparks. 'I bought a book on it, that's how I know. I didn't want to make a mess of things. I wanted tonight to be perfect, but now it's spoiled. Oh, Mollie! How could you?'

Mollie didn't reply. She turned over so she had her back to *him*. She felt cold, so cold, despite the mound of blankets and the thick eiderdown.

That night, she didn't sleep a wink, and neither did Tom. At some time, he got out of bed and, when she looked, he was sitting in a chair by the window, looking out, his chin resting on his hands, a picture of dejection.

Daylight came, the gong sounded for breakfast. They didn't speak to each other while they dressed and went downstairs, the first to arrive in the dining room. The sharp-faced landlady brought them bowls of unappetizing-looking porridge. Other people came into the room and wished them good morning.

'Good morning,' Mollie replied.

Tom didn't say anything, just stared at the porridge with tears streaming down his smooth, boyish cheeks. 'I love you so much, Moll,' he said brokenly.

'And I love you, Tom.' She reached across the table and rubbed the tears away with her hand.

'I don't care what you did before I met you,' he wept. 'I'm sorry about last night. I shouldn't have made a scene. It's just that it came as such a shock. I thought, I thought . . . ' He stopped, unable to go on.

People were staring. Mollie got to her feet. 'Let's go upstairs. I've something to tell you.' It had to be done or their marriage would be spoiled for ever.

'I'd like to kill him,' Tom raged after she'd told him about the Doctor. He was walking back and forth across the room like a madman. 'Policeman or no policeman, I'd like to bloody kill him.' He stopped walking and looked at her sorrowfully. 'Oh, Moll! Why didn't you say anything about this last night?'

'Because I was too ashamed, wasn't I?' she said tearfully. 'I always felt as if it were my own fault.'

He sat on the bed and pulled her on to his knee. 'That was the worst night of me life, that was.'

She stroked his crisp, brown hair. 'I'm sorry.'

'There's nothing to be sorry about, luv. *I'm* sorry I jumped to conclusions.'

There was a knock on the door. Mollie made a face and went to answer it, to find the landlady outside with a tray, her face no longer sharp, but gentle and kind. 'As you didn't have any breakfast, I thought you'd like a pot of tea and some toast.'

'That's very nice of you, thank you very much.' Mollie took the tray. She couldn't have eaten a thing, but was dying for some tea. Tom, who had the appetite of a horse, would eat every crumb of the toast.

'I hope everything's all right,' the woman whispered.

'It is now.' Mollie closed the door. Everything was fine and, from now on, it always would be.

Finn showed Aunt Maggie the room in the cottage she would occupy for the next fortnight, helped Hazel put a sleepy Patrick to bed – he'd been too excited to sleep on the boat and the train – had a bite to eat, then made his way to the Doctor's house to collect Thaddy and Aidan. His aunt was longing to meet them, but had no intention of going anywhere near the Doctor during her stay in Duneathly. 'I'm too scared of what I might do to him if I saw him in the flesh,' she'd said fiercely.

The Doctor's house stood in the square next to that of Mr O'Rourke, the solicitor, on one side, and a tiny bank, which only opened two days a week, on the other. It was a solid, three-storey building with six rooms on each floor. Most of the ground floor was given over to the Doctor's needs: a surgery, waiting room, an office full of files, and a study. There was also a large kitchen and a cloakroom. The family rooms were on the floor above. Long ago, servants had occupied the attic rooms, which had been empty for years when the Kennys first moved in. Finn had been the first to ask if he could sleep upstairs in a room with a sloping ceiling and a window from which you could see for miles and miles. Then Mollie had moved into the next room and Annemarie into another.

Finn noticed the dark-blue paint on the front door had begun to flake. He went inside to find the house uncommonly quiet and the place smelling musty and unused. He recalled the days when five children had lived there and the place was full of noise and laughter.

'Dad,' he shouted and, when there was no sign of his father. 'Nanny, Aidan, Thaddy – is anyone home?'

Nanny appeared at the top of the stairs. She'd been an old woman when she'd looked after Finn when he was a baby and now she looked incredibly ancient, her eyes rheumy in a white face. Her flesh looked as if it had melted, like wax, and lay in deep, uneven creases on her cheeks. She wore a long black dress, a white pinafore, and a white kerchief on her head. 'I sent the lads out, son,' she said in a shaky voice. 'I took them to play with the Patersons: their Cormac is in the same class as Thaddy at school.' She began to descend the stairs, clinging to the banister, each step a terrible effort.

Finn rushed upstairs to help her down and took her into the kitchen where dishes were piled in the sink and the slate floor was badly in need of cleaning. He pulled out a chair and gently sat her down. 'What's wrong, Nanny?'

'It's your father, son. Wasn't he flying as high as a kite last night, drinking whiskey as if it were water, shouting, and throwing stuff all over the place? It frightened the lads, it did. I was worried he'd murder us all in our beds. There's no paraffin left for the lamps and we were stuck in the dark.' Duneathly wasn't connected either to gas or electricity. 'If you'd like to go to his study, you'll see the mess he's made.'

Finn's heart sank to his boots. It was as wrong as wrong could be for this fragile old woman to be left in the house with two small children and a crazy man, but what could he do about it? 'Where is he now?' he asked.

'That I don't know, Finn. He left the house early morning before the sun had risen, slamming the door behind him so hard that all the windows shook. I haven't seen hide nor hair of him since.' Since he'd arrived, Nanny was more her old self again.

'Would you like something to drink, Nanny? A cup of tea perhaps – or would you prefer a glass of the hard stuff?' She was partial to a glass of spirits now and again.

'I wouldn't say no to a nip of gin, lad, thanks all the same. It's in the cupboard under the sink.'

They went into the kitchen. He found the bottle and poured half a glass. 'Is there anything to go with it?'

'I like it neat. I thought you'd've known that by now, Finn Kenny.' Her rheumy eyes twinkled.

'I don't know how anybody can drink neat gin.' He shoved the glass across the table and she seized it eagerly. 'Is there a reason you can think of that sent the Doctor into such a state?' he enquired.

She made a grotesque face and he remembered how Nanny's faces used to terrify him when he was a child. 'People are suspicious of him, son, and he knows it. He's only seeing half the patients he saw before. He hasn't had a receptionist since Mollie left, and he can't get another soul to come and do the cleaning since Fran Kincaid walked out because she could stand the place no more.' She nodded at the dishes in the sink, the dirty floor. 'Everyone's wondering why his girls disappeared the way they did, why you hardly ever come to the house, why Hazel never comes at all, not even to show him his first grandchild, why he didn't go to your Mollie's wedding.' She put the glass down, having drunk half in a single mouthful and looking much the better for it. 'How did the wedding go, by the way?'

'Perfectly, Nanny.' He wrinkled his nose. 'I don't think much of her new husband, he's too big for his policeman's boots by a mile, but Hazel and Aunt Maggie both liked him.' He hadn't realized his father had sunk so low in the eyes of Duneathly.

'I wouldn't mind seeing Maggie while she's home.'

'I'm sure she'd love to see you. Maybe you could meet one morning in the tea shop.'

Nanny's eyes narrowed. 'So, Maggie's not prepared to come to this house, either. I have a good idea why, Finn, though I promise never to share it with a soul. Mind you, there'd be no need; most people have arrived at the same conclusion of their own accord.'

Finn sighed. It was all getting a bit too much for him. 'What time will Thaddy and Aidan be home?'

'Mrs Paterson said she'd bring them around seven. But Finn,' she put a creased hand on his arm, 'I don't fancy another night like the last one. It's not meself I'm worried about, but the lads. If you could've heard the way your father carried on last night, you'd know what I mean.'

'I wonder where he is.'

'Sleeping it off somewhere, I reckon. He must've had the devil of a hangover.'

Finn looked at his watch: nearly half past six. His brothers would be back soon. The cottage was much too small to take another three people: he'd just have to spend the night here. 'I'll stay, Nanny,' he promised. 'I'll just go home and tell Hazel. I won't be long. And I'll bring some paraffin back with me for the lamps.'

Before leaving, he looked in the Doctor's study and discovered a cracked and empty whiskey bottle on the floor, books strewn all over the place, a chair upturned, and a pool of vomit just inside the door. He tried very hard to feel some pity for his father, but found it impossible.

Nanny knew Finn had the ability to sleep through an earthquake. She'd said she'd wake him if the Doctor came home and started carrying on again, but when he opened his eyes in his old bed in his old room it was already morning and the sun shimmered around the familiar curtains. In the distance, a cock crowed. He went down to his father's bedroom, but the bed hadn't been slept in, and he wasn't in the study or any other room in the house. He was beginning to wonder if the Doctor hadn't taken it upon himself to run away, like his girls, when there was a knock on the front door.

It was Willy Keen from Old Mill Farm to say that Dr Kenny had been found floating face down in a pond on the farmer's land.

'No one knows how long he's been there,' he said respectfully, removing his cap and holding it tight to his chest. 'There hasn't been anyone round that way for a few days.' He made the Sign of the Cross. 'May your ould da rest in peace, Mr Kenny. He was a fine doctor, no matter what people might have said to the contrary.'

Levon wasn't sure if it was fear he could see in her big, violet eyes or a wild impatience for the whole thing to be over, for the baby to be born, so that she would have no more to do with it. She hadn't acknowledged the child in her womb, not once, in all the months since the doctor had announced she was pregnant. She rebuffed all Tamara's attempts to talk about it, just turned away or left the room, her face set tight, her pretty mouth a straight line.

He'd engaged a trained midwife, Mrs Sarkadi, for when her time came, not wanting her to go into a hospital for two reasons: first, he was concerned that the strange surroundings and strange people would upset her: second, she was no more than a child herself and there was a chance that questions might be asked about the father, questions that only Anne could answer. The exact date of the child's arrival was unknown, but the doctor had estimated it would be sometime in September.

That summer, Levon had passed the Bar exam and was now legally entitled to practise as a lawyer in the state of New York. He'd rented an office on the Lower East Side and had already acquired a few clients, but, once September came, he'd taken to coming home earlier and earlier, when he should have been staying later and later in order to find more clients to add to his list. He was anxious to be there when the baby came.

Tamara made fun of him. 'You're almost excited as when I was expecting Larisa,' she said. 'Nowadays, she could mention Larisa without dissolving into tears.

Anne's baby arrived in the middle of the night. It was Levon who heard her loud, panicky cry and went to see if she was all right, to find her clutching her stomach, saying, 'I have this awful pain, Lev. I feel as if I'm about to break in two.'

He'd woken Tamara, thrown on some clothes, and raced to fetch Mrs Sarkadi, a big Hungarian woman with a tough face and a kind smile, who lived in East 19th Street, two streets from his own. Her use of English was perfect, but her accent was so thick she was hard to understand.

Mrs Sarkadi had returned with him, examined the girl, who by then was in enormous pain, and said the baby wasn't due just yet. Now she and Tamara were doing things in the kitchen, and Levon was in Anne's room, stroking her brow, holding her hand, telling her everything was going to be fine, though what did he know about it? Did she realize what was happening? he wondered.

She was muttering something under her breath and he bent to listen. 'I don't want to go back,' she was saying over and over. 'I don't want to go back.'

'You're not going anywhere, my angel,' he told her. 'You're staying here — for ever, if that's what you want.'

'I don't want to go back,' she said again. His words had clearly not penetrated her fuzzy brain. Suddenly, she sat up and cried, 'Where's Mollie? I want Mollie.'

'Mollie's not here, darling.' He held her shoulders, thinking how thin they were, and laid her down. 'But *I'm* here. This is Lev, who loves you and will make sure you don't come to any harm.'

She grabbed his hand and held it against her cheek. 'Lev,' she whispered. 'Oh, Lev.'

Mrs Sarkadi came in with a bowl of steaming water, Tamara behind carrying an armful of old towels and sheets. 'We'll see to her now, Lev,' Tamara said.

Levon spent the next hour attempting to read – later, he couldn't remember a single word – drinking black coffee, looking out of the window at the lights of New York, going over the events that had led him to this strange and wonderful place, and listening to the cries and moans coming from Anne's room that ate away at his heart.

Eventually, there came a different cry, not Anne, but from a baby. Levon positioned himself outside the door of her room so that he would be there when it opened and Tamara came out to tell him if it was a boy or a girl. The baby continued to cry and he stamped his feet impatiently. A boy would be called John, a girl Elizabeth, assuming that Anne herself didn't suggest a name, which he felt was most unlikely. Tamara had wanted to give the child an Armenian name but Levon claimed that wouldn't be fair. 'Anne isn't Armenian,' he'd argued. 'Her child should be given a name she might have chosen herself.'

The door opened and Tamara appeared with a tiny baby wrapped in the shawl she had knitted. 'Lev, this is John,' she said, her eyes like two bright stars in her excited face. 'I always wanted us to have a boy.'

Levon looked down at the little, crumpled, bad-tempered face. 'Why is he so red?'

'Lots of babies are red when they're first born.'

'He's awfully small.'

Tamara laughed. 'What did you expect, Lev, an elephant? All babies are small. Mrs Sarkadi thinks he weighs about five pounds.

It's a good thing for Anne he's no bigger, otherwise she'd have had an even worse time.'

'How is she?' He longed to go into the room and see for himself.

'Exhausted. Mrs Sarkadi tried to give her the baby, but she turned away. I doubt she'll want anything to do with him.' Tamara didn't seem upset about it. She was holding the child possessively, like a mother, as if it were *hers*.

'I wonder who the father is?' Levon mused. 'Would he be interested to know he has a son?'

'Do we really care, Lev?' Tamara raised her fine eyebrows.

'I suppose not, no.'

Mrs Sarkadi emerged to say in her rather charming way that Anne was a delicately built young lady, but very fit and strong, and should be left to sleep for as long as she wished. 'I'll come and zee 'er again tomorrow,' she said.

Levon thanked and paid her, then asked if Anne was sleeping now.

'Not yet, but any minute.' She pronounced 'minute' as if it meant small.

Levon showed her out. Tamara was preparing a weak solution of the formula she'd bought, while John lay in a basket on the kitchen table. Levon bent over him, watching, fascinated, as the child yawned extravagantly and bunched his tiny fists into balls. He poked him gently in the stomach, but the child just yawned again. Tamara gave him a glowering look, so Levon left the kitchen and went to see Anne.

She lay on the bed, eyes closed, but somehow he could tell she wasn't asleep. He sat on the edge of the bed and she said, 'Is that you, Lev?'

'Yes, darling, it's me.'

'I know what's just happened, but I don't want to know it. Do you understand what I mean?'

'Yes, I do.' At least, he thought he did.

'I'm not quite as stupid as you think, Lev.' She still hadn't opened her eyes.

'I've never thought you stupid, Anne darling, but you must admit you are a very strange young lady.'

'I've always been strange, at least so people used to say.' Her voice was a soft, feathery whisper. There was a long silence and he thought she had really gone to sleep. She spoke when he got up to leave. 'I love New York, Lev.'

'So do I, Anne.'

'At first, I hated it when I saw it from the boat. I thought it was a dream, a really bad one, but now I never want to leave.'

'Then you never will.'

'Goodnight, Lev.'

Levon softly closed the door and looked at his watch. It was early morning, almost five o'clock, and New York was preparing itself for another day. He changed into what Tamara called his 'lawyer suit': dark-grey flannel with the latest narrow lapels, sloping pockets and narrow trousers. He found Tamara in the sitting room changing John's diaper.

'It didn't really need changing. I just wanted to do it for the first time.' She smiled at him. 'Isn't he beautiful, Lev?'

'Beautiful.' Levon nodded, though secretly he considered the child, with his screwed-up red face, rather ugly. He had massive balls and a tiny penis. His legs were stick-thin and very active.

'He has blue eyes,' Tamara noted.

'They might change,' Levon pointed out.

'I know.' She noticed what he was wearing. 'Are you going to work this early?'

'I thought I might. I need to get started on a few cases.' He gestured at the baby. 'I feel I can now that this is over.'

'I'm relieved it's over, too.' She gave him a dazzling smile. 'We've got a son, Lev. It was the last thing I expected when we came to America, to have a son. We're so lucky. Once I used to think we were cursed, but now I realize how lucky we are.'

Chapter 6

Peggy Perlmann's Academy of Drama, Dance and Song was situated on top of a baker's shop on Hester Street, halfway between Little Italy and Chinatown. The studio comprised a large room that had once been two, with a ballet bar at one end and a mirror covering the entire wall at the other. The only furniture was a small, upright piano. It was tucked between the windows on which the academy's name had been painted in black and gold.

When Levon and Anne arrived, it was early, barely nine o'clock, and half a dozen garishly dressed young people were sitting in a circle on the floor talking animatedly, accompanied by a great deal of dramatic waving of arms.

Peggy had been born in New York and had the accent to prove it. Half-Irish, half-Jewish, she was at least six feet tall and had danced in the chorus of every major theatre in the state. 'Trouble was,' she told Levon when she showed him and Anne into a small room that seemed to double as a kitchen and an office, 'I started out at thirteen, but five years later I was taller than all the girls and most of the men. I tried pretending I was a man for a while, but it didn't work.'

'I'm not surprised,' said Levon. Peggy had the lushest lips, the bluest eyes, and the longest, most shapely legs he'd ever seen. Nobody in his or her right mind would have taken her for a man. She was seated behind a table that held a typewriter, untidy heaps of paper, equally untidy heaps of photographs, and a collection of cracked cups. Her wonderful red hair was piled on top of her head and held in place with a series of colourful combs and slides. She was made up as if she were about to go on stage: black lines around the eyes, blue shadow on the lids, lashes stiff with mascara, and a mouth that reminded Levon of an over-ripe plum. She wore black tights, green shorts, and a knitted top covered in snags and darns. Her high-heeled shoes looked a size larger than his sensible black ones.

'The hours are nine till four,' she informed them. 'Some evenings are involved: I'll explain that later. You can take just one course, or all three. Some kids just take the dancing, the singing, or the drama. Most take the whole damn lot. At the end of each term, we give concerts for the parents – no friends allowed, 'cos we don't have the room. We do two types of dancing: ballet and tap. As you can hear, today we're doing tap.'

Since they'd arrived, someone had started to play the out-of-tune piano with enormous enthusiasm and the young people were pounding the floor so hard Levon half expected the building to collapse. 'What would you like to do, Anne?' he asked.

'Everything,' Anne said promptly. He saw her feet were tapping in time to the music.

'Just a minute, honey,' Peggy said in her loud, raucous voice. 'I don't take just any old body in the academy. You have to audition first. There's some kids who couldn't dance to save their grannie from being eaten by the big, bad wolf, and others whose singing sounds like the whistle on a kettle. I have my reputation to consider. Producers come here all the time if they want a kid in one of their shows.' She transferred her stern gaze to Levon. 'Have you seen *Murder on the Yukon*, Mr Zarian?' When Levon looked at her blankly, she went on, 'It's a movie. A young man called Billy Berry has a supporting role. Billy was one of my drama students the year I opened in nineteen fifteen.'

Levon confessed he'd never been to the movies. 'My wife and I kept meaning to,' he excused himself lamely.

'The whole academy goes once a week, usually Tuesdays – it's included in the fees – and we visit the theatre on the first of every month. It's stimulating for the kids, gives them an idea of what to aspire to. Next week, we're going to see *The Ten Commandments* directed by Cecil B. DeMille. It's in Technicolor, the first of its kind.'

'I'd love to see it, Lev,' Anne said breathlessly.

'First of all, honey, I suggest your pop goes downstairs and has a coffee in the baker's – try their do'nuts while you're at it, Mr Zarian, they'll make your teeth melt – while I see how little Annie does on the dance floor. Then she can sing us a song. You can come back in half an hour.'

The do'nuts were delicious. Levon ate three before deciding enough was enough. He could easily have eaten more, but had been putting on weight since he'd exchanged driving a cab for sitting in an office. In the cab, he'd stopped for the occasional coffee. In the office, he ate at MacCready's, a diner across the street that served the juiciest hamburgers imaginable, or at more salubrious places if he was taking a client to lunch – or the client was taking him.

By now he was making three times as much as he'd done before, a sum that would inevitably increase when he was doing more business. Tamara was already talking about moving from the apartment to a house with a yard for John to play in. 'Brooklyn or Queens,' she'd suggested.

'We'll see when the time comes,' Levon murmured. John was only six weeks old and couldn't sit up unsupported, let alone play in a yard. He liked living in Manhattan and didn't want to leave.

Tamara was so absorbed with John it was almost as if she'd forgotten Levon and Anne existed. She took the baby for long walks and was thrilled when strangers spoke to her and assumed she was John's mother. Although she was forty-six, she still looked capable of having children. There'd been a fierce argument when she'd wanted to register the baby with her and Levon as the parents.

'He may as well be ours,' she pouted when Levon pointed out that Anne was the mother. 'She shows no interest, never so much as looks at him.'

'She might feel differently when she's older,' he said coldly. 'It would be like stealing another woman's child. And, even if Anne doesn't care, John can't be brought up without being told at some time in his life that we're not his parents. It would be extremely deceitful not to tell him the truth, Tamara,' he added rather more gently when he saw the disappointment on her face.

So John was registered as having a mother called Anne Murray, the address the Grammercy Park apartment, and the father 'Unknown'. Tamara secreted the certificate in the drawer that held all their other important papers. 'We'll tell him when he's twenty-one,' she said, 'and just hope he doesn't find out before.'

Time was passing. Levon looked at his watch, then at the do-nuts behind the glass-fronted counter, and managed to resist buying another. It was almost half an hour since he'd left Anne with the statuesque Peggy Perlmann. He left the baker's and went through the narrow door that led to the academy, up the stairs to where the pianist – a tiny old woman who required two cushions on the stool in order to reach the keys – was playing a lively tune that made Levon want to snap his fingers. Anne was at the back of the crowd of dancers, tapping away in her little black boots as if she'd been doing it all her life.

Peggy saw him watching and came towards him, grinning from ear to ear. She grabbed his arm and led him into the kitchen that was also an office, saying loudly, 'She's a natural. Has she had lessons before?'

'Not that I'm aware of. I must explain,' he went on hurriedly, 'that she's not my daughter, but the daughter of a friend, an Irish friend. His wife died and he went bankrupt at the same time, so he sent her to us – my wife and I, that is – to look after. Her name is Anne Murray.' It was a just about credible lie, but there had to be a reason why Anne spoke with an Irish accent, while his was Eastern European. Peggy, however, either hadn't noticed or didn't care.

'She has rhythm, she moves well – you'd think she had elastic in her bones – and she sings like an angel. I'd love to have her, Mr Zarian. All my kids are talented, I wouldn't take them if they weren't, but I only get one a year like Anne. When can she start?' she asked eagerly. 'She still has heaps to learn,' she added, almost as an afterthought.

'Tomorrow?' Levon felt as proud as if he really was Anne's father.

'Tomorrow would be hunky-dory, but she needs a pile of equipment: shoes for ballet and tap, tights, tops, shorts and skirts . . . I'll give you a list. Go to Amelia's on Delancey Street, say Peggy sent you, and she'll let you have a discount.'

'I'll go straight away.' Hang the business: if any new clients turned up while he was away, they'd just have to come back another time.

By the time Christmas came, Levon had engaged a secretary and acquired a telephone. He wasn't sure which thrilled him most: the ability to pick up the telephone and speak to anyone in this exhilarating country who had a telephone of their own, or to have the extremely efficient Miss Emily Lacroix at his beck and call. Miss Lacroix, who was of French descent, had impeccable manners, impeccable typing skills, and impeccable taste in clothes. She sat in the corner of the office wearing a crisp white blouse and a smart black skirt, answering the door when people came and the phone when it rang. In the New Year, Levon was moving to a much larger office and Miss Lacroix would have a room of her own.

On Christmas Eve, he gave her chocolates from Dainty's on Fifth Avenue, noted for their delicious confectionery, and she gave him a grey silk tie from her father's menswear shop in SoHo. At midday, they shook hands and wished each other Merry Christmas, and she departed, a chocolate already in her mouth. Levon intended leaving soon himself: he was taking Anne to Macy's to buy a present for Tamara and one for Anne herself, though she didn't know it. He was reaching for his hat and overcoat when the telephone rang, making him jump – it was unnecessarily loud and could be heard all over the building.

He picked it up. 'Levon Zarian,' he announced; he still hadn't memorized the number.

'Hi, Levon,' said a cheerful voice. 'Ollie Blinker here. My boy, Herbie, and your girl, Anne, are at Peggy Perlmann's academy together.'

'Ah, yes,' Levon replied, rather taken aback by Ollie Blinker's overly familiar approach. 'Yes, she often talks about Herbie.' In fact, she talked about him all the time. They lunched with each other and hung around the local ice cream parlour when the academy finished for the day.

'I'm throwing a party on New Year's Eve,' Ollie Blinker continued, 'and I'd like Herbie and Anne to do a little turn for the guests. I trust you approve. You and your good lady are welcome to come. Herbie says you're a lawyer – you might make a few useful contacts while you're there.'

'That's very kind of you. I'd love to come, though I'm not too sure about Mrs Zarian. We have a small baby, you see.' He felt convinced Tamara wouldn't agree to be parted from John for an entire evening.

'I do know, and I can recommend a sitter if you want – a woman who used to sit for my own kids when they were small.'

'I'll tell my wife that. Thank you . . . Ollie. I look forward to meeting you soon.'

'My apartment is on the corner of Fifth Avenue and Sixty-second Street, top floor. There's a private lift.'

Levon knew the geography of New York as well as the back of his hand; the Blinkers lived in one of the most expensive and exclusive areas in the city.

He rang off and gave Anne the gist of the telephone call later when they met in the top-floor restaurant in Macy's. The place was packed to capacity and, like the entire shop, was lavishly decorated for Christmas. 'God Rest Ye Merry Gentlemen' issued from loud speakers on the wall.

'You don't mind, do you, Lev?' Anne asked, smiling in a way that only the hardest of hearts could have resisted. She looked a bit like a Christmas decoration herself in her blue velvet coat with white fur on the collar and cuffs and a hat to match, little black curls peeking from below the brim and flowing down her back. It was incredible to think that she was a mother. 'The party, I mean. Peggy's coming, and me and Herbie rehearsed the routines all last week.'

'Herbie and I,' Levon corrected. A waitress appeared and he ordered two coffees: one with cream, one without.

'Herbie and I,' Anne continued without a pause. 'We're doing two songs from *No, No, Nannette* – it's a new show on Broadway. Peggy wanted to take us to see it, but she couldn't get tickets.' She put her elbows on the table, her chin in her hands, and said, 'What shall I get Tamara for Christmas?'

'Jewellery, she loves jewellery.'

'I know she does, but I've only about seventy-five cents left.'

'What happened to your allowance? I thought you were saving it to buy presents?' She got two dollars a week. He ducked as a woman nearly decapitated him with her shopping bags.

'Sorry,' she panted. 'Sorry.'

'Well, I *was* saving it,' Anne confessed, 'but a lot went on ice cream and coffees after school – Herbie would pay every time, but I won't let him – and we all clubbed together to get something for Peggy and Mrs Constantine.' Mrs Constantine played the piano at the academy. 'Though I've already bought *you* a present, Lev,' she said a trifle piously, as if that excused the fact she hadn't enough for Tamara's.

'What is it?'

'You won't know until tomorrow, will you?' She laughed teasingly and Levon felt as impatient as a child, wanting to know what the present was.

'Did you buy that with your allowance?' Until now, he hadn't noticed the locket around her neck. It was gold and heavily engraved with scrolls and flowers.

'No, I met Herbie earlier, before I met you, and he bought it me for Christmas. He has loads of money.' She lifted the locket and squinted down at it. 'Thank you,' she said when the waitress

114

came with the coffees. The carol had changed to 'Away in a Manger'.

'Did you buy Herbie a present?' He would be annoyed if she had, leaving a mere seventy-five cents for Tamara.

'I told him I was broke.' She giggled merrily and began to sing, 'The stars in the bright sky looked down where he lay, the little Lord Jesus asleep in the hay . . . '

'I suppose you expect a present from me for Christmas?' he said jovially.

'Haven't you bought me anything yet?' she cried, pretending to be outraged.

'Well, I did think of getting you a box of handkerchiefs, or some bed socks, and giving them to you as a surprise, but decided it would be best to get you exactly what you wanted.'

'Oh, Lev, I'd love a coat,' she said fervently. 'A grown-up one, three-quarter length, with a belt, preferably black. I look like a child in this thing.' She gave the blue velvet coat a look of disgust. He wondered how old she really was. It was almost a year since he'd found her and brought her to his home, but she'd never mentioned having a birthday. Either she'd forgotten, or pushed it to the back of her mind as she'd done so many other things. To most people, she must have given the impression of being a perfectly normal, very exuberant young lady, but Levon knew otherwise.

'All right,' he agreed. 'But we'll look at coats after we've bought something for Tamara, otherwise we might forget about it. And I think I'd better add a dollar or two to that seventy-five cents of yours.' Tamara wasn't partial to cheap jewellery – or cheap anything – and he doubted she'd be pleased with anything that cost seventy-five cents.

As expected, Tamara refused to go to the party on New Year's Eve. She was horrified at the idea of using the sitter Ollie Blinker had offered to provide. 'I don't like the sound of him,' she said. 'What's Ollie short for?'

'Oliver, I guess,' Levon replied.

'Blinker is a very peculiar name. I'm sorry, Lev, but you'll just have to go to the party with Anne, though I would have liked to see her dance,' she conceded. 'She dances for us here, but it'll be different with a partner. You can tell me all about it when you come home.'

At eight o'clock on the night of the party, Levon and Anne set off for the Blinkers' apartment in a taxi, Anne in her new coat with a bag containing her shoes.

'What about a costume?' he asked.

'Mrs Blinker's had some made.'

'Really!' There seemed to be an awful lot going on that he knew nothing about. 'Have you met Mrs Blinker?'

'No, but Peggy has. She's really excited about tonight. They're desperately rich, the Blinkers, and she's hoping Mr Blinker will put up the money for a show written by her young man.'

'Peggy has a young man?' He felt slightly envious.

'Well, she calls him her young man, but I've seen him and he looks quite old, almost thirty.'

'That *is* old,' Levon said gravely, wondering where it put him at fifty-one.

'His name's Rupert something and he's written the music too. The show's called *Roller-Coaster* and it's set in a fairground.'

'It sounds interesting.'

'Yeah, me and Herbie – Herbie and I – are doing one of the numbers: "Dreaming".'

'I'm looking forward to it,' Levon murmured.

The taxi stopped, having arrived at its destination, and he tipped the driver an extra dollar – it was a cold night and last New Year's Eve he'd been doing the same thing, driving folk to their parties and clubs and wishing he were back home with Tamara.

'Wow!' Anne exclaimed when they got out and found themselves in front of an impressive russet-brick building that looked at least a hundred years old. It had arched windows and a large balcony on each floor – six floors altogether, Levon counted. They entered a magnificent foyer with a marble floor, lots of polished brass, and a carved desk, behind which sat a uniformed figure covered in gold braid.

'You for the Blinkers?' he enquired. When Levon nodded, he went on, 'Take the end lift. It should be back any second.'

They joined a small queue and Levon's heart dropped fractionally when he noticed the men were wearing dress suits, something he didn't possess.

The lift came and they shot up to the sixth floor at a speed that made his stomach lurch. The doors opened onto another foyer even more magnificent than the one downstairs, appearing, at first glance, to be considerably bigger, but actually much smaller. Levon came face to face with several versions of himself standing at different angles outside the lift, and even more versions getting smaller and smaller and stretching back for miles, possibly into infinity. He realized it was heptagon-shaped, possibly octagon, or another geometric shape he'd never heard of, and completely lined with mirrors.

'Always gives folks a shock,' chuckled a stocky man with beautifully waved grey hair wearing full evening dress, including a ruffled shirt and a red silk cummberbund. He grabbed Levon's hand and shook it furiously. 'Ollie Blinker, pleased to meet'cha. You're Levon, I presume, seeing as how you're with this gorgeous little lady who can only be Anne, Herbie's dancing partner.' He chucked Anne under her chin and she responded with a cute smile.

Ollie grabbed someone else's hand then, and Levon followed Anne through a door that had suddenly appeared in the mirrors. His coat was taken, Anne disappeared, and he entered a vast room covered with paintings the like of which he'd never seen before and which were comprised mainly of more geometric shapes. The numerous sofas and chairs were covered with white leather and the rest of the furniture was made of wood so pale it was almost white. There was a white grand piano big enough to dance on. A small orchestra was playing a Strauss waltz, though no one was dancing. He was relieved to see a few of the men wore dark suits like himself: the women were draped in silk and satin and precious jewels.

'Drink, sir?' a voice enquired. He turned to find a waiter in a white tuxedo holding a tray filled with glasses of what looked very much like champagne, which he'd only drunk once before in his life.

'Is it real?' he asked stupidly.

'Came over on a boat from France only last week, sir. Genuine vintage.'

'But what about Prohibition?' He felt even more stupid.

The waiter winked. 'Mr Blinker, he ain't ever heard of Prohibition, sir.'

Levon guiltily accepted a glass. He wasn't much of a drinker, but he'd missed having the occasional bottle of wine with a meal since coming to America; Prohibition had arrived in 1920 at about the same time as him and Tamara. It was a crazy law and had brought mayhem to the streets of the major cities, as gangsters fought each other for control of the trade in illicit liquor. His stomach lurched a second time when he wondered if that was how Ollie Blinker made his money. But the champagne, having come into contact with a stomach that hadn't known alcohol for years, was already having an effect. He decided that he didn't care what Ollie did for a living.

He finished the glass, took another, and pushed his way through the well-dressed throng to study one of the paintings: a collection of triangles and squares that meant nothing to him.

A few minutes later a small woman in a plain black evening frock joined him. She wore pearl studs in her ears, her only adornment, a refreshing change from the other women, who appeared to be wearing the entire contents of their jewellery boxes. 'You seem puzzled, Mr Zarian,' she said, 'but if you look closely, you'll see a face in there. It's a portrait of a man called Ambroise Vollard.'

Levon stepped back and studied the painting again. 'Yes, I can see a face,' he said with the excitement of someone who'd just solved a difficult puzzle.

'It's a school of painting called Cubism and was painted by the most famous living artist in the world today: Pablo Picasso. There are three more of his works here, and a couple of Braques. The whole collection cost just under a quarter of a million dollars.' She spoke in an accent he couldn't identify. She was a plain woman of about forty – homely, was how the Americans put it – yet there was something attractive about her face with its slightly crooked nose and too-wide mouth. Her eyes were very large and very dark, her brown hair short and straight, but he could tell it had been cut by an expert.

Levon nearly choked on the champagne. '*That* much!' He wouldn't have parted with a single cent for any one of the so-called works of art. 'How do you know my name?'

'My husband told me.' She thrust out her hand. 'Elizabeth Blinker, Mr Levon, Ollie's wife, though my friends call me Lizzie.'

They shook hands and he said, 'I'm Levon, but my friends call me Lev.' He liked her straightforward manner.

'One of these days, Lev,' she said, nodding at the paintings, 'these will be worth ten, twenty times that much.'

'Is that why you bought them, not because you liked them, but as an investment?'

'Ollie bought them as an investment: he knows nothing about art. Me, I wanted them for themselves.'

He studied the portrait of Ambroise Vollard again. What had been gained by painting a figure entirely in triangles? He couldn't think of anything. 'I suppose you could call it experimental?'

'I suppose you could, Lev.' She linked his arm. 'Come on. I'll introduce you to some of our guests. We have artists, lawyers, bankers, writers, actors, and quite a few crooks here, so take your pick.'

'The lawyers,' Levon said hastily. 'Where are you from, Lizzie?'

'Manchester, England. My mother used to take in washing, so you could say I've come up in the world.'

'Quite a long way up,' he agreed.

He was introduced to a group of lawyers and spent an

instructive few hours discussing the law in the state of New York, until the orchestra stopped playing and Ollie Blinker strolled on to the floor, Peggy Perlmann hovering behind him, and requested everyone to find a seat.

'I've got a little treat for you,' he hollered. 'My boy, Herbie, and his friend, Anne, are gonna dance for you.' There was a smattering of applause; Levon joined in. 'Firstly, they're gonna do "Tea for Two", followed by "Crazy Rhythm", both from the latest hit Broadway show, then a new tune by a new writer and composer who goes by the name of Rupert Coolidge.' He winked. 'No relation to the president, I'm pleased to say. *This* Mr Coolidge is violently opposed to Prohibition.' There was more applause from the heavily inebriated crowd. 'Ladies and gentlemen, I give you Anne Murray and Herbie Blinker.'

Anne and Herbie ran in hand in hand and bowed to the audience. Herbie was as blond as Anne was dark and about six inches taller. A good-looking, fresh-faced young man, he wore a black shirt and pants, and Anne a short black dress. They began to tap-dance to the rather leisurely music, each a perfect shadow of the other, the timing perfect, the moves faultless. The music quickened and so did the dancers. How could they remember the steps? Levon wondered. At one point, Herbie knelt on one knee, Anne sat on the other, and they began to sing, 'Picture you upon my knee, tea for two, and two for tea . . . ' Then they leapt to their feet and finished the number with a series of cartwheels, somehow managing to end up in each other's arms.

There was a thunderous burst of applause as the couple ran from the floor. 'She's a wonderful dancer, that girl,' the man beside Levon cried. He was a lawyer whose name was Carl. 'One of these days she'll make it big time.' He nudged Levon with his elbow. 'What d'you think, fella?'

'Big time,' Levon echoed. He could hardly speak for the lump in his throat. Anne was good. No, not just good. She was brilliant, destined for great things.

It was hardly a minute before she and Herbie re-appeared, having changed into glittering silver costumes: a suit with a bolero for Herbie; a top and shorts for Anne. They both wore top hats, which they immediately flung into the audience. The room darkened, the only illumination left over the space where they were to dance.

'Crazy Rhythm' was a fast number. Levon's eyes were on Anne's face, rather than her feet. Her eyes were bright, her lips smiled, yet he could tell she was lost in the music and the dancing. She was giving it her all, throwing herself into it, *being* it. He could hardly believe this was the mute, white-faced girl who'd climbed into his taxi less than a year ago. What would she be doing now had he driven off and left her outside the apartment in Bleecker Street? It was due to *him* that she was here, dancing and singing in front of a room full of extremely rich people at one of the top addresses in New York.

The number finished with Anne spinning like a top around Herbie while he held on to one of her hands. There was more applause, even louder than before.

'Wow!' Carl muttered. 'What did Ollie say the girl's name was?'

'Anne Murray.'

'I expect to see her name in lights on Broadway one of these days.' He continued to clap, yelling. 'More, more.' Anne had already gained one enthusiastic fan.

The lights came back on and waiters hurried among the guests with trays of drink. Levon helped himself to more champagne: he'd lost count of how many glasses he'd drunk. No doubt he'd pay for it in the morning, if not later that night.

Once again the room fell into darkness. Anne appeared in a green filmy frock and the ballet shoes he'd bought her from Amelia's in Delancey Street. She began to sing, 'I wake up and find, you've been on my mind, and I've been dreaming of you all night through . . . ' Her voice was rich and creamy, a woman's voice, not a girl's.

Herbie strolled on in a green gypsy shirt and pants to match, and began to sing along with her in a pleasant baritone. The dance that followed was sad and forlorn, and ended with Herbie carrying Anne aloft out of the room.

Levon had sensed the audience were getting fidgety. Perhaps they were bored or only liked the fast numbers. The applause was sparse; only Carl and Levon clapped until their hands hurt. Afterwards, Levon felt so giddy he couldn't stand up. He had a feeling that, not long afterwards, everyone joined hands and sang 'Auld Lang Syne', but he wasn't quite sure.

'You're a fool, Lev,' Tamara said tartly, but with a smile, the following morning. 'You should have known to be careful when you hadn't had a drink in so many years.'

Levon groaned and rested his head on the kitchen table. 'I had a great time,' he said weakly. 'I really enjoyed it.'

'I suppose Anne had to call a taxi to get you home.' Anne was still in bed, sensible girl.

'No, Lizzie Blinker, Ollie's wife, sent us in the Duesenberg.' It was a strange conversation they were having: Tamara spoke in their old language, Levon in English.

'Lizzie and Ollie! They sound like a music hall act.'

'They're a really nice couple; very generous.'

'You just claimed the champagne was nice, and look what that's done to you. Have you finished, darling?' she asked John, who was curled on her knee having his breakfast formula. He let go of the bottle and gave Levon a lovely smile.

'Good morning,' Levon grunted, raising his head.

'Would you like some coffee?'

'Are you asking me or John?'

'You. Didn't you notice my tone wasn't nearly so pleasant?' She smiled again. He felt annoyed that she was finding his hangover so amusing.

'I wish you'd been there last night, darling,' he said. 'You'd have loved it. Anne was . . . I can't emphasize enough how good she was: a star in the making, according to my friend Carl. He's a lawyer, by the way.'

'You're a lawyer and I don't trust your judgement any more than I do Carl's.'

'We're having lunch together one day next week. He specializes in property. I'm going to pass some of my clients over to him, and he's letting me have his litigation cases.'

'In other words, the murderers and bootleggers and those sorts of nasty people.'

Before Levon could answer, there was a knock on the door. Tamara put John on his knee and went to see who was there. She came back accompanied by a man he recognized as one of the waiters from the party.

'Present from Mr Blinker.' The man put a cardboard box on the floor. 'With his compliments.'

'What is it?'

'Fruit.' The man winked.

Tamara tried to tip him fifty cents, but he waved the money away and left, crying, 'Happy New Year.'

'If it's fruit,' Tamara said, 'why did it clink when it touched the floor?'

'Open it and see,' Levon suggested.

The box contained half a dozen bottles of French wine. Tamara completely and instantly changed her opinion of bootleggers.

The new office had three rooms: one for Emily, one for him, and a waiting room for his clients. It was situated right behind Union Square, within walking distance of the apartment.

In the spring, when John was six months old, Tamara again began to insist that they move to somewhere more spacious with a garden. She took the baby with her to look at real estate while Levon was at work. She seemed to have settled on Brooklyn and caught a bus across the bridge when the various realtors informed her there was a house for sale or rent – they'd had a telephone installed in the apartment. When he arrived home, she would tell him all about it, show him the details, say that John had loved it and so had she.

'John told you that, did he?'

'I could tell by his eyes, the way they lit up. Oh, and Lev, the one I saw today had a vegetable patch.'

'Would I be expected to look after it?' he asked quickly. The last thing he wanted to do in his free time was grow vegetables. He'd become a fan of the theatre and the movies. Tamara wasn't interested, so he went with Carl, who was unmarried, or Anne and Herbie, or with the Blinkers – Ollie always hired a box at the theatre and invited him along.

'I'll take care of the vegetables,' Tamara said testily. 'By the way, I'm seeing Lizzie Blinker tomorrow. I telephoned and she asked me to tea.'

He was surprised and pleased. She'd shown no interest in meeting the Blinkers before. 'You'll like her,' he said.

'Can we go and view the house with the vegetable patch this weekend?' she asked.

'I reckon so.' He felt defeated.

'I'll arrange it with the realtor,' Tamara said triumphantly.

Anne didn't want to move. She hadn't said anything, but he could tell by her face when the matter was discussed. It closed up, as it always did when it was something she didn't want to hear. When she'd told him she loved New York, Levon knew she'd meant the island of Manhattan with its bright lights, theatres, little streets and wide avenues, Macy's store and Mulberry Street market, Times Square, St Patrick's Cathedral where they sometimes went to Mass – he'd managed to establish that, like him and Tamara, she was a Catholic – and the myriad other things that made this tiny part of America so unique and never-endingly amazing. When the good weather came, he would miss strolling part of the way home from his office, giving five cents to the organ-grinder who only played Italian opera, walking through Central Park in spring when the leaves were in bud, and in autumn when they began to fall. He would miss having the theatres virtually on his doorstep, the restaurants that sold food from virtually every part of the world, the noise and the vibrancy of Manhattan.

'If I look at this house on Sunday,' he said to Tamara the following morning, 'will you do something for me?'

'We're not looking at the house for me, Lev, but for *us*: you, me and John.' He noticed she didn't mention Anne. 'Anyway, what is it you want me to do?'

'Become an American citizen.' He was beginning to think like an American, speak like one. He said words like 'yippee,' and 'okey-dokey.' He called Carl 'pal' and referred to dollars as 'bucks' – but only when he played poker with some of his lawyer pals during an extended lunch-hour every other Friday, something Tamara knew nothing about. He wanted to take part in the next election, vote for the Democrats the same as Carl and Ollie Blinker. He felt American in his heart.

'If that's what you want, Lev,' Tamara said evenly, 'then I'll do it.'

He could tell she was reluctant, but then he was reluctant to live in Brooklyn. Levon felt his sacrifice was the greater of the two.

When he arrived home that night, there was a great bunch of red roses in a vase on the table. 'Lizzie Blinker gave them to me,' Tamara told him. 'As you said, she's very nice.'

'What did you two talk about?'

Tamara shrugged. 'Herbie and Anne mostly. They have another party on Saturday night.' Since New Year's Eve, the youngsters had been hired to entertain at a number of private parties for which they received a hefty fee.

'Is Anne home yet?' It was a quarter after seven and John had already been put to bed.

'Tonight's the night Peggy takes them to the movies.'

Levon missed Anne's delightful smiles and her charming presence, particularly at mealtimes. He made a harrumphing noise and took the satchel containing a heap of files into the dining room – he had work to do later. To his surprise, Tamara followed him. 'Sit down a minute, Lev,' she said. 'I want to talk to you.'

'What about?' He was spreading the files on the bureau.

'Sit down first.'

Irritated, mainly by the fact that Anne wasn't there, he sat at the table.

'I was telling Lizzie we were about to move to Brooklyn,' Tamara said, 'and that Anne didn't want to go, and she suggested she came and lived with them.'

He felt anger rise in his throat and his head began to throb with it. 'Have you asked Anne if she wants to go to Brooklyn?'

'No, but I can tell she doesn't. She freezes over whenever we talk about it.'

'Whenever *you* talk about it. I've never once raised the subject of Brooklyn.'

'Oh, don't be silly, Lev. You know what I mean.'

The anger was beating like a hammer in his chest. He got to his feet and the chair fell back on the floor with a clatter. Tamara jumped and looked frightened. Levon rarely lost his temper and never with her. There was something sly about her beautiful, haughty face that he'd never seen before. She was avoiding his eyes, unwilling to look straight at him, her mouth pulled in a mean line.

'It's why you went to see Lizzie Blinker, isn't it?' he said in a deep, rough voice that sounded strange to his own ears. 'To ask if Anne could live with them. You've taken her child and now you want rid of her.'

It was Tamara's turn to lose her temper, though she kept her voice at a more subdued level, no doubt worried John would be woken by the noise. 'I didn't exactly *take* her child, Levon. If I hadn't looked after John, then who would? I find it uncomfortable her living with us when she completely ignores his existence. It makes for a bad atmosphere.'

'I hadn't noticed a bad atmosphere.'

'That's because you're hardly ever here,' she said coldly. 'If you're not at work, you've gone somewhere with your new friends.'

'I go with other people only because you refuse to come. We

could always get a sitter for John. It would only be for a few hours.'

Her eyes blazed. 'I refuse to leave John with a sitter.'

'Then don't blame me for going out with my friends.' The argument was getting ridiculous. If he'd known she felt so strongly about it, he would have stayed in. His anger was centred on the fact that she'd gone out of her way to get rid of Anne. 'Did you tell Lizzie that John was Anne's child?'

'Of course I didn't.' She wanted everyone to think John was *hers*. 'There's another thing, Lev,' she said, more softly than before. She came towards him, put her hands on his shoulders, and looked at him directly. 'The main reason I want Anne to go is that I believe you're in love with her.'

He laughed incredulously. 'That's ridiculous, Tamara.'

'No, it isn't, Lev.' She put her fingers against his lips: they smelt of formula and the oil she rubbed on the baby when his skin was red. 'Just think a minute, don't speak. How many times a day does Anne come into your mind compared with me, your wife? You're infatuated with the girl, besotted. She's all you talk about and I reckon she's all you think about, too.' She removed her fingers from his lips, but Levon was too astounded to speak. 'I'll go and get dinner: it's meatloaf, a genuine American dish for two prospective American citizens,' she said with a slight, rather sad smile. 'I won't be long.'

They didn't take the house where vegetables grew in the yard – Levon thought it too big for two people and a child – but six months later the Zarians left Grammercy Park and moved into a single-storey house in Brooklyn not far from the promenade. It had two bedrooms and one under the roof for when someone came to stay – he had Anne in mind, but she was already living with the Blinkers in the apartment overlooking Central Park. She never once visited the house in Brooklyn. Levon reckoned she was keeping away from Tamara, whom she'd sensed had turned against her. Maybe she'd even sensed the reason: he didn't know and never would.

He continued to see her at lunch-times, paid the fees for the academy until she left in the summer of 1927. After that, he saw less and less of her, though she would telephone and tell him whenever she and Herbie had a new booking. They toured the East Coast in a show called *High Jinx*, third on the bill, appeared twice at Radio City, did a summer season in Maine.

Peggy's boyfriend, Rupert Coolidge, got backers for *Roller-Coaster*, although Ollie Blinker refused to have anything to do with it. It opened in Philadelphia with Anne and Herbie in supporting roles, but closed within a week after terrible reviews. The music was dire, the plot-line improbable, the costumes lacked imagination. One critic wrote: 'The only thing this show has to offer is the brilliance of its two junior stars: Anne Murray and Herbie Blinker. With her fragile beauty, scintillating dancing skills and enchanting personality, Miss Murray, in particular, is someone to be watched. I expect to see her in a major role on Broadway any time soon.'

Levon's own visits to the theatre and the movies had virtually ceased. He'd managed to see the first talking movie – *The Jazz Singer* with Al Jolson – but hadn't been since. Tamara had made friends who gave regular dinner parties and it was apparently essential that he attend, though he and the friends had nothing in common with each other. Every few weeks, it would be the Zarians' turn to have a dinner party. The neighbours were invited to picnics in the yard or to drinks on Sunday afternoon. Naturally, the invitations were returned. Since John's first birthday, Tamara had condescended to engage a sitter – a young college girl, Colette, who lived next door.

There were always things that had to be done around the house: the screen door needed fixing, a tap wouldn't turn, or a tile was loose on the roof. 'And it would be silly to hire someone to do a small job like that, wouldn't it, Lev?' Tamara would say, smiling sweetly.

It wasn't the sort of life he had ever envisaged and it wasn't the sort of place he'd ever wanted to live. What's more, their relationship wasn't the same as it had been: something had gone and she was punishing him for loving Anne. For he *had* loved her, Levon realized. It hadn't been a sexual love, nor a father and daughter one. It had been love, pure and simple. He had loved Anne, still did.

He and Tamara had made themselves familiar with the history of the land in which they now lived, knew the structure of its government, had studied its constitution, taken the Oath of Allegiance, and were now American citizens. But Levon didn't feel the glow he had expected. Once he'd found life exciting, now it was boring. Each day was the same as the one before and there was nothing new to find. What's more, his hair was turning grey at the temples and he felt old.

One day, two years after the move to Brooklyn, Ollie Blinker telephoned Levon in his office. They hadn't seen each other for months. 'You got any stocks and shares, Lev, old pal?' Ollie enquired.

'No, I don't trust my money anywhere but in a bank,' Levon said primly.

'In that case, drop everything, go to the bank, and withdraw every single cent.'

'Why?'

'Just do it, pal.' There was a click. Ollie had rung off.

Levon sat at his desk, staring at his hands. He didn't have an enormous sum in his account: the mortgage on the house took a huge chunk of his earnings and he'd recently bought a car, an old Maxwell, but there was enough put away for the garage Tamara wanted and to see them through should times ever get hard.

He got slowly to his feet. Somehow, despite his conviction that Ollie Blinker was a crook, he trusted the man. If he removed the money, he'd lose some interest, but it would be better than losing the lot. The Stock Market had been very volatile lately and millions of shares were being traded each day, but he couldn't visualize the banks going broke.

Nevertheless, Levon withdrew his savings. Two days later, the Stock Market crashed, the banks ran out of cash, and thousands of Americans had their entire life savings completely wiped out.

The safe in Levon's office was comfortably full of dollars, but he felt sorry for his fellow citizens. It was if a giant boot had stamped down on the city of New York, squeezing all the life out of it and grinding its heel on Wall Street.

Anne rang late on the day of the crash. Emily had already gone home, and he was trying to think of a reason for delaying his own departure. 'Are you all right, Lev?' she asked. 'I mean financially.'

'I'm fine, darling.'

'Ollie promised to warn you. I don't understand how he knows about these things.'

'Are you at Ollie's now?' Something plucked at his heart at the idea she might only be a taxi ride away.

'We just got back from Boston. Oh, Lev, let's go to dinner! At the Plaza! It'll be my treat. I've never bought you a meal before, but me and Herbie — Herbie and I — just performed at this big political event, a dinner for Boston's finest, and they paid us a small fortune. Will seven suit you?'

'Seven will suit me fine.'

'See you then, Lev.'

'See you, darling,' Levon said, though Anne had already rung off. He immediately dialled his home number. Tamara answered, her voice crisp and business-like. 'I'm afraid I'm going to be late tonight,' he informed her. 'Something's come up, an emergency. I need to go see a client who's in desperate trouble, threatening suicide, according to his wife.'

'But you knew we were having the Di Marcos to dinner tonight,' she said crossly.

'Is dinner with the Di Marcos more important than a man killing himself?' he asked unctuously. He felt, unreasonably, he had right on his side, even though he was lying through his teeth.

'Well, no,' she conceded grudgingly. 'But what am I going to tell them?'

'The truth?'

She sighed. 'Try not to be too late, Lev.'

'I'll try,' he promised, though it was another lie.

Chapter 7

1930

'Hello.'

The man opened his eyes and struggled to a sitting position on the bench. 'Hello, young lady,' he said politely.

'I've brought you some breakfast: coffee and a couple of hot dogs.'

'That's mighty kind of you. Thank you very much.' His hands shook as he reached for the food. The fingernails were broken and full of dirt.

'I asked the man on the stall to put sugar and cream in the coffee. Is that all right?' She sat on the bench where his feet had been. There was a hand-painted placard underneath which said 'Need work – will do anything', and a grey fedora that looked as if it had been trodden on. He'd been using a khaki knapsack for a pillow.

'That's more than all right: sugar gives you energy, so they say.' One hot dog had already gone. 'What's your name, young lady?' he asked with his mouth half-full of the other.

'Anne Murray. What's yours?'

'Robert Edgar Gifford: known as Bobby to my friends. I expect you're still at college, Miss Murray.'

'I've never been to college. I'm a dancer. Please call me Anne.'

'A dancer, eh!' He seemed impressed. 'I don't think I've ever met a real dancer before. I was junior manager in a bank – in charge of the loans department – but the bank went bust and we all lost our jobs. The owner shot himself.' He gave a dry smile.

'Thought about doing it myself for a while, but changed my mind.'

'Oh, I'm so glad you did. You're only young and you're quite good-looking.' He was about twenty-five and badly in need of a wash and a shave – she could smell the dirt on him and the odour of stale perspiration. The suit he wore had been a good one, but now the collar was curled and the pockets torn. His shirt was filthy, but nothing could disguise the fact that he was handsome, if painfully thin. The look in his brown eyes wasn't quite as hopeless as some she'd seen since New York had fallen apart and the streets were full of the hungry and the homeless, mainly men like Bobby Gifford who'd lost not just their jobs, but everything.

He smiled again. 'Are you real, Anne Murray?'

Anne took the question seriously – she sometimes doubted if she were real. 'Yes, I think so,' she replied.

'Do you do this often – feed the down-and-outs?' The hot dogs gone, he was noisily sipping the coffee out of the cardboard cup. A dog bounded up and sniffed the hot dog wrappings. Its owner, an elderly man, smiled at Anne and stared with some surprise at her companion. It was a glorious June morning and there were already quite a few people about in Central Park. Two horse riders could be seen in the distance. She wondered if, on a day like this, Bobby Gifford felt slightly less wretched, or if he was too far gone to notice the weather.

'Only if I see someone sleeping on this bench. I can see from my bedroom window. It's over there.' She pointed to the Blinkers' apartment across the park. 'My bedroom's the second from the corner on the top floor. I always look the minute I wake up.'

'That's a real fancy place to live,' her new friend said enviously. 'Does it mean if I sleep on this bench tonight, I'll get another breakfast?'

'Yes,' she promised. 'What will you do with yourself today?'

He put the coffee on his knee and said thoughtfully. 'I might go to Saks and buy a new suit, have lunch at the Amber Room – they do great salmon, so I'm told – and take in a movie afterwards. Maybe *The Wind* with Lillian Gish, I missed it when it came out. Then I'll meet some old pals for dinner, before heading for Broadway to see a show.' He gave another dry smile. 'Alternatively, I might just look for work.'

'I hope you find some soon,' she said fervently.

'What I'd really like to do is hitch to California – Los Angeles,' he said, creasing his eyes as if he could already see the Pacific Ocean rippling on to the golden sands. 'At least it would be warm. I'm not looking forward to sleeping outside in another New York winter.'

'Why don't you? Go to California, that is.'

He shrugged. 'I'm scared. I was born here, Newark, and it's all I've ever known. Los Angeles is a couple of thousand miles away.'

'*I'd* do it if I were you. You could get a job in the movies.'

He laughed curtly. 'That's easier said than done.'

'Everything's easier to say than to do.' She fished in the pocket of her pink jacket. 'I've got eight dollars you can have. You could get a bus part of the way.'

'I don't want charity.' He scowled and turned away. 'You can keep your money.'

'You ate the breakfast,' Anne gently pointed out. 'That was charity.'

'I wish I hadn't now,' he said churlishly. 'Don't bother looking for me in the morning. I won't be here.'

'It's up to you. I'll look for you all the same. Goodbye, Bobby, and good luck.' She put the eight dollars on the bench and shoved it towards him. She'd hurt his pride, but it was good that he still had some left.

'I've been watching you,' Lizzie Blinker said when Anne went in. 'I wish you wouldn't do that, pet. One of these days you might come to some harm.'

'Did he pick up the money?' Anne asked. 'I gave him money, but he refused to take it, so I left it on the bench.'

'I've no idea. Once I saw you come away, I stopped watching. Have you had any breakfast?' Breakfast was the only meal Lizzie prepared – servants made the others – but it kept her in touch with her roots, she claimed. 'When I was a kid in Manchester, most of the time there wasn't anything for breakfast. When there was, it was only bread and dripping.'

'What was bread and dripping like?' Anne had asked.

'In those days, it tasted delicious, but I doubt if it would now.' Now, she made pancakes and cinnamon toast, scrambled eggs and hash browns. There was always loads of fruit on the table and jugs of juice. 'What would you like this morning, pet?' she asked.

'Everything,' Anne replied. 'I'm starving.'

Together, they walked into the long kitchen with its black tiled floor and white marble tops. There were yellow, slatted blinds on the windows, making the room appear sunny on the dullest of days, and a stove with six black rings that turned bright red when the electricity was switched on. In her worst nightmares, Anne sometimes dreamed that someone was pressing her arm against one of the rings: she could even smell her flesh burning. The table was a round slab of marble supported by a single black support; it always reminded her of a mushroom.

'My friends would like to know how you manage to eat so much, but still stay as thin as a beggar's broomstick.' Although Lizzie had been in America for nearly thirty years, she hadn't lost her Manchester accent.

'She dances the fat off, Ma, that's how.' Herbie came into the kitchen wearing a bright yellow sweater and white pants. He was perfectly turned out, but his room would be in a terrible state, littered with all the clothes that had been rejected. He kissed them both.

'Then I'd better suggest my friends take up tap-dancing.'

'What are we doing today?' Anne asked Herbie. She often forgot.

'Silly girl!' Herbie said fondly. 'We've an audition in two hours, haven't we? It's for that new Broadway show, *Roses are Red* . . .'

'And violets are blue,' Anne sang.

'Sugar is sweet,' said Lizzie, smiling.

'And so are you,' Herbie finished. 'Both of you,' he added with a brilliant smile. 'I don't want to hurt anyone's feelings.'

Lizzie put a pot of coffee on the table, two cups and saucers, a sugar bowl and a jug of cream. The china was eggshell-thin with a gold rim and had a pattern of tiny rosebuds. Herbie poured two cups: black for him; four sugar lumps and a dash of cream for Anne.

'Today's the twenty-first of June,' Lizzie remarked as she made the pancakes, looking slightly incongruous in the exquisite lace negligeée that had probably cost the earth in Bloomingdale's or one of the other expensive shops she frequented. 'That means it's Midsummer, the longest day. When I was little it always made me feel a bit sad, knowing that from then on the nights would get darker and before you knew it, we'd all be sitting in candlelight and there'd be nothing else to do but go to bed.'

Herbie pretended to yawn, something he always did when his mother reminisced about her childhood. She saw the yawn and told him he didn't know how lucky he was. 'You and your sister have never wanted for anything. It'd do you good to go short now'n again.' Herbie's sister, Mabel, was married with two children and lived in Washington where Kurt, her husband, did something very important in the White House.

Breakfast finished, Herbie decided it was time they practised for the audition. He and Anne danced out of the room, along the corridor, past the paintings that had so intrigued Levon and into the mirrored foyer where their whirling, dazzling figures were endlessly reflected, as if they were in a ballroom as big as the world, full of dancing couples identical to themselves. On their way back, Christina, the maid, came out of Herbie's bedroom and told him he should be ashamed of the mess he'd made. Christina, who was black, had been with the Blinkers for a quarter of a century and never hesitated to speak her mind. Herbie just waved and danced by, and Christina smiled. Despite the fact he'd been dreadfully spoiled, he had such a sunny personality that everybody loved him.

'You'll wake the master,' Christina called after them. She

always referred to Mr Blinker as 'the master' in a terribly sarcastic voice that really annoyed him. 'He's still in bed.'

'Who cares?' Herbie shouted back.

They finished the dance with double outward pirouettes back in the kitchen where, having kept in touch with her roots by making breakfast, Lizzie had left the dirty dishes for Christina.

Anne went to her room to get changed for the audition. Through the window, she saw the bench that Bobby Gifford had occupied was empty. She hoped he was already on his way to Los Angeles. Further down the park, well out of sight, were the Hoovervilles, the hastily built shacks that housed the unemployed and their families, named after President Hoover who'd done nothing to help them. She'd only seen them once and they made her want to cry.

Shall I call Lev and tell him about the audition? she wondered. Or wait and see what happened? Wait and see, she decided, though it would be lovely to hear his voice warmly wish her luck. Trouble was, it was something else that made her want to cry because she missed him so much. It was all right living with the Blinkers, but it didn't compare with the months she'd spent with Lev and Tamara before the baby had come along, spoiling everything, reminding her of a time that she mostly managed to forget.

Since she'd met Lev, she'd felt no need to retreat to a world of her own and felt perfectly safe. But she'd found the presence of the baby in the apartment disturbing. She hadn't wanted to look at him, was scared to see whom he might resemble. It had been a relief when the Zarians had moved to Brooklyn and she'd come to live with the Blinkers, though she hadn't dreamed it would hurt so much to be separated from Lev.

It was the third time they'd been to the same theatre to audition for the same show. First there'd been about thirty couples, next fifteen. Now there were only five and a final decision would be made that day. Herbie had been touching wood all week in the hope they'd be hired. Their names would go on the posters after the two main stars: Eric Carrington, who was British, and Patricia Peters. It was Herbie's dream to see their names in lights one day. Anne hoped for the same thing, but mainly for his sake. All she wanted to do was dance and it didn't matter where. When she was dancing, she forgot everything. She just allowed herself to be swallowed up in the music and the mesmerizing sound of their feet tapping on the floor.

As usual, Herbie managed to arrange it so they went on last, a position he insisted was an advantage. After the other four couples had had their turn, a young, rather harassed young man called Jerry, who seemed to be in charge of things, took them on to the stage and shouted, 'Herbie Blinker and Anne Murray, Mr Abel.' Conrad Abel was the producer. He was sitting five rows back in the darkened theatre, a small hunched figure, his face merely a white blur.

'What key do you want, darlings?' the pianist enquired when the music, 'Toot Toot Tootsie Goodbye', was placed in front of him. He had beautiful silver hair and was dressed entirely in purple.

'C,' said Herbie. 'We've marked where we're going to sing and where to speed up towards the end.'

Herbie squeezed her hand, the pianist began to play, and they danced like two people possessed, putting everything they had into the routine they'd been practising for weeks. Anne was never happier than when she danced and it showed in her radiant face and sparkling eyes. She didn't worry that she would take a false step, and her confidence was communicated to Herbie, who often felt nervous on such occasions.

'Thanks,' Jerry said when they'd finished, only slightly breathless. 'If you'd like to sit in the green room with the others, I'll let you know Mr Abel's decision.'

They waited in the green room with the other four couples for what seemed like hours, but was no more than a few minutes, Anne discovered later. Fingernails were chewed, feet studied, legs crossed and uncrossed. No one spoke. One young man rushed out to be sick. Two lives would change for ever as a result of

Conrad Abel's decision. They'd come so far and might never come this far again. The man who'd been sick returned. He reminded Anne a bit of Bobby Gifford with his thin face and haunted eyes, and she traitorously hoped he and his partner would be picked.

The door opened to admit Jerry and everyone tensed. 'Mr Abel would like Herbie Blinker and Anne Murray to stay,' he announced. 'The rest of you can go home. Thanks for coming.'

A young woman jumped to her feet. 'But that's not fair.' She was more than averagely pretty with smooth brown hair and blue eyes. 'Mr Abel promised us we'd get the parts.'

Jerry groaned. 'What's your name?'

'Rosalind Raines and this is my partner, Flip Ungar.' She indicated the young man who'd reminded Anne of Bobby Gifford. 'He promised me, last night, he *promised*.'

'Well, I'm sorry, Miss Raines, but Mr Abel didn't mention either of you.'

'The stinking bastard,' the girl spat. 'He *promised*.'

'The trouble with Mr Abel,' Jerry said as he led Anne and Herbie back to the stage, 'is that he can't keep his trousers buttoned. Them's the times he makes promises that he don't mean to keep. Anyway, I'm the stage manager, so we're gonna see a lot of each other from now on. With Eric Carrington and Patricia Peters starring, *Roses are Red* is sure to be a really big hit.'

'We've done it, Anne!' Herbie threw his arms around her. 'We're gonna be on Broadway.'

'So, you've had a boy at *last*!' Irene snorted. She limped across the sun-drenched room and peered at the baby in Mollie's arms. 'The nurse told me on the way in. A copper called late last night to say you'd gone into labour. Our Tom had asked him to. I didn't sleep a wink thinking about you and praying you'd have a boy.' She chucked the baby under his wrinkly chin. 'He looked a tough 'un. What did he weigh?'

'Eight pounds, two ounces, and I didn't care whether I had a boy or a girl, Irene, and neither did Tom,' Mollie said firmly.

'Men prefer sons,' her mother-in-law stated as if it had been carved in stone, a truth never to be denied.

Mollie didn't bother denying it. She just knew Tom couldn't have loved their daughters, Megan and Brodie, more had they been boys.

'What are you going to call him?'

'Joseph, but Tom's already started to call him Joey.'

'Joey's the gear.' She settled in a chair beside the bed. 'What sort of time did you have, luv?' she enquired, her voice throbbing with sympathy.

'All right.' Mollie winced, remembering. It had been anything but all right. In fact, it had hurt like blazes and gone on for hours, but it was fatal to tell that to Irene, who would then go through her own four labours, every one of which would have been ten times worse than anything Mollie described. Her sisters-in-law, Lily and Pauline, were just as bad, competing with each other for the worst experiences, the most stitches, the longest labours. Gladys was all right. She was married to Enoch and the youngest of the three. Since Mollie had married into the Ryans, Gladys had become her best friend after Agatha.

'I've brought you some oranges,' Irene announced. 'Jaffas.'

'Thank you very much.' Mollie was starving, not for oranges, but for fish and chips soaked in vinegar, preferably wrapped in newspaper. They tasted better out of newspaper than on a plate.

The baby sneezed. 'God bless you,' Mollie murmured. The sneeze must have woken him and he opened his big blue eyes and stared at her vacantly. He was a crumpled little thing with a button nose. 'He looks worried about something,' she remarked, kissing the nose.

'Probably worried where his next meal's coming from. Boys are hungry little buggers, never off the breast. Our Tom was the worst. I had to learn to cook with one arm for a whole year after he was born.'

'Really!' Mollie took everything her mother-in-law said with a great pinch of salt.

The door opened and Lily came in carrying a bunch of

carnations from her garden and said the nurse would be in soon with a vase. Gladys called her Lily the Lampost she was so tall. 'So you've had a boy at last,' she remarked. As well as a long body, she had a long face and a long nose, and was inclined to sniff disapprovingly at everything. She sniffed disapprovingly at the baby, though Mollie took for granted it was just a habit and she didn't really mean it.

'I wouldn't have cared if it had been another girl.' You had what God sent you. She and Tom had picked a name, Jane, in case they'd had a girl, as if she'd have cared any less for the baby in her arms if it had been Jane instead of Joey.

'You're just saying that, Moll.'

'No, I'm not, Lily,' Mollie said through gritted teeth.

'Every man wants a son.'

'Is that so?'

'Leave the girl be, Lily.' Irene rolled her eyes in exasperation, as if she hadn't said exactly the same thing herself a few minutes before. She and Lily didn't get on. They argued over everything, even if it meant one had to discard a lifelong-held opinion in order to win. There were all sorts of tensions in the Ryan family that Mollie hadn't been aware of before she'd married Tom. Not only did Lily not get on with her mother-in-law, she didn't get on with Pauline, either. In fact, they detested each other, though were united in their opinion that Gladys was a hussy who led Enoch a pretty dance.

Enoch's furniture business was prospering and he earned more than his three other brothers put together. Lily and Pauline's opinion of their sister-in-law could have been influenced by the fact that Gladys bought her clothes from George Henry Lee's, whereas they could only afford to shop in Blackler's. Moreover, she had bright-red curly hair, green eyes and a flirtatious manner, and their own husbands always made a beeline for Gladys whenever the families met in the house in Turnpike Street.

The bell rang to indicate morning visiting times were over. Irene and Lily kissed Mollie, then Joey, and promised they'd come again that evening.

The door closed. 'Well, I'm glad they've gone, aren't you?' she said. She opened her nightdress and attached the baby to her breast. He began to suck eagerly. She'd been reluctant to feed him in front of the visitors, who would have told her she was holding him the wrong way or using the wrong breast. 'Your dad's going to do his best to get here in his dinner-hour,' she told him. 'And Agatha's coming tonight after work. You'll like Agatha. She can't wait to meet you.' Agatha had telephoned the nursing home from the chemist's as soon as she got in that morning, so she already knew about Joey.

The nursing home was in Princes Park where Megan and Brodie had been born. The woman who owned it was married to a police inspector and offered special rates to policemen's wives. It was so much better than a hospital where visitors were only allowed twice a week and the wards were crowded, the nurses brusque and not very kind to the new mothers. Here, Mollie had a room to herself. The walls were painted cream and there was a white net curtain and a dark-green blind on the open window. The curtain billowed in and out, touched by the soft breeze, and she could hear the cries of children playing in the park.

'Are you enjoying that?' she asked Joey. He had brown hair, just like Tom's, short and neat, as if it had already been cut by a barber. It felt soft and downy to the touch. Her swollen breasts felt tender and her stomach ached like mad. She stretched out her legs and wiggled her feet, worried she was about to get cramp.

Yet she felt completely happy. It was June – Midsummer's Day, in fact – and the sun was out as if to prove it. Through the net she could see the trees in the park, the leaves shimmering like diamonds. But had it been winter and there'd been snow outside, she would have felt just as happy. Next month, she would be twenty-one, she had three beautiful children, and was married to the best husband in the world.

The door opened to admit the best husband in the world. 'Hello,' Tom grinned.

'Hello.' She wondered if her face wore the same expression as his, slightly bemused, as if they couldn't quite believe their luck in having found each other.

'How's our son?'

'*He's* all right, but he's not doing my left breast much good.'

'Change him to the other one.'

'He's already made short work of that.'

Tom came over and cupped her face in his hands. 'I love you,' he said, kissing her full on the lips.

'And I love you.' She caught one of his hands and kissed the palm. It tasted warm and salty. 'Do you feel tired, darlin'?' He'd stayed until after Joey had been born just after three, but had been due at work by eight.

'Not as tired as you must be.' He sat on the edge of the bed. Joey released her breast and smacked his lips. She handed him to his father. 'Here's your son. You can bring his wind up for the very first time.'

'The first of many.' He hoisted the baby on to his shoulder and began gently to rub his back. Mollie leaned against the pillow, exhausted, thinking what a beautiful picture they made: the handsome young man with the son who wasn't yet half a day old.

'Did you manage to see Megan and Brodie this morning?' she asked.

'They were still in bed, fast asleep.' Their daughters were being looked after by Elsie Hardcastle who lived next door. Elsie was also married to a policeman. She was in her forties and her own children were grown up and married with children of their own.

'I can't stay long,' Tom said. He coughed importantly. 'We're in the middle of this dead interesting case. This avvy, I've got to interview a chap in Smithdown Road whose wife has gone missing. Me, I think she's just run away, but it's got to be investigated.'

Six months ago, Tom had been recommended for the plain-clothes unit and was now a detective constable, using his brain, following clues and relying on his instincts in a way he'd never had to do before. He had re-read all his Sherlock Holmes stories and frequently came up with the most bizarre explanations for a crime that had been committed. Occasionally, he was actually right.

Joey gave a loud, hoarse burp and spurted a little bubble of milk on to the shoulder of his father's dark suit. 'Oh, I should have put a towel over you,' Mollie cried.

Another man might have cursed his newly born son, but Tom just handed Joey to his mother and wiped off the milk with a damp face flannel out of the sink. 'It's all right, Moll, don't worry. Anyroad, it's a badge of fatherhood, isn't it?' His face glowed with pride. 'I'm going for a drink with me mates tonight. We're going to wet the baby's head. But I'll still come and see you afterwards, always assuming the chap in Smithdown Road hasn't murdered his missus and hidden the body in the cellar.'

'You said you thought she'd run away.'

'Yes, but I could always be wrong,' he conceded, though she could tell he seriously doubted it.

Olive Raines was still simmering with rage more than an hour later as she and Flip sat hunched over their cold coffees on a 8th Avenue dinner not far from the theatre.

'He promised,' she said for the twentieth, or it might have been the thirtieth, time.

Flip stroked her hand. 'I know, honey.'

'I never dreamed I'd do anything like that,' she whispered. She hadn't done too badly in New York. At least she could tell people she was 'on the stage', even if a lot of the time she was working as a waitress. Twice she'd been in the chorus of a really big show, had sung in a few tenth-rate nightclubs, and been a magician's assistant in a travelling vaudeville company. But real success had proved as elusive as the Holy Grail. Then *Roses are Red* had come along and she and Flip had found themselves in the last five couples. She'd felt it wouldn't hurt to give the process a little nudge and sleep with the producer. The casting couch, it was called. Lots of women used it to get on in show business.

'I wish you hadn't, Ros. I begged you not to.' She'd never told Flip her real name was Olive. Another thing she hadn't told him was the way she'd used to earn her living back in London. Conrad Abel was a repulsive little man, but sleeping with him hadn't been as much of an ordeal for her as for most women.

'I know you did.' He hadn't begged all that hard. The same desire to succeed burned as strongly in him as it did in her. Had Conrad Abel swung a different way, she knew Flip would have been just as willing to offer himself. She would have begged him not to, but in the same half-hearted way as he'd begged her.

'I bet that Herbie Blinker's folks are loaded,' Flip sneered. 'I could just tell. There was something about him. He looked well fed and pampered; the all-American boy.'

'What about the girl, his partner? What did you think of her?'

'She was OK,' he said grudgingly. 'She looked like a dancer, walked like one.'

'I know her,' Olive said in a low voice. 'At least, I used to. She was on the boat from England.'

'Jeez!' Flip gasped, astounded. 'Why didn't you speak to her? I wonder if *she* did the great Mr Abel a favour?'

'She didn't recognize me. Her name's Annemarie Kenny, not Anne Murray.' Had she thought that one day Annemarie would beat her to such an important part, she would have left the bitch on Ellis Island to fend for herself. 'I doubt if she went anywhere near Conrad Abel.'

'You're probably right,' Flip conceded. 'She looked too classy.'

The comment made her angry. 'And where does that put me?'

He grinned. 'Same level as me, honey. We're two of a kind. We'll do anything to get on. That's why we're attracted to each other. Waiting in that green room, I felt as sick as a dog. 'Fact, I actually threw up in the bathroom.'

They'd met, her and Flip, a year ago in one of the nightclubs where she was singing and he worked behind the bar. They'd clicked immediately. His full name was Filipo Ungaretti, but he called himself Flip Ungar. His folks were Italian, and his dark good looks and lazy manner disguised a feverish ambition to succeed. Within a week, he'd moved into her cold-water apartment on 8th Street. They were good for each other. *Roses are*

Red was the first time they'd auditioned as a couple and they'd done well, if not well enough. Perhaps they should do it again one day.

'There's always other parts,' he said. 'Today's not the end of the world, though it feels like it.' He signalled to the waitress to re-fill their cups for the fourth time. 'After we've had this, let's go back home and join the protest.' The tenants of their building had gone on a rent strike when the owner had tried to double the rent. This morning, when they'd left, there'd been a crowd outside the building with placards and banners. These days in New York, there were protests, marches, and demonstrations against something or other wherever you went.

Olive agreed. 'But I'd like to call my agent first, see what else he's got on his books.'

'Yeah, and I'll call mine.'

Ollie decided to throw an impromptu party to celebrate Herbie and Anne's success. Anne said she'd telephone Lev and invite him.

'I'm sorry, darling, but it's too short notice: we're having people to dinner and they'll be arriving soon,' Lev said. He sounded old and tired. 'I would have loved to be there. I promise faithfully to come and see the show. When does it open?'

'September. We start rehearsals next week. I'll send you tickets for the opening night.' She doubted if Tamara would come with him.

'Thank you, darling. I'd better go. Tamara's making faces at me, I'm still not properly dressed. Anyway, congratulations to you and Herbie, I'll be thinking of you tonight.'

She replaced the receiver, feeling sad. This exciting life she was leading was entirely due to Lev, yet he was unable to share it. She sighed, changed into a red silky dress, and combed her shoulder-length hair. It was even curlier since she'd had twelve inches cut off because it got in the way when she danced.

The doorbell went: the guests had already started to arrive. She imagined them sitting by their telephones earlier, hoping for a call and an invitation out. There were voices outside close to her window: people were on the balcony, the best place to be on such a beautiful evening. What would the inhabitants of the Hoovervilles think, she wondered, if they could see the rich, well-dressed folks sipping cocktails while they lived in squalor? It hardly seemed fair. It *wasn't* fair. Lights exploded in the corners of her eyes and she hoped she wasn't getting one of her headaches. She'd been having them a lot since she came to live with the Blinkers. Sometimes, the pain was so great she wanted to scream.

There was a knock on her door. It was Herbie. 'What are you doing in there?' he shouted. 'Peggy Perlmann's arrived and wants to see you.'

Anne sighed again and went to join the party.

Peggy was doing the routine that went down well at parties: dancing while pretending to be a scarecrow, flopping all over the place. It probably helped that she was, like most people there, a bit drunk. The only ones completely sober were Anne, who didn't drink, and Ollie Blinker, who was never without a drink in his hand – only his wife knew it was the same drink he'd been carrying around all night. Ollie's life had been, still was, a dangerous one and he liked to remain in complete control of his senses.

When Christina, the maid, came in during Peggy's performance to tell him there was a telephone call and that the caller had refused to give his name, Ollie guessed immediately who it was. 'It's the phone in the den,' Christina said.

The den was where Ollie made his business deals, played pool, smoked cigars – Lizzie couldn't stand the smell – and went for some peace and quiet when Lizzie was entertaining her friends or when the kids had been young and making a row. He went in now and picked up the receiver. 'Ollie Blinker here,' he said cheerfully.

'It's me, Conrad Abel,' said a surly voice.

'This is a wasted call, Mr Abel. The cheque's already in the post.' He'd heard through the grapevine that the producer was a

147

gambler – not a very good one – and owed big money to a dangerous character who went by the name of Al Capone.

A satisfied grunt came from the other end of the line. 'Does your boy know I was persuaded to give him the part in my show?'

'It's not *your* show, Mr Abel,' Ollie said stiffly. 'You're just the producer, and my boy thinks he was picked on merit. You and I are the only ones who know the truth. If you tell a living soul, you'll be finished in the theatre. And my boy and his partner were down to the last five when I made my offer, so there's a good chance they'd still have been given the parts.'

'The partner, yes – she's a peach of a girl, a real humdinger – but not your boy. He's good, but he's not brilliant. For one thing, his knees are too stiff. There was another young fellow came today: him and the girl would have gone perfectly together, but I turned him down.' Ollie sensed regret in his voice. 'That girl carries your son, Mr Blinker. He'll never get anywhere without her.' The receiver at the other end was abruptly replaced.

'Swine,' Ollie muttered. But it was an opinion that he'd already reached himself.

Two weeks later, Mollie and Joey were allowed home to find everywhere full of flowers and as clean and neat as a new pin. Irene and her sisters-in-law had descended on the place and scrubbed and polished every surface, including the floors.

The house was in a small cul-de-sac off Heath Road in Allerton. There were five pairs of semi-detached properties, all for the families of policemen. There was electricity, and a boiler in the kitchen that provided hot water, so there was no need to light a fire when the weather was warm. They also had an indoor lavatory, a proper bathroom, and handkerchief-sized gardens front and back.

'Oh, Tom,' Mollie had gasped five years ago when he'd carried her over the threshold and she'd run like a child around the spacious rooms. 'I'm so glad I married a *policeman*.'

It was a relief to be home again and to find the place looking and smelling so nice, with Tom's family there to greet her and her new son. Lily, sniffing disapprovingly, felt obliged to point out there'd been cobwebs hanging from the ceiling on the landing.

'Well, I don't suppose the girl felt like touring the house with a feather duster while she was in the club,' Pauline said with a disapproving sniff of her own. Pauline was small and round. Although only twenty-nine, she already had a double chin. For a reason she was unable to fathom, her face reminded Mollie of an onion.

Elsie Hardcastle came in with Megan and Brodie, who looked as if they'd also been given a scrub and a polish. 'We thought you were *dead*, Mammy,' Megan complained. She was four and had inherited her grandmother's tendency towards exaggeration.

'How could you think that when Mrs Hardcastle brought you to the nursing home every single day so we could wave to each other through the window?' Mollie asked. Children hadn't been allowed inside. 'Come and say hello to your new brother. You too, Brodie, love.' Brodie was hanging back, as always. The girls, with their fair, curly hair, blue eyes, and little oval faces, were very alike, but only in looks. Megan's forward ways and outgoing personality made her the centre of attention, whereas two-year-old Brodie seemed to live in the shadow of her louder, more aggressive sister.

'Is he ours?' she whispered when Mollie pulled her against her knee where Joey lay fast asleep, his tiny mouth curved in a smile, though it was probably wind.

'Of course he's ours.' With a jerk of her hip, Megan shoved her sister out of the way.

Mollie put her arm around her younger daughter and pulled her back. Children and in-laws required enormous patience and loads of diplomacy. 'Yes, love. He's come to live here for always, along with you, me, Dad and Megan.'

'Why he is all wrinkled like Grandma?' Megan wanted to know.

Irene hooted. 'One of these days, young lady, you'll be just as wrinkled as Grandma. Unfortunately, I won't be around to see it.'

'Where will you be?' Megan enquired. She was a child who had to know everything.

'In me grave, luv: dead and buried.'

'Don't frighten the child, Irene,' Lily remonstrated.

Megan looked indignant. 'I'm not frightened, Auntie Lil.'

'As if I'd ever do anything to frighten a child.' Irene contrived to look hurt.

Mollie began to wish they'd all go back to their own homes, apart from Gladys, who was doing things in the kitchen.

A whole two hours later they did, and only then did Gladys emerge from her hiding place. She wore one of Mollie's pinnies over a smart blue summer frock. Her brown legs were bare and her toenails were painted bright red. Lily and Pauline regarded red toenails as the very depth of depravity. 'What on earth have you been doing out there?' Mollie asked as she opened her blouse to feed Joey. Megan and Brodie looked on with bright, fascinated eyes.

Gladys managed to wrinkle her nose and roll her eyes at the same time. 'Keeping out the way. If I see too much of that lot, one of these days I'll explode.'

'They're very kind, Gladys. I mean, they didn't have to come and clean my house, did they?' That sounded terribly sanctimonious when she'd been praying for them to leave.

'Oh, they're kind, all right: kind of awful.' Gladys grinned. 'But their hearts are in the right place and you know you can always rely on them in an emergency. When our Kevin was born, he bawled his little head off for three whole months and Lily and Pauline took turns in coming round so me and Enoch could have a decent night's sleep.' Gladys had two boys: Kevin and Little Enoch. 'Anyroad, Mollie, I've done things to your kitchen I wouldn't dream of doing to me own: all your shelves and cupboards have been lined with fresh paper, your cutlery set's been polished, as well as the things you use every day, and I took the lampshade down and washed it. I even gave the inside of the dustbin a scrub. The dustman'll think you've bought a new one. Oh, and there's a casserole in the oven for you and Tom when he comes home, save you having to make a meal. It's on a really low heat so it should be ready about eight o'clock.'

'Thank you, Glad,' Mollie said gratefully. 'Just a minute, sweetheart.' She helped Brodie to squeeze on to the armchair beside her. Megan immediately tried to squeeze in the other side.

'Any time.' Gladys waved graciously. 'Come on, Megan, sit on your Auntie Gladys's knee.' When Megan looked reluctant, she added, 'I'll let you play with me powder compact, if you like, but you'll have to fetch me handbag out the kitchen.' Megan shot out of the door.

'I'll do the same for you when you have another baby,' Mollie promised.

'There's not much chance of that, Moll. Two kids are enough for me and Enoch.'

'But how can you stop having children unless you stop . . . you know.' Mollie blushed.

Gladys winked. 'There's ways and means, Moll.' She hoisted Megan on to her knee. 'Here you are, luv. It's a new one.' She delved in her bag and brought out a gold compact. 'Just think, Moll,' she went on. 'You're not yet twenty-one, but you've already had three kids. At that rate, by time you're thirty-five you'll have had fifteen: eighteen all together.' She grinned fiendishly. 'How would you fancy that, eh?'

'I wouldn't,' Mollie said faintly. She wondered what Gladys meant by ways and means.

Megan stopped powdering her nose. 'If you had eighteen kids, Mammy, would I still be the oldest?'

'Don't even think about it, Megan.'

'But—' Megan began.

'I said don't even think about it.'

'I can't help it, Mammy.'

'Would you like me to make the kids' teas, Moll?' Gladys offered.

'No, thanks, Glad, I'll do it. It's time I did something.' She'd been sitting in the chair like an old cabbage, nursing Joey, since she'd come home, allowing herself to be waited on hand and foot.

It was time he sampled the cot upstairs. It had been put in her and Tom's bedroom, where it would stay for a few weeks until he settled in, then moved into the smallest bedroom, which had been freshly painted white for his arrival.

He was still asleep when she laid him down. He was such a tiny bundle it was hard to believe that one day he'd be as big as his father. There was the suggestion of a lump in her throat at the idea of leaving him upstairs on his own, entirely defenceless, unable to do a single little thing for himself. She left the door wide open in case he cried.

She made Megan and Brodie poached eggs on toast. In the larder, she found jelly and blancmange that someone had made, but forgotten to tell her about.

Gladys left to see to her own children's teas. The other policemen's wives popped in one by one to see the baby and she let them peep at him through the bedroom door. They stayed for a cup of tea before going home. Brodie was put to bed, and Megan went shortly afterwards. Joey woke but didn't cry, just gave a tiny whimper. She was in the middle of feeding him when Agatha came and apologized for being late.

'And I can't stop long, either. I'm meeting Walter in half an hour. We're going to the Savoy to see *The Love Parade* with Maurice Chevalier. It's a talkie.' She stared rapturously at the baby attached to Mollie's breast. 'Oh, is this him? Is this Joey?'

'Of course it's Joey, you idiot,' Mollie snorted. 'I'm not likely to be feeding another woman's baby, am I?'

'Can I bring up his wind the way I did for Megan and Brodie?'

'You might not have enough time.'

'I'll make the time. To hell with Walter. I don't like him anyroad. I'm thinking about giving him his marching orders.' Agatha had had plenty of boyfriends, but so far there hadn't been one that she'd fancied living with for the rest of her life.

She stayed, brought up Joey's wind, then went to meet Walter half an hour late, saying she hoped he'd got fed up and gone home: 'Save me the job of chucking him.'

Mollie was still nursing Joey when Tom came in. He took the

baby, while Mollie served up Gladys's casserole. It smelled delicious, though she still had a fancy for fish and chips soaked in vinegar.

Later, Joey back in bed, they sat hand in hand on the settee, staring out the window at their tiny garden with its neat privet hedge and patch of lawn.

Mollie said, 'The nights have already started getting darker.'

'Six months from now, and they'll start getting lighter.'

The future stretched before them, a long, smooth road free from sudden bends and dangerous bumps. They would travel along the road together – Tom, Mollie, and their children – growing older and hopefully wiser. There'd be good days and bad days, memorable days and days you wished had never happened. Christmases would come and go, birthdays would flash by. The children would get married and have children of their own, by which time Tom would have been promoted to detective sergeant or even inspector. And all this while Mollie would have been caring for them, loving them, because that was all she wanted to do: look after her family.

'Shall we turn in, Moll?' Tom grunted when the sun had disappeared, leaving the sky a breathtaking mixture of red, green and purple.

'All right, darlin'.'

He went into the kitchen to bolt the back door and Mollie went upstairs.

Chapter 8

Finn and Hazel now lived in the Doctor's house with Patrick and their two younger sons, Kieran and Eoin. At first, the house looked no different from how Mollie remembered it since she'd shut the door on that cold February night more than five years ago to start the journey to America with Annemarie.

Yet it *was* different. She sensed a new, lighter atmosphere when she stepped inside, Joe in her arms and Tom holding Megan and Brodie's hands, Finn behind with their suitcase. He had a car now, Finn, and had picked them up from the station in Kildare. Tom and the girls had seemed overwhelmed as they'd been driven along the narrow, mainly deserted country lanes with hardly another vehicle or a house in sight, just fields of emerald-green grass and gentle hills. Until then, the furthest they'd been was Southport and across the water to New Brighton.

It was September, and they'd come to Duneathly because it was more than five years since Mollie had seen her brothers, Thaddy and Aidan. Before she knew it, they would be men and have forgotten all about their sister – two sisters, although Annemarie had apparently vanished off the face of the earth. Finn said he was always expecting a letter to land on the mat, either from Aunt Maggie to say she'd been found, or from Annemarie herself, explaining the reason for her mysterious disappearance. After a long courtship, Aunt Maggie had married Sergeant McCluskey and moved to a place called Queens.

The doctor's surgery had been turned into an office for Finn who'd had his own business in Duneathly as an accountant since

Doric Kennedy, who'd done the job before him, had passed away. Another person who'd passed away was Nanny, dying peacefully in her sleep two years ago on All Souls' Eve. And the Doctor himself, of course, had also gone to meet his maker, but whether it was by accident or design no one would ever know. Father Byrne had allowed him the benefit of the doubt and given him a Christian burial (suicides were forbidden to rest in consecrated soil).

Hazel cared for Thaddy and Aidan as if they were her own. 'Five boys and possibly another on the way,' she said to Mollie, smiling as she patted her bulging stomach. The new baby was expected in November.

Now ten, Thaddy hugged his sister as if she'd never been away. He was tall and brown-eyed, just like Mollie, a pleasant-faced boy, not exactly handsome, whereas seven-year-old Aidan was another Finn – good-looking and fine-featured, his blue eyes with a hint of mauve that reminded her of Annemarie. He was shyer than his brother, maybe because he was only two when Mollie had left and his memory of her had slowly faded.

On their first night there, Finn took Tom across the square to O'Reilly's pub, leaving Mollie and Hazel at the kitchen table, the dishes having been washed and the tiny kitten, Bubbles, finishing the remains of the delicious lamb stew they'd had for their tea. Apart from Thaddy, who was in the dining room doing his homework, all the children were in bed. Ten-week-old Joe was due for a meal before Mollie went to bed herself.

'Are you intending to have a fourth, Moll?' Hazel enquired, once again patting her stomach. She lit the lamp on the dresser – Duneathly was still without electricity or gas, though telephone lines had been connected a while ago.

'I'd quite like four children, it's a nice, round figure,' Mollie replied, 'and I'd prefer a boy as a playmate for Joe, but I wouldn't mind a bit if it were another girl.'

'Me and Finn would like a girl, but we don't mind if it's another boy.' Hazel laughed, happiness shining out of her rich brown eyes.

'You're lucky,' Mollie said, 'having Finn working on the premises. Tom's out all hours. Sometimes he works nights and has to sleep the next day. Not that I'm complaining,' she added hastily. 'I knew what to expect when I married a policeman.'

'I'm lucky all round,' Hazel said simply. 'You know I was brought up in an orphanage, don't you?' Mollie nodded and Hazel went on, 'I was six when I first went, right after me mam married a feller who wasn't prepared to bring up another feller's bastard. For the first few years, I was punished every day for the fact I'd been born out of wedlock, but whenever they hit me I just laughed in their faces. Their weapon was a cane: mine was laughter. Oh, but Mollie,' she said with a shudder, 'I was so miserable. No one knew I cried meself to sleep night after night. After I left, I got a job in a hotel in Kildare where they worked me to death, washing and cleaning, carrying in the luggage, waiting on the tables. I laughed all the time, as if I were having a grand old time. That's where I met your Finn. We were fighting over a suitcase that he insisted on carrying himself, him being a real gentleman, like, when it dropped on me foot. Instead of yelping and moaning about it, I laughed. By then, it had become automatic, but it made him laugh, too. He actually tried to pick up me foot and stroke it! I laughed again, but this time I meant it, possibly for the first time in me life. And that's how it began with me and Finn. We haven't stopped laughing since, and a day never goes by when I don't count me blessings and realize what a lucky woman I am.'

'I'm sure our Finn does, too,' Mollie said gently. She gave a start when Bubbles leapt on her knee and began to wash. 'Is it a boy or a girl cat?' she asked.

'A boy, else the house would soon be invaded with kittens that I couldn't bring meself to give away.'

'He's pretty.' Bubbles was a long-haired tabby, a miniature tiger of a cat. She stroked his thin, delicate back. 'I wouldn't mind us having a cat. The girls would love one.'

'Bubbles has a number of brothers and sisters. You could take one back with you. Nona from the post office is desperately looking for good homes. You'd need a cardboard box for carrying after making a few holes in the top so he or she can breathe.'

'He,' Mollie said hastily. 'I'd hate giving kittens away, too.'

Tom and Finn came home and, at the same time, Joe began his subdued little whimper. Hazel rushed round lighting lamps all over the place. Mollie fed the baby in the bedroom where later she and Tom would sleep, modesty preventing her from exposing her breasts in front of her brother, though Finn was so used to seeing his own babies fed he probably wouldn't notice.

When Joe had decided he'd had enough, she took him downstairs so his father could bring up his wind, something Tom insisted on doing when he was around. Hazel had made a pot of tea and a plate of cold, lamb sandwiches.

They sat and talked until it was nearly midnight, while a deathly silence fell over the village of Duneathly, the sort that was strange to a place like Liverpool where there were always people about and traffic of some sort on the roads. A similar silence had reigned the night Mollie and Annemarie had crept across the icy square towards Finn's cottage, never dreaming what might lie in store.

'I like it here,' Tom said when they got into bed. 'I wouldn't mind retiring to Duneathly when the time comes.'

'Oh, Tom, that's at least forty years off.' She snuggled against him and he wrapped his arms around her so tightly she could hardly breathe.

'Well, it doesn't hurt to plan for the future,' he whispered.

As she drifted into sleep, she could hear Finn and Hazel laughing in the bedroom next to theirs.

Monday was sunny, but with a slight nip in the air, as if autumn was sending a signal that it was on its way. Mollie toured the village with the children – Hazel had loaned her a pram for Joe – saying hello to old friends and meeting a few new ones. Ena Gerraghty had sold the dress shop and it now stocked more modern designs, though there was nothing in the window Mollie would have been seen dead in.

She felt as if she were mending in a hole in her life when she shook hands with Billy Adams in the butcher's and Roddy Egan in the baker's. Two girls she'd been to school with came rushing out of Ye Old Tea Shoppe when they saw her pass. They kissed extravagantly and exchanged their life stories within a matter of minutes. Mr O'Rourke, the solicitor, opened his window and shouted he'd come across and see her in his lunch-hour.

She'd left the village and the people in it so abruptly, not saying goodbye to a single soul and leaving loose ends all over the place, but most were now neatly tied. She had a whole week to tie the rest.

Everyone asked after Annemarie. 'She's in America. I don't hear from her all that often,' Mollie replied over and over again. It was what Hazel had told her to say, what she and Finn said to people when they were asked the same question. Hardly anyone mentioned the Doctor.

She called on Nona in the post office and asked for a kitten. The girls were thrilled to pieces and Megan wanted to take home all five. But there were only two males left and Mollie chose the one identical to Bubbles. 'We'll collect him on Saturday,' she told Nona.

The other male was black and smooth, not nearly so pretty as his brother. She felt convinced she could see tears in the tiny creature's eyes. 'He looks so sad, he knows no one wants him,' she murmured. She shooed the girls out of the shop before she could say she'd take them both.

Megan suggested they also call their kitten Bubbles, but Mollie said she'd sooner they thought up a name of their own. 'What about Winnie, like in *Winnie the Pooh*?'

'Winnie stinks,' Megan said scathingly. 'Anyroad, Winnie the Pooh is a *bear*.'

'Tiddles?'

'Tiddles stinks worse.'

'Dandelion, Mammy,' Brodie piped up. 'Our kitten is like a dandelion.'

'Dandelion is a lovely name.' Mollie clamped her hand over

Megan's mouth before she could say how much Dandelion stank. 'Let's see what your dad has to say about it, shall we?'

'Will Patrick be home when we get there?' Megan enquired. She'd fallen head over heels in love with her cousin at first sight.

'No, he's at school.'

'Next year, can I go to the same school as Patrick?'

'No, love. It's too far away.'

'If I came to live with Auntie Hazel and Uncle Finn, could I go to school with Patrick then?'

'If that's what you want, Megan, yes.' She felt like giving her daughter a quick blow to the head to shut her up.

After earnest consideration, Megan decided it wasn't what she wanted after all. Perhaps she'd been taken aback that her mother appeared so willing to let her go. 'I'd feel sad without you and Dad and Brodie – and our Joe,' she said.

'That's good, love, because we'd prefer you stayed with us.'

'And I think we should call our kitten Dandelion.' She could be so sweet when she was in the mood.

'That's good, too. Clever old Brodie.' She patted her small daughter's head. 'Dandelion's perfect.'

Hazel set an extra place at the table when Mr O'Rourke turned up at lunch-time. They sat down to cheese and onion pie followed by fruit salad and cream. Megan, usually so picky with her food, ate every mouthful, and Brodie, who rarely opened her mouth in company, described Dandelion to her father. 'He's striped all over, Dad, like a jumper, and he's got big hairs growing out of his mouth.'

'Whiskers, luv,' Tom said fondly. 'They're called whiskers.'

'Everyone knows they're called whiskers, Dad,' Megan said in a haughty voice.

'Brodie didn't, and neither did you when you were two,' Tom pointed out.

'I bet I did.'

Tom didn't answer. Sometimes, the best thing to do with Megan was ignore her.

Mollie went to the door with Mr O'Rourke when it was time for him to return to his office. 'I'm pleased everything's turned out well for you, Mollie,' he said, squeezing her hand. 'There were all sorts of dark rumours floating around after you and your sister left. But that husband of yours is a fine young man and I'm sure he takes good care of you.'

'The very best, Mr O'Rourke,' she assured him.

That afternoon, she took the children to the convent to show the nuns, who fussed over them in the way women did when they didn't have children of their own, kissing them and stroking their arms, exclaiming that the girls were the prettiest they'd ever seen and Joe the bonniest baby.

Brodie, scared, hid behind her mother's skirt, only emerging when Sister Francis produced a doll she'd knitted for the Christmas bazaar. Megan refused a doll, saying that she'd grown out of them, causing shrieks of amazed laughter and comments that she was old long before her time.

Eventually Mollie left, exhausted. Patrick was home from school when they got back to the house and Megan was struck dumb for the rest of the day, much to everyone's relief.

Tom and Finn were getting on like a house on fire. Whatever hostility Finn had felt for his brother-in-law had gone. He merely smiled when Tom continued to boast about his triumphs in the police force.

On their third day in Duneathly, the men offered to look after the children while their mothers went to Kildare to do some shopping. Mollie made a bottle for Joe and left it in the larder, and she and Hazel caught the half past eight bus.

'I feel desperately odd without the kids,' she admitted to Hazel, as the little single-decker made its winding way towards Kildare.

'Me, too. I feel as if vitally important parts of me are missing, like me arms and legs.'

'Will we ever feel any different, I wonder?' Mollie mused.

'I hope so. I'd hate to feel like this when I'm eighty.' Hazel began to laugh. 'I expect the time will come when they'll grow away from us and won't need us any more, then we can do things like swim the English Channel. Some woman did a few years ago.'

'Or get elected to Parliament.'

'Learn to fly an aeroplane.'

'Climb Everest. Some other woman did that.'

'Today, let's forget we're mothers with hordes of small children,' Hazel said firmly, 'and think of no one but ourselves, after we've bought the kids a few sweets, that is. Me, I'm going to buy a hat, a winter one: the old one's got moths in it.'

'And I'll get the wool to make myself a jumper with a Fair Isle yoke.'

It was a lovely day out. They stopped for morning tea, then stopped again for lunch: roast beef with Yorkshire pudding, and apple charlotte and cream for afters. Hazel insisted on paying for the meal, so Mollie bought her a pair of knitted gloves to match her new blue hat.

They caught the three o'clock bus back to Duneathly, earlier than planned, neither prepared to admit they were worried about the children – rightly, as it happened.

Joe had positively refused to touch his midday bottle and hadn't stopped crying since. Bubbles had scratched Megan and she no longer wanted a kitten, particularly one called Dandelion, upsetting Brodie, who'd had her head buried in a cushion ever since. Kieran had got stuck up a tree in the garden and refused to come down until his mother came home, and Eoin had hurt his leg trying to join his brother up the same tree.

'Thank God you're home, Moll.' Tom's normally neat hair looked as if he'd been trying to tear it out and Finn had aged twenty years in the matter of hours. They flatly refused to believe that, for their wives, it would have been a perfectly normal day.

'I think it'll be a while yet before we get to swim the English Channel or climb Everest, don't you, Moll?' Hazel muttered with the suspicion of a grin.

'A long while.' Mollie grabbed her screaming son and took him upstairs to feed. She'd sort Megan and Brodie out later, then she'd see to Tom.

It was a lazy holiday, if not exactly quiet. Mollie looked up more old friends, and spent as much time with Thaddy and Aidan as she reasonably could. Tom and Finn visited the pub every night, leaving her and Hazel to discuss life and all its ups and downs and twists and turns. Inevitably, they talked about Annemarie and the Doctor. Mollie said that, no matter how hard she tried, she couldn't imagine what her sister was doing in New York: 'That's if she's in New York: she could be anywhere by now.' As for the Doctor, she didn't know what to feel. 'He wasn't a bad father,' she confided, 'though he never petted us or played with us the way Tom does with our children and Finn does with yours. Perhaps Mammy dying was a terrible blow that he never recovered from.'

'You're too forgiving, Mollie,' Hazel said harshly. 'What the Doctor did to you and your sister was a crime. If I'd had me way, he'd have swung for it.'

'Is it possible to be too forgiving? Didn't Christ say, "Forgive them, Lord, they know not what they do?"'

'He also said, "Vengeance is mine."'

The next day, Mollie went alone to visit the Doctor's grave. She knew that Finn, after much soul-searching, had decided not to put him in the family grave with Mammy, which must have provoked much speculation in the village.

The graveyard lay behind St Saviour's church, where Mollie had made her First Holy Communion and been Confirmed (she'd chosen Theresa as her Confirmation name). She found the simple white stone with just the Doctor's name, the year he was born, and the year he'd died engraved in gold: there was no message like 'Sadly Missed' or 'A Dearly Loved Father'. Weeds had spurted through the smooth, white gravel and she plucked them out, then laid a single rose from the bunch she'd bought for

Mammy. She tried to think of a prayer to say, but couldn't. 'Rest in peace,' she said softly.

Mammy's grave was very different. It was well cared for, with not a weed in sight, and there were fresh flowers in a stone vase. She wondered if Finn and Hazel looked after it, or one of Mammy's friends from the Legion of Mary. The names of the grandparents she'd never met were engraved above her mother's on the headstone: Padraic Cormac Connelly, who died in 1855, when he was only twenty-five; and Margaret Brigid Connelly, who'd lived on, a widow for almost fifty years, dying in 1904, the year that Finn was born.

She put the roses in the vase, but still didn't say a prayer. She didn't believe in visiting graves. Mammy was dead and she thought about her frequently, sometimes talking to her in her head. No amount of flowers would bring her back and she got no comfort from knowing her mother's remains lay six feet under the soil. She made the Sign of the Cross and went home.

'You know what I think,' Tom said on Friday morning when they were getting dressed. They were due to return home the following day. 'I think you and the children should stay for another week.'

'Without you?'

'I'm due back on Sunday, so I have to leave on Saturday, but you haven't, luv,' he said earnestly. 'It'll be a long while before we come to Duneathly again, at least a year. Why not stay? You're obviously enjoying yourself, the kids are having a whale of a time, and it'd be nice to spend more time with your brothers.'

'But I don't want to stay without you!' Mollie wailed. She was sitting on the edge of the bed pulling on her stockings.

Tom sat behind her, put his arms around her waist, and nuzzled her neck. 'And I don't want to go without you, but it'll only be for seven days. The weather's the gear, and you know mam will be only too pleased to look after me. She'll feed me up and I'll weigh another stone by the time you come home.'

'Oh, I don't know, Tom.' He was right, though. The children

163

were enjoying themselves, the weather was lovely, and it seemed selfish to deny them another week. 'But you can never tell; Finn and Hazel might be longing to see the back of us.'

But when Tom made the same suggestion over breakfast, Hazel looked only too delighted. 'I'd love you to stay, Moll. Finn will miss Tom now they've become such good mates, but having you and the kids for another week will make up for that.' Megan gave the idea her approval, putting a seal on the matter.

So, the next morning, after a week that had been only too short, Mollie and her daughters waved goodbye to Tom as he climbed into her brother's car. Finn was taking him to the station in Kildare. His clothes were in an old carpetbag that had been found in the attic; it would save Mollie having to carry them. A nervous Dandelion had been placed in a cardboard box punched with holes so he could breathe.

Mollie knew she would feel sad to see Tom go, but hadn't dreamed the sadness would be so intense as she watched Finn drive out of the square with everyone, Tom included, waving madly until the car disappeared. She could feel the pressure of his final kiss on her lips. It didn't help when Brodie began to cry for her dad and Megan called her a cissy.

'*I'm* not crying,' she bragged. Seconds later she burst into tears.

'What if the boat sinks and Daddy's on it?' Megan asked when she'd more or less recovered.

They were sitting on a bench in the big garden full of apple trees. Windfalls lay plentifully on the grass – Nanny had used to collect them and put them in a box outside the door for people to help themselves. Mollie thought she might do the same thing later if Hazel didn't mind. Her sister-in-law was too busy to do it herself.

'Ferries don't sink, darlin',' Mollie lied.

'The train might crash into another one.'

'That's most unlikely to happen. Trains hardly ever crash into one another.'

'Where will our dad be now, Mammy?' Brodie enquired tearfully.

'He'll just about be on the train and Uncle Finn should be back soon. Don't forget, your dad's going to ring from a phone box when he reaches Liverpool to say he's arrived safely.'

'Can I speak to him?'

'Yes, Megan, and Brodie can, too.'

Hazel said it was a good idea about the windfalls. 'Though be careful the wasps haven't got at them,' she added. Kieran and Eoin came to help and there was already a box by the front door with a notice saying 'Please help yourself' by the time Finn returned. Nanny had always put 'pleese' but no one had liked to tell her she'd spelt the word wrong.

Finn confirmed that Tom had been alive and well when he'd got on the train. He disappeared into his office, saying he'd been neglecting his work lately and needed to catch up. Hazel made sandwiches for his dinner and he didn't emerge until it was time for tea.

Every now and then, the telephone in the office would ring and Mollie and the girls would tense, waiting for Finn to call and say it was Tom.

They were sitting down to their tea when Tom rang. 'Whose idea was it for me to come home on me own?' he asked mournfully.

'Yours, darlin',' Mollie told him.

'Well, it was a daft idea and I wish I hadn't had it. I'm not looking forward to sleeping in an empty bed in an empty house.'

'It won't be for long, only another seven days,' she said tenderly.

'*Seven*! Jaysus, I won't be able to stand it.' He sniffed. 'I think I'm going to cry.'

Megan and Brodie were pulling at her skirt. 'I want to speak to him,' Megan demanded crossly.

'Look, Tom. The girls would like a word with you. I'll say goodbye for now. Perhaps you could call again tomorrow? Look after yourself, won't you?' She handed the receiver to Megan before she burst a blood vessel.

Megan wanted to know if Dandelion was all right. Apparently, Tom had taken him out of the box on the ferry and given him a cuddle. Brodie didn't say a word, just listened, astounded, to her father's voice saying how much he missed her. Then, all of a sudden, the line went dead: Tom must have run out of pennies.

On Sunday afternoon, not long after they'd come back from Mass, the sun disappeared behind a nasty black cloud, the heavens opened, and the rain came down in buckets. The downpour persisted for three whole days: it was no wonder the grass in Ireland was such a brilliant green. The temperature dropped and the house felt uncomfortably cold. In the worst of the winter, Mammy used to have fires lit in every room.

All the children, Hazel's included, grumbled because they couldn't play outside. Mollie read to them until her voice became hoarse. She taught them how to play Snap, but they soon got bored, apart from Megan, who won every game. Hide and Seek turned into a nightmare, as it was such a big house with so many places to hide that finding people was well-nigh impossible. Joe was grizzly and she wondered if he was expecting an early tooth. Bubbles must have decided he didn't like the rain: he stayed indoors and weed on the mats.

Tom telephoned every night to ask how they were. 'Fine,' Mollie said heartily. She'd wait until she got home to tell him that his idea they stay another week was the worst he'd ever had.

On Wednesday it was still raining lightly when she went into the kitchen and found Hazel propped against the kitchen sink, her face as white as a sheet. 'Help us to a chair, Moll,' she croaked. 'I feel as dizzy as a top.'

'It's not the baby, is it?' Resisting the urge to panic, Mollie grabbed a chair and helped Hazel to sit down.

'No, it's just me legs refusing to support me any more.'

'I'll fetch Finn.'

Finn came, took one look at his wife's pale face, and

telephoned the doctor, who came straight away. Dr Kavanagh looked no more than twenty-one, but had two children and a wife who was expecting another child at Christmas. He examined the patient, informed her she was doing far too much, and she was to go to bed and stay there for at least forty-eight hours. 'Mrs Kavanagh is exactly the same,' he complained. 'She refuses to listen when I tell her she must rest.'

The doctor went, Finn helped Hazel upstairs, and Mollie took over the housework, cursing the ancient stove that was such a pain to use compared with her neat little gas stove in Liverpool. 'This thing belongs back in the nineteenth century,' she grumbled to Finn, giving it a kick. 'No wonder Hazel's tired.' She shovelled more coal into the stove. 'It's like living in the Dark Ages.'

'I'll get someone in to give her a hand,' Finn promised. 'She's always refused to have help, but it's a big house, she's got five lads to look after, and she's pregnant. From now on, I'll make her lie down every afternoon, even if I have to carry her upstairs and lock her in the room.'

Two days later, Rosie Hume came to work for Hazel and Finn. She was a big, red-cheeked woman with heavily muscled arms and a willing manner. Her husband worked the land, she told Mollie, and she had thirteen children, four of whom were married: the other nine still lived at home. In no time, she'd made fires in Finn's office and Hazel's room, while Finn was still struggling to make one in the living room, then started on the dinner, peeling the potatoes twice as fast as Mollie had seen them peeled before. It made her feel very inadequate.

Hazel felt well enough to come down for dinner, looking almost her old self again, and grateful for Rosie's help. 'I *had* been doing too much,' she confessed, 'but I've promised Finn I'll take things easy from now on. But this week hasn't been much of a holiday for you, Moll, what with the weather the way it's been, and me stuck in bed half the time.'

'I haven't minded,' Mollie assured her stoutly, though she was glad the week was almost over and tomorrow they would all go back to Tom.

★

The children were as good as gold on the way home. Megan was already missing Patrick and gave a little sniff from time to time. Brodie couldn't wait to kiss Dandelion and her dad. Perhaps Joe understood he would shortly see his father and didn't grizzle once.

Tom had said he'd meet them at the Pier Head if he could get away, but there was no sign of him when they got off the ferry. It meant he was unlikely to be at home when they arrived. Mollie caught the number eight tram to Allerton, no easy task with a baby, two small children, and a suitcase. By now, Megan seemed to have forgotten about Patrick, and both girls were in a state of high excitement at the idea of being back in their own home.

They danced alongside her as she walked up the path and unlocked the front door. 'Dandelion,' Brodie called, 'we're home.'

'Mind he doesn't get out,' Mollie warned. 'Come on, everyone: in we go.' Leaving the suitcase on the step for now, she carried Joe inside, longing to get the weight off her feet. The minute he was fed, she'd make the girls their tea. They must be starving and she wouldn't mind a bite to eat herself.

At the door of the living room, she stopped, convinced she must be seeing things; the room was full of people, who were staring at her as if she were a ghost. For several seconds, no one spoke, until one of the people – it was Irene, her mother-in-law – burst into tears. 'Mollie! Oh, Mollie, girl,' she wept, 'we didn't know how to get in touch with you. All we could do was wait for you to come home.'

'Why?' Mollie wanted to laugh. Tom's three brothers were there, their wives, and a young policeman in uniform whom she'd never seen before. They all looked so ridiculously solemn you'd think the world was about to end.

Gladys darted forward and seized Mollie by the arms, waking Joe who began to cry. 'Mollie, luv. I'm ever so sorry, but Tom is dead.'

'Don't be daft,' Mollie snorted. What a terrible thing to say! 'I only spoke to him last night on the telephone.'

'I'm afraid he is, luv. It happened in the early hours of this morning. He was shot.'

'*Shot!*'

As if the word had been a signal, the room sprang to life. Someone took Joe away and half a dozen arms helped Mollie to an armchair where she was patted and kissed, her hair stroked, and told to cry as much as she liked. 'We're all here for you, luv,' a sickly voice said.

Mollie seemed to be the only person there who wasn't crying. She jumped to her feet, infuriated by the intrusive hands and the whining, cloying voices. 'Tom's not dead.' She shook her head. 'It's not true, is it?' she demanded of the policeman, who was standing clutching his helmet and looking as if he'd sooner be anywhere else on earth.

He nodded awkwardly. 'I'm afraid it is, Mrs Ryan. Your husband disturbed a couple of burglars. He died in the line of duty. He was a very brave man.'

Was. Tom *was.* Tom really was dead? She shook her head again. 'Where is he?' she demanded angrily.

'The undertaker's, Moll.' It was Gladys again. 'They'll bring him home, if that's what you want, and lay him out in the parlour.'

'What I want?' She wanted Tom – the real, live Tom – to kiss her and fold her in his arms, welcome her home, say how much he'd missed her and that they would never be parted again. She kept waiting for this to happen, for Tom to open the door and walk in, because she was finding it impossible to believe that she'd seen him for the last time.

She ordered everyone to go away, to leave her alone with the children – her and Tom's children. She needed to think, reason things out in her head, not listen to other people wail and cry. Her own tears were mounting and she'd sooner shed them in private, not in front of Tom's relatives, who were only waiting for her to cry so they could pounce and start stroking and patting her again.

'I think we should do what Molly wants,' Gladys said sensibly. 'If she wants us to leave her and the kids alone, then that's what we should do.'

'But she can't possibly be left on her own,' Pauline protested. 'Not at a time like this.'

'But it's what she wants,' Gladys insisted.

Lily bridled. 'Who are you to tell us what to do?'

'Don't argue,' Mollie screamed. 'Just *go*!'

At that, they went, shuffling out uncomfortably, glancing at her doubtfully, as if expecting her to change her mind and ask them to stay.

The front door closed and then only Mollie and her children were left.

Someone had put Joe in his cot upstairs. She fetched him down, sat on the settee nursing him, and indicated to the girls to sit each side of her. 'Do you understand what's happened?' she enquired, unsure if she understood herself.

'Grandma said our dad's gone to heaven and we won't see him again, not ever.' Megan's face crumpled. 'But I *want* to see him again, Mammy. I'd sooner he'd stayed with us.'

'So do I, sweetheart. So does everyone, but I'm afraid that's not going to happen.' She found it hard to believe her own words. 'But your dad will be happy in heaven, I know he will. For the rest of our lives, he'll be keeping an eye on us, making sure we're all right, because he loves us more than words can say.'

'And we love him, Mammy, just the same.'

At this, Mollie broke down and the tears she'd been suppressing came in a flood that threatened never to stop. Megan cried just as hard and eventually so did Brodie. Mollie wasn't sure if her two-year-old daughter actually realized her dad had gone for good.

After a while, they were too tired to cry any more. Brodie asked if Dandelion had gone to heaven, too. Mollie had completely forgotten about the kitten. She despatched Brodie to look for him and he was found in the kitchen, fast asleep in a basket that Tom must have acquired from somewhere, along with a little blue collar that had a bell attached. He woke up and regarded them sleepily with his round blue eyes, then jumped out and began to rub his tiny body against their legs, the bell tinkling all the while, as if a fairy had come to stay. The girls took him into the garden while Mollie made the tea.

There were two eggs and a few slices of bacon in the larder, enough for the girls. She couldn't have eaten a thing to save her life. She scrambled the eggs and fried the bacon, but Megan must have felt like her because she left most of the food. Mollie cut it into little pieces and gave it to Dandelion – there was a Bakelite dish by the basket – amazed that she could do these simple, everyday tasks knowing that Tom was dead.

She fed Joe, tidied the room, put the dirty washing she'd brought back from Duneathly in the boiler to soak, read to the girls, helped Brodie get undressed and into her nightie. The house felt uncommonly, eerily quiet: twice someone knocked on the door, but she ignored it. Tomorrow, she must let Finn and Hazel know about Tom.

At eight o'clock, with both girls and Joe sound asleep, Mollie went to bed herself, knowing that sleep was impossible, but it was the place where she would feel closest to Tom. She lay nursing the pillow where his head had lain. It smelled faintly of soap and of Tom himself.

He'd died a hero, the policeman had said. He'd finished his shift, gone for a drink with his mates, and told them he intended to walk home because his missus and the kids were away so there was no point in hurrying. Along the way, he'd noticed a window open at the side of the Westminster Bank on Woolton Road and, like the brave man he was, had decided to wait for the burglar to appear. It turned out there were two of them: one had been armed and shot him in the head. He'd died on the spot.

He'd always hoped to interrupt a bank raid, Mollie recalled. And he wasn't brave, but downright stupid. Why had she listened when he'd suggested she and the children stay another week in

Duneathly? Had they come home when they'd planned to, right now he would have been lying in bed beside her.

The door opened and Megan came padding in. She climbed into bed without saying a word and fell asleep immediately. A few seconds later, Brodie did the same. Mollie lay listening to their quiet, even breathing, conscious of their warm bodies pressed against hers. Joe whimpered in his sleep and she reached through the bars of the cot and stroked his cheek. She felt as if she and her children were stranded on a desert island and would never be found. With this thought in her mind, she eventually dozed off.

At some time during the night she woke with such an ache in her heart that she could scarcely breathe. She sat up, remembered what had happened, and the ache got worse. She began to cry then: huge racking sobs that threatened to tear her apart. A feeling of emptiness fell over her. From now on, it would always feel like this; nothing would change.

In a bedroom thousands of miles away, Annemarie woke with a similar ache. She too sat up in bed and began to cry, nursing the ache with her arms. Something terrible had happened to Mollie. She could feel it.

At that moment, she remembered her old life with the utmost clarity. It rolled in front of her eyes like a silent film, starkly black and white: the house in Duneathly with apple trees in the garden; Mollie, not just her sister, but her best friend in the whole wide world; Finn, who'd taught her how to skim stones on the pond behind O'Reilly's pub; Thaddy, whom *she'd* taught how to draw. Then there was Aidan, born at the same time as her darling Mammy had died and gone straight to heaven. She recalled the convent where she'd gone to school, the shops in the square, and the dirt-poor people she's always felt so sorry for who worked on the farms. They were always included in the prayers she'd said every night before she went to sleep.

Smiling now, she watched the record of her life roll by, but then the picture began to get murky and she didn't like it any more. She put her hands over her eyes, not wanting to see, but still the film rolled on, and she witnessed the Doctor commit a mortal sin against her, saw herself and Mollie tiptoe through the moonlit village on their way to Finn's cottage. She remembered the ship, the *Queen Maia*, and the reason Mollie had missed it.

Suddenly, without warning, the film finished, the end flapping noisily around the spool like a bird trying to escape its cage.

She got out of bed and sat by the window. Right now, she wasn't quite sure where she was. Was that a forest across the road lit by the occasional lamp? Cars drove by and she wondered what time it was. What was she doing here? Whose house was this? What had happened to Mollie?

'My name is Annemarie Kenny,' she said aloud. 'I have a sister and three brothers and I come from a village in Ireland called Duneathly.' She shivered and felt desperately cold.

After a while, she returned to bed. When next she woke, it was daylight, she was Anne Murray again, and had no memory of the previous night, just a slight pain in her chest that had gone by the time she sat down to breakfast.

Chapter 9

The letters arrived together, both from Liverpool Constabulary. The first advised her that, as Tom had died in the line of duty, she was being awarded a pension of twelve and sixpence a week: the second requested that she vacate the house in Allerton by the end of December. It was merely official confirmation of what Elsie Hardcastle had warned her about. Tom had hardly been in his grave a week, but Elsie thought it best she be prepared.

'These houses are for policemen, not the widows of policemen,' she said ruefully. 'You'll be allowed three months to get out. Me and Charlie will have to leave when he retires.'

Mollie and the children were going to live with Irene in Turnpike Street. The furniture she and Tom had bought together was to be sold. Everything was being left until the very last minute because Mollie wanted to spend one final Christmas in the house where she and Tom had lived for five blissfully happy years.

Lily and Pauline, agreeing for once, thought she should leave straight away, only too pleased to see the back of the place that was so full of memories of Tom. Mollie couldn't be bothered to explain that was precisely why she wanted to stay. She felt convinced that Tom's spirit was still there, keeping his family warm at night and safe during the day. Also, she wanted to delay going to Turnpike Street for as long as possible: she wasn't looking forward to it in the least.

Finn, who'd come to the funeral, had tried to persuade her to return to Duneathly with him — not for the first time. 'There's loads of room, Moll, and the girls loved it there. Hazel insisted I try to talk you into it.'

Mollie firmly shook her head. 'Hazel's already got Thaddy and Aidan to look after as well as her own three. And soon you'll have four. You can't burden her with more children, Finn. I'd do my share and Rosie Hume will help, but the responsibility for running the house will still fall on Hazel.' What's more, she'd feel in the way. Hazel and Finn were entitled to some privacy and where would she put herself during the evenings and at weekends? 'Anyway, Irene expects us to move in with her. She's really broken up over Tom: he was her baby and her favourite. I'd feel awful taking his children away. Anyway, I love Liverpool and I don't want to leave.' She was a Ryan now and felt her place was with Tom's family rather than her own.

Finn had kissed her on the forehead. 'Life's unfair, sis. If ever anyone deserved to be happy, it's you.'

'Nobody could have been as happy as I was with Tom, and it lasted for five whole years. I've been lucky, Finn. Even if I never smile again, I've been a very lucky woman.'

The words were said purely for Finn's benefit. She didn't want him sitting in Duneathly worrying and feeling sorry for her. Mollie couldn't describe exactly how she felt, but in truth 'lucky' was the last word she would have used. As the weeks passed and Christmas approached, she felt only half alive. There seemed no point to anything any more apart from taking care of the children. She fed them, kept them and the house clean, and managed to do the same with herself.

With December came the realization that she was expecting another child. For some women, this might have been the last straw, but it lifted Mollie's spirits just a little. She just knew it was going to be a boy and she would call him Tom. It rather upset her plan to get a job of some sorts when they moved in with Irene, but that would just have to wait.

Irene came daily, upsetting the girls with her mournful face and noisy tears, her son's death as fresh and raw in her mind as if he'd only died the day before. Mollie didn't know what to do with her. She didn't have the capacity to comfort her mother-in-law and preferred to grieve alone. Lily and Pauline considered her very hard. They told her she'd taken the loss of her husband extremely well. 'You hardly seem upset at all,' Lily said with one of her irritating sniffs.

She saw little of Gladys, whose sons had come down with mumps, followed shortly afterwards by her husband, Enoch, then Gladys herself. 'I'm keeping well out of the way of your kids, Moll,' she said. 'That last thing you'll want is a house full of invalids on top of everything else.'

Agatha came two or three nights a week. She'd taken up dressmaking and usually brought her sewing with her. Mollie helped with the hems. Her friend made her realize that a world existed outside the house in Allerton, a world where it was possible to be happy and enjoy yourself, something she forgot a lot of the time.

One night Agatha brought her a piece of material. 'A remnant,' she claimed. 'I thought you might like to make yourself a new frock for the summer. One of those shifts, completely straight. You wouldn't even have to bother with sleeves.'

The material was dark-blue linen and, as Mollie sewed, she imagined herself wearing the frock in another seven or eight months when the weather was fine. There would be no Tom around, but it was evidence that life went on, that summer would come, followed by winter, then summer again, and so on until the end of time. She thought about it while she patiently embroidered a row of tiny white flowers around the neck of the frock, remembering how much Annemarie had hated embroidery or stitching of any kind because it was so slow. She preferred to draw and could dash off a picture in five minutes. Agatha declared the flowers made the frock look dead expensive.

'You could make a hat out of the bits left over and wear it to our Ellen's wedding next July. Your baby will have been born by then and you'll be the star of the show.'

By now, all Agatha's sisters were engaged or married. She was an aunt twice over, though showed no sign of settling down, despite being the eldest. Even Mrs Brophy had married again: the bridegroom an old friend of her late husband.

Agatha didn't care. She wasn't prepared to marry just anyone to get a ring on her finger. 'If I'm going to be an old maid, I'll be a happy one,' she said gaily.

She was there the night Philip Fraser called on Mollie to see how she was. Philip was the young constable who'd been present the day she'd returned from Duneathly to be met with the terrible news that Tom was dead. When she was told his name, Mollie remembered he and Tom had been good friends. This was the third time he'd called to see her. He wasn't quite as tall as Tom, or as handsome, at least in Mollie's eyes.

She introduced him to Agatha, whose face was red from the fire. Her brown hair was piled in an untidy heap on top of her head, and her spectacles were resting on the tip of her nose, as she looked up from the piece of scarlet material she was sewing.

Philip stayed longer than Mollie had expected. When Agatha announced it was time to go, he jumped to his feet with alacrity and asked if he could walk her as far as the tram stop. A few days later, Agatha told her that the next night they'd gone to the pictures and to a dance the night after that. In no time at all they were going steady.

Watching her friend and Tom's friend fall more and more deeply in love was yet another reminder that the world didn't stop turning every time a tragedy occurred. She would just have to get used to things being the way they were. Tom had gone and if she didn't accept that fact then she had a pretty dire future ahead of her.

First though, she wanted to spend one more day with him.

Somehow, by being stubbornly insistent, she had arranged to have Christmas Day with just herself and the children in the house. From early morning, she could sense Tom's presence in Megan and Brodie's bedroom while they opened their presents, and beside her when she walked to Mass. She set a place for him at table at dinner-time and imagined him on the floor with his girls when they played with the doll's house their Uncle Enoch had made. Dandelion was crouched outside the tiny front door, ready to pounce on any creature smaller than himself who might emerge. Joey sat on Mollie's knee, chirping like a bird and waving his arms at absolutely nothing – though perhaps he, too, could see his dad and he was waving at him.

It was a quiet day, serene and uneventful. The children enjoyed themselves and Mollie said goodbye to Tom, knowing he would never be so close to her again. Soon, people would come and take the furniture, and she would have to pack away the clothes and toys ready to go to Turnpike Street. In another seven days, she would close the door on a period of her life that had been too wonderful for words. She squared her shoulders: she was quite prepared.

Anne wasn't the only member of the cast in the wings watching Zeke's solo with fascination and a measure of disbelief. Some of the moves looked physically impossible: the way he ran up the wall, and somersaulted backwards; the perfect cartwheels in a circle around the stage; the incredible leaps on and off the counter, which must have been almost five feet off the floor. A sign above it said 'Reception' – it was supposed to be the lobby of the hotel in which *Roses are Red* was set. Zeke played a bellboy, and wore an emerald green uniform with gold buttons and a round, pillbox hat secured under his chin by a strap. The show had been running for over three months and the hat had fallen off just twice. Zeke had covered by throwing it on to a coat hook where it stayed put.

The audience were spellbound. Anne could only see the faces of the first few rows where people were watching, open-mouthed, as Zeke leapt from the counter on to a luggage trolley and careered across the stage, stopping only inches from the orchestra pit. There was an audible gasp and the musicians held up their hands in horror – it was all part of the act. The trolley was scooted in the direction of an ornate staircase where Zeke danced to the top at an incredible speed, slid down the banister, and landed on the trolley with such force that it rolled back to Reception and he jumped back on the counter with a grace of a cat. There was a grin on his face and a glow in his eyes that showed he was having the time of his life. He finished by dancing on his hands with incredible skill, double-somersaulting to the ground, and finishing with a magnificently ostentatious bow.

The curtains closed for the end of the second act and the audience shouted for more, but they were to be disappointed: Conrad Abel, the producer, didn't allow encores until the show was over. Zeke came off stage, his face dripping with perspiration. Anne could have sworn she could see steam rising from his body. His father, who was also his dresser, waited for him with a jug of water, which he drank without pausing for breath. He tore off his hat and undid the buttons on his tunic, then noticed Anne watching.

'Hello, there,' he said with a grin.

'Hello.' She grinned back. She really liked Zeke. Along with Herbie, the three had become the best of friends. 'Every night you get even more fantastic. I'm not entirely convinced you're human.'

Herbie came and pumped Zeke's arm. 'I go along with that, pal,' he enthused. 'Tonight you were truly out of this world.'

Zeke bowed and rolled his eyes. 'Well, yo see, massa and missus, I'se a nigger, and some folks already think I ain't really human fo' that reason alone.'

His father dug him sharply in the ribs. 'Don't talk like that, boy.'

'Sorry, Pops. Just trying to fit the stereotypical picture that white folk have of us niggers.'

'And don't say nigger, either,' his father said disapprovingly. 'You're a black man and you should be proud of that fact.' Zeke's dad, Lemuel Penn, had been a sergeant in the Army and had fought in the Great War. A bullet in his hip had left him with a slight limp. In the day, he worked in a hardware store in Harlem. Zeke and his eight brothers and sisters had done well at school, and Zeke had been the first black student to attend Peggy Perlmann's academy. Some parents had removed their children in protest, but the numbers had quickly returned to their usual level.

Despite Zeke being a phenomenal performer, Conrad Abel had taken a risk hiring an eighteen-year-old black man for such a big part in a white show, but the reviews had been good and Zeke Penn was considered a triumph. *Roses are Red* wasn't in the same class as *Show Boat*, a landmark musical written by Jerome Kern and Oscar Hammerstein, but the story of two rich middle-aged people – played by Eric Carrington and Patricia Peters – and their respective children – Herbie and Anne – struggling to bring their parents together, had struck a chord with New Yorkers. Even if it hadn't happened to them, they all knew people who'd lost everything, and it was nice to escape to the theatre for a few hours and watch the wealthy cope with their not-very-important problems in a five-star hotel. *Roses are Red* was fully booked for the next six months and expected to run for at least a year.

Zeke went to get changed for the third and final act, and Anne and Herbie did the same. Anne found a large box of chocolates from Dainty's in front of her dressing-room mirror marked, 'Happy Christmas, Anne. Love from Eric', and a much smaller box from Patricia – she was notoriously mean. There were presents from other members of the cast, but nothing from Zeke. She'd bought him a white silk scarf with a long fringe.

There was a knock on the door and she called, 'Come in.' The door opened, but the person didn't enter. She saw the tall, distinguished figure of Lemuel Penn standing outside. He bowed slightly, though there was nothing obsequious about it.

'Zeke would like to know if you would be offended if he gave you a gift for Christmas?' he said courteously.

Anne regarded him with astonishment. 'Why on earth should I?'

'Some women might.' There was a reproachful look in his eyes, as if to say she must surely be aware of the slights and insults he, his son, and all black people were subjected to on a daily basis.

'Well, *I* wouldn't,' she said stoutly. 'And I've got something for him.'

'Thank you, Miss Murray,' he said, as though on Zeke's behalf. 'Another thing—'

She interrupted, 'Why don't you come in, Mr Penn?' She cleared a chair of clothes and indicated that he sit.

'I think it wiser if I stayed outside.' He gave her the reproachful look again. 'I am not the only person who should be careful in this sort of situation, Miss Murray. You have your reputation to consider and I would advise you never to invite a black man into your dressing room.'

'I'll bear that in mind, Mr Penn.' She had heard some of the stagehands call him 'boy' or 'nigger'; he pretended not to hear. 'What was the other thing you wanted to talk to me about?'

'Mr Blinker is having a party at his home tomorrow and all the cast have been invited. Herbie insists Zeke has been included, but I wanted to make sure.'

'Zeke is definitely included. We've worked out a routine between the three of us and we're going to put on a bit of a show.'

'Is that so?' He frowned, clearly annoyed. 'Zeke didn't mention it.'

'We only thought about it the other day.'

'I see.' He made to close the door. 'It's time you got changed for the next act, Miss Murray. I hope you have a very enjoyable Christmas – and Herbie, too, if I don't see him before I leave.'

'And the same to you and your family, Mr Penn.'

Anne hadn't seen a black person in her life until she came to America. After five years there, she still couldn't think of a single reason why anyone should be treated differently because of the colour of his or her skin. It was surely not what the Lord Jesus himself would have wanted, for hadn't he created people in his image, and wasn't he a dark man himself? Lev had understood, but she'd noticed he didn't have a single black friend. 'It's just not *done*, Anne,' he'd remarked when she'd asked him why.

There were states in the South where black people had to sit in their own section at the back of buses, and weren't allowed in certain restaurants and shops.

It shocked and sickened her, quite literally gave her a headache, when she thought about black people being treated with such contempt. It was just as bad that other people who'd done no harm to anyone were reduced to living in the Hoovervilles. Wasn't God supposed to keep an eye on what was happening on earth?

Anne donated half her income to charity. She would have given more but Ollie Blinker advised her against it. 'You need to think about the future, baby. You won't always be a dancer and you don't want to end up in a shack in Central Park like that family you've adopted, do you?'

'Well, no,' Anne conceded. She felt guilty that she could buy clothes whenever she liked and eat whatever she fancied, but the problem of the poor wouldn't be solved by becoming poor herself, at least so Ollie said, and Lev agreed when she asked him.

On Christmas Day, she got up early and immediately looked out of the window where the sky was a gentle grey spotted with white puffy clouds. Central Park was covered with frost and the road glittered as if it had been sprinkled with diamonds. A few cars crawled along and a man walking his dog was the only person on foot. She was conscious of the warmth in the room coming from the iron radiator on the wall. There was a boiler downstairs that heated the entire building. A memory surfaced, of another Christmas, waking up to find toys on the floor beside the bed, and sweets and fruit stuffed in one of her grey school socks. That room, she recalled, was freezing. The memory flitted away as quickly as it had come.

She put on a thick, wool frock, boots, and a fake fur coat with a hood that made her look like a teddy bear, picked up a carrier bag full of brightly wrapped parcels, and made her way to the kitchen where Christina, still in her dressing gown, was waiting with a

my husband to have a job and my children new clothes. I don't want to spend Christmas in this awful place with people like you bringing us food when I'd sooner buy our own.'

Today, the woman was looking ill again. 'Thank you,' she said in a sullen voice when she'd looked through the food: candy, a Christmas pudding, and enough turkey and vegetables to feed eight. It would only need re-heating later on top of the little round fire, the fumes from which were making Anne choke. Somehow, the place managed to be warm and cold at the same time. Draughts were sweeping up her coat, yet her face felt hot. She hoped she wasn't getting another headache.

'There's a present for you, Ma,' Gail shouted, 'and one for Dad.'

'It's just scarves and gloves,' Anne muttered. She didn't like being Lady Bountiful: it made her feel embarrassed. Next time she had a parcel, she'd get someone else to bring it.

'What do you say to Miss Murray?' Mr Schultz raised his thick black eyebrows at the children. Having opened his own present, he was winding the brown knitted scarf around his neck as if to prove how appreciative he was. Mrs Schultz was shivering badly as she opened her own gift. Anne wished she'd brought something prettier; jewellery, for instance.

'Thank you, Miss Murray,' the children chorused. She'd bought dolls and clockwork cars for the younger children, a set of paints for Gail, who was very artistic, and, on the advice of Herbie, a knife with lots of blades for Vinny.

'Would you care to sit down, Miss Murray, and take a cup of tea with us?'

She sat down, but refused the tea saying she'd prefer a cup of hot water. Although she longed to leave, she courteously sat in one of the chairs and waited for the kettle to boil.

'Where's your coat, miss?' Eric enquired almost half an hour later when Anne returned to the car.

'I gave it to Mrs Schultz; she was desperately cold.'

Eric tutted. 'Now *you're* desperately cold.' He got out the car, took a rug out of the trunk and wrapped it around her shoulders. 'Do you still want to go to church?'

'Yes, please.'

'I'll stop at the apartment and ask Christina for another coat,' Eric said. 'Or would you sooner collect it yourself?'

'You do it for me, please.' If Lizzie were up, Anne would have a job getting out again. Lizzie, who never went near a church, couldn't understand the importance of going regularly to Mass. 'How can it possibly be a sin to miss it?' she would argue.

Eric drew up outside the apartment and returned a few minutes later with a red and white check coat. 'Christina put a hat in one of the pockets,' he said.

Anne put on the coat and pulled a little white beret out of a pocket. 'Thank you, Eric,' she said. 'You and Christina are very thoughtful.'

'Someone's got to look after you,' he said gruffly. 'Going round, scattering money all over New York, giving your clothes away. Lord knows what you're likely to do next.'

The city was coming to life. More people were walking through the park, the traffic had increased a little, but it would be nothing like a normal day. It was a complete contrast to yesterday, Christmas Eve, when the stores had been so busy there was hardly room to move and the streets had become clogged with traffic. Carols had competed with the impatient honking of horns to make the most noise. Today in Fifth Avenue, a few people window-shopped, but most were making their way towards St Patrick's Cathedral for Mass.

Eric drew up outside the massive building with its Gothic spires and white marble façade. She told him there was no need to collect her, that she'd walk home.

He simply snorted. 'It's too cold to walk. Christina said you ain't had so much as a cup of coffee yet. I'll wait for you down Fifty-first Street.'

She thanked him. Walking home would have been a penance for vague sins she may, or may not, have committed. On entering the church, she dipped her fingers in the holy water and made the

Sign of the Cross. She knelt at the back, feeling tiny and humbled by the vastness of the church, which smelled of incense and the Blood of Christ. Waves of pain were sweeping through her head, advancing and receding like an ocean tide, and it felt as if a hole was being bored in her skull next to her right eye.

She joined the queue for Communion, returning to her seat with the Host resting on her tongue, her throat too thick to swallow it. She worried she might choke.

Half an hour later, she was home, though she couldn't remember having got there. Christina made some strong, sweet coffee, and Lizzie gave her an eye mask and rubbed lavender oil on her forehead to help with the pain. 'Have you had your drops today?' she enquired, and Anne assured her that she had. The shades drawn and the door closed, Anne lay on the bed, hoping the headache would have gone by it was time for the party.

In the kitchen, Christina was getting the dinner ready. Lizzie was setting the table, taking extra care with a floral display and silver cutlery because Ollie had invited some business friends and their wives. Ollie, who never went to bed until well into the small hours, was still asleep, and a bored Herbie, who'd been expecting Anne's company that morning, was playing pool in his father's den.

As so often happened when she was alone in the dark, when the only sounds were muffled and far away, Anne's brain commenced a turbulent, dizzying journey, soaring like a bird over mountains and valleys, across oceans, and through forests. Sometimes, she would find herself in a familiar, though nameless, place, like a crowded church where there was a coffin covered with white flowers. She was the only one there who wasn't crying because she knew the person in the coffin had gone straight to heaven and they would meet again one day. In another, much smaller place, a girl pushed a piece of paper in her hand and said, '*Hold on to this, darlin'*.' Then she was on a boat and a little boy was clinging to her skirt, sobbing his heart out, but she had no idea how to comfort him. '*Where are you from, Miss Anne Muray?*' asked a voice, but that was real: it was Lev and they were in a taxi. Her memory only stretched back that far. The other things might have happened or they might not. Anne tried not to think about them too deeply in case she remembered something she'd sooner not.

Her hand was taken and tucked inside a bigger, warmer one. She wasn't sure if it was real or imagined. 'Is someone there?' she whispered.

'It's Lev, darling, come to wish you Merry Christmas.'

'Lev!' She tore the mask off her eyes and saw him smiling down at her. His thick, wavy hair was almost entirely grey and his brown eyes sparkled with affection. She wondered if he loved her as much as she did him. 'I wasn't expecting to see you today,' she cried, throwing her arms around his neck. 'Is that the only reason you're here, to wish me Merry Christmas?'

'Well, no,' he conceded. 'I've something important to tell Ollie, but he's still in bed, so I came to see you instead. Lizzie said you had a headache, but I thought it wouldn't hurt to just hold your hand. I've put your present under the tree: it's a white kimono.'

'I've always wanted a white kimono. Your present's under the tree, too. It's the latest William Faulkner novel.'

'I look forward to reading it.' He kissed the tip of her nose.

'I was just thinking about the night I got into your taxi,' she said. 'Did I ask you to take me somewhere?'

'No, darling. You just sat there without opening your mouth, refusing to answer my questions. I had no idea what to do with you, so I took you home to Tamara. I suppose I should have tried to find out who you belonged to, but you seemed quite happy to stay with us so I didn't bother.'

'I'm glad you didn't.'

She appeared quite satisfied with his answer. There were times when Levon couldn't get over the enormity of what he'd done, actually kidnapping her off the streets. Should his crime ever be discovered – and it *was* a crime, a serious one – then he would be put in prison and the key would be thrown away – Tamara, too.

She'd been an accessory to the crime. Then there was the fact that they'd stolen Anne's baby.

What he should have done was take Anne to Bleecker Street the following morning, taken her every day, if necessary, until there was someone in, and handed her over to the person who'd been expecting her all along.

But he and Tamara had been too excited at the notion they'd found a daughter to replace their dead one. It was as if fate had intervened on their behalf; Anne was meant for them and they for her. No one outside their little circle had mattered.

He wondered if her question meant that, after five years, she was suddenly interested in knowing where she came from, where she belonged, but she didn't pursue the matter.

'Can you stay for tonight's party?' she asked.

'I'm sorry, darling, but Tamara's expecting me back for Christmas dinner. She was annoyed enough I missed breakfast, but I have this news for Ollie.'

In fact, Tamara had been as mad as hell. She seemed to expect him to be there every minute of every day when he wasn't at work. The news for Ollie was important, but it could have waited a few more days. He'd felt the need to visit Manhattan – no, dammit, he'd wanted to see Anne. He really *had* come just to wish her a Merry Christmas.

She sat up. 'My headache's better,' she said. 'It's seeing you that did it.'

'Good.' Pleased, he folded her small, cold hands inside his and saw a small amount of colour had come to her white cheeks. 'I'll see if Ollie's up yet, then I suppose I'd better get back to Brooklyn.' He sighed. He would far sooner have spent the day with the Blinkers. 'I'll come and see you before I go.'

Ollie was sitting behind the desk in his den wearing a gold brocade dressing gown over navy-blue silk pyjamas. He was smoking a long, fat cigar. His grey hair, normally so neat, stood out like a halo around his head. He'd put on weight with the years and the dressing gown didn't quite meet around his waist.

Considering how wealthy he was, Levon wondered why he hadn't bought a new one.

'Hey, there, Lev.' He waved the cigar, creating a circle of white smoke. In contrast to the rest of the house with its pale furnishings and light walls, the dark wood panelling of the den belonged to a different era. Cosy, with old, well-worn furniture and a mixture of smells – cigars, liquor, the musky cologne Ollie used – it always made Levon yearn for a den of his own. Unlike Ollie, he wouldn't have wanted a dartboard, a pinball machine, or a pool table, just a nice comfortable chair and a desk on which to spread out his books and not feel in the way. 'What can I do for you, old chap?' Ollie enquired.

Levon looked at Herbie, who was noisily playing pool at the other end of the room, and slightly shook his head.

Ollie took the hint and requested his son make himself scarce: 'Me and Lev have got something confidential to talk about.'

Herbie rolled his eyes good-naturedly and did as he was told. He was a nice young man; Levon liked him enormously.

'How's that boy of yours?' Ollie asked when his own boy had gone. He shoved the box of cigars in Levon's directions, but he declined. He liked the smell of cigars, but if he smoked one he'd be sick for a week.

'John's five now; he started school last year.' According to Tamara, he was the cleverest in the class. John going to school had provided another reason for Levon's continual presence at home. There were childish concerts to attend and childish games to watch, even if John was too young to play. 'It's to support the school,' Tamara claimed after they'd watched an incredibly tedious football match. At Hallowe'en there'd been a party; and at Christmas a Nativity play in which John had been one of the three kings. There was something called Little League.

Levon knew that Ollie wasn't interested in John, just being polite. 'I came about Judge Seabury's investigation into City Hall,' he said. 'I've got a client who works there. Last night he called to tell me one of the witnesses had been murdered. I'm not sure where you stand in this, Ollie, but I just thought I'd let you know.'

'Why should I want to know about that, Lev?' Ollie asked levelly.

'I understand you've been called as a witness yourself.'

'Yeah, I have,' Ollie admitted with a nonchalant shrug.

Levon could tell the nonchalance was put on. Only a fool would be unperturbed by the news. For more than a year, the United States Attorney General, Charles Tuttle, had been looking into the affairs of City Hall. He had discovered an alarming level of corruption in the Mayor's administration. It was no secret that Mayor Jimmy Walker and Ollie Blinker were the best of friends – Levon had met Mayor Walker in this very apartment several times in the past. Ollie had made his fortune out of building: flooring, cement, foundations, something like that. He even had something to do with the Empire State Building currently going up on 34th Street. But Ollie sailed very close to the margins. If the Mayor went down, he was very likely to go with him.

Just then, Ollie slapped his knee with a fat hand, making Levon jump. 'Thanks for telling me. There's quite a few people who'd like to see me go down with the sinking ship, but not you. Thanks again, Lev. You're a good friend.'

'You warned me about the Stock Market crash,' Levon mumbled. 'I'm just returning the favour.'

Ollie grinned. 'You're still a good friend. Would you like a drink? I've got some Irish malt that goes down the throat like liquid gold. Tell you what,' he said generously, 'I'll give you a bottle to take with you.'

Levon nodded his thanks. If he had to spend the rest of the day at home, it would be preferable to do so in a mildly alcoholic daze. Ollie went to a run-down cabinet with leaded windows and removed a bottle and two glasses. There was a row of photos on top, of Ollie and Lizzie's wedding – the groom looked positively skinny – the children, Herbie and Mabel, in various stages of development, and a charming grey-haired couple staring lovingly at each other.

'Are they your folks?' he asked. He knew nothing about the man's past.

'I like to think they might be.' Ollie chuckled. 'Lizzie found the photo in a book she borrowed from the library, so I kept it. It was only supposed to be a joke, but they've been here for years.' He picked up the photo and studied it. 'Good-looking pair, aren't they?' he said with a smile. 'I expect they're someone's folks, but not mine. Me, I was found abandoned in a waiting room on Penn Station. I never knew my ma and pa. I don't know what sort of blood runs through my veins. I'd been circumcized, so I might be a Jew. The dame who found me brought me up. Her name was Edna Blinker. She was OK, but she looked nothing like this.' He flicked the photo with his finger. 'She died when I was fourteen and I was left on my own. I used to find it scary, not knowing a single thing about myself, but after I met Lizzie and had kids of my own, it didn't seem to matter all that much.'

'In the long run, I don't suppose it does,' Levon commented, 'but I think I'd find it scary, too.' Somewhere in the apartment, Herbie said something and Anne responded with a laugh. It was an attractive laugh, full-throated and completely natural.

Perhaps Ollie had heard. 'What does Anne know about her background, Lev?' he enquired.

'Nothing and everything.' It was Levon's turn to shrug. 'It's all there in her head, buried deep down, but something happened that made her forget.' He recalled the drawings she'd used to do. '*I'm not as stupid as you think*,' she'd said just after she'd had John. 'One of these days I reckon it will all come flooding back; when she's older, maybe, and more resilient.'

Ollie handed him an inch of whiskey in a tumbler. He went to the door and yelled for ice, then returned to his seat behind the desk. 'That stuff Tamara told Lizzie years ago, about Anne being the daughter of an Irish friend who went bankrupt, well, I don't believe a word of it, Lev.' He waved his hand in a gesture of dismissal. 'Not that it matters. I don't give a damn what the truth is.'

A bad-tempered Christina came in with a bowl of ice cubes,

complaining she was far too busy to be fetching and carrying while she was in the middle of making dinner. 'You want anything else, Master Blinker, you fetch it yourself.'

'What would you say,' Ollie said slowly after the door had slammed shut, 'to Anne and Herbie getting married?'

Levon jumped. 'How long have you had that idea?'

'About two and a half minutes. They really like each other.'

'Aren't people supposed to love each other when they get married? And shouldn't the idea come from Herbie?'

Ollie drummed his fingers on the desk. 'Perhaps he needs a bit of encouragement.'

The idea was taking some getting used to. Levon continued to think of Anne as a child, though she must be about nineteen or twenty by now. 'Another thing, Ollie,' he said, 'I'm not Anne's guardian. It's not up to me who she marries.'

'No, but she listens to you. You're the person she talks about more than anyone. If Herbie proposed, first thing she'd do is ring and ask what you thought.' He reached for the whiskey. 'What's the drink like, Lev? Does it go down smoothly or not?'

'Very smoothly, Ollie.' He could feel it caressing his throat.

'Does Anne have papers – birth certificate, passport, stuff like that?'

'No, nothing.'

Ollie winked. 'I won't ask how she got into the good old US of A.'

Levon didn't wink back. 'It wouldn't be any good asking; I don't know. She's not legally adopted. We just came across each other accidentally.'

'I'll have some papers made up for her, use what little influence I've still got with City Hall before the Mayor quits his job. It's bound to come in useful one day, like if she decides to become an American citizen.'

Levon thought it was time he made a move. He got to his feet. 'You look after yourself, Ollie. Don't forget the murdered witness.' The conversation had taken a surprising turn, from corruption in City Hall to Anne and Herbie getting married. About the latter, Levon didn't know what to think.

Zeke arrived for the party that night in a dark-blue velvet evening jacket and blue bowtie. With his beautiful brown eyes, pink cushiony lips, and breaktaking smile, he looked so handsome it almost took Anne's breath away. His ma, he explained, had borrowed the jacket from a piano player who was laid up with an unidentifiable chest complaint.

'Got some bad news,' he added darkly. 'Pops said there's no way a nigger can be seen dancing with a white woman – actually *touching* her with his evil nigger hands. I'm afraid our performance tonight is off.'

Anne was bitterly disappointed. 'But I was looking forward to the three of us dancing together!'

'So was I!' said Herbie. 'Do you have to do as your pop says, Zeke?'

'He was deadly serious and made me promise on my mom's life I wouldn't dance with Anne.' He looked sober for once. 'He said the trouble with me is I have too big an opinion of myself and don't know my place. There's some folks who'd like to take me down a peg or two. In the South, a nigger could be lynched just for touching a white woman.'

'Jeez!' Herbie gasped.

'That's disgraceful,' Anne said hotly. 'And stop saying "nigger". Your father doesn't like it and neither do I.'

Zeke moodily stuffed his hands in the pocket of the velvet jacket. 'Pops said the place to live is Paris, France, where no one cares whether you're black or white. I might go there one day.'

'We'll all go,' Anne declared. 'We'll all go to Paris if that's the only way we can dance together and be friends.'

Two days later, Herbie slipped on the icy pavement outside the theatre and sprained his ankle. His understudy, Nelson, who normally danced in the chorus, partnered Anne that night. There'd been hardly any time to rehearse and Nelson put in an adequate performance under the circumstances. But he tried too hard and it showed. His face was fixed in a tense smile that vanished the minute the dance was over.

Next morning, Anne and Nelson met early in the theatre so they could practise. To Anne's surprise, Conrad Abel was already there, along with a seething Nelson, and a starved-looking young man who seemed familiar.

'Anne, this is Flip Ungar,' the producer said. 'He's filling in until Herbie's ankle is better. I got him along to watch the show last night so he knows what to do.'

'I remember you.' Anne smiled. 'You auditioned the same time as we did. While we were waiting, you had to leave the room to be sick. I hope you don't feel sick now.'

'It was the waiting that did it.' He had dark, smoky eyes, hollow cheeks, and a wide, thin mouth that twitched slightly in an answering smile. His body moved with the lazy grace of a cat.

Nelson flounced away close to tears when Conrad Abel said impatiently, 'Come on, let's get started.'

They were born to dance together, the producer realized after a mere few minutes. When she danced with Herbie, it was Anne who led, Anne who had the personality that inspired her partner to greater things, but with Flip Ungar, neither led: they inspired each other. There was a sexual chemistry between them. Herbie was the boy next door; Flip was the predator looking to get his partner to bed.

Conrad Abel rubbed his hands together gleefully. He'd always deeply resented giving the part to Herbie Blinker, even though it had been his own weakness had led him to do it. This would be one in the eye for Herbie's old man.

Lizzie brought the paper into the den for Ollie to see. It was the *East Coast Herald* and mainly dealt with matters in New York. 'Read this,' she said, pointing to a small item on the arts page:

An understudy filling in for a performer with a sprained ankle is hardly worth a reviewer's comment, except when the understudy puts

*in a performance of such calibre as can be found in Roses are Red
at the Classic Theater on 42nd Street. Flip Ungar (standing in for
the injured Herbie Blinker), partners the superlative Anne Murray,
treating the audience to a display of such sublime perfection that it
lifts the soul. It is rare for two dancers to be so in tune with each other
as Murray and Ungar . . .*

'Shit!' Ollie laid the paper down. He'd already got the picture and
there was no need to read any more.

'Let's hope Herbie's ankle gets better soon,' Lizzie said dryly,
'or he'll be out of a job.'

'Over my dead body,' Ollie growled.

Lizzie left. Ollie put his head in his hands and thought about
their son. It had been a relief when, at an early age, Herbie had
said he wanted to go into show business, preferably as a dancer.
He was unlikely to set the world alight with his brain. Not even
the most experienced tutors his father engaged could make him as
interested in conventional lessons as he was in clothes, movies,
and the theatre. There was no point in sending him to college.
With Ollie's wealth, he could have funded the most up-to-date
gymnasium or the best-stocked library in the country and got
Herbie in that way, but his son wouldn't have emerged one whit
cleverer than when he went in.

Ollie wasn't the sort of parent who believed in making things
tough for their kids. If Herbie wanted to be a dancer, then a
dancer he would be, and Ollie would do everything in his power
to smooth his path.

At sixteen, Herbie went straight from high school to Peggy
Perlmann's academy in Hester Street. Peggy had been honest
right from the start. 'He's exceptionally good-looking, has loads of
personality and plenty of talent,' she'd told Ollie. 'I'm sure he'll
make it into the chorus of the top shows. He might even be
picked for a solo spot if he's lucky.'

From that, Ollie took it that there was little chance of Herbie
becoming a star. He just didn't have it in him: the extra shine, the
final bit of polish that separated the mundane from the uniquely

talented. He felt disappointed, both on his own and Herbie's behalf. A dancer sounded much better than a chorus boy.

Anne started at Peggy's during Herbie's second year. *She* had the extra shine, the final bit of polish in spades. And she was capable of lifting Herbie to her own dizzying level. Seeing them dance together had made Ollie wonder if they could be launched as a couple: Herbie Blinker and Anne Murray – Blinker and Murray.

When Tamara had approached Lizzie about Anne moving in with them, it had seemed like the answer to a prayer. He liked Anne, she was a sweet kid, and once she was living under his roof it seemed quite legitimate – responsible, even – to look after her career. He had engaged an agent, Joe Squires, and impressed upon him that Herbie and Anne were a team. They came together like coffee and cream. Neither could be booked without the other.

Now all Ollie had to do was make sure it stayed that way, except Herbie had sprained his ankle, and he couldn't very well demand that Anne be withdrawn from *Roses are Red* until the ankle got better. It worried him that one of these days, someone like that creepy producer, Conrad Abel, would advise her she could do much better with another partner.

The sound of applause was still ringing in his ears as Conrad Abel made his way along the dusty passage to his office beneath the stage. He felt exceedingly pleased with himself. *Roses are Red* was a trite show, but his daring in engaging the astonishingly gifted Zeke Penn had lifted the production out of the ordinary. Now the pairing of Anne Murray with Flip Ungar was attracting attention. After the piece in the *East Coast Herald*, the demand for tickets had increased and quite a few reviewers were coming back for a second look.

'Good evening, Mr Abel,' a voice said from behind.

He turned to find himself being followed by a rotund individual in evening dress. 'Mr Blinker!' He stood aside to allow the man into his office, which was hardly bigger than a cupboard.

Every single inch of wall was covered with posters. 'What can I do for you?'

'I'll not beat about the bush,' Blinker said in a flat, unemotional voice. He put a white envelope amidst the papers on the untidy desk. 'There's a thousand bucks in there. I want that Ungar chap out of the show. Tomorrow, Anne can go on with the chap from the chorus, whatever his name is.'

'Nelson.'

'That's right, Nelson. I don't know how long my Herbie's going to be out of action, but I'll give you another thousand for every week you do without him.'

The producer shook his head. 'I don't want your money, Blinker. I wouldn't have taken it that other time if I hadn't been in such a hole.' It was the first and only time he'd done such a thing and he hadn't touched a playing card since. He felt a spurt of anger at the cheek of the man. 'How dare you come here telling me what to do with my own show,' he said hotly.

The anger was wasted on Blinker, who just glowered. 'Two thousand, then.'

'I wouldn't do it for ten thousand, not even a hundred,' he sneered. 'I thought Ungar was the right choice months ago when he auditioned.' He'd loathed turning the young man down in favour of the only moderately talented Herbie. Ungar's girlfriend had tried the old trick of seducing him, but she was just one of a long list who'd done the same. He took the sex when it was offered, but it was rare a girl got what she was after.

'Have you got kids, Abel?' Blinker enquired in a friendlier tone, a touch wheedling, as if he were trying to reach Conrad through his heart, unaware the producer didn't possess the sort of heart that could be reached by anything on earth.

'Not that I'm aware of.'

'If you had, wouldn't you do everything in your power to help them make a success of their lives?'

'It all depends,' said Conrad Abel. He was enjoying their positions being reversed. 'If a kid of mine wanted a part in one of my shows, they wouldn't get it in a million years unless they were up to it. The general public pay good money to visit the theatre and they're entitled to the best there is. Do you seriously think *Roses are Red* would still be running if the entire cast were made up of second-raters like Herbie? It'd have closed within a week. As for my career, it'd have gone down the toilet a long time ago.'

Blinker winced. 'I could have your legs broken, Abel,' he said threateningly.

'I know,' the producer said with a cynical smile. 'Better still, you could have Flip Ungar's legs broken so he'll never dance again. If you get rid of enough competition, your Herbie could well get a part on his own accord. Oh, and forget about Anne. It won't matter that she's never stretched, never dances with someone of the same calibre. Just use her as you are now, as one of the props to help your Herbie's pathetic career. You might like to tell your precious son that it's no use him expecting to come back when his ankle's better. The part's been filled by a *real* dancer and it's going to stay that way.'

Ollie was in his den, his feet on his desk, chomping on a big cigar. He wrote the word '*Hollywood*' in the air with smoke, though the H had disappeared by the time he wrote the D.

He'd always wanted to go to California and get involved in the movies. Some of his business friends swore they were the coming thing and the theatre was quite likely to die on its feet in the not-too-distant future. He'd commission a writer to come up with a movie script for Herbie and Anne, demand it be done by yesterday. It was a way of getting Anne out of the clutches of Conrad Abel and avoiding Herbie being embarrassed when his ankle was better and he expected to return to *Roses are Red*. And it wouldn't hurt to get himself out of the way of that investigation into City Hall. He'd feel safer on the other side of the country. And that was a real good idea he'd had about Herbie and Anne getting married. Lev hadn't been all that enthusiastic when he'd come up with the idea at Christmas, but he hadn't been against it either.

Chapter 10

It was like a scene out of . . . well, a movie. Levon watched Anne and Herbie being filmed from the other side of the heart-shaped pool. The cameraman's head was bent over the view-finder, shielding it with one hand, while turning the handle with the other. Another camera filmed the wedding guests coming and going through a white flowered arch. Waiters hovered on every path and corner with trays of pink champagne – how Ollie managed to break the law so openly, he would never know. Prohibition was still in force. Someone very important must have been persuaded to turn a blind eye.

Quite a few of the guests were household names – no doubt the unfamiliar ones were producers and directors. After all, this was Los Angeles and Hollywood was only a few miles away. Levon recognized quite a few faces: Douglas Fairbanks, for instance, more handsome in the flesh than on the screen. The woman in the floaty blue outfit and big sunglasses was his wife, Mary Pickford, and the one draped in leopard skin – despite the heat – was an actress who'd just arrived from Germany and was reputed to have had five hundred lovers.

'All at the same time?' Levon had quipped when told this startling fact, to be met by stony-faced silence from an avid fan, who clearly fancied being the five hundred and first.

So far, it had been the strangest weekend of his life and quite likely to get even stranger. He'd flown – actually *flown* – from Newark to Los Angeles in a Fokker plane that normally carried mail. It had taken more than fourteen hours and was an experience he would prefer not to repeat, although he would have to tomorrow if he wanted to get home. He could always return by train, which would take several days, but at least he'd feel safe, even if business would suffer from his long absence. It depended on how courageous he felt when the time came.

He felt conspicuously alone, one of the few people present not connected with show business. It had been all right on the plane. Peggy Perlmann had been invited to the wedding, as well as some of the youngsters who'd been at the academy at the same time as Anne and Herbie, and the Blinkers' daughter, Mabel, who had driven down to New York from Washington with her husband, Kurt, and their two children – the children had been the only ones who'd enjoyed the flight.

Tamara had been invited, but Levon hadn't shown her the invitation. He was confident she wouldn't come, yet at the same time worried that she might. A trip by private plane to a Hollywood wedding would be hard for most people to resist and would certainly give her something to boast about to her numerous friends.

But Anne and Tamara hadn't come face to face since they'd lived in the apartment in Grammercy Park. Levon had no idea if Anne bore a grudge for having been so unceremoniously evicted when Tamara judged she'd served her purpose – he didn't know if Anne was capable of bearing a grudge – but reckoned her wedding day wasn't the time to find out. Moreover, Tamara would want to bring John. Lord knows what sort of effect the sight of her five-year-old son would have on Anne when she'd done her very best to pretend he didn't exist. He'd told his wife he was visiting Ollie for business reasons.

The newly married couple were posing for the photographers, who were circling around them, cameras held like weapons, in the hope of getting a good shot. Ollie had invited representatives of every newspaper, every agent, every single person who was likely to give Anne and Herbie's wedding publicity. It was all tied in with a movie he had planned.

And as if the plane journey hadn't been strange enough, Los

Angeles was just as odd: unnatural in Levon's view. The single-storey house that Ollie had rented was set on a hill amidst an exotic garden planted with palm trees and bushes with blooms as big as faces. In the distance, the Pacific Ocean gleamed a silvery turquoise, in contrast to the Atlantic, on the East side, which was usually the colour of mud. The grass was too green, the sun too big and hot in the too blue sky. The house itself was as pink as a baby and set like a blancmange on the top of the hill. Last night, Levon had slept in an entirely white room with lace curtains and lace covers on the bed. It had its own private bathroom, also all white.

The women appeared to guard their complexions from the cruel heat, but nearly every man had a glorious suntan. Levon thought he must look pale and sickly beside so many healthy, brown-skinned males with their flashing white teeth.

A woman caught his arm. 'Darling, were you in *Hangman's House* with Victor McLaglen?'

'No, madam,' Levon replied courteously.

The woman frowned. 'Are you sure?'

'Positive.'

'Do you know if Mr McLaglen is here today?'

'I'm afraid I wouldn't recognize him if he were. I don't belong to the . . . film industry,' he added lamely after the woman had rudely walked away without waiting for him to finish.

'Lev!' Lizzie Blinker shoved her arm inside his. 'It's lovely to see a familiar face. I'm fed up shaking hands with folk I don't know from Adam.'

'How did Ollie manage to make friends with so many people so quickly?' Lev asked. 'There's hundreds of guests and you've only lived in Los Angeles for a couple of months.'

'You and Peggy are the only *real* friends. Ollie put someone in charge of the wedding arrangements and told them to invite everyone who was anyone in Hollywood. Fortunately, only about a quarter came or we'd be over-run.' She squeezed his arm. 'Are you happy for Anne, Lev? I know you look upon her as a daughter.'

Levon glanced at Anne. She and Herbie were still posing for pictures. They were standing on a round, white platform and looked like figures on a giant cake, laughing and holding hands. 'She looks happy enough,' he said to Lizzie. 'Herbie, too.'

'Yes, but are *you* happy, Lev?' Lizzie persisted.

'I suppose so.' He wasn't sure. Ollie had said Herbie needed encouragement to ask Anne to marry him. It had seemed funny to Levon at the time and still did. Herbie was a handsome, healthy young man of twenty-two and, if he was in love, shouldn't have needed encouragement. He and Anne had lived under the same roof for over five years and were fond of each other, there was no doubt about that. But in love? Levon wasn't sure.

'We'll look after her, Lev, I promise,' Lizzie said. 'Anne's not exactly your average young woman and she needs looking after. Don't you agree?'

'Well, yes.' There still seemed something not quite right about it.

He thought the same thing later when Anne and Herbie began to mingle among the guests, eventually arriving at him. Instead of Anne flinging her arms around his neck as she usually did, she merely kissed his cheek. He was convinced there was something in her beautiful eyes, right at the very back, a lost, scared look that worried him. Had Ollie pressurized her into marrying his son?

'Congratulations, darling. And you Herbie.' He shook the young man's brown hand. 'I hope you'll be very happy together.'

'We will, Lev,' Herbie said confidently as he led Anne away.

Levon spied Peggy sitting at a table alone, a bundle of spangled pink net with a pink flower in her voluminous red hair, attracting a great deal of admiring looks from the men in the vicinity. With a sigh of relief, he quickly went and sat beside her before someone else got there before him. 'I thought you'd be making contacts and that sort of thing.' He waved his hands vaguely.

'Oh, Lev, I feel a bit like Alice in Wonderland.' She seemed as pleased to see him as he was her. 'These people terrify me. I can't wait to get back to New York where everyone's more civilized. I hope Ollie keeps an eye on Anne or she'll be eaten alive.'

'What makes you say that?' he asked, alarmed.

'Well, this company he's making the movie with, they turn out complete trash,' she said darkly. 'Ollie seems to think if he's putting up the money, they'll do as he says. If he wants a nice, tasteful musical with Anne and Herbie as the stars, he's gonna have a battle on his hands. All Hughie Vandervelt is interested in is making a quick buck. He owns the company, if you didn't know.'

Levon felt even more alarmed. 'Does Lizzie know about this?'

'I've no idea, but Lizzie has complete faith in Ollie. Let's hope it's justified.'

Despite this worrying news, Levon was very conscious of Peggy's luscious red lips and plump white arms. Her face shone with perspiration and tendrils of red hair curled around her ears and clung to her glistening brow, gathering in little clumps on her long, white neck. She was like a goddess, a magnificent pagan goddess. He recalled how smitten he'd been when they first met.

'You look extremely beautiful today, Peggy,' he murmured.

To his surprise, her face turned almost as red as her hair. 'Why, Lev, you've never said anything like that before.'

'I've thought it,' he confessed.

She looked at him provocatively through lowered lids. 'I've always considered you the handsomest man I know.'

Something very peculiar was happening to his stomach, peculiar and exceptionally pleasant. He managed to raise a quizzical eye. 'More handsome than Douglas Fairbanks?'

'Ten times handsomer.' She laughed. 'You should have gone into the movies.'

'Then *I* would have been eaten alive.' He sniffed pathetically. 'I'm not as tough as I look.'

'I know you're not. You're like a chocolate with a soft centre, all gooey and sweet inside.'

Quite how it happened, Levon could never remember, but within a very short space of time, he was making love to Peggy in the white bedroom with the lace curtains. 'I've always wanted to do this,' he groaned as he lowered himself on to her glorious, throbbing body.

'And I've always wanted you to,' Peggy gasped.

Later in the afternoon, Levon left the room to collect a bottle of champagne. A few hours afterwards, Peggy went to fetch another. That night, they slept together on top of the lace cover – it was too hot to get underneath – making love with an inhibited passion that Levon, for one, had never known before. The following day, they decided to return home by train. He booked a sleeping compartment with two bunks and they made love all the way to New York.

'Thank you, Peggy,' he began, as they stood in Grand Central terminal, joshed by the crowds, in everyone's way. The noise was horrendous. After all they'd been to each other, he was scared to touch her in case anyone he knew might see.

Peggy put her fingers over his mouth. 'Don't thank me, Lev, and I won't thank you,' she whispered. 'We both have done exactly what we wanted. And, Lev, I don't expect us to do it again now we're on home territory. You're not the sort of man to have an affair, I know that.' She shrugged her majestic shoulders. 'But should you ever feel the urge, you know where I live. 'Bye, my darling.' She kissed him briefly on the lips and was gone.

'Tamara, my love, I have brought you another daughter.'

For some reason, Levon kept remembering the words when he returned from Los Angeles, the tropical paradise where nothing seemed real. He recalled the night he'd taken a couple to a ship moored by the docks. 'We're going to Europe,' the man had told him. He'd been unloading their luggage when a young woman had asked him to take Anne to Bleecker Street.

When he'd arrived home with Anne, Tamara had emerged from the bedroom wearing the bloodstained frock she'd had on the night they'd found Larisa. He'd loved Tamara then, and she'd loved him. But Anne had come between them and would always be there, even now when she was thousands of miles away. It was scarcely Anne's fault that their marriage had faltered. But who *was* to blame? Tamara had shown a side to her personality that he'd never known existed, a ruthless, selfish side. Perhaps he too had acted in a manner she found repugnant. He'd loved Anne in the same way as he'd loved Larisa, but Tamara hadn't looked upon her as a daughter, only as another woman, a rival.

And now it was worse. She was cross with him for staying away so long, scorned him for coming home by train. 'I'd made arrangements, Lev,' she complained. 'It was Dean Miller's party and I promised we'd be there.'

'At a child's birthday party?' Had he been expected to play Blind Man's Buff and Musical Chairs?

'All the parents were there – apart from you.' She glared at him. 'We had cocktails in the lounge while the children played downstairs.'

'So, I should have risked my life on a plane so as not to miss Dean's party?'

'Oh, don't be silly, Lev.' She twisted her shoulders contemptuously.

The gesture offended him, and the nasty expression in her eyes. 'Am I to have no life of my own, Tamara?' he asked coldly. 'Do you expect me to be at your beck and call every minute I don't spend in my office? Would you like me to retire so I'm available twenty-four hours a day? And don't say, "Don't be silly, Lev" again, or I shall walk out of this house and never come back.' He half hoped that she would, in which case he would go and live with Peggy in her apartment over the academy and be happy again.

Instead, after a few seconds of contemplation, she said, 'I'm sorry, Lev, but we took on John and he has the right to have his father around. I would have thought you'd understand that,' she added, her voice not quite so harsh. Perhaps his threat had frightened her.

'No, Tamara, *you* took on John. I don't recall you asking my opinion on the matter.' He walked out of the room, feeling as if he'd scored a victory, but not wanting to score anything, not with Tamara, whom he'd once loved with all his heart, but no longer loved at all. He wondered what it would be like if he'd never brought Anne home. Would they still be living in Grammercy Park, quietly, uneventfully, mourning their lost daughter, growing old, but still loving each other in the old, sad way? He wasn't quite sure if that's what he would have preferred.

On Tuesday, he went to the theatre to see *Roses are Red* for the third time. It was easy to buy a single seat at the box office on the night. He had a feeling Peggy would be there with her students. They'd seen it once, but she wanted them to see it again with the new dancers in place of Anne and Herbie. 'I've heard the man is brilliant, not nearly as good-looking as Herbie, but with loads of charisma. The girl's not a patch on Anne.'

But there was no sign of Peggy or her students in the cheap seats they usually occupied. He'd either got the wrong day or the wrong week. He'd wanted them to meet as if by accident, just to see her lovely, expressive face, reminding him of the way things had been over the few blissful days they'd spent together. Peggy had made him feel like a man again: with Tamara he was a mouse.

With a sigh, he settled in his seat and looked at the programme. Herbie's part was now being played by a Flip Ungar and Anne had been replaced by Rosalind Raines.

Peggy was right, he realized two and a half hours later when the show came to an end. Until tonight, he'd considered Herbie to be a fine dancer, but Flip Ungar had the fire of genius in his lithe frame, the ability to express the subtlest emotion by a single movement or the expression on his face. Rosalind Raines was more than adequate, but she didn't have her partner's passion or Anne's unique talent.

Zeke Penn had put in his usual brilliant performance, but Levon noticed he didn't appear at the end to take the curtain call. He recalled the other times he'd seen the show when Zeke had stood between Anne and Herbie, holding hands. Anne had loved Zeke, insisting on referring to him as her friend. Was it possible he was too embarrassed to come on without her and Herbie? Or were the rest of the cast, all white, shunning him?

Levon determined to go backstage and shake Zeke's hand. It's what Anne would have wanted. She'd be upset if she knew Zeke was missing out on the applause that was his due.

He waited until most of the audience had gone before venturing behind the curtain where he asked a stagehand manipulating scenery the whereabouts of Zeke Penn's dressing room.

'You mean the nigger?' the man curled his lip. 'He's gone. Goes every night halfway through Act Three when his part finishes. Good thing, too. The producer should've got a white guy for the part. I'm not the only one here who don't like mixing with niggers.'

Levon turned away. The prejudice against Negroes in America appalled him. He wanted no part of it, but was reluctant to speak out, worried he'd be called a 'nigger lover'. It was possible to lose friends that way, not to mention clients.

The stagehand was eyeing him with animosity. The mere fact he'd asked for Zeke had put the man's back up. Levon ignored him and made for the stage door rather than return through the theatre; it was easier to get out that way. He followed a crowd of excited young people whom, he understood, were on their way to the nearest coffee bar. They made him wish fervently that he were young again. The one at the rear, a boy of about eighteen, held the door for him, and Levon did the same for the man following behind.

'Don't I know you from somewhere?' the man asked when they were outside in the grubby little alley that ran behind the theatre. He was a small, hunched figure with long greasy hair combed over a bald spot.

'I was at the opening night party.' They pushed their way through the small crowd of admirers waiting for Eric Carrington and Patricia Peters to emerge. 'I'm a friend of Anne Murray – and the Blinkers.' A memory clicked into place. 'You're the producer, aren't you? I'm sorry, I didn't recognize you at first.'

'Yeah, Conrad Abel. Are you really a friend of Ollie Blinker's?' The man looked at him keenly. 'If you don't mind my saying, you don't look the type.'

Levon wasn't sure whether to be flattered or annoyed. 'Anne and Herbie were at Peggy Perlmann's academy together. That's how we met.'

'That's right, you were Anne's guardian or something. How come you let her go live with the Blinkers? That guy is an out and out crook. Ended up fleeing the state in order to avoid that dirty business with the Mayor. Least, that was one of the reasons.'

'I wasn't Anne's guardian,' Levon said stiffly. 'She merely lived with my wife and I when she first came to America.' He felt the urge to walk away, to escape the producer's offensive questions, but something prompted him to stay. For all his faults – and there were many – most people seemed to like Ollie. He was keen to know what this man had against him.

There was a roar from behind; the two leads had come out of the theatre together. The crowd fell upon them, demanding autographs. Conrad Abel moved a few feet away; Levon followed. 'What did Ollie do to make you dislike him so much?' he asked bluntly.

'Dislike!' The word was almost spat out. 'I don't dislike the bastard, I hate him. He took Anne out of the show without a moment's notice. She just didn't turn up one night. When I phoned the apartment, the maid said they'd all gone to California. It wasn't just the Mayor he was running away from, but the show's backers. They were insisting I keep Flip Ungar and tell Herbie to get lost when his ankle got better. Blinker found out and wasn't prepared to see his precious son dumped.' The man was virtually apoplectic; spittle was running down his chin. 'I only took Herbie in the first place because Blinker pressurized me into it.'

'I knew nothing about this,' Levon stammered.

'Not many people did.' His fierce expression softened. 'I liked Anne, she's a nice kid, not a bit like the fucking prima donnas – male and female – I usually have to deal with. Ollie's only using her to sell his own kid: "You can have Anne Murray, but only if you take Herbie Blinker with her."' This was said in a perfect imitation of Ollie's New York accent. 'And now I hear they're married. That's a laugh.' He snorted.

'Why is it a laugh?' Levon asked.

'Herbie Blinker slept with five girls from the chorus that I know of. He might well have been through the lot. One got pregnant and had to leave the show. I suspect his fond daddy paid her off.' He snorted again, an ugly sound. 'I suppose Ollie thought it'd be safer if his sex-mad son had a wife: it'd mean no common or garden hoofer could get her claws into him. So the devious bastard arranged for him to marry Anne.'

There was another furore outside the stage door. Flip Ungar had come out and half a dozen young girls were throwing themselves at him. His partner, Rosalind Raines, stood to one side, ignored, and clearly not very pleased about it. She caught Levon's eyes upon her and made a little moue with her brightly painted lips.

Close up, Levon thought she looked familiar, but fireworks were exploding in his brain and he didn't give the woman a second thought. All he could think about was Anne and what had happened to her – and what was going to happen in the future.

'Who was that guy talking to Conrad in the alley?' Olive asked Flip when they turned into 42nd Street. Her name wasn't yet amongst those in the lights that twinkled outside the theatres, but it was fourth down on the posters pasted to the walls: Rosalind Raines.

'I've no idea,' Flip replied.

But Olive never forgot a face and she already knew who the man was: the taxi driver she'd paid to take Annemarie to Bleecker Street all those years ago. He didn't look like a taxi driver now, all done up in a posh suit. How come he knew Conrad Abel?

Oh, what did it matter? All that mattered was she had an important part in a Broadway show. It hurt a bit that Flip was getting all the glory – nobody ever waited outside the stage door for *her* – but it was a small price to pay and she didn't really care. Well, not all that much.

*

'Nowhere,' Ollie Blinker screamed, 'nowhere in the script does it say that Anne is a hooker and Herbie a pimp. Are you trying to turn this into a dirty movie, Collins?'

'No, sir, but Mr Vandervelt thinks the script is too bland. He wants to give it a bit more fizz.' Abe Collins rubbed his perspiring brow with the back of his hand. It was murder having two people yelling directions in his ear: Ollie Blinker during the day; Hughie Vandervelt at night when he watched the rushes.

'Fizz!' Mr Blinker's red face turned purple. 'What the hell's fizz? I want to make an entertaining movie, one that will make people laugh and feel happy. According to the script, Herbie and Anne are at college; they wanna put on a show to raise funds for an operation for a dying kid. The concert's a success, the kid gets better, and Herbie and Anne get married. The End. *The End,*' he repeated forcefully. 'There's no hookers, no pimps, no tight skirts or low-cut frocks, no nightclubs with Anne singing suggestive songs. All the songs are *nice* songs, the sort that folks'll want to sing to their kids. That's why it's called *When Angels Sing,* not *When Angels Sin.* It's gonna be a *nice* movie. Tell Mr Vandervelt to shove *his* script up his scrawny behind. We're using *mine* from now on, otherwise I'll take *my* script to another company and get *them* to make the movie. Understand, Collins?'

'Yessir, Mr Blinker, I understand.'

'This is like having cream cakes shoved down your yapper for the best party of ninety minutes,' Hughie Vandervelt roared that night, as he and Collins watched the rushes. A tall, extremely thin man in his forties, his hair had turned prematurely white. Not that anyone could remember it being any other colour. Hughie Vandervelt wasn't a popular man in Hollywood and his strange hair was put down to the fact he had acid running through his veins instead of blood. 'It makes me wanna puke. It'll make the entire audience wanna puke. It's got no soul. It's got no *fizz.*'

'Mr Blinker said he's pulling out if we don't do it his way,' Abe said nervously.

'He won't pull out,' Vandervelt sneered. 'He's already spent too much and he can't afford to start again with someone else.'

'I can't see Mr Blinker going with the hooker and pimp line, Mr Vandervelt, sir, I really can't.' Abe was desperate. He couldn't stand another day like today – and yesterday and all the days before. Being a movie director wasn't quite the dream job that people supposed. 'He wants a blue skies movie where the sun never stops shining and nothing bad ever happens.'

Hughie reached for the script to make more changes, but must have thought better of it. He withdrew his hand. 'In that case, let him have it,' he said contemptuously. 'I can always disown his stupid movie. But wrap it up as fast as you can, Collins. We've already wasted enough time.' He snapped his fingers, as if expecting his director to wrap it up there and then.

But Ollie Blinker refused to be rushed. He demanded an orchestra to accompany the songs, dismissing the piano in a rage. 'It's pathetic,' he screamed. 'Pathetic.' He wanted more costumes, more extras, grander sets. Staircases had to be built or borrowed from other companies' sets, a balcony was required for Herbie to swing from, a church for Anne to sing in, a hospital for the kid who was sick, and an angel in full regalia to visit him during the night he thinks he's about to die, while a choir sang full-throated in the background.

Abe Collins, used to shooting Hughie Vandervelt's tawdry, dimly-lit movies in a couple of rooms with a single camera and a handful of actors, and taking no more than a fortnight to do it, was beginning to enjoy himself. This was what being a director was all about; using his imagination, improvising now and then, creating something that might not exactly be a work of art, but was a million times better than the crap he normally churned out. Mr Blinker, whom he was beginning to like, provided another two cameras, extra lighting, and an overhead gantry.

Hughie Vandervelt had stopped watching the rushes, but fumed at the ever-increasing costs – Blinker paid for the equipment, but he was responsible for the wages of the actors and crew. Costs were mounting daily, he complained between gritted teeth. Abe pretended to sympathize, but privately he was indifferent to everything apart from the making of *When Angels Sing*.

'How Ollie and Herbie can play golf in this weather is beyond me,' Lizzie panted. She wore a full-length kaftan, a straw hat as big as an umbrella, and sunglasses, leaving the minimum amount of skin exposed. It was Sunday afternoon and the movie had been put on hold for the day. Ollie would have continued, but the crew had mutinied and insisted on a break.

Anne said it was beyond her, too. The men had really taken to Los Angeles, but the women couldn't get used to the place. With Lizzie, it was the heat. She couldn't bear to go out and remained in the house all day on her own, feeling lonely without her New York friends. Anne didn't mind the heat, but she didn't like making movies.

She and Lizzie were sitting in canvas chairs on the patio at the back of the house where the sun only shone in the morning and it was as cool as it was possible to be on a Los Angeles afternoon. The heart-shaped pool shone brightly in the distance. Anne wouldn't have minded a swim, but she didn't want to desert Lizzie: Sunday was the only day she had company.

'How's the movie going?' Lizzie enquired. 'Whenever I ask Ollie, he just goes into a tirade about that Vandervelt chap, and Herbie says he doesn't know.'

'I don't know, either,' Anne confessed. 'It's such a muddle, you can't tell. The scenes aren't shot in the order they're in the script, but all over the place. Yesterday, we did a scene from the middle and one at the end – it was something to do with having the choir present and saving money having to hire them again. I much prefer the theatre. At least you know where you are.' The worst thing was the dance sequences were frequently interrupted when she was in full flow and she had to do them again and again, sometimes commencing halfway through a number, which meant she was unable to get back into the swing of things. It bothered her so much that the headaches she thought she'd got rid of had started again.

Lizzie nodded. 'The theatre's live, the people are real, there's a lovely atmosphere. A movie just doesn't compare. Oh, Anne,' she said with a throb in her voice, 'I don't know about you, but I badly miss New York.'

'So do I.' She missed it so much she wanted to cry when she woke up and saw through the window the blue waters of the Pacific rolling on to a golden beach, when she would have far preferred Central Park with the sun shining, the rain falling, or the entire park covered with snow. She missed the shops, she missed Lev, but most of all she missed the theatre, in particular the last few weeks of *Roses are Red* after Herbie had sprained his ankle and Flip Ungar had become her partner.

She would never have said it to a soul, certainly not Herbie's mother, but dancing with Flip had been sheer bliss, like dancing with another version of herself, who knew exactly what to do next and how to do it. She hadn't been looking forward to Herbie's ankle getting better and having to dance with him again. In a way, Herbie was a liability. She worried all the time he'd make a mistake and she'd have to cover it with a mistake of her own so no one would notice. Flip never made mistakes.

Then, one night in February, very late, Ollie had got into one of his terrible rages and began to curse Conrad Abel for all he was worth. 'It's all his fault, he's behind it,' he yelled at Lizzie, 'But I'm not going to let him get away with it. I'll get the bastard, you'll see.'

No one except his family – and Anne – knew about Ollie's rages, the way he threw things about and kicked the furniture. When people were there, he was all sweetness and light. Once, he'd smashed one of Lizzie's paintings against the wall, breaking the frame and making her cry. The rages never lasted long, though, and afterwards he was as nice as pie.

When he was cross, Anne would shut herself in the bedroom till he'd stopped shouting, but on that particular night she was already in bed and was surprised when there was a knock on the door and Ollie said, 'Can I speak to you for a minute, honey?' He no longer sounded mad, but then he was never angry with her.

He came in and told her to start packing first thing in the morning. 'We're going to California,' he told her. 'I've been planning it for a long while, just felt like a change from New York. I'm gonna produce movies.'

'But what about the show?' she protested. 'I can't let everyone down.'

'You won't be,' he said abruptly. 'It's closed. I've just had a phone call. The backers have dropped out.'

'But we were doing so well.' She'd understood they were booked solid for six months. Did it matter if the backers had dropped out so late in the day? It didn't make sense. And why tell Ollie rather than her or Herbie? It was nothing to do with him. But Ollie didn't look in the mood to explain.

The next morning, she packed her clothes, leaving most behind for Christina to send on. Lizzie positively refused to give up the apartment and Christina was being kept on as caretaker, though Eric would have to find another chauffeur's job after he'd arranged to have the Deusenberg put away in a long-term garage.

Anne wished she could have said goodbye to the Schultzes and wanted to ring the theatre to speak to someone, but the telephone in the lounge didn't appear to be working and Ollie was monopolizing the one in the den.

Eric drove them to Grand Central. Lizzie was almost in tears, but Herbie was his usual sunny self. Ollie had recovered his temper and showed them a script he'd commissioned. 'It's called *When Angels Sing*. It only arrived the other day. When I heard about the backers pulling the plug on the show I decided it was now or never. I've been putting it off long enough; it's time for action.' He smacked his lips, pleased with himself.

'I think I'll make another cold drink,' Lizzie said now. She removed her hat and fanned herself with it. Her hair was soaking. 'One of these days I'll melt away to nothing.' She went indoors.

Anne felt genuinely sorry for Lizzie, who was now her mother-in-law and had always been so kind. She reached for a magazine that lay under her chair and saw it was open on the page that carried a photo of her and Herbie's wedding.

It had been a shock, Herbie asking her to marry him. They'd been in Los Angeles only a couple of weeks and were by the pool studying the script of *When Angels Sing* when, all of a sudden, he'd fallen on one knee beside her and proposed marriage.

'But why?' she'd asked, not very romantically.

'Because I love you,' he'd said, brushing away the lock of blond hair that always hung over his eyes. 'And you're already a member of the family. Why not become a fully paid-up member – Mrs Herbie Blinker? You'll never want for anything, darling. It means I'll stop worrying that one day you'll go away, desert us, and I'm not sure if I can live without you. Don't you love me just the teensiest little bit?'

'Well, yes,' she conceded.

'There then,' he said gleefully. 'If we love each other, the obvious thing for us to do is get married.'

'No.' Anne shook her head. 'I don't want to marry you,' she said vehemently. 'I don't want to marry anyone. I'll never get married; never, never, *never.*'

Herbie had been taken aback by the force of her words. 'Whyever not, darling?' he asked gently. When she didn't reply, he went on. 'Something bad happened to you in the past, didn't it? I think I understand. If you're worried about a . . . a certain side of marriage, then I promise on my heart I won't touch you till you're ready.'

'But what if I'm never ready?' she cried.

'I'll take a chance on that, darling. There's more to marriage than just the things people do in bed. There's loving and caring and just being there for somebody.' He kissed her hand. 'Please marry me, Anne. I love you so very much.'

How could she have refused? Six weeks later they were married and nothing, apart from her name, had changed. Even then, everybody still referred to her as Anne Murray – the name that would appear on the screen when – if – *When Angels Sing* was shown in the cinema. She still slept in the same bedroom on her own and Herbie slept in his.

But she belonged, she had a family, and she didn't feel quite so lost.

Three weeks later, the movie was finished. 'That's a wrap,' Abe Collins shouted when the very last scene was shot. That night, they had a party on the set. Anne was relieved it was all over, at least, that her part in it was. All sorts of things had to be done to the film before it was ready to be seen by an audience. As far as she was concerned, she never wanted to make another movie for as long as she lived, but Ollie was already talking about the next one. It made her feel physically sick. She desperately wished Lev were there to talk to.

It was another Sunday afternoon and Ollie and Herbie were playing golf again. 'I never thought a game like golf would appeal to either of them,' Lizzie complained. 'It's too strenuous. They're a pair of lazy buggers, and until now all they've ever played is pool or darts.' It was June and the weather was getting even warmer. Lizzie was talking about going to New York for a while.

'It'll be just as hot there,' Anne warned. New York summers were notorious for their blistering heat.

'Not as much as it is here.' California had done Lizzie no good at all. She looked pale and quite ill. 'Anyway, the walls of the apartment are so thick it always felt quite cool inside. Trouble is, I don't like deserting Ollie.'

A few days later, Lizzie changed her mind about deserting Ollie when a packet of photographs of him and Herbie cavorting in a pool with two buxom blondes, all of them naked, came through the post.

'Funny sort of golf,' Lizzie sneered when she showed them to Ollie, who blamed Hughie Vandervelt for sending them. He and Lizzie had a flaming row that lasted most of the night. Herbie shut himself in his bedroom.

Next morning, Lizzie told Anne that she was leaving Ollie and returning to live permanently in New York. 'We're not getting divorced – believe it or not, I still love the wretched man and he loves me – but from now on we're going to lead separate lives and just see each other occasionally. Are you coming with me, Anne?'

'To New York?' Anne asked, startled.

'Where else, pet?' Lizzie looked triumphant. 'Any other time, I'd've cried meself to death over what Ollie's done, but it doesn't feel nearly so bad if it means I can escape from Los Angeles.'

'But Herbie and I have only been married a few months.' Nevertheless, a little worm of hope crawled into Anne's brain. She didn't care that Herbie had been unfaithful.

'So what, pet? Herbie's my son and I know I shouldn't say this, but he's let you down, just like Ollie did me. You don't have to get divorced: no one will see anything odd about a wife pursuing her stage career in one part of the country, while the husband makes movies in another. Come on, pet,' she urged, eyes shining in a face that was no longer pale, 'pack your bags and we'll go home together.'

Christina was delighted to see them back. The Duesenberg was resurrected from the garage and Eric returned to work for the Blinkers. Lizzie immediately threw herself into the campaign to elect Franklin Delano Roosevelt as the next President of the United States. Not only had he promised the country a New Deal, but had vowed to repeal Prohibition.

For the first few days, all Anne did was stroll dreamily through Central Park where children played and lovers kissed and people picnicked or slept inside the long shadows that spread over the grass, breathing in the fresh scent of flowers, the smell of cut grass and the hint of cigars. She was pleased to discover that Mr Schultz had got a job and no longer lived in the Hoovervilles. Lev came to the apartment for dinner and she described to him the horrors of Los Angeles compared to the pleasures of New York.

One morning, she woke up to the smell of greasepaint and the sound of a thousand feet tapping away – possibly the remnant of a lovely dream that had lost itself in sleep. She jumped out of bed, threw on some clothes, and caught a cab to 42nd Street. *That* was where she belonged, not just in New York, but Broadway: theatreland. As the cab neared its destination, she felt the same rush of excitement as she did while waiting for the curtain to go up or was about to do a number that would stop the show.

She alighted from the cab when the driver turned into 42nd Street from Times Square and looked to see what was on: *Girl Crazy* with Ginger Rogers and Ethel Merman; *Mourning Becomes Electra*, a new play by Eugene O'Neill. Her eyes popped when she saw the posters outside the Classic for *Roses are Red*. 'But Ollie said it was closing,' she said aloud. She walked up and down in front of the theatre, studying the posters. Flip Ungar had third billing after Eric Carrington and Patricia Peters, followed by Rosalind Raines. There was no mention of Zeke Penn. It was too early for the box office to be open, but there was no doubt that the theatre was still in business. *Roses are Red* hadn't closed. Ollie had lied.

Why?'

'Because Herbie was about to be dumped, that's why,' Lev explained when she went to see him in his office. She hoped she wasn't interrupting anything important and was relieved when he appeared extremely pleased to see her. In return, she wanted to cover his face with a hundred kisses. 'Conrad Abel told me. He didn't want Herbie to be hurt, so he decided to move his entire family to California.'

'*I* wasn't part of his family, not then,' Anne said indignantly. 'I could have gone later when my understudy was ready to take my place.' She frowned. 'I might not have gone at all. Ollie didn't give us time to make up our minds.'

'He did that deliberately, darling. It was imperative that you went with them because Herbie needed you. He'd never have got as far as he did in the theatre without you.'

'But he's much better in movies than me, much more natural.

It didn't bother him when we had to shoot scenes over and over again.' Her face broke into a delighted smile. 'That means he and Ollie won't mind that I've come back to New York, will they?'

'Not all that much, no.'

They both decided that Ollie wasn't nearly as bad as Conrad Abel painted him, or as nice as they'd always thought him, but somewhere in between. He was still Anne's father-in-law and Levon's friend.

Anne was beginning to feel restless. Her feet itched to dance and her throat to sing. It was a relief when Conrad Abel called and invited her to dinner.

'I'm leaving *Roses are Red* in the fall,' he announced during the meal. 'I've been asked to produce a new show, *Orchids for My Lady*. It opens in December and I'd like you for the leading lady. Flip Ungar's already accepted the leading man's part. You wouldn't have to audition; I just know you'd be perfect.' He flicked the ash of his cigar onto the carpet. 'Think about it, Anne. I need to have your decision at the very earliest.'

'You can have it now,' she said, her voice thick with excitement. 'It's yes.' She couldn't wait to get back on the stage. 'Yes, yes, yes.'

Chapter 11

1935

'Mammy, why can't I have a bed of me own?'

'My, Megan; say *my* own, not me own.'

'Mammy, why can't I have a bed of *my* own?' Megan repeated with a smirk.

'Because we haven't got the room.'

'It could go in the corner.'

This was true, except it would leave no space to move around. 'I can't afford a new bed,' Mollie said.

Megan pouted. 'Joe and Tommy have beds of their own.'

'That's because they're boys and they have a room to themselves.' Mollie rolled her eyes in exasperation. 'If I've had this argument with you once, Megan, I must have had it a million times. There isn't the room to put a bed and, if there was, I haven't the money to buy one.'

'I'm fed up being kicked all night long.'

'So am I and so is Brodie, but I'm afraid there's nothing I can do about it.' It was extremely uncomfortable sleeping three to a bed. They took turns: two at the top and one at the bottom, the worst place of all because you had two pairs of feet attacking you. This week it was Megan's turn to sleep at the bottom, hence the demand for another bed.

'It's all right for us, Megan,' Brodie said quietly. 'All we have to do is go to school. Mammy has to look after Mr Pettigrew every morning and do lots of housework. She needs her sleep more than we do.'

Mr Pettigrew was a ninety-year-old curmudgeon. His fond

granddaughter, Philomena, his only relative, didn't like leaving him alone all day when she went to work. Another woman took over from Mollie at one o'clock and stayed until Philomena returned home.

'Huh!' Megan stalked out of the room, but Mollie knew she'd soon be back to say sorry.

She wiped her forehead with the back of her hand – the day was oppressively hot – and went into the parlour to make sure Joe and Tommy were all right playing in the street. Joe was very timid and easily bullied – once, he'd had his shoes stolen – but Tommy did his best to keep an eye on his elder brother. Four-year-old Tommy had taken to street life as if he'd been born to it, which he had in a way, as she'd been living in Turnpike Street when he'd arrived.

It was the school holidays and the street was full of kids, ranging from the clean to those who hadn't seen soap and water for quite a while. Either they were over-dressed in thick jerseys and trousers, quite unsuitable for the weather, or they wore hardly anything at all, just a pair of shorts or a skimpy frock. One boy wore wellies that were far too big and flopped against his pitifully bandy legs. Some women looked after their children as best they could, but others just gave up, not just on the children, but on themselves. Life was just one long, wretched struggle, as they tried to survive from one day to the next.

Her own boys were playing 'tin can' football with two lads of about the same age from the house opposite. It was the bigger lads who caused the trouble.

The sleeves on Joe's shirt were much too short. It was time to turn it into a proper short-sleeved shirt. And Megan was growing out of her only decent summer frock and there was no more hem to let down. Mollie wondered if she could add a band of ribbon or a frill before Megan noticed her knees were showing and demanded a new frock. It was August; in a few weeks' time the summer would be over and Megan and Joe would need warmer clothes when they returned to school in September.

She sighed. It meant a visit to Paddy's Market and she resented dressing her children in other children's cast-offs, although it had seemed fun when she and Agatha used to do it for themselves. Poor Brodie and Tommy were doubly unfortunate, as they inherited the cast-offs that Megan and Joe had grown out of. Not that Brodie seemed to mind, and Tommy had yet to start school and didn't care what he wore.

Irene appeared with a shopping bag. She saw Mollie in the window, took out a package, and waved it exultantly. 'Mince,' she shouted. 'Only a penny a pound in Maxwell's.'

Mollie opened the door to let her in. 'How old is it?' she asked.

'I didn't ask, luv, but it looks quite fresh.' She opened the package. The meat was more grey than pink. Maxwell's butcher's, known locally as Mucky Max's, had a terrible reputation and was only frequented by the grindingly poor. It was rumoured that the rabbits they sold were, in all probability, cats. The first time Dandelion had disappeared, Mollie had a horrible feeling he'd ended up at Mucky Max's, but Dandelion had returned quite safely. Now no one worried when he took off for long periods, apart from Brodie, who cried herself to sleep every night until he came back, fatter and more smug than when he'd left. Mollie could only assume he had two homes.

She looked doubtfully at the meat now, wondering what sort of animal it had been before being slaughtered and fed through the mincer. 'I'd sooner not use it, Irene,' she said. 'I'll make potato cakes for our tea.'

'Oh, don't be daft, Mollie,' Irene said scathingly. 'Growing kids need meat. It makes stronger bones. I'll get the veg ready for a nice stew. I bought an onion while I was at it.' She went into the kitchen, singing at the top of her voice.

Mollie returned to the parlour to keep an eye on the boys. Although she loved her mother-in-law, there were times when Irene set her teeth on edge. She didn't want the children eating suspect meat; they weren't so poor they needed to shop at Maxwell's. They could at least afford fresh mincemeat from an identifiable animal. But, as usual, she'd given in, though it seemed cowardly to risk the family's health rather than make an issue of it.

The trouble was Irene was very touchy and there could easily have been a row, followed by a bad atmosphere for days.

She froze. A lad she'd never seen before had jumped on Joe's back and seemed intent on dragging him to the ground, but was foiled by Tommy, who kicked his bottom with considerable force. The lad fell off and Tommy faced him, fists raised, an infant pugilist ready for a fight, but the attacker just wandered off, rubbing his behind.

Mollie smiled. Tommy wanted to be a bobby when he grew up, just like the dad he'd never known. Irene had shown her a photograph of Tom when he was a little boy and Tommy was so like him it made her want to cry. Irene made a desperate fuss of him. In her eyes, her youngest grandchild was another Tom and could do no wrong. She completely ignored the other children, except to criticize, in particular Megan, whom she didn't appear to like. But Megan wasn't prepared to be disliked without doing something about it. She turned against her grandma and didn't hesitate to answer back whenever Irene said something she didn't like. The first time this happened, Irene had slapped her and Megan had slapped her back. Mollie had given her a good telling-off, then done the same to her mother-in-law when there was no one else around.

'You're never, *never* to hit one of my children again,' she said angrily. She was shaking inside. 'If they need to be smacked, *I'll* do it, not you.'

'That Megan is a cheeky little madam,' Irene said, just as angrily.

'I know she is, but you must stop picking on her all the time, telling her to blow her nose, sit up straight, take her elbows off the table, walk not run, not speak until she's spoken to. She's only a little girl, Irene, an extremely irritating, arrogant little girl, but her heart's in the right place.'

'Mammy,' Megan said from the door now. She came into the parlour, oozing martyrdom.

'Yes, darlin'?' She knew what was to come.

'I don't really want you to buy another bed. I know you can't afford it and there isn't the room. I don't mind being kicked all night, honest.'

'I know, love.' Mollie held out her arms and Megan ran into them. 'We'll be able to afford a new bed one of these days, I promise.'

'Why can't Grandma turn the parlour into a bedroom?' Megan enquired in a slightly injured tone. 'And she has a big bed and the biggest bedroom all to herself. It's not fair. My friend Sheila Nelson sleeps in the parlour with her sister.'

Mollie didn't answer. She'd often wondered the same thing herself. Perhaps Irene didn't realize how uncomfortable they were, or she didn't want to get rid of the over-stuffed settee that closely resembled a hippopotamus, the glass-fronted cabinet full of dishes that were never used – just like the parlour itself – or the piano that the children weren't allowed to touch, though they did when Irene was out and Mollie didn't stop them. They weren't doing any harm and what was a piano for except to play?

'Grandma's making something really smelly in the kitchen,' Megan whispered. 'I hope it's not for tea.'

Mollie groaned inwardly. 'If it is, you must promise not to make a face when you eat it,' she whispered back. 'Pretend it's really nice.'

'Yuck!' Megan pushed her plate away after the first mouthful. She made the most dreadful face imaginable. 'It's horrible.' From his perch on the sideboard, Dandelion watched with interest, hoping for some scraps.

'Eat it up this minute,' Irene commanded. 'There's kids in this street who'd give their eye teeth for a stew like that.'

'No, they wouldn't.' Megan turned away and managed to make an even worse face. 'It tastes like worms.'

'Megan—' Irene began, but Mollie interrupted.

'She's right, Irene. It doesn't taste very nice. What about you others, do you like it?'

Brodie and Joe shook their heads, but Tommy said, 'I like worms,' and shovelled a spoonful into his mouth.

'There!' Irene said triumphantly, as if this proved something.

Mollie removed Tommy's plate. 'You're not to eat it, any of you. I'll go and buy some fishcakes and chips.' She couldn't afford fish. 'How about you, Irene? Would you like some?'

'No, thanks. I'll eat this.' To Mollie's horror, two huge tears were slowly making their way down the woman's wrinkled cheeks. 'I was only trying to do me best,' she sobbed. 'Trying to make up for the fact I don't contribute a penny towards keeping this place going. You pay for everything, Mollie, even the rent, when you've already got four kids and yourself to feed. I thought it'd help if I made dead cheap meals.' She sniffed tragically. 'I'm a burden, aren't I? A terrible burden. If it weren't for you, I'd have to go on the parish.'

Mollie hastily reached for her purse and sent all four children to the chip shop. 'Buy six of everything and be as quick as you can coming back so it won't get cold,' she told them.

'I'll have to carry them, won't I, Mammy, because I'm the oldest?'

'Yes, Megan, but try not to get grease on your frock.'

'Irene,' she said when the children had gone, 'you're not a burden. You're Tom's mother and I love you, we all do.' She doubted if she was speaking for Megan. 'We're poor, but not so poor we have to buy our meat from Maxwell's – or use leftover vegetables from St John's Market.' Irene often turned up with squashed tomatoes and potatoes that had rolled onto the floor, or bruised fruit.

'I thought I was helping,' Irene wailed.

'You are. I don't know what I'd do without you. How could I look after Mr Pettigrew if you weren't here for Tommy – for all the children when they're on holiday from school?' But while she was away, she was worried sick what might be going on between Irene and Megan, given that she wasn't there to act as referee.

'I used to think meself so well off when the boys sent money.'

'Well, they can't now, can they?' Brian had lost his job when the Liverpool Tool Company closed down. Mike hadn't had a wage rise in years, and Enoch's furniture business wasn't doing nearly as well as it used to. There were over two million unemployed in Britain and it had become virtually impossible to get a job. Mollie, who read *The Times* to Mr Pettigrew every morning, knew it had all started with the Stock Market crash in America in 1929. The ripples had spread, affecting the entire Western world. She felt lucky to have a roof over her head, a pension of twelve and sixpence a week, and the ten shillings she earned from sitting with Mr Pettigrew. Agatha's mother, Mrs Brophy – now Mrs Raymond – had put her in touch with the company she'd sewed gloves for and she earned a little extra from that. Put together, it meant they could just about scrape by. She even managed to put a few coppers aside each week to save for the children's clothes.

'I really appreciate you making the meals,' she said to Irene. 'I'd never manage to do the cooking on top of everything else.' She *would* have managed, but she wasn't going to admit it to Irene. 'But I'd sooner you stopped buying meat in Maxwell's.'

'All right, luv.' Irene looked pathetically grateful. She spent the time until the children came with the chips bemoaning the fact that Tom was dead, yet it was almost five years since he'd gone to meet his maker. Mollie just listened, making little comforting noises when it seemed necessary. She preferred to think of Tom when he was alive, full of energy and plans for the future.

After tea, she took the family for a walk along Scotland Road. Joe and Brodie held her hands, while Megan marched confidently in front, as if she were leading a procession. Tommy trailed behind, kicking stones and making grotesque faces at himself in shop windows.

It was cooler now and the sun was slowly sinking. The salty air felt fresh and invigorating. Mollie took a huge sniff. It was a relief to get away from her mother-in-law and the tensions in the house for a while. It had been peaceful when she'd left, but she didn't doubt another crisis would arise before the week was out.

Scotland Road was frantically busy. Trams, packed to the gills, rushed both ways, swaying unsteadily on the tracks. Cars and lorries edged more slowly along. Quite a few shops were still open. A small queue had formed outside Tanner's bakery to buy leftover bread at half-price. There was a pub on every corner, already doing good business. Children, some little more than toddlers, hung outside in the hope of cadging a coin off any drunk who might appear, though it was a bit early for that. They'd still be there at closing time, poor little mites, in filthy, ragged clothes, their feet bare, their eyes huge in their too-old faces. Mollie thought of the stew that she'd only recently thrown away and felt guilty. Her own children were immeasurably better fed and better dressed in comparison, and her own life was more comfortable than that of most women. Those lucky enough to have a job worked for twelve hours or more in stinking factories, or laundries where it was almost too hot to breathe.

A crowd of men pushed noisily past, half on the pavement, half in the road, their heavy boots beating against the cobbled surface. Drivers sounded their horns, angry at this invasion of their territory. One of the men slowed down and began to walk alongside Mollie. She felt Joe shrink against her fearfully.

'Hello, Moll,' the man said with a roguish grin. He was an attractive individual of about her own age, as thin as a post, with black curly hair and smiling brown eyes. He wore a clean, threadbare shirt and corduroy trousers tied up with rope.

'Oh, hello, Harry, I didn't realize it was you. Where are you off to?' More men passed, clearly in a hurry. One said, 'Get a move on, Harry. Can't you forget the women for five bloody minutes?'

'The blackshirts are marching along Vauxhall Road, Moll. Me and me mates are off to tear them up for arse paper.' His brown eyes sparkled. 'Would you like to come along?'

'With four kids?'

'It's never too early to learn about politics, Moll.'

'Politics is one thing, fighting blackshirts is something else altogether.' But she didn't doubt that Megan and Tommy would have been willing to have a go.

'Never mind, then. See you, Moll.' He strutted away, full of himself, shoulders back ready for a fight.

Mosley.' Mosley was the leader of the British Union of Fascists to which the blackshirts belonged.

'Me, I wouldn't work five minutes for a bastard like that.' He leapt upon a tin and crushed it with his boots, as if it were Oswald Mosley's head, then continued to walk, like a child, with one foot in the gutter and the other on the pavement, hopping from one to the other.

'Well, you're not me; you haven't got four children and a mother-in-law to feed. The money I get puts bread on the table and that's all I care about.'

'There's such a thing as dying on your feet and living on your knees,' he said a trifle pompously, reminding her of Tom.

It was her turn to laugh. 'For goodness' sake, Harry. I'm not working for Hitler or Mosley, just a ninety-year-old man who can hardly walk. Sometimes, I worry he'll die and I'll lose the ten bob a week. I just hope he stays alive until I don't need the money any more.'

'I like it when you laugh.' He stood in front of her. Mollie's stomach lurched at the look in his eyes. They'd reached the end of the street where the lamp hadn't yet been lit and the cobbles glistened in the pale moonlight. Before she realized what was happening, he was kissing her on the lips. She pulled away a fraction later than she should have.

'Don't do that!' she said sharply.

'Didn't you like it?' He sounded surprised.

'No.'

She turned on her heel and walked quickly back to the house. She didn't look back. When she got in, she discovered Irene had gone to bed, in a huff no doubt. There was a cup of faintly warm tea in the pot and she took it into the parlour. If she didn't finish both gloves tonight, it would prey on her mind and she'd never sleep. She lit the gas mantel, drew the curtains and discovered her heart was racing. Harry Benedict was only the second man in her life to kiss her like that and she felt ashamed. 'Tom,' she groaned for no reason at all. 'Oh, Tom.'

Her hands were shaking too much even to thread the needle,

let alone sew. There was blood on her palm where she'd pricked it; she'd wash it later. 'I don't love him,' she whispered, 'but he makes me feel like a woman.' It was a long time since that had happened, since a man had wanted her and told her she looked nice. Tom used to say that she was beautiful.

The door opened and Brodie crept in. Her little face was flushed and she'd been crying. 'Dandelion hasn't come home,' she said in a subdued voice. 'I rattled his saucer on the step for ages, but he still didn't come. Grandma gave him her worms to eat, and I heard him being sick in the yard. I think he might be dead.'

Mollie lifted her daughter on to her knee; she felt hot and clammy. 'It wasn't really worms, darlin'; it was mincemeat, though not very nice. It was probably some other food he'd eaten that made him sick.' Dandelion was a terrible scavenger. 'But he'll come back. Doesn't he always come back?'

'Yes but, Mammy, I worry about him something awful.'

'I know you do, Brodie. We all worry.' But not as much as Brodie, who loved Dandelion as much as any mother loved her child. Mollie dreaded that he might come to some harm, more for Brodie's sake than her own. She was too sensitive for her own good, Joe too. Both were easily hurt and not fitted to live in Turnpike Street where children needed to be hardy and resilient like Megan and Tommy. Brodie's sweet, sad face plucked at her heartstrings. 'Tell you what, darlin', shall I make us a cup of cocoa?' It wasn't often she had time alone with her youngest daughter and she'd finish the gloves tomorrow.

'You're late,' Mr Pettigrew snapped when she arrived the following day. He said the same thing every morning and Mollie always gave the same reply.

'No, I'm not. It said quarter to nine on the clock in London Road. Your own clock must be fast.' The grandfather clock, showing ten past nine, was squeezed between a giant sideboard – its shelves almost reached the ceiling – and an equally giant wardrobe. Mr Pettigrew's bed, which he only left to visit the lavatory, had been placed beneath the window. A round table at the side was covered with a dark-brown chenille cloth and heaped with the newspapers he refused to be parted from until they were a month old. Mollie was often obliged to search through them for an item he wanted read to him again.

'Would you like a cup of tea?' she enquired.

'Yes, and make it strong. You know I only like it strong.'

'That's why I always make it strong,' she replied. She went into the kitchen where Philomena had left a tray with two cups and saucers, a bowl of sugar cubes, a small jug of milk and a plate of biscuits, which her grandfather always ate with great relish. With its bright yellow walls and pretty flowered curtains, the room couldn't have been more different from the one in which Mr Pettigrew was living out the last few years of his long life, but he refused to have a single item of furniture removed or the horrid olive-green wallpaper with navy-blue stripes changed for something brighter. He even preferred the ceiling, which looked as if it hadn't been painted since the last century, to stay the same disgusting dirty yellow. Philomena, a spinster of about forty who part-owned a jewellery shop in Southport, would inherit the big house in Copperas Hill when he passed away.

Mollie returned with the tea. 'You could stand your spoon up in this,' she said cheerfully, but was given a sour look in return. 'Which paper would you like me to start with this morning?' she asked.

'The *Herald*,' he said grumpily. He never addressed her by her name. 'What does the headline say?'

'"Hitler bans German–Jewish marriages,"' she read.

'Quite right, too.' He peered at her with old eyes that could hardly see. 'Are you Jewish?'

'No, I'm Irish. Can't you tell by my accent?'

'They're almost as bad, the Irish,' he grumbled.

Mollie resisted the urge to throw the tea in his face, reminding herself that he was a very elderly invalid, and that his sickening views didn't matter. 'George Bernard Shaw is an Irishman,' she said, 'And Keates and Synge and loads of other famous people.' The old bugger liked an argument.

'Shaw's a playwright.' He sniffed disdainfully. 'I could never stand the theatre, couldn't see the point of it. The other two are poets and I could never see the point of poetry either.'

'Is there anything you do like, Mr Pettigrew? If so, I'll try to think of an Irishman who does it.'

The glimmer of a smile passed over his skull-like face, remarkably unlined for a ninety-year-old. He had a full head of dark-grey hair that still retained streaks of black. His hearing was perfect and his brain razor-sharp; only his eyes and his legs no longer worked as well as they might. He must feel frustrated, lying in bed day after day, but nothing could excuse his monstrous opinions.

'I have to go to the lavatory,' he announced.

Mollie buried her head in the paper and didn't watch as he attempted to get up; he couldn't abide to be helped. She could hear him grunting as he struggled to make his legs reach the floor.

'Dressing gown,' he barked. 'That stupid girl's hung it behind the door.' By 'girl', he meant Philomena. The dressing gown was supposed to be left at the foot of the bed so he could easily reach it.

She fetched the dressing gown, gave it to him, and buried her head again in the paper while he endeavoured to put it on. Then he shuffled out of the room to the lavatory that Philomena had had installed on the ground floor especially for him.

'The sun's out,' he said when he came back. She thought there was a wistful note in his crusty voice.

'Would you like to sit in the front room? It'll be lovely and sunny in there.' He lived at the back looking out over a small yard, which the sun only reached very early in the morning and never in winter. 'I could read to you there and we could watch the traffic pass by.' He was completely cut off from the world outside and must feel very isolated.

'I have no wish to see the traffic pass by, thank you. I am not a child. I would not be amused at the sight of a bus or a motor car.' He removed his dressing gown with aching slowness and got back into bed. 'Read me the letters in *The Times*, if you please, and remember, should I ever wish to sit in another room, I am perfectly capable of suggesting it myself.'

'I can't help feeling sorry for him,' Mollie said a few hours later to Agatha, who, five years ago, had married Tom's policeman friend, Philip Fraser, and now had two small children; Donnie, three, and Pamela, who was almost twelve months old. After four hours spent with Mr Pettigrew, she wasn't in the mood to go home and face her mother-in-law's wrath, so had caught a tram to her friend's house off West Derby Road. Having witnessed the plight of Tom's widow, Phil had turned down the offer of a police house and rented one instead. If anything happened to him, at least his wife and family would be left with a roof over their heads.

'He sounds horrible.' Agatha shuddered.

'Oh, he's revolting, but I still can't help being sorry for him.' She hadn't come to complain about Mr Pettigrew, but to tell her friend about the events of the night before. 'Irene did her nut when she saw us talking through the window,' she finished indignantly. 'If it hadn't been for her, I probably wouldn't have gone outside. All we did was walk down the street a bit, discussing politics, but now Irene will have a face on her for days.' She didn't mention Harry's kiss. 'She drives me up the wall, Agatha, but I suppose her heart's in the right place. I'm always saying that, aren't I? Irene, Lily, Pauline, all their hearts are in the right place, and our Megan's, too, the little monkey. Yesterday, she was nagging me again for a new bed.'

'I don't know how you stand it, Mollie, I really don't.' Agatha's face creased with sympathy, while trying to prevent Pamela from tearing her hair out by the roots. 'Phil's mam and dad are all right, but I wouldn't fancy living with either of them for very long. His sister lives in Chester, so we don't see all that much of her.'

'I probably wouldn't mind Irene if I didn't see so much of *her*,' Mollie moaned. She couldn't have described exactly how she felt about Tom's mother – a mixture of love, resentment, irritation and admiration for her fighting spirit.

'It's a pity you can't go back to Duneathly. Mind you, I'd be dead upset if you did. I'd miss you horribly.' She put Pamela on the floor and the baby immediately crawled across to Mollie and demanded to be picked up. Mollie hauled her on to her knee.

'You're spoilt, you are,' she told the tiny girl, who immediately made a grab for her hat. 'Is that a new tablecloth, Agatha? It's very pretty.' The cloth was lavender and white gingham with a *broderie anglaise* frill.

'I needed a new one for second best. I got that from Blackler's.'

Mollie couldn't imagine shopping in Blackler's again, even buying anything *new*. She was envious of Agatha, who had a husband and a house of her own, who could buy tablecloths whenever she wanted and clothes for her children that hadn't been worn before. She'd had the same things once and if it hadn't been for Tom's recklessness, she'd have them still.

'I'd better go,' she sighed. 'I only popped in for a minute to get everything off my chest. The later I get home, the angrier Irene will be.'

But when she arrived back at Turnpike Street, Irene greeted her with an enormous smile. 'There's a job going,' she said in a rush, 'and it'd be perfect for you. You know Betsy Evans from across the street?'

'Of course I do.' Betsy was the young girl who'd admired her hat all those years ago. Since Mollie had returned to live there permanently, she and Betsy, now nineteen, had become good friends. Mollie had shown her how to turn an old hat into something really fashionable with the addition of a length of ribbon, a piece of net, or a flower.

'You know where Betsy works, don't you?' Irene went on.

'She's an usherette at the Rotunda,' Mollie said patiently.

'That's right. Well, she came round earlier to say the lady in the box office has decided to retire early; she's got rheumatism somewhere or other and can't sit down for long. They want someone well spoken and trustworthy in her place, so Betsy recommended you to the manager. If you're interested, you're to go there around six o'clock for an interview.' Irene could hardly contain her excitement. 'You'll never guess how much the wages are, Moll.' She paused for effect. 'Thirty-five bloody bob a week! You *are* interested, aren't you?' she added when Mollie stayed silent, too stunned to speak.

'Yes,' she said weakly after a while. 'Of course I'm interested. Oh, but what shall I wear?' she wailed. 'I haven't got anything decent.' She seemed to live in a plain black skirt and an assortment of blouses that had seen better days.

'What about your blue going-away frock?'

'I've already worn that to death and it's going thin under the arms. The pink one shrank in the wash and it's too tight around my chest.' It was Irene's fault; she'd boiled the damn thing. 'I haven't got any more frocks except winter ones and I'd melt to a puddle if I wore one of them in this weather; besides, they're as old as the hills.'

'Here, take this.' Irene pulled off her wedding ring. 'Take it to Uncle's and pawn it, then buy yourself a frock.' It wasn't unusual for Irene to pawn her ring. When Mollie had been expecting Tommy and unable to work, the ring had been in and out of the pawnshop like a yoyo, sometimes accompanied by Mollie's own.

'Have I got time to get to and from Blackler's?'

'Just about. Buy yourself some stockings, too. While you're gone, I'll boil some hot water for you to get washed in. You can use that *eau de cologne* Pauline gave me for Christmas and take one of the little embroidered hankies that Lily got me. Oh, and wear that pearl necklace and earrings you got off your auntie in New York.'

By the time Mollie returned, the children had become aware that something of importance was happening. They crowded around their mother in the kitchen when she stripped down to her pants and bra to get washed.

'Why are you getting washed in the afternoon?' Megan wanted to know.

'I've got an important interview, love.'

239

'What's an interview, Mammy?' Joe enquired.

'A meeting with someone.' She rubbed the flannel under her arms. 'Mammy's meeting a man about a job.'

'A job where?' asked Brodie.

'In the Rotunda Theatre, love.'

'You didn't wash behind your ears, Mam,' Tommy said accusingly. 'You're always telling me off for not washing behind me ears.'

'*My* ears, Tommy,' Megan said haughtily. 'Not *me* ears.'

'Fuck off,' Tommy said.

Mollie stopped washing herself and stared aghast at her son. 'Tommy Ryan, how dare you? How dare you use that word? If your dad was alive, he'd put you over his knee and spank you.'

'What's wrong with it?' Tommy stared belligerently at his mother. 'Everyone says fuck off.'

'I doubt that very much, Tommy. Some boys might say it, but they're very wrong to do so.' She'd have to keep an eye on him in the future, or he'd turn into a proper little scally. 'You're not ever, *ever*, to say it again. Do you hear me?'

'Yes, Mam.' He looked torn between telling her to fuck off again or bursting into tears, something he only did once in a blue moon, as he was too tough for tears. She was glad when he started to cry, though didn't have time to comfort him.

Irene came to the rescue. 'He probably doesn't know the meaning of the word.' She took Tommy's hand, which was filthy, and led him out of the kitchen. 'Come on, lad. Give your mammy a bit of space while she finishes getting washed. You've only got another thirty-five minutes, Mollie,' she warned. 'It won't look good if you're late.'

'I'm nearly ready.'

The frock she'd got from Blackler's wasn't as pretty as some they'd had – beige moygashel with a collar, short sleeves, a gently flaring skirt, and a narrow belt – but it was smarter than most and it suited Aunt Maggie's pearls.

'How do I look?' she asked the children, who'd been following her around the house.

'Beautiful, Mammy,' Megan and Brodie said together.

'Nice,' said Joe.

'You look the gear, Mam.' Tommy burst into tears again.

Irene ushered her out of the house. 'Good luck, luv, I'll be keeping me fingers crossed till you come back.'

They kissed fondly. 'I love you, Irene,' Mollie said.

'I know you do, Moll, and I love you.'

Chapter 12

1936

There was always a big queue on Saturday night, mainly for the cheapest seats, the wooden benches at the back of the balcony that only cost threepence. The front balcony was sixpence, and the stalls, where the seats were upholstered, were ninepence and a shilling. Everyone wore their best clothes and were always in a particularly good humour as they looked forward to the show, giving every act a rowdy welcome and cheering wildly when it ended, though there were occasional boos for a poor performance.

The buskers entertaining the queue were sometimes better than the acts on stage; Jonty the Juggler, for instance, who worked in insurance during the week; Spit and Spat, who did a brilliant sand dance; John Lloyd, who was only fifteen but had a fine voice.

Mary Blunn, who had a face like a rosy apple, sold faded fruit. In the warmer weather, an ice cream man on a bike did a roaring trade, though the cones had to be eaten quickly as they weren't allowed inside the theatre for fear of the mess they might make on the thick red carpet in the foyer and on the stairs. The foyer was round, like the theatre itself, and the walls were faced with red velvet, the woodwork painted gold. A chandelier glittered on the ceiling.

In the box office, a little cubby-hole behind a sheet of glass, Mollie waited for the doors to open and the queue to come pouring in, which would happen any second now on the dot of half past seven. The performance would begin at eight. Instead of the usual fare – an assortment of singers and acrobats, comedians and magicians – this week the Rotunda was presenting a play: *Maria Marten: Murder in the Red Barn*, starring Tod Slaughter. The theatre had been full to capacity all week, with many patrons coming twice, or even three times to see it.

Mr Samson, the doorman, splendid in his maroon uniform adorned with yards of gold brocade, opened up, and the people streamed inside. For the next half-hour, Mollie was frantically busy as she tore off the different-coloured tickets: yellow for the cheapest seats; blue for the front balcony; red and pink for the stalls. She didn't sell many for the stalls, as the seats could be pre-booked. These rather better dressed personages presented their tickets to Mr Samson, who accepted them with a majestic bow and a quiver of his waxed moustache.

'Hello, Mollie, two for the gods, please.'

'How are you keeping, Daisy?' She'd got to know many of the regulars by name. Daisy O'Connor and her daughter were always near the front of the queue for the second performance on Saturday. 'Next, please,' she sang without waiting for Daisy's reply. There wasn't the time.

By eight o'clock, her fingers aching from counting coins and tearing tickets, the door to the auditorium had closed and the foyer was unnaturally quiet. The orchestra weren't playing their usually lively music, but something darkly dramatic that was more appropriate to the play. Every seat in the house had been sold: any latecomers would be out of luck. Mr Samson had put a sign, 'Theatre Full', on the door.

'Phew!' she said to no one in particular. She flexed her fingers and twisted her head to ease the pain in her neck. Her back hurt. In a minute, she'd sort the individual coins into one-shilling piles and put them into their own separate bags – the farthings and ha'pennies, the pennies and the threepenny bits, and so on – with a label to say how much was in each, then add up the totals. The children considered her something of a wizard to be able to carry out such a complicated task.

'It's easy when you know how,' she told them.

There was a burst of applause from inside the theatre; the

curtain must have gone up, and Tod Slaughter, who played the wicked Squire Corder, would be rubbing his hands gleefully as he confided in the audience the evil deeds he had planned. They responded with a chorus of boos – it was all part of the fun.

Mollie loved her job. She'd been there for seven months and it was almost, although not quite, like being in show business. Some of the stars were very friendly and came round and introduced themselves to the staff when they first arrived. Malvolio the Magician had shown her how he sawed his pretty assistant in half. 'It's all an illusion,' he explained, as if she'd actually thought it real.

The wolf in the Christmas pantomime, *Little Red Riding Hood*, had been *too* friendly. He'd had the cheek to ask her out. 'I'm a married woman,' she'd said indignantly. She'd displayed her left hand. 'Can't you see my ring?'

'One of these days, you'll be sorry you turned me down,' he said frostily. 'You'll kick yourself when I'm topping the bill at the London Palladium.'

'I doubt it.' She also doubted if he'd ever top the bill anywhere. His voice wasn't very strong and a few people had complained the wolf couldn't be heard up in the gods.

She pulled down a black blind over the glass and began to count the money. She was deeply involved, her head buzzing with figures, when she heard the door to the auditorium burst open and the place become full of voices. It must be the first interval.

Fifteen minutes later, silence reigned once again, but not for long. There was a bang on her window. She hastily wrote down a figure before she forgot it, and let up the blind.

'I've come to take you home,' said Harry Benedict. Mollie felt cross with herself when her heart gave a stupid little jerk. He hadn't stopped pursuing her since the night he'd gone after the blackshirts and she'd been silly enough to let him kiss her. He was forever stopping her in the street and suggesting they went for a walk after one of his inevitable meetings. She'd refused every time. Tonight, he wore a polo-necked jersey full of snags and a thin tweed jacket with frayed cuffs. She couldn't see his trousers, but assumed they were just as shabby.

She shook her head. 'I've not finished, and I'm going home with Betsy Evans, like I usually do. She only lives across our street.'

'Betsy's got a date with her young man,' he said smugly. 'She just told me. They're going for a stroll along the Docky; there's a liner there, the *Queen Mary*, on its way to America.'

'America – you mean, New York?' Her heart jerked again, but for a quite different reason.

'I reckon so. I've always wanted to go there. What's the matter, Moll? You've gone quite pale.'

'Nothing – nothing at all. It was just the mention of a ship sailing to America. It reminded me of something, that's all.' Nowadays, she went days, weeks, without thinking about Annemarie. 'Look, Harry, I'm sorry, but I have to get on with this.' She pulled down the blind. For a few minutes, she sat staring into space. The mention of a liner sailing to America had vividly brought back the memory of the *Queen Maia* and the single night she and Annemarie had spent on board together. The following morning she'd gone to buy digitalis and never seen her sister again. Next month, on 1 April, Annemarie would be twenty-five, no longer a girl, but a fully-grown woman. She'd always liked the idea of being born on April Fools' Day, not any old day, but a special one, almost as good as being born at Christmas.

There was a burst of thunder that, at first, she thought was real, then remembered it was part of the play; there'd be lightning, too. The audience screamed. Mollie sighed and continued to count the takings.

She left during the second interval after Betsy had confirmed she was meeting her boyfriend. His name was Dave and he worked in a warehouse on the Dock Road – or the Docky as most people called it. Mollie had already seen the final act and she'd sooner go home and think about Annemarie. Tonight, she seemed very real. She tried to imagine what her sister would look like now that she was eleven years older, but couldn't. In her mind, she would always be thirteen, with long black hair and violet eyes.

If only she could talk to someone about it, but there was only Agatha and she couldn't call on her at such a late hour. Irene knew about her failed attempt to reach New York, but was inclined to come up with a dozen different fates that could have befallen Annemarie, none of them happy and some quite gruesome.

It had started to rain. The lamps were on and their reflections made little orange smudges on the wet pavements. She was hurrying in the direction of Turnpike Street when a voice said, 'Didn't I say I'd take you home?' and Harry Benedict appeared beside her. He must have been waiting outside the theatre all this time.

'Are you following me?' she asked exasperatedly. The raindrops on his dark curly hair shone like diamonds. Why wasn't he wearing a cap?

'It's not safe for a woman on her own in Scottie Road late at night.'

'Don't be an eejit, it's as safe as houses. And it's not at all late; it's only half past nine.'

'Are you in a hurry?'

'Of course I am. It's raining and I'm wearing a new hat.' It had cost nine and eleven in T.J. Hughes's and she didn't want it spoilt.

'Come in here a minute.' He took her arm and almost dragged her into a fish and chip shop. The girl behind the counter looked as if she were about to swoon when she saw him.

'Hello, Harry,' she said coyly. 'What can I do for you?'

'I'd like two teas upstairs as quick as you can, Rita.'

'Straight away, Harry. It'll hardly take a mo.'

'The stairs are over there, Moll.' He gave her a little push.

'I can see them. What the hell are you up to, Harry Benedict?' She climbed the narrow staircase and entered a small room furnished with an assortment of tables and chairs that didn't match. Her heel caught in one of the holes in the lino and she nearly tripped. An elderly man was sitting in a corner eating chips out of a paper bag. He gave them a curt nod. Harry said, 'What'cha, Bill. How're y'diddling?' and got a shrug for his pains. There was salt and pepper and a bottle of vinegar on each table, but no cloths. 'This reminds me of the Ritz,' she said.

'Are you always so sarcastic?' he asked when they sat down.

'No,' she confessed. 'The only person I'm sarcastic with is you.' Then she wondered why. Perhaps it was her way of putting him off, keeping him at a distance. If so, it didn't seem to be working.

Rita, true to her word, arrived immediately with two mugs of tea. 'Would you like some chips, Harry?' She fluttered her lashes invitingly. 'They're on the house.'

'No, ta, Rita. Tea's enough.'

The girl departed, swinging her hips and looking back at Harry to see if he was watching, but his eyes were on Mollie. 'I went to a lecture earlier tonight,' he said.

'What was it about?' she asked, interested.

'Hitler and the threat he poses to Europe.' For once, he looked deadly serious.

'Does Hitler pose a threat to Europe?'

'A really big threat, according to the lecturer, Doctor Stein.' Harry cleared his throat importantly. 'He teaches at some university in London. Germany has done away with the Treaty of Versailles, brought in conscription, and has a big re-armament programme. Hitler wants to expand. He'll take over Austria first, then the Sudetenland. Who knows where he'll go next? Wherever it is, Fascist Italy will go with him.'

'You mean he might try to involve this country?' Mollie could hardly believe what she was hearing.

'Not without a fight.' Harry smacked his lips, as if he couldn't wait.

'A fight? A *war*? But it's hardly five minutes since the last one.' She pushed away the tea and made to get to her feet. 'I don't want to hear this, Harry. I'd sooner not know.'

'You can't close your eyes to it, Moll.' He looked at her regretfully, as if he'd considered her made of sterner stuff.

'I can if I want,' she said stubbornly, but sat down again.

'Trouble is,' Harry said, 'the government's closing its eyes too. This country needs to start re-arming. Instead there's some people talking about appeasement.'

'I'm not sure what that means,' she confessed.

'It means letting Hitler do whatever he wants as long as he doesn't touch us.' Harry looked so angry she didn't like to say that sounded a sensible, if somewhat cowardly approach.

The old man was leaving. 'Would you like a fag, Bill?' Harry offered.

'Wouldn't say no.'

Harry produced a packet of Woodbines. 'Take a couple. Have you got matches, mate?'

'I've got some at home. Ta, Harry, you're a sport.' The old man shuffled away.

'Could we talk about something different?' Mollie asked when his footsteps could be heard slowly descending the stairs.

'All right,' Harry said, lighting a ciggie for himself. 'Let's talk about why you went as white as a sheet when I mentioned the *Queen Mary* was sailing to America. You asked if it was going to New York; have you ever been there?'

'I nearly did – once.' She explained what had happened, leaving out, as she always did, anything to do with the Doctor and finishing, 'I've never seen Annemarie since. My brother, Finn, went to New York to look for her, but had no luck. I've an auntie there who still keeps an eye out. I'd love to go myself one day, but I'll have to wait until the children are older.'

'Perhaps we could go together?'

This seemed so unlikely that Mollie thought it wouldn't hurt to say that perhaps one day they could. She looked around the squalid room with its odds and ends of furniture and dirty, steamed-up windows. Where was Annemarie right now? What sort of room was *she* in? She hoped it was a better one than this, but at least she couldn't fault the company.

'What does your brother Finn do?'

'He's an accountant back in Ireland; a village called Duneathly where we were born. He'd married to Hazel and they have eight

248

children: four boys and four girls.' Mollie smiled. On average, Hazel produced a new baby every fifteen months. 'My young brothers live with them, Thaddy and Aidan, so they've got a houseful.' She'd had photos of the new children, but would love to meet them – and see Hazel again. She hadn't seen her sister-in-law since she'd been to Ireland with Tom, the girls and Joe. Finn had come to Liverpool twice, but that was the only real contact she'd had with her family. 'I really should be going, Harry.'

'I'll ask Rita for some newspaper to protect your hat.' A grin crossed his thin, handsome face. 'See, I can be quite gallant when I want.'

The three Ryan brothers, their wives and children descended on the house on Sunday. Irene was in her element as she served tinned salmon sarnies, with cold stewed apple and cream for afters. Mollie had insisted she use butter, not marge, on the bread.

They hadn't exactly become rich overnight once she'd started work at the Rotunda, but money was no longer the nagging worry it use to be. She'd given up making gloves, though had continued to read to Mr Pettigrew. After a while, it had dawned on her that it was unfair to keep the job, when a man or woman whose need for an extra ten shillings a week was much greater than hers could do it. To her surprise, the old man had been upset to learn she was leaving.

'You read very well,' he said. 'You put expression into the words. It's like listening to a play.'

She didn't remind him that he'd told her he didn't like plays, couldn't see the point in them. She promised to drop in whenever she was in town, but when she'd called one day soon after Christmas, he'd been too unwell to see her.

'He seems to sleep most of the time,' the woman, an ex-nurse who'd taken her place, told her. 'I usually end up reading the papers to meself.'

Three months later, only half listening while Lily and Pauline made digs at each other, Mollie realized how much she missed being kept up to date with the latest news bulletins. From tomorrow, she'd start buying the *Daily Herald*, if only to keep track of what Hitler was up to. All that stuff Harry had come out with last night had really taken her by surprise.

Tom's brothers were talking about the new King, Edward VIII, yet to be crowned. It was rumoured he was having an affair with a married woman who'd divorced one husband. 'The British people are being kept in the dark,' Enoch said indignantly. 'I met this chap the other day who knew another chap who'd just come back from France. He said it's in all the papers over there. She's an American with a dead funny name.'

'What does divorced mean, Mammy?' Megan whispered.

'I'll tell you later. Why don't you play out in the street with your cousins, love?' Mollie whispered back.

'I'd sooner stay here. S'interesting.' Megan was the nosiest child under the sun.

Irene looked just as indignant as Enoch, but for an entirely different reason. 'I don't believe it,' she declared. She was a devout royalist. 'The King would never have an affair, let alone with a woman who's already married.'

The lads groaned.

'Our mam thinks royalty can do no wrong,' Brian snorted. 'They're just human beings, Mam; they go to the lavatory and wipe their arses, just like us ordinary mortals. And have affairs with married women.'

It was Pauline's turn to be indignant. She claimed that sounded as if Brian was speaking from experience and had actually had an affair with a married woman.

'I should be so lucky,' Brian muttered underneath his breath.

'I heard that,' Pauline spat.

'Bloody hell, Pauline, he was only joking,' Lily said with a sneer.

Irene glared. 'If you're going to swear, Lil, I'd sooner you did it in your own house.'

'I'll make more tea.' Mollie left the room, feeling she might explode. She was pouring water in the kettle when Gladys joined her.

'Shall we laugh, or shall we cry?' she asked mournfully.

'Oh, let's laugh. It'll do us more good than crying.'

'I wouldn't mind divorcing Enoch if it meant I'd see no more of that lot. How you stand living with Irene I'll never know – and if you say her heart's in the right place, I'll kill you.'

'All right, I won't say it, though it is.' Mollie dodged out of the way when Gladys came towards her making a throttling gesture with her hands. 'They all mean well. They just have a funny way of showing it.'

'*I* don't find it funny.' Gladys groaned. 'How can we avoid Lily and Mike's twentieth wedding anniversary the Sunday after next?'

'We can't,' Mollie said crisply. 'We both married a Ryan and we'll just have to grit our teeth and bear it.'

Mollie's anniversary present to Lily and Mike was two front stall tickets for the Rotunda on the night before the do. 'The show's called *Parisian Music Hall*,' she told them. 'It sounds really good.'

Outside the theatre, last week's posters had been torn down. The replacements showed a row of colourfully clad women doing the cancan. Mollie hoped the sight of twenty-four legs clad in black stockings and suspenders and exposing a great deal of naked thigh wouldn't offend Lily. There were Chinese acrobats, an Indian snake-charmer, a Russian choir, Apache dancers, roller-skaters, and a ballerina called Mimi. The star of the show was a young man called Zeke Penn, a tap-dancer, who'd actually starred on Broadway. Mollie couldn't wait. She'd only managed to see the last part of the show, but she'd do her best to count the takings in record time and get into the auditorium as soon as she possibly could.

The Chinese acrobats seemed literally to fly through the air, as if, unlike ordinary people, they'd been granted the gift of flight. Mollie stood at the back of the theatre beside Betsy and watched, open-mouthed, hands on cheeks, terrified one of these human birds would plunge to the ground and break every bone in his body. And how Mimi could twirl around so fast and so furiously without getting dizzy and falling flat on her face she would never know.

Then the cancan dancers came on, six from each side of the stage. They met in the middle, kicked their legs, and shook their frilly skirts. Where did they get their energy from? Mollie wondered. She felt exhausted after half an hour of selling tickets. They finished with the splits, making her wince, then the stage went dark until a single spotlight revealed a young black man, Zeke Penn, dressed in white, who began to dance on the spot, faster and faster, his shoes clicking at an incredible rate. Suddenly all the lights went on and the girls came back, having changed into brief, glittering frocks. The young man danced with them one by one, each time doing a different step. The ballerina danced and he danced with her. Everyone seemed to be having an extraordinarily good time, laughing and clapping their hands. The audience joined in and laughed and clapped with them.

Mollie felt moved, exhilarated, excited, as if she, too, wanted to rush on to the stage and dance. The Russian choir – she'd only heard them before as she sat in her cubby-hole counting money – filed on at the very back and began to sing, then the jugglers came on, followed by the Apache dancers and the skaters. The acrobats flew overhead, and still Zeke Penn danced, a look on his face that said he was enjoying every minute. The stage was a mass of moving, singing people. Then, all of a sudden, as if a lever had been pulled or a switch turned, they stopped singing and moving, Zeke Penn stopped dancing, and the orchestra ceased to play. For a few seconds, they all stood as still as statues, until the curtain fell.

The audience leapt to their feet and began to cheer wildly. For the regulars, it was the best show they'd ever seen at the Rotunda and they could only wonder if they'd ever see another like it.

Harry Benedict was standing outside the theatre. 'What was it like?' he asked.

'Out of this world,' she said, linking his arm. 'You should come one night. I'll keep a ticket aside so you won't have to queue.'

'You'd do that for me?' He looked both surprised and pleased.

'Of course.' She'd like them to become friends. Unlike most men, who spent every spare minute in the pub, Harry wanted to make the world a better place. He cared about people. Since the night he'd walked her home, her feelings for him had become clearer – she would quite like him to kiss her again. How things would proceed from there, she had no idea. They could never marry, not only because he was a Protestant, but because he had a miserable, dead-end job where he no doubt earned peanuts. Where would they live? Anyway, marriage, to her or any other woman, might be the last thing on his mind.

'Fancy a cuppa at Charlie's?' he asked. 'We could talk.'

'All right,' she said happily. Charlie was dead, but his wife still managed the chippy where they'd been a few times, much to Rita's delight.

Tonight, there was a different girl behind the counter who looked just as pleased to see him. Her name was Issy and she brought the tea just as swiftly as Rita had.

'What happened to your mam and dad?' Mollie asked as soon as they sat down. She felt the urge to know everything about him.

'They died in the big 'flu epidemic after the war along with me two little sisters. I was nine. We'd always lived with me gran, so I just stayed there and she brought me up. She's where I got me politics from, me gran.' He smiled fondly, his dark eyes far away, as he thought about the erect, silver-haired woman who'd raised him. So far, Mollie had merely passed the time of day with Mrs Benedict. 'She's a Socialist through and through, kept giving me books to read. When she was a young woman, she got sacked from a jam and pickle factory in Vauxhall for trying to organize a strike for better working conditions.'

'She sounds wonderful,' Mollie murmured.

'She is . . . wonderful.' He said the word as if he'd never used it before. 'What about your mam and dad?'

'They're both dead, too. My dad was a doctor—'

'A doctor!' Harry broke in with a guffaw. 'A doctor for a dad, an accountant for a brother, and a copper for a husband; I never realized I was in such exalted company. I'd better mind my Ps and Qs from now on.'

'Don't be ridiculous, Harry.' She felt annoyed. 'We both live in the same street, don't we?'

'Yeah, but I was born there. You only landed there by accident.'

Mollie had no idea how the conversation – or was it an argument? – would have continued, had there not been the sound of someone rapidly climbing the stairs two at a time and a young black man leapt, smiling, into the room. It was Zeke Penn, who'd just danced so brilliantly at the Rotunda. He lit up the dreary little room, his eyes shining and his skin glowing. His teeth were the whitest she'd ever seen. 'What on earth are you doing here?' she gasped.

'I'm hungry, ma'am,' he replied politely, the smile fading just a little, 'and there wasn't a sign outside saying "No Blacks Allowed".'

At this, Mollie felt so horrified she nearly dropped her tea. 'Oh, I didn't mean that,' she stammered, 'Only I've just seen the show and I thought you'd be staying at a desperately posh hotel with its own restaurant.'

'I am staying at a desperately posh hotel, but the meals take a helluva long time coming.' He sat at the next table, crossing his legs elegantly. He'd changed into well-cut brown trousers, a brown jersey, and a heavy suede jacket with fur lining. 'First there's the soup,' he said, holding up a finger. 'You have to wait until they've slaughtered the ox and cut off its tail, or caught the mulligatawny – whatever a mulligatawny may be.' He raised another finger. 'Then there's another long wait for the main course.' A third finger was raised. 'The dessert appears about midnight, followed by the coffee,' another finger, 'which last night was cold. When I came out of the theatre, I saw this little diner across the street and thought I'd eat here. I'm sure as hell hungry,' he added a trifle pathetically.

Issy appeared with a plate heaped with chips and two pieces of battered fish. 'I'll bring the tea in a minute, luv,' she panted.

'In Liverpool, all the women call me "love",' Zeke Penn remarked. He removed his coat and tucked into the food.

Mollie smiled. She turned away to let him eat in peace and told Harry the events of the day before. 'When everyone had gone, Megan only asked her grandma for a divorce. "I don't want to live with you any more," she said. Irene nearly went through the roof.'

'It must be funny having kids,' Harry mused.

'You can meet mine, if you want. They're coming to the first house at the Rotunda on Saturday. You might like to come at the same time.'

'Will your mother-in-law be there?' When Mollie confirmed that was the case, he said hastily, 'I'd sooner go to the second house.' On reflection, Mollie thought that was probably a wise decision.

Zeke Penn had finished his meal in record time. 'What did you think of the show?' he enquired.

'I loved every minute,' Mollie enthused. 'At least, every minute that I managed to see. I'm in the box office and I missed the first half.'

'Why don't you bring your tea over here and drink it with us, mate?' Harry suggested.

'"Love" and "mate"; I like that.' He put his tea on their table and sat next to Harry. 'It's a big improvement on what I was called back in the States by white folk. It was more usually "nigger" or "you dirty nigger", or names that I can't repeat in front of a lady.'

'*All* white folk?' Mollie's brow puckered. 'My auntie lives in New York and she'd never call black people names like that.'

'No, not all white folk,' he conceded. 'I suppose I got over-sensitive about it. I had some really good friends who were white, but they moved to California. Not long afterwards, I left to live in Paris. It's different there; I'm treated as an equal.' He gave a joyful sigh. 'You'd have to be black yourself to know how good it feels, though I badly miss my family back in New York. Whereabouts in New York does your aunt live, ma'am?'

'Oh, please call me Mollie and this is Harry,' Mollie cried. 'Aunt Maggie used to live in Greenwich Village, but now she's in Queens.'

'I lived in Harlem; 'fact I was born there, but I know Greenwich Village well. There's clubs there, jazz clubs, that admit blacks.'

He seemed ready to chat all night, but after a while Mollie said reluctantly that she couldn't stay another minute. Irene would have been expecting her home ages ago. Zeke said he'd catch a taxi back to the hotel, but Harry informed him he'd have a long time to wait for a taxi, as not many cruised along Scotland Road in the hope of picking up a fare.

'Best thing is to take a tram into town. I'll come with you, show you to the door of your hotel. It'd be a bit risky to go wandering round town looking like that. I'm talking about your coat, mate, not your colour. There's some scallies who'd give their right arm for a coat like yours; they'd have it off your back before you could turn around.'

The audience must have gone home and told their friends about the show, and the friends told their friends. The following night, the queue was longer than Mollie had ever known. At least a hundred people had to be turned away. The night after, the queue was even longer. Some who'd queued for hours sold their tickets for twice as much to people at the back.

'Couldn't you stay another week?' she asked Zeke when he turned up at Charlie's for the third night in a row. The room was almost full. It seemed to have got around that Zeke Penn graced Charlie's with his company after the show.

'Sorry, Mollie,' he said regretfully. 'I must say I'm enjoying Liverpool, but we're due in Manchester next week and Birmingham the week after, then three other cities – I can't remember the names. We finish at the Palladium in London around the end of May. We've been given to understand the King of England will be there.'

'Lucky old you,' Harry said scornfully. 'I hope you don't bow and scrape to him. Don't forget you were born in a country that got rid of kings and queens a long time ago and became a republic. As for France, they chopped the buggers' heads off.'

Zeke's eyes twinkled merrily. 'I shall probably bow, Harry, but I certainly won't scrape.'

'Where did you learn to tap-dance, Zeke?' someone shouted.

'I went to a stage school in New York.'

'Does anyone know if there's a stage school in Liverpool?'

No one did, but Mollie said loudly there were plenty of dancing teachers around.

'I wouldn't mind our Rosie learning to tap-dance. I wonder how much it costs?'

The questions continued. Zeke, the centre of attention, seemed perfectly happy to answer them. Yes, he really had starred on Broadway, he confirmed: 'It was in a show called *Roses are Red*; I played a bellboy.'

As the week progressed, more and more people packed into Charlie's, and the chip shop, unused to doing so much trade at such a late hour, required extra help. The late Charlie's wife, who only worked during the day, came to supervise. A tiny, wizened woman, who wore a dirty white overall and too much lipstick, she sat at the top of the stairs, watching the charismatic young man entertaining her customers with tales of New York and Paris.

Harry continued to accompany him on the tram and deliver him safely to his hotel. 'What do you talk about?' Mollie asked.

'All sorts of things.' Harry shrugged nonchalantly. 'Football. He'd like to see a match on Saturday – Everton are playing Chelsea – but he'd have to leave at half-time and it wouldn't be worth it. He's worried about the situation in Europe – Hitler loathes Negroes as much as he does Jews. Oh,' he grinned, 'and we talked about you. He thought you were me wife.'

Mollie claimed to be offended. 'If I were your wife, I wouldn't let you go around looking like a tramp. I'd've chucked that jersey a long time ago and bought you a new pair of trousers and a pair of socks – *two* pairs of socks. Doesn't your gran look after you?' she asked exasperatedly.

'She'd like to, but I won't let her. I'm all right as I am, Mollie. Don't fuss.'

'I'm only fussing because Zeke thought I was your wife.'

Saturday night was sad enough seeing the show for the final time, but even sadder at Charlie's where a crowd had gathered to say tara to Zeke. The atmosphere was gloomy. Zeke was like a star that had briefly shone on their minuscule part of the universe and was about to move on. Unless a miracle happened, they would never see his like again.

'Manchester and Birmingham and all those other places will seem very dull after Liverpool,' Zeke said to Mollie.

'Liverpool will seem dull without you,' she told him. She put her arm around his neck and kissed his cheek. 'Goodbye, Zeke, it's been lovely knowing you.'

Everyone went outside to see him and Harry off on the tram, cheering and banging the windows. Mollie watched the tram make its rackety way towards town. The magic was over and life was about to resume its normal dull routine.

Actually, life wasn't all *that* dull. Her job at the Rotunda continued to enthral her, although the shows weren't a patch on *Parisian Music Hall*. Harry met her every night and they became regulars at Charlie's, but never bought more than two cups of tea, which they drank while sorting out the problems of the world.

She felt convinced it must have got back to Irene that she was seeing Harry, but her mother-in-law didn't say anything. For months now, putting aside the occasional tiff between Megan and her grandma, an air of tranquillity had filled the house in Turnpike Street. Mollie and the girls enjoyed a decent night's sleep, having swapped bedrooms with Irene, who'd moved into the middle bedroom. Mollie had bought an extra bed. No doubt due to the provision of better food, Dandelion hadn't found it necessary to fill his stomach elsewhere, so Brodie was happy. Furthermore, after seeing *Parisian Music Hall*, Mollie had heard Megan and Brodie saying how much they'd love to dance, not like Zeke, but Mimi. She found a ballet teacher who taught in St Oswald's church hall, Old Swan, and booked the girls in for two hours on Saturday mornings. The cost was sixpence an hour for both and she was thrilled at the idea of being able to spend an entire shilling without having to cut back on other things. She made the little frilly frocks herself – they were called tutus – and visited Paddy's Market to look for ballet shoes. She'd actually found some that only required a small amount of darning on the toes.

Mollie would far sooner Tom were still alive and they were living in the house in Allerton. But Tom was dead and she had to make the best of things the way they were. Tommy was now five and would start school in September and be able to keep an eye on his brother; she worried about Joe when he was at school. Brodie was such a sweet little girl and the other girls seemed to like her. Megan didn't care if they liked her or not. As for Irene, she relished her weekly visits to the Rotunda with the children; they went to the first house every Saturday. The only fly in the ointment was Harry Benedict.

They couldn't go on the way they were. He was young, virile, and exceptionally good-looking. If he bothered to comb his hair now and again and dress more smartly, he could have had any woman he wanted. As it was, enough girls went weak at the knees at the mere sight of him. Mollie knew he wouldn't be content for long with tea in Charlie's and a stroll along Scotland Road. Much to her disappointment, he hadn't tried to kiss her again. Even if he did, the time would come when he'd want more than just kisses. She tried to visualize going to bed with Harry Benedict, but her imagination refused to let her; she was too attached to the memory of Tom.

The crunch came months later, in August, when the children were on holiday from school and the theatre had closed for a month. She still met Harry. At half past nine, when it was beginning to grow dark and the children were in bed, she'd say to Irene, 'I'm just going for a walk, I won't be long.'

Irene didn't ask where she was going or why hadn't she gone

for a walk in daylight, just, 'All right, luv. I'll probably be in bed by the time you get back.'

Harry would be in Charlie's, the tea already paid for. Rita or Issy would bring it up as soon as she arrived. 'Hello,' Mollie would say, touching his shoulder lightly then sitting opposite him at the wobbly table.

'Hello.' He in turn would touch her hand.

On the night in particular, when the crunch came and everything changed, Harry was hunched over the table and didn't move when she sat down.

'What's the matter?' she asked. 'You look very glum.'

'Glum!' He sat up straight and gave her a caustic smile. 'I'm not glum, as you put it,' he said angrily. 'I'm on top of the world. I'm going away. I'm going to do something proper with me life for a change, stop fiddling round at the edges trying to put things right and wasting me bloody time.'

'Going away?' It was the only part of the diatribe that she understood. 'Going away where?'

'Spain. I'm going to join the International Brigade and fight the Fascists, who are trying to overthrow the legally elected Socialist government. We got a letter asking for volunteers.' His face changed, became softer. 'Mollie, luv, I've always wanted to do something like this: fight for what's right, *really* fight, not just attend meetings, sign petitions, and go on marches, but meet the enemy face to face, deal with them at first-hand.'

'You mean kill them before they kill you?' She was horrified. She didn't want him to go away and risk his life, however worthy the cause. 'What about us?' she asked in a small voice.

'Us?' He was angry again. 'There is no "us". We both know I'm not good enough for you, that there'll never be an "us". That's another reason I'm going. I love you, Moll, but we're going nowhere.' He picked up the tea that Issy must have brought without her noticing, took a sip, and returned the cup to the table with a bang. 'No bloody where at all.'

'But, Harry,' she said meekly, 'there's nowhere for us to go.'

'We could get married.' He looked at her challengingly and the expression on his face, so full of love and longing, made her want to weep.

'Oh, Harry, you know we can't.' She was almost weeping now. 'There's so many things against us: religion, for one.'

'Religion! Huh! I've no time for religion; lighting candles, saying prayers to statues, listening to a priest drone on in Latin, which no one understands.' The table was banged again, this time with his fist. 'Marx said religion is the opium of the people and he was right. Me, I'm an atheist. I don't believe in anything except meself and the goodness in people's hearts, if only they were allowed to get on with their lives without interference from the capitalists and the politicians – and the bloody priests.'

She wanted to argue that he was wrong, that most people weren't as good as he thought, that he was looking at the world through rose-tinted spectacles. He was prepared to die for a cause he believed in, but not many men, or women, would do that.

'It's not just religion, Harry,' she whispered. 'Say if we got married and I had more children and had to give up my job. What would we live on? Tell me, how much do you earn a week?'

'Twenty-five bob,' he muttered. 'We could move into the country, and I could get a job on a farm – though a farm worker's wages are disgraceful.' His shoulders drooped as the sense of what she had just said sank in. 'It's hopeless, isn't it?'

'Yes, love.' She stroked his hand.

'I want you,' he said. 'I want you so much that I'd go back on the docks if they'd take me, and keep me big mouth shut this time. I wish you weren't so prim and proper, Moll,' he said childishly, 'and more like other girls.'

'In what way, Harry?' She had no idea what he meant.

'You know what way.' He refused to meet her eyes.

The penny dropped. 'You mean make love with you?' She felt herself blush, but pressed on. 'Where? In the back entry of Turnpike Street? In my mother-in-law's house while she and the children are asleep? Would that keep you here, Harry, if we were able to make love?'

'It might. That, or the thought that we'd be together one day. I won't always be an odd job man. I read books, I know about things most people don't, I could learn to talk proper, more like you.'

'Oh, Harry, don't! I love you – yes, I do.' She nodded as if she were telling herself, not just him. 'I love you, but it'll never work. I've got four children and I have to put them first. Their lives have already been disrupted enough.' At least Megan and Brodie's had: Joe and Tommy had no memory of their father.

'So, unless I turn up in a few years' time driving a Rolls-Royce and wearing a Savile Row suit, there's no hope for us?' To her surprise, he managed the trace of a grin.

'There'd be no need for posh cars and posh clothes, but there's always hope, Harry. We'll just have to see.' Her eyes filled with tears. 'I don't want you to go away.'

'There's nothing else for it, Moll. I've got to.'

'When?'

'There's the tickets to arrange and that sort of thing. I'll be off as soon as I can.'

Perhaps she was too sensible, too set in her ways. The only risk she'd ever taken in her life was leaving Ireland with the intention of going to America – and look at the mess she'd made of *that*! However hard she looked at it, in however many ways, she couldn't come up with a single solitary reason for marrying Harry Benedict other than they loved each other, which might have been enough for some women, but not for her.

She imagined writing to Finn and saying she was about to marry a Communist with a hopeless job – he'd been shocked enough when she told him she was marrying a policeman. As for her mother-in-law, Irene wouldn't have stood for it, if only on religious grounds. She would be so incensed she could well throw Mollie and her children out of the house, not caring that she'd be cutting off her nose to spite her face and have to go on the parish to pay the rent and feed herself. As for Lily and Pauline, they'd never speak to Mollie again, and she wasn't even too sure about Gladys.

Harry had an address in Barcelona where he would stay. He was catching a train to London, and another to Dover, then he would cross the channel and journey through France on more trains until he reached Spain. 'Barcelona's not far from the border,' he told her. His gran had paid for the tickets. She'd been saving a few coppers a week out of the money he'd given her over the years for housekeeping.

'I bet she doesn't want you to leave,' Mollie commented.

'You don't know me gran. She's all for it. She said she'd've come with us if she were younger.'

Mollie had the feeling he was taking his time making the travel arrangements in the hope that she would change her mind and agree to sleep with him, or marry him. Even if she had been prepared to sleep with him, where would they go? Only a hotel, and she couldn't think of a single reason on earth she could give for staying out all night.

She bought him a jumper and two pairs of socks. 'Have you got a suitcase?' she asked worriedly. She still had the old carpetbag Finn had found in the Doctor's house for Tom when he'd returned to Liverpool, leaving his family behind in Duneathly.

'Don't need one, Moll. I won't be taking all that much.' He was in high spirits and full of himself. Perhaps he'd be glad to see the back of her. Maybe he felt trapped in a situation that couldn't be resolved, and this was the only way out.

The tickets were bought; he was leaving on Monday on the first train out of Lime Street. In four days he would be gone out of her life, possibly for ever. Mollie wasn't sure if she could bear it. She too was trapped, but for her there was no way out.

'Irene,' she said. 'Agatha's invited me to tea on Sunday. I was going to take the children, but Agatha suggested we go to the pictures afterwards to see Fred Astaire and Ginger Rogers in

Roberta. Phil's offered to stay and look after the children and I wondered if you'd mind looking after mine?'

'Of course I wouldn't luv,' Irene said warmly. 'It'll make a nice change for you and Agatha to go out together.'

Mollie set off on Sunday wearing the frock she'd bought for her interview at the Rotunda. Since then, she'd always thought of it as her 'lucky' frock, for nothing even faintly unpleasant had happened when she wore it. There were butterflies in her stomach and her legs felt unsteady. She had never done anything like this before.

She alighted from the tram in London Road and walked quickly in the direction of Lime Street station where Harry was waiting underneath the clock as she'd asked him to. He was better dressed than she'd ever seen him in a navy-blue suit with chalk stripes, a pale-blue shirt, and a dark tie, though there was something odd about the outfit that she couldn't quite put her finger on.

'Why couldn't we have come together on the tram?' he asked when she stood in front of him. His face split into the familiar grin that she loved. 'I know, you were worried someone like your flamin' mother-in-law would see us together, weren't you?'

'Yes,' Mollie conceded. 'You look nice. Where did the suit come from?'

'It belonged to me dad. It's the one he wore when he married me mam. Gran kept it in the wardrobe all this time.' That was why it looked so odd. The suit was about thirty years old, the lapels were unfashionably wide, and the waistcoat buttoned too high. The legs were an inch too short, but that was nothing to do with fashion, just that he was taller than his father had been. 'Where are we going, Moll? I hope it's not the pictures, because I've never had much time for them. They're just a way of keeping the population pacified, like giving them sweets when they're hungry and telling them it's proper food.'

'It's not the pictures, Harry.' She linked his arm. 'Come with me.'

Ten minutes later, they entered the little hotel in Seymour

Street where she'd booked a room the day before. The room was on the second floor. The wallpaper was patterned with purple grapes on the vine, the furniture the cheapest you could buy, but the bed looked comfortable and everywhere was scrupulously clean.

Mollie locked the door. Harry was looking at her, totally bemused. 'What's this all about, Moll?'

'You're awfully slow on the uptake, darlin'.' She held out her arms. '*This* is what it's all about.' It wasn't enough to prevent him from going away, but it would be something he — and she — would remember until the end of their days.

'The only photo I've got of him is the one taken at his christening.' Kate Benedict handed her a small, faded photo showing a young couple, the man very like Harry, and the pretty woman beside him holding a baby in her arms. The baby wore a bonnet and a long christening gown. His face couldn't be seen. 'It doesn't tell you much, does it?'

'Not really,' Mollie agreed. 'It's hard to imagine Harry in a bonnet, even as a baby.'

'He never cared a fig how he looked — and he never felt the cold. I gave up insisting he wore a scarf and gloves in winter. I wonder how he's getting on?' she mused.

Harry had been gone a month. By now, the children were back at school and Mollie was feeling very low. She'd called on Mrs Benedict — who insisted she call her Kate — to ask if she'd heard from her grandson, but so far a letter hadn't arrived.

Kate Benedict was eighty, but looked much younger. There was fire in her eyes and her small, pink, surprisingly unwrinkled face was animated and full of life. She was an older, feminine version of her grandson. She took Mollie into the parlour, which was full of books. 'I was just writing something,' she said. There was a pen, a bottle of ink, and an exercise book on the table in front of the window.

'Is it a letter to Harry?' Mollie asked.

'No, luv. I wouldn't know where to send it, would I? He'd no intention of staying at that place in Barcelona. It's the minutes of a meeting held last night in this very room: the Socialist Sisters of Liverpool. We meet once a fortnight. The local Labour Party meet here every month. Harry never came: he hadn't much time for Labour. Mind you, neither have I, but the Communists are a bit too wild-eyed for me and there's something about that Joseph Stalin I can't abide. Would you like a cup of tea, Mollie?'

'Yes, please.'

From then on, she called on Kate Benedict at least once a week, but, by the time Christmas came, there was still no word from Harry. She read the *Daily Herald* from cover to cover. The International Brigade was made up of thousands of Europeans as well as volunteers from Canada, America, and Australia, most of whom had never touched a rifle in their lives. They were no match for the many more thousands of experienced troops from Italy and Germany led by the Fascist General Franco. The fighting was bitter and brutal. It was a war of ideas and ideals.

In April, the small town of Guernica in northern Spain was attacked by German Heinkels, followed by the much heavier Junkers, dropping bombs a ton at a time, tearing the town apart, slaughtering its innocent people, machine-gunning those who'd managed to escape to the countryside. The onslaught continued for three hours. A full account of the dead and injured was never made, but it was in Guernica that Harry Benedict died.

Three weeks later, a letter arrived for Kate from a Liverpool man: Frank Davenport. The writing was cramped and illiterate but, when Mollie read the letter, she felt love for Frank Davenport that filled her heart. He wrote about his 'dear friend Harry', his 'comrade in arms', and how he had died a 'hero's death', trying to save a child from German bombs: ' . . . I'm not ashamed to say it – I cried when Harry died. I still cry whenever I think of him. He talked a lot about his gran and a girl called Mollie who he loved. Yours in sorrow, Frank Davenport.'

Kate sighed now, folded the letter and returned it to the envelope. Her eyes were bright, but she hadn't shed a tear. Her grandson had died a death to be proud of, not weep over. She handed the letter to Mollie. 'You keep this, luv. Oh, and someone gave me a poem the other day; it was printed in the *New Statesman*. I'll give you that an' all.' She slipped the cutting into the envelope with Frank Davenport's letter.

Mollie read the poem when she got home, hardly able to see through her tears. The last line read, '*We will remember Guernica when black birds descending, OUR cities are on fire.*'

It was an ominous warning of what was to come should Hitler turn his evil gaze on Europe.

Chapter 13

'Happy birthday,' Mollie cried when Annemarie went into the kitchen. 'Your present's on the table; it's a blouse. Sinead Connolly made it and I embroidered the flowers down the front.'

Annemarie took her seat at the table and opened the parcel. 'Oh, Mollie, it's desperately pretty. I wish I could embroider like this.' She touched the little pink rosebuds, so neat and perfect.

'You're too impatient, sweetheart,' Mammy said. 'You sew as if you're racing against time. If I were you, I'd stick to drawing.' Mammy was expecting a baby and her stomach was like a little mountain. If it was a boy she was going to call it Aidan, and Calla if it were a girl. She looked tired and Annemarie impulsively reached across and stroked the black, curly hair that was so much like her own. Mammy caught her hand and squeezed it. 'Happy birthday, darlin',' she whispered.

'April Fool!' Finn shouted gleefully. 'It's not your birthday after all.'

'Indeed it is my birthday,' Annemarie said firmly. Finn said the same thing every year. 'I'm eleven – and where's my present from you, I'd like to know.'

'I haven't got you anything. I forgot.' Finn said that every year, too. 'Oh, all right.' He took a tiny box out of his trouser pocket. 'Here it is.'

'A ring! I can just tell it's a ring.' Annemarie took the lid off the box. Inside, nestling on a lump of cotton wool, there was indeed a ring with a green stone. 'Is that an emerald?' she asked.

'Not likely, sis. I'm not made of money. It's jade.'

'Jade's unlucky,' Nanny said in doom-laden voice. 'That ring will bring the girl nothing but grief.'

'Please don't say things like that, Nanny,' Mammy said sharply. 'It's a really pretty ring and I think it's opal that's unlucky, not jade. Put it on, sweetheart, let's see what it looks like.'

Annemarie slipped the ring on to the middle finger of her right hand, half expecting the ceiling to fall in while she did so. Fortunately, nothing happened. She spread her hand and showed it to Mammy and Finn. Mollie, who was making toast so Mammy could rest, came over to have a look, and they all remarked how lovely it was. Nanny, who was busy stirring the porridge and seemed determined to spoil things, said Finn should have bought a ring with an amethyst stone, 'to go with her eyes', but Annemarie said she'd much prefer green.

'The porridge is ready,' Nanny said in the same doom-laden voice, as if the porridge was heavily laced with poison and everyone was about to die.

'Where's Thaddy?' Mammy enquired. 'Didn't I wake the lad half an hour ago? I reckon he's gone back to sleep.'

Mollie put a plate piled high with buttered toast on the table, along with a bowl of damson jam that Nanny had made the year before. 'I'll fetch him,' she said, but there was no need, for three-year-old Thaddy came staggering in carrying a giant cardboard structure that turned out to be a fort. He had built it for Annemarie on her birthday.

'Thank you, Thaddy darlin'.' She kissed him warmly on both cheeks. 'It's lovely. Just what I wanted.'

'I nearly fell downstairs and spoiled it.' His eyes shone with love for his sister and made her want to cry.

Instead of crying, she kissed him again. 'That would have been desperately awful,' she said. 'I'll take it up to my bedroom in a minute and play with it when Mollie and me come back from Kildare.'

It was going to be a wonderful day, her birthday. They were on holiday from school for Easter, and Mammy and her da had given her a whole five shillings. Very soon she and Mollie would catch the bus to Kildare to spend it, along with Finn who worked there. They would meet Finn for lunch and he would put them on the bus home.

'Is the Doctor not joining us for breakfast this morning?' Nanny enquired.

'He's in the surgery with a patient,' Mammy replied. 'Didn't one of Mr MacDonald's farm workers go and nearly cut off his foot with a *scythe? He's sewing the poor man back together again. He'll be a while yet.'*

Annemarie was glad – not because the poor farm worker had nearly cut off his foot, but because her da wouldn't be joining them for breakfast. His presence would cast a shadow over the room. She always sensed it, though Mollie said this only proved how daft she was. She sensed nothing at all.

A pale sun shone through the window, making the jug of bluebells on the sill look even bluer. A feeling of sheer happiness overwhelmed her and she had to stop herself from laughing out loud or Mollie would think she was even dafter. It really was going to be a wonderful day.

April 1940

'Good morning,' said a voice.

Anne opened her eyes with the feeling she'd just had a lovely dream. The voice belonged to a man who was looking at her as if he knew her well. For a moment, she lost her bearings, then realized with surprise that she was in Central Park sitting on the bench opposite the apartment and had actually fallen asleep. She'd been on her way somewhere, but couldn't resist stopping to savour the fresh April sunshine. 'Hello,' she said. He was a fine-looking man with a boyish face, brown crinkly hair, and brown eyes.

He smiled. 'You don't recognize me, do you?'

She screwed up her eyes and tried to remember where she'd seen him before, but gave up. 'No,' she admitted.

'Robert Edgar Gifford, known as Bobby to my friends.' He doffed his hat, an off-white Homburg. 'And you're Anne Murray. Do you remember me now?'

'Of course,' she said delightedly. She'd found him on the very same bench ten years ago and given him hamburgers and coffee. 'You look very different now.' Then, he'd looked like the scarecrow out of *The Wizard of Oz*. Now, he wore a smart grey pinstriped suit with a plain grey waistcoat. She patted the bench. 'Sit down.'

'You've hardly changed,' he said when he was seated beside her. 'I'd've known you anywhere.'

'I knew I'd seen you before,' she confessed, 'but I just couldn't remember where. You were much thinner back then. Did you go to California?' She remembered giving him the eight dollars that she had in her pocket. 'Are you still cross with me for giving you money?'

'I was very rude. It seemed demeaning to take money off someone so young. But I still took it. I'm sorry,' he said abjectly. 'And no, I didn't go to California. I hitched a lift as far as Springfield, Illinois, where I had my suit pressed and mended, and my shoes polished. I bought a fresh shirt, called in the local barber's for a shave and a haircut, and got a job on the local paper, the *Springfield Star*. Now I'm the editor,' he said proudly, 'and it's all due to you, Miss Anne Murray.' He nodded at her left hand with its thick gold ring. 'Though I see you're no longer a miss, but a missus.'

'Mrs Herbie Blinker, though Anne Murray is my professional name and most people call me by that.'

'What does your husband do?'

'He's in the movies; he's what's called a movie star.' Ollie produced a movie once a year with Herbie in the leading part. They would never win an Oscar, but were very popular and made a big profit. 'He lives in California most of the time, Los Angeles, and I live in New York. We don't see much of each other.'

'Do you mind?' He made a face. 'Sorry, that's a very intrusive question. Forget I asked.'

'It's quite all right.' She liked talking to him. 'No, I don't mind a bit that Herbie and I don't see much of each other. I'll ask you a question, shall I? What are you doing in New York?'

'I'm here for a job interview, assistant editor on the *New York Standard*.' His boyish face shone and she could tell he wanted the job very much. 'It's a much bigger paper than my present one with a wider circulation, and it's a daily, whereas the *Star* only comes out once a week. The interview's not until tomorrow. Today, I'm looking up a few old friends – starting with you.'

She looked at him, puzzled. 'I'm very flattered,' she said, 'but you could hardly call me a friend. We only spoke to each other for about ten minutes.'

'You're the best friend I've ever had,' he said in a heartfelt tone. 'You completely changed my life around. If it hadn't been for you, Lord knows where I would have ended up. I owe everything I have to you, Anne Murray.'

Anne felt herself blush. 'Did you actually expect to find me on this bench?'

'No, but you told me where you lived. Your bedroom's the second from the left in that apartment building directly opposite. I intended to enquire if you still lived there so we could meet and I could thank you and apologize for being so rude, but found you in exactly the same place as you found me.'

'Well, now we've met, you've thanked me, and I've accepted your apology. What happens now?'

'How about lunch? Or is it too early?' He paused and put a finger to his chin. 'I know, how about a drink in the Plaza and we'll just hang around until it's time for lunch? Or were you planning on doing something different? Are you in a show? I seem to recall you said you were a dancer – no, I don't *seem* to, I recall very well.'

'I'm resting between shows. I start rehearsing a new one next week.' Her smooth brow furrowed. 'I think I was going shopping,' she said vaguely. She couldn't remember what she was going shopping for, so it couldn't have been anything important. 'It's my birthday,' she announced then, taking herself by surprise. How did she know? She looked down at her right hand, half expecting to see a ring with a green stone, but the hand was bare. She shrugged. She had so many strange dreams that sometimes she couldn't tell the difference between what was real and what was not, but she was certain it was her birthday. Lizzie had mentioned this morning it was April Fools' Day, so it must be. She was probably twenty-nine. Lev had reckoned she was about fourteen when he'd found her. They'd used to pretend it was her birthday on a different day each year. Lev had gone to Washington for a conference, but she'd telephone as soon as he got back and tell him she'd remembered her birthday.

'Many happy returns,' Bobby Gifford said warmly.

'Thank you. Shall we walk to the Plaza?'

'What a good idea.'

Without thinking, she tucked her arm inside his and they strolled across Central Park in the April sunshine. Anne just knew it was going to be a really wonderful day.

After a long lunch, during which they'd talked non-stop, hardly noticing what they were eating, she took him back to the apartment to introduce him to Lizzie. She'd already told him that Lizzie was her mother-in-law and Ollie her father-in-law, 'but he spends as much time in Los Angeles as Herbie – he produces Herbie's movies.'

'That's a very strange arrangement,' Bobby opined. 'Wives on one side of the country, husbands on the other. You couldn't be further apart.'

'It's also a very happy arrangement. It means that Ollie and Herbie can get up to whatever they like without interference from their wives.'

'I won't ask what they get up to,' Bobby said darkly.

Anne laughed. 'I wouldn't tell you if you did.'

When they arrived, Lizzie was having a bath. Christina offered to make coffee while Anne showed Bobby around the apartment. He paused in front of the paintings, hugely impressed. 'Is that really a Picasso?' he asked, and Anne assured him that it was. He touched it reverently. 'A genuine Picasso. It must have cost the earth.'

'It didn't when Lizzie bought it. She's had it for years. And most of these.' She waved at the canvases done by other artists whose names she couldn't bring to mind. Like Lev, she preferred paintings in which the figures had two eyes, a nose, a mouth, and recognizable bodies with arms and legs in the right places.

'Are you admiring my art collection?' Lizzie sailed in wearing tailored slacks and a polo-necked jumper.

'It's stunning, Mrs Blinker,' Bobby said appreciatively. 'Like having your very own art gallery.'

'Not bad for a girl who was born in the back streets of Manchester nearly sixty years ago, is it?' Lizzie said heartily. 'Call me Lizzie. And who are you?'

'Bobby Gifford, ma'am — Lizzie. Anne and I found each other in the park.'

Lizzie laughed out loud. 'All I ever seem to find in the park is old cigarette packets and the occasional glove. I shall definitely go there more often if there are more young men like you waiting to be found.'

Christina came in with the coffee and they sat around and talked for ages. Lizzie said there was a breathtaking new work by Picasso in the Museum of Modern Art. 'It's called *Guernica*. It's the name of a little town the Germans bombed during the Spanish Civil War. Have you heard of it, Bobby?'

'I've heard of Guernica, yes, but not the painting.' Bobby slapped his knee impatiently. 'That's why I'd like to work for the *Standard*. The *Star* is very parochial. I want to deal with world events, not local council matters and church affairs. I doubt if anyone in Springfield knows there's a war going on in Europe.'

'Ah, yes, the war,' Lizzie said gravely. 'I have relatives in Manchester that I still write to. Apparently, it's been the coldest winter they've ever known and they're short of virtually everything. I've been sending food parcels.'

'I always make a cake,' Anne put in. She was beginning to feel a bit out of things.

'And so you do, pet. They're probably the richest fruitcakes ever made and they weigh a ton. Well, I'd better be off.' She got to her feet. 'I'm secretary of the Committee to Re-elect the President and I'm due at a meeting. Eric will have the car outside by now.'

'She's nice,' Bobby said when Lizzie had gone. 'You're very lucky to have her for a mother-in-law. My mother-in-law was a witch. I'm convinced she practised the black arts in the kitchen of her house in Queens and put spells on people she didn't like, including me.'

'I didn't know you were married.' For some reason Anne's heart gave a mournful little tug. She didn't know why. After all, *she* was married, so why should it matter if Bobby was?

'I'm not sure if I'm married or not,' he said frankly. 'I was married when I first met you, but my wife had gone back to live with her mother after I'd lost my job and was about to lose our apartment. *I* wasn't invited. Not that I would have gone,' he added hastily. 'I'd sooner have shot myself than live with my wife's mother. She might have divorced me by now – my wife, that is, not her mother. I suppose I'd better find out.'

Anne giggled. 'It sounds very complicated.'

'It's not as complicated as *your* marital situation.'

'My marital situation is completely straightforward. Herbie – and Ollie – come to stay at Christmas. Lizzie and I go to Los Angeles when Ollie is about to release one of Herbie's movies, but I can't go if I'm in a show, so I've only been three times.' She was glad. The less she saw of Herbie the better, even though she still liked him. But it was useful being married. It kept other men at bay. Apart from Lev, Anne had never had much time for the opposite sex. Bobby Gifford, she realized, was the first man she'd really felt attracted to. There was something wholeheartedly nice about him, as if the niceness went right down as far as his toes.

'What would you like to do tonight?' she asked. 'Shall we see a show?' Too late, she remembered he'd come to New York to look up old friends. Anyway, it was the man who was supposed to ask the woman out, not the other way around. The trouble was, she had little experience of such things. She couldn't flirt to save her life and was useless at small talk. 'I forgot, you've got other people to see, not just me.'

'The other people don't matter,' he said bluntly. 'I'd sooner be with you.' He gave her a look that sent a delicious shiver running through her body.

'And I'd sooner be with you.' She shouldn't have said that.

Women were expected to play hard to get, but Anne didn't know how, nor did she know what to say next.

Bobby must have noticed her confusion. He came over and kissed her softly on the lips. 'You're married,' he said, 'but I get the impression you're not madly in love with Herbie? Is that true?' She nodded vigorously. 'I might well still have a wife, but I'm not in love with her either. I might not get that job tomorrow. If I don't, I shall just have to find another so I can be in New York near you.' He raised his eyebrows quizzically. 'Shall we leave it like that and see what happens next?'

Anne nodded again. She leaned against him, he put his arms around her, and she could feel his cheek pressing against her hair. They stayed like that for a long time, neither speaking, but both knowing how the other felt.

Levon was having the worst time of his life. Why was he so weak? Why did he give in to Tamara every time she wanted to do something and he didn't? He supposed it was to avoid an unpleasant atmosphere and her endless nagging. The trouble was that, in doing the thing he didn't want, he ended up being even more miserable than if he'd refused.

Look at the present situation. He'd been looking forward to the lawyers' conference in Washington, had planned to travel by train with a few lawyer friends who were all staying at the same hotel, anticipated getting slightly drunk each night in the hotel bar, swapping stories and telling jokes. It was only going to be three days and would make an enjoyable break.

Then Tamara had decided she'd like to come. 'I've never been to Washington. I'd love to see the White House.'

'But what about John?' Levon pointed out.

'John can stay with one of his friends. He's fifteen and will probably have a lovely time.'

At the expense of mine, Levon thought darkly. Then, as if that wasn't enough, Myra Grimaldi, Tamara's best friend, decided she'd also like to visit Washington with her husband, Art.

'Art will take us in the car,' Tamara informed him. 'It means you'll save the train fare.'

Levon didn't give a damn about saving the train fare and he loathed Art Grimaldi more than any other human being on earth. Art was a big man with a big voice who dominated every conversation with his right-wing opinions. Other people weren't allowed to get a word in. But Lev's objections to the Grimaldis' presence were witheringly demolished by a determined Tamara, who was working out a programme of what they would do in Washington. She'd already booked a different hotel where all four of them would stay.

'Will I be allowed to attend the conference?' Levon asked sarcastically while he watched her make a list.

'Of course, Lev, but we can meet outside and have an early dinner. Do you think you could get away for lunch?'

'No,' Levon growled.

'Don't be so bad-tempered. Anyone would think you didn't want me to come.'

If only he could tell her! If only he could bring himself to say, 'I don't want you to come. I don't want you to be my wife any more. I don't want to live in Brooklyn. I want to live with Peggy Perlmann in Manhattan. By the way, Peggy and I have been having an affair for years, ever since we went to Anne's wedding in Los Angeles.'

But he couldn't. He was too much of a coward. Not only that, he didn't want to hurt her. Once, she'd been the love of his life and he couldn't bring himself to let her down. He tried to insist they went in his car, not Art's, so at least he'd have some control over events. But apparently Art's Oldsmobile was bigger, more comfortable, had eight cylinders and, what was more, was only a few months old, far superior to Levon's ancient Maxwell, of which he'd grown extremely fond.

Art sang at the top of his voice all the way to Washington. Tamara and Myra discussed what they would buy in the shops. Levon sat miserably in the back. Every now and then, Tamara would mouth at him, '*Say something*,' but Levon could think of nothing to say.

The enjoyable break became three days of sheer torture. He would leave the conference and his lawyer friends to find Tamara, Myra and Art waiting for him in the lobby. 'Ah, here he is,' Art would boom. 'The sinner returneth.' They would go for a meal at an expensive restaurant where only minuscule portions were served, when Levon had been looking forward to steak and fries in a greasy spoon, or heaps of spaghetti somewhere cheap and Italian accompanied by warm, red wine.

But now at last they were on their way home. It was a beautiful day, full of sunshine. Art was singing and driving too fast, the car windows were wide open and the stiff breeze was making Levon's ears ache. 'Would you mind closing the windows?' he asked mildly.

'The fresh air will do you good, pal.' Art turned around and gave him a look bordering on contempt. 'You're as pale as a fish.'

'For Christ's sake, man, look where you're going!' Levon yelled, as the car swerved wildly across the road while Art was looking the other way.

Myra screamed, '*Art!*'

Tamara flung herself at her husband and he caught her in his arms as the Oldsmobile and the tanker coming directly towards them met head on. Seconds later, both vehicles burst into flames.

John Zarian was a handsome young man, almost six feet tall and well built with broad shoulders and perfect limbs. He had a pleasing disposition, was considered quite clever, though more with words than with figures. He played soccer and basketball for his school, where he was very popular with both the boys and the girls.

He'd been staying with his pal, Scott Ives, for the Easter break when the news came of his parents' deaths in a car crash on their way back from Washington. As Scott's mother, Angie, told her husband when he came home that night, 'He took it very well – unnaturally well, in my view. He just said, "Thank you, ma'am,

278

'It's be best if I made the necessary arrangements from there,' he said. 'Then I'll have any papers to hand that might be needed. Your pop's office should be informed, his bank. Do you want to come with me, son?'

'No, thank you,' John said politely.

Mrs Ives came and gently told him that breakfast was ready. Yesterday, she'd just yelled, 'Grub's up!'

John's appetite had disappeared completely. All he wanted was coffee, which he didn't normally like. 'Have you heard of a woman called Anne Murray?' he asked Mrs Ives when he was on his third cup. Connie stared at him with her eyes full of tears. So far, John hadn't shed a single tear.

'Anne Murray? Why, yes. I saw her once on Broadway; she's a wonderful singer and dancer. I think your pop knew her. It was him who got us the tickets. She married someone, a film star.' She frowned deeply as she tried to recall the name. 'I know, it was Herbie Blinker, so she might have gone to live in California, but if she's still on the stage she could have stayed in New York. Why did you want to know, John?'

'There was a letter from her back home,' John improvised, 'but it didn't have her address on. I just wondered who she was.' He was beginning to feel trapped at the Iveses' house. He was desperate to find Anne Murray, even if it meant going all the way to California. First, though, he'd try to find her in New York, call in all the theatres on Broadway. Someone somewhere must know where she is. It dawned on him that his task might be made much simpler by looking in the telephone directory.

But even that proved difficult. When he asked for the directory, Mrs Ives offered to look the number up for him and he didn't want her to know it was for Anne Murray. He said he'd changed his mind and fancied a ride on his bike – he could look up the number in the post office – but she asked Scott to go with him, so John changed his mind again. It was no good saying he'd like to go home for a while, because Mr Ives was there.

In the end, he just rode away when no one was looking. It was rude, but he didn't care. He had something vitally important to do and nothing on earth was going to stop him.

He left his bike with Mrs Engels, who taught history at school. She lived not far from Brooklyn Bridge and let him look at her directory without interference, though remarked she hoped he'd done his Easter homework. John said that he had, which was a lie. She didn't know about his folks and he didn't break the news about the accident.

There were loads of Murrays in the telephone directory, six with the initial 'A', and no indication as to whether they were male or female. He remembered Mrs Ives had said Anne Murray had married someone called Blinker, so looked up that as well. There was only one, an E. Blinker who lived on Fifth Avenue at 62nd Street.

It wasn't the right initial, but Fifth Avenue seemed an appropriate address for someone who appeared on Broadway and had a film star for a husband. He supposed the proper thing to do would be ring the number and ask for Anne Murray, but he preferred to come face to face with the woman who might be his mother – if she were there.

He caught the bus across the bridge, then another to 62nd Street. It was a swell day, sunny and warm, and he had to remove his jacket on the bus. The address turned out to be an imposing building with swing doors opposite Central Park. His pop had loved Manhattan and had sometimes taken him to the park on Sundays if Mom hadn't had something else arranged, usually to do with church or school. His pop had seemed a distant figure, but John had loved him. Had he been allowed more say in things, he reckoned Pop would have taken him to all sorts of places like museums and theatres and movies, the sort of trips that didn't interest Mom.

He pushed through the swing doors and went inside.

Christina was in the kitchen preparing lunch, Lizzie was out for the day, and Anne was waiting for Bobby to return from the offices of the *New York Standard* and say he'd got the job as assistant editor. To pass the time, she was playing pool in Ollie's den. She was good at pool: Herbie used to get quite cross when she beat him. Sometimes, she would lose just to placate him, but he would guess she'd done it deliberately and be even crosser.

'There's no pleasing you,' she would laugh.

She and Herbie still got on well when they met. In Hollywood, he was forever getting entangled with different women, and a photo of him and the latest woman, usually referred to as a 'starlet', would appear in the scandal rags. Sometimes Anne was mentioned as his 'long-suffering wife'. She didn't give a damn what Herbie did.

The phone in the den rang. 'Bobby!' she cried aloud. The cue slipped and nearly ripped the table. It was the desk downstairs. 'There's someone down here to see you, Miss Murray: a Mr Zarian.'

It wasn't Bobby, but Lev, which was just as good, as she could introduce them to each other. 'Send him up,' she said, and put down the phone, wondering why Lev hadn't been automatically allowed up. Everyone downstairs knew him. Perhaps there was someone new on the desk, though it had sounded like Jimmy who'd worked in the building for ever.

The lift stopped and the doors opened on to an oddly shaped lobby lined with mirrors, like something out of a fairground. John was met with a hundred reflections of himself, all at a slightly different angle. He was so dazzled by the assortment of images that he failed to notice the slender, dark-haired girl waiting for him until she spoke.

'Who are you? I was expecting Lev,' she said.

'I'm John Zarian. Are you Anne Murray?' It hardly seemed possible; she looked so young – young enough to be his sister – and was incredibly pretty with black, curly hair just like his own and enormous violet eyes. He'd never seen eyes such a lovely colour before. She wore a plain white frock and white sandals. 'I'd like to see Anne Murray.'

'That's me. What do you want? Who are you?' She spoke in a

whispered hiss and looked so terrified that he wondered if she knew exactly who he was: it made him go hot and cold at the same time.

He took the birth certificate from his pocket and held it in both hands so she could read it. 'I'm John Zarian,' he repeated, 'and it says here that you're my mother.'

'I can't possibly be your mother, or anybody's mother,' she said coldly. 'I've never had a child. Where's Lev? I thought you were Lev.'

'Levon, my father, is dead. I found this.' He waved the certificate in front of her eyes. 'See, it says, "Mother – Anne Murray".' He hadn't had time to wonder what sort of reception he would get. Perhaps there was another Anne Murray. But no, he'd got the right one. This woman, this girl, was his mother, no matter how much she might try to deny it.

'Lev's dead?' Her eyes widened in shock. 'But he can't be. He's in Washington. Oh, he can't be dead, not Lev.' She began to cry – loud, heartrending sobs. 'I can't live without my darling Lev.'

A black woman appeared, all concerned, and put her arms around the younger one. 'What's wrong, honey? Tell Christina what's the matter.'

'Lev is dead, Christina.' It came in a long, drawn-out wail. 'What am I going to do?'

'Come and sit down, honey, and I'll make a cup of coffee.' She beckoned to John. 'You too, young man. Are you a friend of Mr Zarian's?'

'I'm his son.'

The admission shocked Christina. 'Oh, you poor soul. I reckon you could do with some coffee, too, and a few hugs and kisses wouldn't come amiss.' She ushered them both into a palatial room full of pictures and funny-shaped chairs covered with white leather. 'Anne, honey, this young fellow's just lost his father. I know you're upset, but try to spare a thought for him. He's got more reason to cry than you.'

She left to make the coffee. Her words seemed to have had some effect on Anne, who wiped her nose and said quietly, 'I'm sorry; you must be devastated. I bet Lev was a wonderful father. How is Tamara taking it?'

'She's dead, too. They died in a car crash on their way back from Washington.'

'Dear God!' Her tear-stained face was contorted with horror. 'When did this happen?'

'Yesterday.' For the first time, John felt tears come to his eyes. 'All I've got left is you.'

'You're wrong.' She shook her head. 'I really feel for you, but I assure you I'm not your mother.' She paused and seemed to cast around for something to say. 'You can stay here for a while; there's plenty of room. You're Lev's son and I want to help.'

'It says on my birth certificate "Father Unknown".''

'I don't know anything about that.' If she shook her head much more it would fall off.

'It's strange my family knowing two Anne Murrays.' He felt anger rise like bile in his throat.

She shrugged. 'Strange things happen all the time.'

'As you seem to have known my pop so well, perhaps you can tell me where to find the other Anne Murray?' Now he was even angrier and put all the sarcasm he could muster into his voice. He knew he was being very rude – his parents would be shocked if they could hear him.

'I don't know anything about that,' she said again, tightening her lips stubbornly.

Christina came in with the coffee. Neither spoke while she put the tray on the table. She looked at them worriedly, but departed without a word. John could tell she wanted to do or say something, but didn't like to interfere.

Anne pushed a drink in his direction. He didn't pick it up. 'What am I going to do?' he asked. Instead of anger, now there was a wobble in his voice. All of a sudden, he felt like a little boy who wanted his mom. 'Where's the bathroom?' he asked croakily.

'This way.' She virtually ran out of the room, as if she wanted to get away from him, for her life to return to normal. He followed, hardly able to walk because he felt so sad and so very alone. She was his mother, yet was determined to deny it. From now on, he knew he would always be alone: he had no one.

'This is a bathroom.' She flung open a door in another lobby, this one without mirrors, then disappeared. John entered the room, bolted the door, sat on the pan, and bawled his head off. His sobs were raw and full of pain, like the last cries of a dying animal. He fell face forward on to the floor, curled up in a ball, and willed himself to die.

Anne closed her bedroom door and put her hands over her ears to shut out the sound. If she allowed herself to acknowledge that he was her son, she would have to acknowledge that other thing that wavered constantly on the brink of her mind and that she always pushed away, convinced that if she let it in she would go completely mad.

But she could still hear the sound of the boy crying and it tore at her heart. He *was* her son, her own flesh and blood – but he was someone else's flesh and blood, too.

Now there was another sound, banging. Anne removed her hands from her ears. It was Christina knocking on the bathroom door and calling, 'Come on out, honey. I knew your daddy well and we can talk about him.'

It wasn't up to Christina to sort out Anne's problems. 'Dear God, please help me,' she whispered as she left the room. 'I'll see to him,' she told Christina, who looked at her oddly and said, 'The poor young man's beside himself. I'd've gone in, bathroom or no bathroom, but he's bolted the door. I wish Lizzie was home; she'd know what to do.'

'*I* know what to do.' She waited until Christina had gone into the kitchen before sitting on the floor outside the bathroom and tapping on the door. 'It's me, Anne.'

The crying stopped. 'What do you want?'

'For you to come out.'

'Why?' His voice was as deep as a man's, yet he was only fifteen, still a child inside.

286

'Because you can't stay there for ever; you've got to come out sometime.'

'I want my mom and pop,' he said in an anguished tone. '*I want my mom and pop.*' He was shouting now, his voice hoarse with rage.

'But they're dead, darling.' She shouldn't have called him that, but there was a tenderness in her that she hadn't wanted to convey.

'*You're* not dead,' he said pointedly. 'Why won't you admit that you're my mother?'

Anne began to cry, very softly. She bent her legs, wrapped her arms around them, and hid her head behind her knees. 'I can't, I just can't.'

The door opened and he came out and dropped onto the floor beside her. 'Why not?'

She lifted her head and looked at him straight in the eyes. She felt dizzy, muzzy, and could hardly think. 'The Doctor had grey eyes,' she whispered.

He pounced on the words. 'Who's the Doctor?'

'My father.' Everything swam – the walls, the floor, the ceiling, the boy's face, her own hands. She gasped, 'My father was your father.' He'd come into her bedroom, laid on top of her, pushed himself inside her. The pain was indescribable. She'd begun to scream . . .

'Stop!' Someone was holding her shoulders, shaking her, but it wasn't the Doctor. The Doctor had been drunk and hadn't cared about her screams, just continued to pump away inside her until she'd fainted from the pain, the shock, and the horror of it all. No, it was John who was shaking her, tears pouring down his cheeks, while, behind him, Christina waved her arms, looking close to tears herself.

Between them, they carried her to a different bedroom and laid her on a different bed. 'Lord Almighty, I wish Lizzie was here,' Christina cried plaintively.

'It's all right, she'll be all right now,' John said gruffly. 'Perhaps you could make more coffee.'

'Right away, son.' Christina looked only too pleased to have something to do.

'How do you feel?' John asked. He was sitting on the bed looking down at her. The child had gone and he was now a man.

'Awful,' she said limply. 'I'm sorry. As if you haven't had enough to cope with over the last few days without me having hysterics.'

'I'm sorry, too. I wish I hadn't come now. I should have waited until I didn't feel so upset about everything. Mom always said I was too impulsive.'

'You didn't have anyone else to turn to, did you?' Her lips quivered in a reluctant smile. 'Only me, and I'm useless.'

'No, you're not,' he said stoutly. He hesitated before speaking again. 'Is it . . . is it OK to ask if you meant what you said – about your father being my father?'

She shuddered. 'Yes, I meant it.'

'Golly!' It seemed an inadequate word to use.

'Do you mind?' Not that there was anything she could do about it if he did.

He looked at his shoes and sighed. 'It isn't much use minding now, is it?'

'I was thirteen.' She could remember that now, but not how many years had passed in between.

Elsewhere in the apartment the phone rang and Christina answered. Seconds later, she popped her head around the door. 'It's Bobby Gifford who came yesterday. He's downstairs and wants to come up.'

'Tell him to go away, I don't want to see him.' She didn't want to see anybody. Right now, she could hardly remember who Bobby Gifford was.

Christina frowned. 'Are you sure about that, honey?'

'I don't want to see anybody, Christina.'

'You shouldn't have shouted at her,' John said when the woman had gone and could be heard relaying Anne's message to the desk.

288

'I didn't realize I'd shouted.' Poor Christina had also had an upsetting day. 'I'll apologize later.'

'Can I use the phone? I need to tell some people, the Iveses, that I'm OK or they'll be worried.'

'Of course, there are phones all over the place.'

'When I come back, I'd like us to talk.' He paused at the door and looked at her searchingly. 'You're more like my sister than my mother.'

'But I *am* your sister, aren't I? Your sister *and* your mother.'

John told Mrs Ives that he was in Manhattan: 'I'm staying with one of Pop's friends, I hope you don't mind.' He got the impression that Mrs Ives could well have minded very much, had the circumstances been different. But he'd lost his folks and his rudeness was excused.

When he got back to the bedroom, Anne was fast asleep. He looked at her compassionately. It sure was a weird story. She'd been through a lot but, from now on, *he'd* look after her. Having a husband in California wasn't much use.

He sat on the bed, watching her, but in a while his eyes began to blink and he lay down beside her and fell asleep.

Christina came, wondering why everything had gone so quiet. She'd heard everything, but the only person she'd tell was Lizzie. She smiled with relief when she saw them asleep on the bed: mother and son; sister and brother. Softly, she closed the door and helped herself to a large glass of Mr Blinker's best whiskey. The last few hours had possibly been the most traumatic of her life.

Chapter 14

Anne wanted John's parentage kept secret. Because of Herbie, her name had already appeared in the scandal rags. 'Can you imagine the headlines?' she said, shivering. '"ANNE MURRAY, WIFE OF THE INFAMOUS HERBIE BLINKER, IS RE-UNITED WITH LONG-LOST SON." There'd be reporters round and they'd insist on having all the horrid details.' Only Lizzie and Christina were allowed to know, though Ollie and Herbie would have to be told eventually.

Lizzie, who was very nice and very capable, returned with John to Brooklyn to take over the funeral arrangements from Dick Ives. 'We can't very well leave it in the hands of strangers,' she said.

His mom and pop were buried together in Holy Cross Cemetery, Brooklyn, after a Requiem Mass in the old St Patrick's Cathedral. Hundreds of people turned up: his mother's friends from Brooklyn, John's friends from school – school was still out – and his father's friends from Manhattan. John hadn't dreamed his pop had been such a popular man – Mom had always made out he was a bit of a failure – but there were other lawyers, the staff from his office, the manager of MacCready's diner where Pop had always lunched, some of his old clients, people from show business. Lizzie's husband, Ollie Blinker, came all the way from Los Angeles to say goodbye to his best pal, Levon Zarian.

'There'll never be another guy like Lev,' he said tearfully, and everyone within earshot said, 'Hear, hear.'

When it was over, John and the Blinkers went back to the apartment on Fifth Avenue. John had been sleeping in Herbie's room where the closet was full of clothes that he wouldn't have been seen dead in; flashy suits, loads of white pants, and gaudy sweaters. Blown-up pictures of Anne and Herbie dancing had been stuck to the walls. In his opinion, Herbie looked a bit of a dork, and his hair was too long. Had *he* been given a say, he would have been against Anne marrying him.

It had been established that he would live in the apartment from now on and that the house in Brooklyn would be sold. When Herbie came back – and he only came at Christmas – he could sleep in the room that used to be his sister's. 'If he doesn't like it, he'll just have to lump it,' Lizzie said in the funny accent she'd managed to keep after spending over two-thirds of her life in New York. She'd asked Christina to empty the closet and give the clothes to a thrift shop. 'They're too old-fashioned for Herbie; he'll never wear them again,' she said. 'I don't know why he left them behind in the first place. I suppose he thought he'd buy a whole new wardrobe in Los Angeles.' In future, the closet would be used for John's clothes, though he doubted if they'd fill a quarter of the space.

He enjoyed being fussed over by Lizzie and Christina – his mom had been a very practical person and didn't hold with fuss. Anne didn't fuss, either, but John reckoned it was because she was too used to people fussing over her and wasn't experienced at it. She just drifted around looking vague and beautiful with a slight smile or a wistful look on her face. She read the theatre section in the paper, but nothing else. Sometimes, she sat by the big white piano, playing with one finger while she sang in a deep breathy sort of voice that sent prickly sensations up and down his spine. 'I sang that in a show once,' she'd tell him, or: 'This is from my new show. We haven't started rehearsals yet. Oh, and what do you think of this one? "*Oh, Danny boy,*"' she sang, '"*the pipes, the pipes are calling, from glen to glen and down the mountain side . . .*"' That's my very favourite song. I used to sing it when I was a little girl.'

So far, no one had mentioned school. When they did, he'd say he'd like to go back to his old one. Lots of people travelled from Brooklyn to Manhattan every day, so it wouldn't hurt to go the opposite way. He would enjoy telling his pals that he was now living on Fifth Avenue with one of Pop's old friends. And he was of Irish descent, not Armenian, though he couldn't tell them that.

The day after the funeral, Anne announced she was off to start rehearsing for a new show.

'Can I come with you?' John asked. He didn't want to be parted from her for a single minute.

'You'll only be bored.' She was packing shoes in a bag and wore a strange outfit comprising black tights, a short skirt, and a skimpy sweater. There was a red bandana on her black curls. She'd look silly dressed like that on public transport, but it turned out Eric was taking her in the car.

'No, I won't,' he argued. He was convinced he would never be bored with her.

'You can come if you want. If you are – bored, that is – you can always go out and take a stroll around Broadway.'

The show was all about Prohibition, some stupid law that had been passed in the 1920s banning the population from drinking alcohol. When Franklin Roosevelt became President, he'd repealed the law and become the most popular guy in the whole of America. He probably still was, although not with the right-wingers, who didn't believe in real democracy, as Pop had been fond of saying.

John sat near the back of the theatre. In a row near the front there was a man who kept shouting instructions. A woman with a feather in her hair played a beat-up piano. From what John could understand, most of the male cast were gangsters, and the women, including Anne, were gangsters' molls. On stage, she was a different person, lithe and sensuous, dancing with such passion and energy that it amazed him, as if this was the only place where she was truly alive. This incredible woman was his mother. She fascinated him. When they were together, he couldn't take his eyes off her. He'd hardly grieved for his mom and pop because he was so enamoured with Anne. He watched her twirl across the

292

stage, as light as a feather, to be caught in the arms of a guy who held her aloft for a second, then threw her to the floor and began to kick her. John's fists tightened and he was about to hurl himself down the aisle and break every bone in the guy's body, when he remembered it wasn't real; he was in a theatre where nothing was real.

On the way home in the car, she asked if he'd like to go to stage school. 'You could go to the same one I went, Peggy Perlmann's. Peggy was at the funeral yesterday. She was the tall, red-haired woman who cried the whole time.'

John confessed he'd never nursed any ambition to go on the stage. 'Pop wanted me to be a lawyer like him, and Mom wanted me to teach, but I don't think I fancy either. I'm not sure what I want to do when I leave school, but I'd sure like to work in Manhattan, the same as Pop.' Then he would never have to leave her. He could cut the grass in Central Park, drive a bus, work on the subway – and live in the apartment on Fifth Avenue for the rest of his life.

Anne's eyes snapped open. She looked at the clock on the bedside table. Its luminous hands showed that it was ten past four. Outside, it was still dark. She'd just remembered something. Her name was Annemarie Kenny and she was born in a village in Ireland called Duneathly. Oh, if only Lev were alive and she could ask him where the name Anne Murray had come from. There were still blank spaces in her mind. She remembered boarding a big white boat in a place called Liverpool and Mollie putting her to bed, but nothing more until she'd found herself in Lev's cab and he'd called her Anne Murray. She'd accepted the name because she didn't want to be Annemarie Kenny any more. She was a new person without a past, except she'd brought part of the past with her in the form of her father's baby.

It was such a relief that she could let herself think about it, talk about it with Lizzie. She'd blocked so many things out of her mind, even John, who wasn't really part of the past. It was hard to believe that the tiny baby she'd turned her back on had grown into such a remarkable young man. She was so proud of him that she really wished she could tell everyone that she was his mother.

Something else she'd remembered was that she had an aunt in New York, Aunt Maggie, whom she and Mollie had been going to stay with. Her other name was Connelly and she was a teacher, but Lizzie had hired a private detective who could find no trace of her. 'Perhaps she's gone back to Ireland, pet,' she'd said.

Anne had felt a tiny bit glad. Aunt Maggie was bound to write and tell the Doctor where she was, and just imagine if *he* wrote to her! Her flesh crawled at the idea. She'd love to contact Mollie and her brothers again, but she'd have to tell them about John and how could she put that in a letter? She wasn't sure if she could ever bring herself to do it.

It was a full two weeks later before she remembered Bobby Gifford, the way he'd kissed her and said, '*Shall we leave it like that and see what happens next?*'

John had happened next. John had arrived and taken over her life, releasing so many memories, which kept seeping in a few at a time, that she couldn't cope with anything else apart from rehearsals for the show; they came before everything. She had a feeling that he'd phoned when she'd been unable to speak to him and wondered why he hadn't phoned again. Had he got the job he'd wanted on the *New York Standard*? In fact, she'd telephone the paper right now and find out. When she did, she discovered he was working for the paper, but was now thousands of miles away in another country altogether. The woman who answered the phone refused to give her his address, but Anne didn't mind. They would meet again one day, she felt quite sure of it.

Jeez! Being in London was like stepping back in time. Some of these buildings were hundreds of years old. Even the more recent ones looked as if they dated back to Victorian times. The cars and the big red buses were very much out of place in such ancient surroundings.

Bobby Gifford turned away from the window of the hotel in Parliament Street, right opposite the Foreign Office. The windows, like every other one in London, was criss-crossed with tape, which was to prevent the glass from shattering in the event of a bomb dropping nearby. The United Kingdom was at war; he was actually in a war zone.

His room was like something out of a museum: a thick carpet, a ponderous bed covered with a tasselled velvet quilt on which his suitcase waited to be unpacked, furniture that looked as if it would require a crane to lift. He wondered how many images and fashions the slightly spotted, gold-framed mirror over the marble fireplace had reflected over the years. At the desk, he'd been asked if he would like a fire in his room, but had refused.

Tomorrow, he would start looking for an apartment, something small and comfortable in the centre of the city, for Bobby was now the European correspondent for the *New York Standard*, based in London, but shortly off to Paris. Having captured Norway and Denmark, German troops were now approaching the borders of Belgium, Holland, and France, and it was anticipated these countries would be invaded at any minute. As an American, Bobby assumed he would be safe to assess the situation on the ground and send reports back home.

Two and a half weeks ago, Bobby had got the job of assistant editor on the paper. Outside, the interview over, he'd whooped with joy and caught a cab to Anne's apartment. He could hardly wait to tell her. He was thirty-five, but hadn't had a great deal of experience with women. His wife hadn't exactly instilled him with confidence the way she'd abandoned him when he'd lost his job through no fault of his own, and there hadn't been much time for socializing in Springfield. In fact, he'd deliberately buried himself in his work, not wanting to get involved. But he'd never forgotten Anne and her kindness. When they'd met again he'd realized this was it. She was the woman he'd been waiting for all his life. There was something otherworldly about her, an artlessness that must be unique in someone who'd made a career in show business, but this only strengthened the attraction she held for him; an attraction that he had believed he also held for her.

But it turned out he was wrong. He'd asked the guy on the desk to announce he was downstairs, and had imagined the way her lovely eyes would light up when he told her he'd got the job he was after, that in another month he would be living in New York.

Boy, had he been wrong. The guy on the desk reported that she didn't want to see him. 'But why?' Bobby had asked, but the other man had merely shrugged.

'I dunno, feller, do I?'

'Is she sick?'

'I dunno that, either. I sent another young feller up there a couple of hours ago, and he hasn't come down again. Maybe she's busy with him.'

'Should I come tomorrow?'

'That's up to you, but if some dame told me to go away, I'd stay away.'

Which is precisely what Bobby did. Feeling as if his heart had broken, and hurt more deeply than he'd ever been before, he'd gone back to the paper, asked to see the editor, and told him he didn't want the job after all. All he wanted to do, though he didn't say it, was return to Springfield, bury himself in the *Courier*, and forget about women for the rest of his life.

The editor was remarkably sympathetic and intuitive. 'Is it woman trouble?' he'd asked.

Bobby nodded. The man had a kindly face and was old enough to be his father. He had a job stopping himself from bursting into tears and telling him the whole story. Instead, he said, finding it hard to keep his voice steady, 'Strange how quickly life can change: when I left your office, I felt as if I were on top of the world. Now, it's as if the bottom's dropped out of it.'

'That can happen to anyone, son. Take Skip Hillier, f'rin-stance, our European correspondent. He was driving down some little country lane in Suffolk, England, as right as rain, when he took a bend too fast, crashed into a wall, and ended up with two broken legs, three cracked ribs, a smashed collarbone, and a sprained wrist. He'll be in traction forever and a day,' he finished ruefully. 'Now we've got another vacancy on the books. I can manage without an assistant, but not without a guy in Europe, not when there's a war raging over there, the British Prime Minister's in deep shit and the population want Winston Churchill to take over. That guy Hitler's on the prowl and Christ knows what country he'll take over next.'

'Can *I* do it?' Bobby asked impulsively.

The editor – his name was Bill Flanaghan and he still had a trace of an Irish accent – shook his head. 'You haven't had the experience, son. How much do you know about the war?'

'*Everything*,' Bobby said emphatically. 'I read your papers from cover to cover every single day. I've read all Skip Hillier's reports. I know what the situation is with the British government and that the Brits are having a hellish time, losing hundreds of their ships. It makes me mad when some folk over there refer to it as a "phoney" war; there's nothing phoney about being torpedoed. The next country the Germans will invade will almost certainly be Norway. The main reason I wanted to leave Springfield is because it's too parochial for me – I told you that before.' Thinking about it now, he didn't want to go back; he didn't want to bury himself anywhere. Bill Flanaghan would consider him a no-brainer, turning down one job and demanding another, but the idea of living in London and reporting on the war was the best job on earth and, if anything would help him forget Anne, it would be that.

The editor smiled. 'I'm impressed with your enthusiasm – and your knowledge. Let me think about it and give us a call in the morning.'

The next day Bobby had called and had been told he had the job. He'd gone rushing back to Springfield where he'd stayed a while to make sure the *Courier* was in good hands – there wasn't time to work out a month's notice – and now here he was in London. He hadn't forgotten Anne and never would, but the excitement of his sudden move to another continent had certainly cushioned the blow of losing her.

Having rented an apartment in Dover Street, off Piccadilly, Bobby went to see Skip Hillier, his predecessor, in a hospital in Suffolk at the request of Bill Flanaghan: 'It'll cheer the bastard up, let him know the paper's thinking about him.'

He went by train – he hadn't even tried to hire or buy a car; petrol was difficult to get in England and likely to get more difficult as the war progressed – and was dazzled by the soft green fields, the thatched cottages that had probably stood there for centuries, the great Tudor manor houses, and quite a few horse-drawn carts driven by men dressed like peasants. He was fully aware, however, that there were many parts of the country that weren't so picturesque; cities like Birmingham, Liverpool, and Manchester, where Anne's mother-in-law had come from, places that he would still like to see, however.

The only part of Skip Hillier that wasn't bandaged was his head and the tips of his fingers; otherwise he bore a strong resemblance to an Egyptian mummy. His face was full of old bruises that had turned a nasty shade of yellow.

'I've brought you some smokes,' Bobby said after he'd introduced himself.

'I can't smoke, I can't bend my arms,' the man said sourly – understandably, 'I could do with some liquor, though. I could drink through a straw if someone held it for me. Will you arrange to have some sent?' He sniffed pathetically. 'I'm dying here.'

'I'll do my best,' Bobby promised, a promise he had no intention of keeping. (According to Bill Flanaghan, the reason for the accident was almost certainly due to Hillier's liking for booze. 'He was probably sozzled to the roots of his teeth when he crashed the car,' his editor had said. 'Don't give him anything to drink, whatever you do.')

He lit a Marlboro and held it to the man's still swollen lips. Hillier breathed in hungrily and blew the smoke into Bobby's face, then began a tirade against England, the English, English food, rationing, the hard job he'd had finding cigarettes and decent booze, the fact his girlfriend had dropped him since he'd had the accident – she'd had a title of sorts, or her cousin had: 'He was an honourable something or other; a gormless bastard with teeth like gravestones.' The job was as boring as hell, the blackout stank, and he felt sorry for Bobby from the bottom of his heart. 'In another few weeks, you'll be bored out of your skin and wishing you were back in the good old US of A.' He then began to cry for his mother. Bobby patted the bandages and assured him it wouldn't be long before he was fit enough for the paper to fly him home. He helped him smoke another six Marlboros and went back to his flat in Dover Street, feeling that his duty had been done.

Boring! He couldn't think of anything less boring than sitting in the press gallery in the House of Commons the following day listening to a motion of confidence in the Conservative government led by Prime Minister Chamberlain. The atmosphere was electric. When the debate was over and all the speeches had been made, thirty Conservatives followed the opposition into the 'no' lobby, meaning the motion was lost. Chamberlain was out and Churchill was in.

Bobby called the *Standard* from a phone in the lobby and dictated a report. He left the building feeling as if he'd just witnessed an event that would go down in history. After today, the course of the war could well change, affecting not just Europe, but the entire world.

In the meantime, *his* little part of Europe had been plunged into a darkness so dense that it looked impenetrable. He now had the task of negotiating the blackout so he could return to his apartment.

Two days later, Germany attacked Holland and Belgium and made for France. Bobby didn't know a single soul who didn't think it inevitable that France would fall, leaving just the narrow strip of water called the English Channel separating the enemy from the country he was quickly growing to love. That night, he packed his bag and left for Paris. It meant travelling by boat to Spain and passing back up through the French border.

Jeez! This was one helluva job.

The country had been at war for almost a year before the bombs came. At first, they fell harmlessly in fields on the outskirts of Liverpool, but in September they began to drop on houses, cinemas, hospitals and churches. People were being *killed*.

In quiet moments, Mollie had furious arguments inside her head with Harry Benedict. 'So, this is what you wanted, is it, Harry?' she would rant, often giving herself a headache. 'Are you happy now? We could have come to an agreement with Hitler that he wouldn't attack this country, then we wouldn't have been at war, and people could still sleep peacefully in their beds. There'd have been no such thing as ration books, no blackout or shortages, no bloody bombs. Betty's husband, Dave, and Mrs Oakley's son would still be alive, along with hundreds of other people's sons and husbands.' They had been merchant seamen who had all been lost when their ships were sunk.

Of course, she knew Harry was right and she was wrong. Hitler had to be stopped. He couldn't be allowed to conquer country after country while Great Britain just sat back and watched it happen. That would have been shameful, but the arguments with Harry helped her cope with the fear and frustration she felt – that everyone felt – whenever the air raid warning siren sounded, followed by the rumble of planes overhead. Then the bombs would start to drop. The children would have to be roused from their beds and taken to the nearest shelter – ordinary brick buildings that she reckoned were no safer than the house they'd just left. The shelter would be crowded and they'd have to sit on the floor and listen to explosions all over Liverpool, everyone ducking when one sounded particularly close. Brodie insisted on bringing Dandelion, nursing him in her arms, and he would struggle to escape. He hated the noise. When the siren went he would hide under the table and bury his head in his paws. Mollie bought him a new collar and wrote his address on the inside just in case he ran away and got lost.

Some families slept all night in the shelter, arriving early so they could get the best spots, but Mollie knew that she would never manage to sleep on a hard, wooden bench or a concrete floor, no matter how thick the bedding, and neither would Irene or the children. When the pubs closed, the shelter was invaded by hordes of noisy drunks who urinated against the walls, making the place stink to high heaven.

The air raids weren't all the population had to worry about. There was also the ever-present threat of Britain being invaded by the German Army, which was poised on the coast of France. Church bells had been banned and wouldn't ring again until the war was over – or if German troops landed. Then the bells would ring to signal an invasion had begun.

Finn kept writing to insist she and the children come and live in Duneathly, actually accusing her of being irresponsible for not coming. Southern Ireland wasn't involved in the war. 'You'd be perfectly safe here. You're putting your own and your children's lives at risk,' he wrote.

At the end of October, a month when there'd been a raid almost every night – and some during the day – Mollie decided it was time she took the children to Ireland. She didn't intend to stay herself. Irene was approaching seventy and becoming increasingly fragile, both mentally and physically. She was terrified of the raids, clinging to Mollie's arm with a vice-like grip until the all-clear went, positively refusing to move in with any of her three sons who lived in less vulnerable areas of Liverpool. She wanted to stay in her own home with Mollie.

Mollie had to keep reminding herself that Irene was Tom's mother and Tom had been her favourite son. He would have wanted her to look after his beloved mam – she'd been telling herself that for the past ten years. But neither would he have wanted his children to be in danger when there was no need.

On 3 November, she and the children, laden with suitcases containing all their clothes and toys, caught the boat to Ireland, the train to Kildare, and the little bus that sputtered through the deserted country lanes to Duneathly. Nothing had changed, except that the trees were perhaps taller and the door of the cottage where Finn and Hazel had once lived had been painted dark blue, when it had used to be dark brown.

The bus stopped in the square outside O'Reilly's pub and a whole crowd of young people came pouring out of the Doctor's house, from the very tall to the very small, followed by Hazel, who was stouter than when Mollie had last seen her. The children stood in a row, the tallest at one end, the smallest at the other, while Hazel called out their names. 'I'll start with Patrick, at fifteen he's the eldest, then Kieran and Eoin – you've met them before. Do you remember your Auntie Mollie, lads?' The boys grinned and nodded vigorously. 'Then there's Sean, Kerianne, Noreen, Finola, and Bernadette. Bernadette's the baby; she's only three. Say hello to Aunt Mollie, everyone. She's brought her children to stay with us until the cruel war across the water is over.'

'Hello, Aunt Mollie,' the children chorused. 'It's very nice to meet you.'

Hazel grinned. 'They've been practising that all day, and standing in a line. Finn had an appointment, but he'll be along soon. Thaddy and Aidan are still at work.'

Mollie introduced her own children, who were immediately taken into the house, surrounded by their cousins. She and Hazel came behind with the luggage. 'I wish you were staying for more than two days, Moll,' Hazel said.

'So do I.' Mollie glanced around the square. Not a single window had been taped, there were no sandbags, no barrage balloons in the sky, no chance of a siren going off to warn of an imminent air raid. It was half past four and the light was beginning to fail, yet all the shops were brightly lit, whereas in Liverpool, the blackout would be in force. 'It's so peaceful here. But when I told Irene I'd be away for a little while, she went berserk. She needs me, Hazel, I can't let her down.' For all her faults, she genuinely loved her mother-in-law.

'It hardly seems fair.' They entered the house and deposited the suitcases in the hall.

'It hardly seems unfair, either. Irene's entitled to be looked after in her old age, and it won't last for ever, nothing does.' She followed her sister-in-law into the kitchen. Bubbles immediately came and rubbed himself against her legs. 'This is a big improvement on the last time I was here,' she gasped when she saw the electric stove in place of the horrible one she'd been apt to kick from time to time. 'Finn wrote and told me Duneathly had electricity at last.'

Hazel gave the stove an affectionate pat. 'Now, all we have to do is switch on the light when it's dark. I was glad to see the back of those filthy oil lamps. At first, I kept switching the lights on and off to convince meself they actually worked.'

Mollie blinked at the sight of a tray of twenty-four eggs on the table: *two dozen*. Back home they were rationed to one egg each a week. There was also a bowl of fruit: oranges, apples, and a bunch of grapes. She couldn't remember when she'd last seen a grape, and oranges were almost as rare. The children would love it here.

'Kerianne is the image of Annemarie,' she remarked.

'Isn't she?' Hazel agreed with a smile. 'Quite a few people have remarked on that, the ones who can remember Annemarie. Time seems to stand still in Duneathly and they talk about her – and you – as if you'd only gone last week.'

'Tom said once he'd like to live in Duneathly when he retired.' He'd said it ten years ago in the bedroom upstairs where they'd slept.

'Oh, Moll, that would have been lovely, having you and Tom living here all the time.'

'But it wasn't to be, was it?' Mollie said sadly.

Not long afterwards, Finn came rushing in and gave his sister an enormous hug, followed shortly afterwards by Thaddy and Aidan, who both worked in Kildare. They were young men now. Thaddy was twenty and Aidan seventeen. They were pleased to see her and their nieces and nephews. Mollie felt sad again, wishing she and Annemarie hadn't had to leave Duneathly and they could have all grown up together, but then she wouldn't have met Tom. She might have married someone else and had quite different children.

Two days flashed by. Duneathly was buried in a wet mist that gave the village a ghostly quality, blurring the lights and making the buildings appear to be suspended in mid-air. Mollie bought flowers, big russet chrysanthemums, and walked alone through the mist to put them on Mammy's grave, did a tour of the shops to say hello to the people she knew, and visited Nona in the post office to tell her Dandelion was doing just fine, except he didn't like the air raids. Most importantly of all, she took the children to the convent where they would go to school and introduced them to the nuns. Megan, who was fourteen, had left school that summer and had been working in a florist's shop on Scotland Road, but Mollie wanted her bright, argumentative daughter to have two more years' education.

Sister Francis remembered the girls and Joe well. 'I can tell this one's a little monkey,' she said, looking at Tommy's tough, mischievous face. She suggested they start the following Monday to give them time to get used to Duneathly. She'd never been to Liverpool, but imagined it being very different.

'Very different,' Megan agreed in her grown-up way.

Next morning, it was time for Mollie to go, but she found it a wrench to tear herself away from a house so full of warmth and good humour – and twelve children. Finn and Hazel weren't rich, but neither were they poor. They could afford to pay for help with the cleaning, the cooking, and the mountains of washing that had to be done. The food was plain but nourishing.

The other children had gone to school, except for Finola and Bernadette who were too young. Mollie looked at the mournful faces of her own four and told them how much she would miss them. 'But it won't be for long,' she added. 'I'll be back at Christmas, though it will only be for a few days.' Somehow or other she would get away, even if it meant bringing Irene with her.

'Dad went back to Liverpool,' Megan pointed out, 'and we never saw him again.'

'Well, that's not going to happen with me,' she assured them, wishing Megan had kept her big mouth shut. 'You'll be happy with your Auntie Hazel and Uncle Finn. You'll have loads of cousins to play with, lots of lovely food, and there'll be no more air raids.' She wanted to cry. She'd never thought a time would come when she would be separated from her children. 'Oh, you'll have a fine time, I feel sure of it,' she said, her voice breaking slightly.

'What about Dandelion?' Brodie's lips quivered. 'We should have brought him with us. Who'll take care of him in the raids?'

'*I* will,' she promised. 'Dandelion's a town cat. He's not used to the countryside. I was worried he'd run away in such a strange place. What would you have done then, Brodie?'

'I'd have cried,' Brodie said simply.

'Well, now there's no need to cry, and you can help Auntie Hazel look after Bubbles – don't forget he's Dandelion's brother. Anyway, I'm not going to the shelter again. From now on, Grandma and I will sit under the stairs with Dandelion when there's a raid.' She was fed up with shelters. Lots of people took refuge under the stairs. She turned to Joe, who looked very pale. ''Bye, son. As I just said, Mammy will be here for Christmas and I'll bring some lovely presents for you all.'

'I don't want presents, Mammy, I want you.' He was on the verge of tears. If he cried, then so would she.

'I want presents, Mammy, *and* I want you,' Tommy declared.

Hazel yelled, 'The bus has arrived, Mollie. You'd best get a move on. I'll run out and tell the driver you're coming.'

Mollie virtually ran out of the room. She boarded the bus, sat on the back seat, and sobbed her heart out all the way to Kildare. She was still shedding the odd tear when the boat docked in Liverpool.

*

Irene objected fiercely the following night when Mollie put on her coat and announced she was going to the Rotunda. When the war had first started, she'd thought she was out of work as the government ordered all the theatres and cinemas to close. She'd been desperately looking for another job when the government had changed its mind and announced they could re-open.

'What happens if a raid starts and you're not here?' Irene's eyes were wide with terror. It had happened twice before at the Rotunda; the manager had come on to the stage and advised the audience that the siren had just gone. A few people had left. The rest including the performers, preferred to stay where they were. 'At least we'll die having a good time,' someone had said. Mollie had had to wait until the money had been counted, then race like a mad woman along Scotland Road to be with her family.

'Irene, love,' she said patiently, 'I can't leave the theatre, can I? We'd have no money to live on.' Once a month, she intended to send a postal order to Duneathly. Finn would object, but she didn't care. It was a matter of pride that she contributed towards the upkeep of her children.

'But, Mollie, what will I *do*?' Irene persisted.

'You'll just have to go next door for a while, or sit under the stairs by yourself. It won't be for long and I've made it nice and comfortable in there.' She'd bought two canvas garden chairs from a second-hand shop, brought down some of the bedding from the children's beds, and provided a tin of biscuits and some bottles of lemonade. 'I'll be back as soon as I possibly can.'

There was a play on that week, *Gaslight*; it was dark and creepy and full of atmosphere. The audience, their nerves more on edge than normal, gasped so loud that Mollie could hear them in the box office where she was sorting out the takings. As soon as she'd finished, she took the bags to the manager's office and left the theatre.

It was a beautiful, moonlit night – perfect for a raid. Every building was clearly visible from the sky, including the docks, the lifeblood of the city and the prime target of enemy bombs. There were few people about, though the pubs, shrouded in darkness, were full of revellers. 'We're gonna hang out the washing on the Siegfried Line,' they sang. 'When the lights go on again, all over the world,' they were singing in the next pub she passed.

In Duneathly, O'Reilly's customers would be singing 'Danny Boy', or 'The Black Velvet Band'; Finn and Hazel would be listening to the wireless, most of the children would be in bed, and Thaddy and Aidan would be out with their girlfriends – Thaddy was getting engaged at Christmas, but Mollie hadn't had time to meet his girlfriend, Ellen.

She wished she was with her children so much that it hurt. She noticed Charlie's fish and chip shop on the other side of the road, but couldn't tell whether it was open or not, and wished Harry were still alive, even if all they did was talk. 'If wishes were horses, then beggars would ride,' someone used to say, almost certainly Nanny.

A tramcar passed, going slowly, the windows painted black and the headlights barely visible. It was like something out of a nightmare and she imagined it being full of ghouls and banshees behind the darkened glass. The emptiness of the road, the fact that there wasn't another human being in sight, was getting to her.

Tomorrow, she'd go and see Agatha, cheer herself up a bit. Surely Irene wouldn't object to her going out during the day? The trouble was that Agatha reminded Mollie of all the things she'd lost when Tom had died. Phil was now in plainclothes and a detective sergeant. In August, they'd gone on holiday to Blackpool where, Agatha said, you'd hardly believe there was a war on apart from the blackout. The fairground was still open and the kids had had a lovely time. They'd all gone to the pictures to see *The Wizard of Oz*. In the hotel where they'd stayed, they'd had dances and floorshows. 'So it didn't matter about the blackout,' Agatha had enthused. She'd sent Mollie a box of kippers and sticks of Blackpool rock for the children.

No, she wouldn't go and see Agatha. It would only make her more miserable than she already felt.

The children sent letters saying how happy they were living with their Auntie Hazel and Uncle Finn. Brodie drew a girl in a tutu on hers and said she was going to ballet lessons with Kerianne, and Tommy drew a lion devouring a nun. According to his letter, it was Sister Swastika whom he didn't like. Mollie assumed he meant Sister Scholastica, who'd taught at the convent when she was there. She hadn't liked her, either. Megan claimed she was top of the class: 'I know all sorts of things the others don't.' Joe was missing his mammy badly and really looking forward to Christmas.

Hazel enclosed a note of her own:

Megan's in love with Patrick again. She insists she's going to marry him one day. How do you feel about cousins marrying? I don't mind if you don't, though Finn's not sure. Brodie has adopted Bubbles and takes him to bed with her in a blanket. He's enjoying the fuss, as our children are inclined to torment him. Tommy's really settled in, but Joe's still a bit tearful. I give him a cuddle every night and feel confident he'll soon be all right.

Mollie was upset to think that another woman was cuddling her son, even if it was Hazel. It should be *her* doing it. She lost her temper with Irene when she gave her letters to read and she remarked that Megan was a snooty little so-and-so: 'And cousins *can't* get married. The church wouldn't stand for it.'

'Then the church can go to hell.' She recalled Harry's caustic comments about the church, that religion was the opium of the people.

Irene took offence and disappeared into the parlour. Mollie stayed in the living room simmering with anger until it was time to leave for the theatre. When she came home, Irene was in bed. At three in the morning, the siren went and the women sat under the stairs, listening to the bombs falling. Irene clutching Mollie's arm so tightly that she had to prise her fingers loose when her arm started to go numb.

'I'm sorry, luv,' Irene said humbly. 'I didn't mean what I said before. Megan's a lovely kid. It was my fault we didn't get on. And I really appreciate you staying with me, girl. I'm just a daft old woman who's got no right to keep you from your family. I know how much you must be missing them. Go to Ireland, Mollie,' she said stoutly. 'Go tomorrow. I can manage on me own.'

Irene had offered her an opportunity to escape, but Mollie couldn't bring herself to take it. It just wasn't in her to desert her mother-in-law at such a time.

During November, the raids got worse and lasted longer, culminating in one terrible night at the end of the month when 180 people were killed in a single incident. It was a night when it seemed as if the whole of Liverpool was on fire, and the sky turned red from the flames. Ambulances and fire engines raced through the city, which resounded to the sounds of bombs exploding, buildings collapsing, and the sinister crackle of fires.

It was an unexpected relief when the first three weeks of December passed without a single raid. Mollie went to town and shopped for presents for the children – sometimes Irene came with her. Despite the worsening situation, Irene had become less clinging of late. Mollie could tell she was determined to be brave. She didn't object to her going to Duneathly for Christmas and had agreed to stay with Brian and Pauline while she was away.

When it came to toys, there were few to be had in the shops. The country was at war and factories had turned to producing more important things. Mollie managed to get Tommy a camouflaged aeroplane and a popgun, which he would no doubt use to frighten the cat. Brodie loved clothes, so she bought her a pretty frock and a lacy cardigan. At ten, Joe had become a voracious reader and Mollie was thrilled when she found a collection of virtually new boys' adventure books and comics in a second-hand shop. It was Irene who discovered the perfect gift for Megan: a dressing-table set comprising a hand mirror and brush with flowers painted on the backs and a matching comb.

'She's a young lady now and won't want toys,' Irene said,

adding tearfully, 'I wish we'd got on better when she was home. I scolded her too much. I know that now.'

The presents were wrapped in red and green crêpe paper and put on top of the piano ready to take to Ireland, along with bags of sweets and chocolate for Mollie's nieces and nephews – she'd been saving her sweet coupons for months. Now all she had to get was something for Irene.

Lily had come up with the idea that they buy a present between them for their mother-in-law. 'We could get her a nice piece of jewellery,' she said. 'She'd be more pleased with that than talc, posh soap, and a box of hankies from each of us.'

Mollie, Pauline, and Gladys were inclined to agree. They met in town one afternoon a few days before Christmas and toured the jewellery shops, eventually choosing a gold St Christopher medal on a chain. Feeling satisfied with their purchase, they went into the Kardomah for coffee. Everyone was in good mood; the war had brought people closer together. Lily and Pauline rarely bickered these days and had been getting on better with their mother-in-law. Gladys was far more tolerant of her husband's family.

It was Gladys who suggested they all went to the pictures. *Goodbye, Mr Chips* with Robert Donat is on the Forum. It'll be a nice treat; this is the first time the four of us have been out together.'

Lily looked dubious. 'What if there's an air raid?'

'There hasn't been one for ages,' Gladys replied. 'Personally, I think we've seen the last of them.'

'Irene will be worried if I'm late home,' Mollie said, but Pauline argued that Mollie was a grown woman and entitled to a life of her own.

'Anyroad, it won't be all *that* late. It's not quite four o'clock now.' Gladys got to her feet. 'Let's go round to the Forum and see what time it starts.'

Minutes later, they were studying the times in the cinema foyer. The supporting picture still had half an hour to go and would be followed by the Pathé news and the interval. *Goodbye, Mr Chips* started at five to five and finished at quarter to seven.

'You'll easily be home by seven, Moll,' Gladys pointed out.

'Oh, all right.' Irene would be expecting her home before it went dark. She hoped she wouldn't be too upset. After all, Mollie wasn't a little girl who had to answer to her mother. There was very little excitement in her life these days – in fact, none at all that she could think of – and a visit to the pictures was just what she needed.

The film was incredibly moving. Mollie's handkerchief was soaked with tears in no time, yet she was enjoying it immensely. She'd never seen Robert Donat before; he had a kind, gentle face and the most beautiful voice she'd ever heard. The film was about three-quarters of the way through when a notice appeared on the screen to say a raid had started. The audience groaned and a few people stood to leave, Mollie amongst them, ignoring the pleas from her sisters-in-law to stay and see the film through to the end.

Outside, the blackout took her by surprise. It always did. She was never quite prepared for the intensity of it, of sometimes not being able to see her hand in front of her face. It was like being buried in black cotton wool.

Somehow, she managed to find her way to the tram stop where she waited, hoping and praying a tram would come soon. It was up to the driver whether or not to continue once a raid had started. Most kept on the move; it was no more or less dangerous than standing still. There were other people waiting at the stop. A man struck a match to look at his watch. A woman said, 'Well, I can't see any sign of a raid, can you?'

The words were hardly out of her mouth when the heavy drone of planes could be heard. Mollie felt sick to her stomach. She'd never been out in a raid before. A tram glided up and the conductor shouted cheerfully, 'Come on, let's be having yer.' Everyone climbed on, the conductor rang the bell, and the tram set off.

They'd hardly gone a minute when bedlam broke out and the

earth erupted, as if every plane had dropped a bomb at the very same minute. The tram swayed. 'Looks like we're in for a rocky ride,' the conductor quipped. A few people laughed.

The tram continued to sway as it journeyed along Byrom Street – at least, Mollie assumed it was Byrom Street; she couldn't see a thing through the painted windows. The conductor was calling out the names of the stops, so there was no chance she'd get off at the wrong place. She could hear the urgent clang of a fire engine as it raced by. There were explosions all around them. The tram's brakes creaked and then it suddenly stopped. The conductor got off and went to speak to the driver. He returned within minutes.

'Sorry, folks,' he shouted, 'but the lines are up ahead. I'm afraid you'll all have to get off and walk. Either that, or stay on the tram till the all-clear goes. It's up to you. The tram's going nowhere, but me and Bert are off to The Grapes on the corner for a bevy.'

Mollie alighted with the other passengers, most of them grumbling about what they'd do to Hitler given half a chance. 'Me hubby'll moan like hell if his tea's late,' a woman complained.

The conductor winked. 'Well, he knows who to blame it on, doesn't he, missus?' His unremitting cheerfulness was getting on Mollie's nerves.

She stepped off the tram into a world made red by fire and bright by flares, and began to run, coming soon to the place where a bomb had fallen, leaving a crater in the middle of the road that stretched from pavement to pavement. Inside it, she could see the twisted remains of tramlines. The shops on either side had had their windows and doors blown in. She stepped over the rubble and began to run again, passing the florist's where Megan had worked. It meant she wasn't far away from Turnpike Street. More people were running; the raid had taken everyone by surprise. It was unusual for air raids to start so early and perhaps, like Gladys, they'd thought they'd seen the last of them. Mollie had been more hopeful than optimistic.

Turnpike Street at last! She'd actually turned into the street, was hurrying down it, breathless, when the bomb fell, the explosion threw her backwards, and she lost consciousness.

When she came to, she was lying on the ground and her eyes and nose were full of dust. She raised her head and saw that about half a dozen of the little terraced houses had been reduced to debris. One of the houses had belonged to her mother-in-law.

Two days later, the day before Christmas Eve, Lily and Mike saw her on to the Irish ferry. Finn met her at the other side and drove her back to Duneathly. Her head was bandaged and her arm in a sling – it was only a bad sprain and expected to get better soon.

Irene's body had been found and her sons would see to the funeral. Mollie had wanted to stay, but they wouldn't hear of it.

'You've been through enough, luv,' Enoch had said the day before when the three brothers had come to collect her from the hospital where she'd spent the night. 'And you've done enough an' all. You've looked after our mam for ten long years, and she wasn't the easiest person to get along with, we all know that, though we loved her to bits, all three of us. You go back to your kids and be with them for Christmas.'

She'd spent the next night with Lily and Mike, an horrendous night during which she didn't sleep a wink, not only because her head and arm were hurting, but because there was a raid that lasted ten hours and didn't finish until gone five in the morning. It was just as bad, if not worse, than the one that had killed Irene.

Mollie was tormented by the thought that Irene had died alone yet, had the tram not stopped, had Mollie been there, she would be dead too, and her children would be motherless. As it was, she'd been left with only the clothes on her back and the coppers in her purse. She thought about the Christmas presents that had been stacked on the piano and the money in an old handbag in the sideboard that she'd been saving towards a holiday next year. But none of these things mattered when she was still alive.

It had been poignant saying goodbye to Tom's brothers and their wives, not knowing when they would see each other again.

She said she'd do her best to get to the wedding of Mike and Lily's son in September, but couldn't promise anything.

Over Christmas, Mollie wasn't allowed to do a single thing except sit in a chair and eat – and drink the occasional sherry. They all went to early Mass on Christmas Day and since they'd returned, the house had been in chaos while the children played with their new toys. As soon as Finn had received the news from Liverpool, he'd gone to Kildare and bought extra presents for her own four, who wouldn't let their mammy out of their sight. Megan insisted on bathing her wrist with warm water several times a day, though Mollie couldn't imagine it doing any good. Brodie kept asking if Dandelion had gone to heaven with Grandma, and was assured, over and over, that this was certainly the case. All Joe did was sit on her knee, and Tommy couldn't stop poking her for some reason. Perhaps he just wanted to make sure she was really there.

The months passed peacefully, without incident, apart from the miraculous return of Dandelion, who everyone had thought was dead. He'd been found wandering along Scotland Road six weeks after the bomb had fallen on Turnpike Street. He must have been out for an evening stroll when the siren went and had hidden in someone's back yard, only to find his home destroyed when he returned.

Fortunately, because his name and address had been written on his collar and nearly everyone in the street had known Irene's three sons, the cat was saved. Mike and Lily had been astounded when a strange man turned up with a tabby cat that looked very much the worse for wear. Dandelion had been despatched to Ireland in a secure cardboard box with holes so he could breathe – the same way, in fact, that he'd gone the other way a decade before except now the box was much bigger. Finn had driven to Dun Laoghaire to collect him. When he'd opened the box, back home, Dandelion had leapt straight into Brodie's arms. At first, he and Bubbles hadn't taken to each other, but the brothers were now on good terms.

Easter came and went and suddenly it was spring. Duneathly burst into life and the trees were full of buds and tiny green leaves. There was the suggestion of blossom on the apple trees in the garden.

By this time, Mollie had found herself a job, spurred on by the fact she hadn't a penny to her name and hardly any clothes. Lily, Pauline, and Gladys, aware of her predicament, had bought her underwear for Christmas, and Hazel and Finn's present was to ask Sinead Larkin to make her a frock. But Mollie had turned down Finn's offer of a weekly allowance; it would have been too much like charity. As it was, Finn bought all her children's needs.

As there wasn't a job of any sort to be had in Duneathly, she travelled to and from Kildare on the bus to work in a bank, adding up figures and preparing statements for someone else to type. It was as boring as a job could be and she hated every minute. The time crawled by, but at least she was paying her way and in a position to buy things for her family and herself.

Gladys and Enoch had a telephone, and Mollie called regularly to ask how everyone was. In May, there'd been a week of air raids that made them wonder if the world had come to an end. 'Parts of town have completely disappeared, Moll,' Gladys said soberly. Almost two thousand people have been killed and no one knew how many were seriously injured. Of all the famous buildings that had been destroyed, Mollie was most upset to learn that the Rotunda had burnt to the ground.

She couldn't quite understand why this news made her feel restless. The very last thing she wanted to experience was another air raid but, at the same time, she felt she was missing out on something.

One morning, a letter arrived from Agatha. Mollie felt more and more guilty as she read it. It appeared her friend had thought she was dead.

'I didn't know Turnpike Street had been bombed until days afterwards,' she wrote:

Phil went to look and said your house had gone. I couldn't believe it, Mollie. For some reason, I kept thinking about the day you got married and I went to the house with my plum bridesmaid's frock, shocking your sisters-in-law no end.

Then the other day I was in Woolworth's and I met Lily. She told me you weren't dead after all and had gone back to live in Ireland. She gave me your address. Oh, Mollie, how could you have gone away without telling me? I know we hadn't seen each other for a while, but we were friends!

With Donnie and Pamela both at school, I felt determined 'to do my bit' and now work on the production line at Garston Electrics where they make wirelesses and walkie-talkies for the Army. The wages are five times as much as I used to earn in the chemist's and the women I'm working with are dead funny. Just think, if you were still in Liverpool we could have worked there together! They're always short of staff.

Phil and the children are very well and I hope this letter finds you the same.

With all my love,
Agatha.

Mollie immediately wrote back. She said she truly had intended writing to say where she was, but had kept forgetting. 'Everything's been so upside-down for the last six months,' she explained, but didn't say that she'd been resentful of her friend having a husband, a nice house, and being able to afford holidays in Blackpool. How small-minded could a person be? She recalled she'd even felt envious of Agatha's new tablecloth!

Agatha's letter had made her feel even more restless. This time she told her sister-in-law how she felt. The women were in the kitchen where Hazel was kneading bread and Mollie rolling out pastry for steak and kidney pies. The kitchen was the place were all their serious conversations were held.

'What do you mean, "restless"?' Hazel asked.

'I really don't know,' Mollie confessed. 'I think I want to do something towards the war.'

'Well, you can't do that in Duneathly.'

'I know that, Hazel, and it's probably why I feel restless.'

'Now we're back where we started. The only way you can do something towards the war is to go back across the water and get a job like Agatha's.'

'But what about the children?'

'I'll look after them, you know I will. I love them and they love me – not as much as they do their mammy,' she added hastily. 'But you left them once before and they managed to get used to it. They'll get used to it again.' She kissed Mollie on the cheek. 'You've been a mother since you were seventeen, Moll. Now you're nearly thirty-three. It's about time you did something for yourself. Before you know it, you'll be too old. You'll be sitting doing your knitting and wondering where the years have gone.'

Mollie furiously attacked the pastry while she considered Hazel's words. Eventually, she laid down the rolling pin. 'I'll ask the children,' she said, 'and see what they have to say about it. If they don't want me to go, then I won't.'

The following night, she took the children into the parlour and told them she wanted to ask their advice. Megan, now fifteen, nodded wisely, as if it were only natural for their mother to seek their guidance from time to time: Brodie appeared surprised; Joe looked worried, and Tommy as if he couldn't care less about anything.

Mollie cleared her throat. 'I want to know if you'd mind if I went to work in Liverpool for a while – I'm not sure for how long. The truth is, I'd like to do war work of some sort. It probably sounds silly, but I actually miss the war. I could come and see you regularly, at least once a month, but more often if you wanted. I'm leaving it to you to decide. If you'd sooner I stayed, then that's what I'll do. The last thing I want is for any of you to be unhappy.'

'But you might get killed like grandma!' Joe burst out.

'The raids have all but stopped, darlin'. There's only been a handful since May and then only little ones.'

'I think we should be left to discuss the matter between ourselves, Mammy,' Megan said importantly. 'Come back in half an hour and we'll let you know our decision.'

'All right,' Mollie said meekly.

She went in the kitchen. 'Irene was right,' she said. 'That Megan is a snooty little so-and-so.' She sat chewing her nails while Hazel made a pot of extra-strong tea to calm her nerves. After half an hour had passed, she returned to the parlour.

Megan had clearly taken charge of the meeting. She coughed importantly and suggested Mollie sit down. 'We think you should go to Liverpool,' she said. 'We all understand that you miss the war, because we miss it a bit, too. Duneathly is nice, but not very exciting. We know you don't like your job in the bank and we want you to have a more interesting one. We'd also like it if you came and saw us once a month, but you must promise to come home for Christmas and write to us every week.'

Mollie nodded. 'I promise faithfully I'll do both.' She looked at her other children. 'Do you all feel the same as Megan?'

'Yes, Mammy,' they chorused. She studied their faces one by one and was quite happy with what she saw. They would miss her, she could tell, but they wanted her to be happy because they loved her. She kissed them and hugged them, then went upstairs to have a good cry.

Two weeks later she set sail for Liverpool.

Chapter 15

1941

Liverpool was where she had spent the best and the worst times of her life. *This* was home, not Duneathly. She caught her breath at the sight of the three buildings that stood like sentinels looking out over the River Mersey in the dusk of a beautiful September day. Two had been damaged in the horrendous May air raids, but still stood, proud and welcoming. The first time she'd seen them had been from the deck of the *Queen Maia*.

She caught a tram to Agatha and Phil's house in West Derby Road where she had arranged to live. Her sisters-in-law had each generously offered a room when they knew she was coming, but Mollie reckoned she was bound to offend the two whose offers she rejected. Staying with Agatha meant there'd be no hurt feelings. Besides, she'd already hurt Agatha's feelings, so it was a way of making up to her for not having written to say she was in Ireland.

Both women cried when they threw their arms around each other. 'Oh, it's so good to see you, Moll,' Agatha sobbed. 'I should've gone to Turnpike Street more often, not always waited for you to come here.'

'And I should have come here more often and not waited for you to come to ours.'

Phil rolled his eyes and said they were making him feel embarrassed, so Mollie threw her arms around the man who'd been Tom's friend and kissed him on both cheeks in order to embarrass him even further, whereupon Phil announced he was going to the pub and hoped they'd both calmed down a bit by the time he came back.

Donnie and Pamela were in bed. Mollie said she'd brought them presents and looked forward to seeing them in the morning. Agatha had kept her a dinner in the oven and after she'd eaten they settled down to a chat about old times and new times. They recalled their wedding days, the films they'd been to see, Mollie's time in Roberta's hat shop and Agatha's in the chemist's.

'I loved working in Roberta's,' Mollie reminisced, 'but not as much as I loved the Rotunda.'

'It burnt down during the May blitz. Did you know?'

'Gladys told me.'

'It was terrible, Moll, the blitz.' Agatha shuddered. 'After the first awful night, Phil took me and the kids to stay with his auntie in Ormskirk. We came back each day to see if the house was all right, and do you know, there'd always be a bottle of milk standing on the step outside. No one stopped working; the milkman and the postman still came, the *Echo* was published, even though the offices were bombed. The people were tremendous, so brave. I was really proud to be a scouser then.'

'I'm almost sorry I missed it,' Mollie murmured.

'Oh, you were best out of it, particularly with the children. It's them you worry about far more than yourself. It was then I decided I had to do my bit and went to work for Garston Electrics. By the way,' she continued, 'I told Mrs Havelock about you – she's the personnel officer – and she'd like you to come for interview the day after tomorrow. I thought you'd like a day to settle in before you thought about work.'

'Thanks, Agatha.' Tomorrow, she'd see about getting a new ration book then have a wander around the shops and look for a frock for Lily's son's wedding. Gerald was getting married the Saturday after next. 'Do you finish early enough to be here for Donnie and Pamela when they come home from school?'

Agatha shook her head. 'Our Blanche's two go to the same school, so she picks them up and gives them their tea and I collect them on the way home from work.' She grinned. 'In return,

I take Blanche's kids all day Sunday while she works as an auxiliary nurse in Smithdown Road hospital. Our Cathy, Dora, and Ellen are all working at something or other and helping each other out, fitting together like a jigsaw puzzle.' She jumped to her feet. 'Come on, I'll show you where you're going to sleep. You know it's in the parlour, don't you?'

'Yes, you said in your letter, but I hope it's not inconveniencing you in any way.'

'Not a bit,' Agatha said easily. 'It's only used on high days and holidays.' She flung open the door. 'I've folded the table and pushed it against the wall and Phil's put two of the chairs in the attic. The sideboard's been emptied so you can use it to keep your clothes in and hang the bigger things behind the door.'

'You didn't buy a new bed, did you?' The single bed had a pretty patchwork cover.

'No, I borrowed it and the bedding from Mam – she's dying to see you, by the way.'

'I'm looking forward to seeing her – and your sisters.' All of a sudden, Mollie felt very emotional, remembering the time when she'd first met the Brophys, only days after she'd lost Annemarie and weeks before she'd found Tom.

Mrs Havelock, a jovial-looking woman of about fifty with a bountiful mop of grey curly hair and enormous breasts, greeted Mollie with a broad smile and waved the application form she'd just completed in her face. 'You're exactly the sort of person we're desperate for, Mrs Ryan. Sit down and make yourself comfortable.'

'Thank you.' Mollie sat on the chair on the other side of the desk.

Mrs Havelock rested her breasts on the desk and folded her arms in front of them. She smiled again. 'We're badly in need of another pair of hands in wages and you sound perfect; you've worked in a bank and the Rotunda box office – I used to go there regularly when I was young – so you're used to handling money and would be perfect for the vacancy. The wages are four pounds, ten shillings and sixpence, and there's always overtime available if you want it.'

Mollie felt intensely disappointed. 'But I was hoping to work on the production line with Agatha Fraser, the woman who told you about me.' There was something faintly romantic about working on a production line during a war and she'd been looking forward to writing and telling the children about it. There was nothing remotely romantic about making up wages.

'But, Mrs Ryan,' Mrs Havelock protested mildly – she was still smiling and knew darned well she was about to get her own way – 'we *need* someone like you in wages, someone who's good with figures. You'd be doing us an immense favour if you took the job. On Fridays, pay day, I have to go in the office myself and help because the staff are so overwhelmed, which means I'm neglecting my own work in the process.' She leaned forward and said in a hushed voice, 'Don't tell Mrs Fraser I said this, but you only need half a brain to work on the production line – and the money isn't quite so good.'

Mollie burst out laughing. 'Oh, all right, I'll take the job, but I have to know something first: can I have Christmas week off? I promised faithfully I'd go to Ireland and see my children.'

'You can indeed,' Mrs Havelock said graciously. She held out her hand. 'Welcome aboard, Mrs Ryan. Now, if you'd like to come with me, I'll ask Mr Parrish to show you the ropes.'

'You want me to start straight away?' She'd intended going back to Bon Marché to buy a frock she'd seen the day before, but supposed it was more sensible to start earning money rather than spending it.

Mrs Havelock didn't answer, just grasped her arm and almost dragged her along to the wages office, as if worried she might escape.

Mr Parrish was a dear little man, almost seventy, with soft silver hair and a pink, babyish face. He had retired from his job at an accountant's five years ago and had been pleased to discover his services were needed again when the war started and there were vacancies galore because so many men and women had joined the Services.

'I felt lonely at home,' he told Mollie, his blue eyes watering slightly. 'My wife, Mary, died in her fifties and we hadn't been blessed with children. It had been our intention to retire to the Scilly Isles – have you ever been there, Mrs Ryan?'

Mollie confessed she hadn't. Not only that, she didn't even know where they were.

'A short boat ride from Land's End,' he told her. 'We were going to buy a cottage there, but Mary's medical care cost so much I can't afford to do it now.'

He was a thorough, conscientious worker, but agonizingly slow, writing with such neat precision that the words almost looked as if they'd been printed on a machine.

There were two other people in the office: Esme Fitzgerald, who'd only been married a fortnight when her soldier husband had been despatched to Hong Kong; and Dolly Birch, who was fifteen and spent a lot of time examining her pretty face in the little mirror she kept in her bag. Dolly went on the odd message, collected the time cards that the workers used to clock in, fetched tea from the trolley that came round twice a day, and disappeared for long periods to chat to her various friends around the factory.

On Friday, Mollie accompanied Mr Parrish to the local Lloyd's bank and they were waiting outside when the doors opened. Apparently, the women took turns to go with him, whether as protection, or to make sure he didn't run away with the money, Mollie wasn't sure. He collected well over a thousand pounds in notes and a bagful of silver and coins to make up the wages. Garston Electrics had 227 employees.

The rest of the day was spent stuffing little brown envelopes with money and a wage slip, and writing the name of the recipient on the outside. At around half past four, Mr Parrish, Esme, and Mollie sailed forth, each with a tray of envelopes, and delivered them individually to each worker in different sections of the factory. A few complained they hadn't been paid enough, that they'd worked forty-six hours and had only been paid for forty-four, for instance. Mollie had been advised to tell them to come to the office on Monday and it would be sorted out.

Although she hadn't expected to, she quite enjoyed her job. She loved Mr Parrish, Esme quickly became a friend, and it was impossible not to like the impossible Dolly.

Something else unexpected was discovering how much she'd missed the Ryans – and how much they seemed to have missed her. Lily and Pauline burst into tears when she turned up for the wedding, and Gladys gave her a hug and said how nice it was to have her back. Tom's brothers kissed her with real affection and she realized she was still as much a part of the Ryan family as she was of the Kennys.

The ceremony was very touching – there was something poignant about two young people getting married in the middle of a war. Barely twenty-one, Gerald was in the Merchant Navy, and his eighteen-year-old bride, Lucy, had nearly been killed in an explosion in the munitions factory in Kirkby where she worked. No one could be sure how long they'd have together in such dangerous times.

Mollie felt a lump come to her throat when the priest pronounced them man and wife. She desperately wished that Irene had been alive to attend her grandson's wedding and welcome a new Mrs Ryan into the family.

Two weeks later she went back to Duneathly. It was Saturday, the children had known what time she was coming and were waiting for her when the bus stopped in the square. Minutes later, she was sitting on the sofa while they piled on top of her, plying her with kisses, stroking her hair, and listening while she described her job, the people she worked with, the wedding, all things she had already told them in her letters, but which they wanted to know again. They were particularly interested in Dolly, whom they seemed to admire enormously; she couldn't think why. Tommy asked if she would bring her to see them next time she came and Mollie said she'd try, but couldn't promise anything.

The weekend flew by and, on Sunday afternoon, she sailed

back to Liverpool, feeling as miserable as sin. But she cheered up as soon as she reached the Pier Head and caught the tram to Agatha's.

This was now the pattern her life would follow. She didn't know how long it would be this way, but she was beginning to enjoy it.

Five days before Christmas, Bobby Gifford flew to New York. Since his last visit, the entire face of the war had changed. Two weeks ago, Japanese aircraft had attacked Pearl Harbor, virtually destroying the American fleet. The full extent of the losses, both of ships and lives, was being kept secret. Days later, Hitler allied himself with the Japanese and declared war on America.

Bobby hadn't been expecting anyone to meet him at the airport. He caught a cab to the Harrington, a small, comfortable hotel on Canal Street; Bill Flanaghan had cabled to say a room had been reserved in his name. As soon as he was shown to his room, he rang Bill to tell him he'd arrived.

'We're having a conference tomorrow,' Bill told him, 'but tonight, you, me, and two other guys on the paper that you haven't met, Ben Overton and Chay Dennis, are having a night on the town. I've got tickets for a show and a table booked at Jerome's Fish Bar afterwards. Until then, your time's your own.'

They arranged to meet in the foyer of the Gaiety Theater on 42nd Street at half past seven. Bobby looked at his watch; just gone four. He knew exactly what he wanted to do in the meantime.

Half an hour later, he was in Bloomingdale's admiring the decorations, listening to the carols being played over the loud-speaker, and looking for a gift for Bill and for Karen, the Swedish girl he'd been going out with for the last six months. He wished there were more people he could buy gifts for. His folks had been dead a long time and he had lost track of his sister during the Depression. It had been a relatively simple matter to discover that his wife was no longer his wife, having divorced him on the grounds of desertion in 1937. She had since re-married.

He had a childish love of Christmas, always had. Until he was twelve, he had stoutly refused to accept that Father Christmas didn't exist. After getting Bill a scarf and Karen some very expensive perfume, he decided to treat himself to a shirt and a couple of ties. He left the shop, looked for a bar, and ordered a whiskey and soda.

Next time he came back, he wondered, would America be shrouded in blackout the same as Britain? Would Hitler, aided by the Japs, bomb the hell out of New York as he'd done London? Washington might well be the capital, but Bobby had always looked upon New York as the hub of the world.

Outside again, he strolled part of the way back towards his hotel. A bitter wind blew, making his eyes water. He was conscious of the bright lights in every window of every shop, the streetlights, the headlights on the stream of passing traffic. A man coming towards him paused to light a cigarette. You couldn't even do that in London without someone yelling, 'Put that bloody light out.' New York without lights was impossible to imagine. There was a song in England: 'When the lights go on again, all over the world . . . '

Bobby sighed and hailed a cab. Back in the hotel, he changed his suit, put on the new shirt and a tie, and made his way to 42nd Street.

The show was a musical – he was glad; he wasn't in the mood for anything heavy – so he shouldn't have been all that surprised when Anne came dancing on to the stage. He caught his breath and leaned forward in his seat. Bill had got them good seats in the front stalls, so they weren't all that far apart; except he could see her and she couldn't see him.

He hadn't forgotten her, he never would, but he thought he'd gotten over her. He reminded himself that there was nothing to get over. More than a decade ago, she'd given him a couple of hamburgers and a coffee. A decade later, they'd spent a day together. Another year later, here he was, watching her dance, listening to her sing, and realizing that she was the woman for him. But hadn't she refused to see him when he'd called to tell her he'd got the job on the paper?

The show was about a pair of hoofers, played by Anne and a guy who appeared to be double-jointed, trying to make their names on Broadway. It was a trite story, but the songs were tuneful and the entire cast threw themselves into their parts with such blazing enthusiasm that Bobby was awed. He wondered if he should go backstage and talk to Anne when the show was over. But what was the point? She'd already made it clear she wanted nothing to do with him. He was just an ordinary Joe with nothing much going for him. She was Anne Murray and could have any guy she wanted. No, he wouldn't go backstage, at least not tonight. Perhaps another night, when he was by himself. He was in New York until after Christmas. He'd still like them to have a talk, and it would give him time to rehearse what to say. It might, just might, be possible to persuade her to change her mind.

Jerome's Fish Bar was on the first floor of an expensive hotel overlooking Times Square, only a short walk from 42nd Street. Bill had booked a table in a part that had windows on three sides so the gaudy lights of the square flickered on and off all around them: adverts for liquor, cars, banks, shows. Tickertape messages flashed across buildings announcing the state of the Stock Market, giving the latest news headlines, and wishing everyone a Merry Christmas.

Ben Overton insisted on ordering a magnum of champagne. 'While we can,' he said darkly. He was a patrician gentleman in his seventies who wrote learned articles on every subject under the sun, though of late had concentrated on the war that had now widened to include America itself. 'Can you get champagne in London, Bobby?'

Bobby confessed he'd never tried. 'Since France fell, there's been a shortage of table wine all over the country. Spirits are hard to get and the bars over there – they call them pubs – often run out of beer.'

Ben shuddered and said it sounded like Prohibition all over again.

The other man present, Chay Dennis, was a good thirty years younger than Ben, and had got the job of Bill's assistant when Bobby had turned it down. He said he understood that beer in Blighty was served without ice. 'It sounds a heathen practice to me,' he said.

'You quickly get used to it,' Bobby assured him.

They ordered the food from a rather sullen waitress – back in London, she'd have been described as someone who'd 'lost a pound and found a sixpence' – and Bill asked Bobby if it would be possible, considering the changed circumstances, to visit France again.

'Anything's possible, Bill, but I wouldn't like to try it now I'm one of the enemy.' He laughed, though there was nothing funny about it. 'If I were stopped, I'd be charged with being a spy. I'd probably be tortured and shot. If they didn't shoot me, I'd end up in a prisoner of war camp.'

Chay leaned across the table and said in a hushed whisper, 'Hey, guys, see who's just come in. Isn't that the girl from the show, Anne Murray?'

Everyone turned to stare, then quickly turned away when they realized how rude it looked, except Bobby whose chair was in a position where he could see the people entering the restaurant, five of them altogether. He recognized the woman in the front as Lizzie, Anne's mother-in-law, followed by Anne in a white fur coat, and three men, one small and stout, one tall and slender with golden-blond hair and foppish good looks, and, bringing up the rear, a very tall young fellow still in his teens.

Ben leaned forward. 'The little tubby guy's Ollie Blinker: he was in cahoots with Mayor Jimmy Walker. He either took backhanders or dished them out; it's a long time ago and I can't remember all the facts. Whatever he did, he got away with it.'

'So did Jimmy Walker,' Bill reminded him. 'His punishment was being sent on a long holiday to Europe. Not every corrupt politician is so lucky.'

Bobby was watching Anne remove her coat and give it to a star-struck waiter. Underneath, she wore a long black dress with narrow shoulder straps. Her skin shone like satin and he could see the colour of her marvellous eyes from here. She sat down, patted the seat beside her, and the teenager took the chair. She stroked his cheek affectionately and he flushed with pleasure.

Could there be anything between them? The kid looked very young, but so did Anne, though she must be going on for thirty. His eyes drifted to the other people on the table. Ollie Blinker was Lizzie's husband and the blond, good-looking guy was almost certainly Herbie. 'We only see each other at Christmas,' she'd told Bobby.

'What do you think about it, Bobby?' Ben asked.

Bobby had totally lost track of the conversation. 'I'm sorry, I wasn't listening.'

'Oh, let him be,' Chay said jokingly. 'He's only got eyes for Anne Murray; hasn't stopped looking at her since she came in. Must be love at first sight.'

Lizzie had noticed him! She waved madly and mouthed 'hello'. Bobby waved back. The other guys looked startled and Chay muttered, 'What the heck!' Then Lizzie said something to Anne, who looked across, saw him, immediately got to her feet, and came over to his table, her long dress swishing against her ankles. She wore shoes that appeared to be made entirely of diamonds on her small feet.

'Why didn't you come to see me as you promised when you got the job on the paper?' she asked in a loud, clear voice. 'I called the paper, but they said you'd gone abroad to England.'

'But I did come to see you.' Bobby's foot became entangled with a leg of his chair when he tried to stand. 'I came exactly when I promised.'

He became aware his three companions had stopped talking and were watching the proceedings with considerable interest, as was the sullen waitress. He said to Anne, 'Let's get out of here.' Taking her arm, he led her out of the restaurant, along a short corridor, and into the hotel bar. There was standing room only, but he found an empty corner, dark and private.

For what must have been an entire minute, they stood looking at each other, neither saying a word. God! She was so beautiful, Bobby thought: strange, but beautiful. He doubted if there was another woman who would have spoken to him the way she just had. She was completely without guile, just said what she thought, regardless of whether it was the right time or the wrong time.

She was the first to speak. 'I've missed you,' she said in a husky voice. 'We were only together a matter of hours, but I've still missed you.'

'I came, Anne, when I promised,' he assured her, 'but the guy on the desk called upstairs and said you didn't want to see me.'

'John was there, that's why, but I expected you to come again. I only didn't want to see you right *then*.'

He didn't try to explain that he couldn't be expected to see into her mind and know exactly how she felt. He merely said, 'Who's John?'

'My son. That was him sitting next to me at the table.' Her eyes shone with pride. 'Would you not agree that he's the most desperately handsome young man in the entire world?'

She'd suddenly acquired an Irish accent. 'I would agree, yes,' he said faintly. Her *son*! That great hulking youth was her *son*! He hadn't thought she'd been married to Herbie long enough to have a child that old and she hadn't mentioned having a son when they'd met before.

'Oh, Bobby!' She slid her slim arms around his neck. 'All sorts of things have happened since we last saw each other. Apart from John, Herbie and I are divorced. Isn't that wonderful? It was him who asked for it. He fell in love with a girl and wanted to marry her straight away. Ollie knows all about these things and arranged for us to get divorced, so Herbie got married, and now the girl wants a divorce.' Her expression sobered. 'Poor old Herbie, he's awfully upset. She was only after his money.'

330

He didn't give a damn about Herbie. 'Does that mean you're single? I mean, you haven't got married again, have you?'

She giggled. 'Of course not, silly, I've been waiting for you all this time. You see, I knew you would come back to me one day, I just knew.'

Bobby gulped. 'Does that mean if I asked you to marry me you'd say yes?'

'Yes,' she said simply, and kissed him.

He had no idea how long they stayed in the dark corner, kissing and making plans for the future, but when they returned to the restaurant everyone had finished eating. Lizzie had appropriated Bobby's chair and was deep in conversation with his colleagues.

'Bobby and I are getting married,' Anne announced in a voice loud enough for the entire room to hear. The other diners looked up from their food and there was a sprinkling of applause. 'We're getting married by special licence on Christmas Eve. Ollie will arrange it for us, won't you, Ollie, darling? There's nothing on earth that Ollie can't do.'

'With pleasure, Anne.' Ollie came over and kissed her, followed by Herbie, then John. Over the next few minutes, it seemed as if the entire room was kissing or shaking hands with each other.

'You take care of her now,' John growled when he shook hands with Bobby. He didn't exactly add, 'or you'll have me to answer to', but Bobby could tell from the look on his face that the threat was there.

'You've no need to worry,' he assured the boy, 'though it'll be you who'll be doing the caring until this crazy war is over. I'm going back to London after Christmas and your mother's staying in New York.'

It wouldn't be a conventional married life, but he wasn't marrying a conventional woman. He couldn't imagine her making him a meal or ironing his shirts. He chuckled, remembering the way his mother used to fuss around his father, insisting he wear a scarf when it was cold, keeping his slippers warm by the fire, taking him tea in bed every morning. With Anne, it'd be him doing the fussing and taking the tea.

It was an hour before both parties left for the Blinkers' apartment where the celebrations would continue. Anne paused by the door, bowing graciously to the people left behind, who laughed and applauded. A man shouted, 'Best of luck, Anne.'

No one noticed her slip something into the hand of one of the waitresses on the way out. If they had, they would probably have wondered why she'd tipped the unpleasant, scowling one, the one who looked as if she'd sooner be anywhere else in the world rather than Jerome's Fish Bar.

The waitress opened her hand: a hundred-dollar bill! Anne had recognized her. Was it from the boat, or from the theatre where she'd been Flip Ungar's girlfriend? Or was it both? For the briefest of seconds, she wanted to run after the girl and throw the bill in her face, but what good would that do? It would only mean other people would be witness to her shame and she'd be without a hundred bucks. Not that there was anything shameful about an actress waiting on tables in between parts. Trouble was, she hadn't had much in the way of parts for nearly five years. She'd thought she'd made it when she took over Anne's role in *Roses are Red*, but she'd only been riding on Flip's coat-tails – he'd told her as much when he'd walked out and shacked up with another dancer.

She went into the nearest bathroom and examined her thirty-four-year-old face in the gold-tinted mirror. It was unlined but, somehow, producers could tell she was no longer young. 'You're too old,' she'd been told bluntly when she'd auditioned for some crummy job in the chorus.

Her hand curled around the bill. A hundred dollars! Maybe it was about time she left New York and started again somewhere new like Hollywood. The weather would be better and she could lie on the beach and get a tan. Thirty-four wasn't all *that* old.

She'd ditch her American accent for a posh English one. Brits did well in Hollywood.

There was a knock on the door and the maître d' shouted, 'Are you in there, Miss Raines?' Without waiting for an answer, he went on, 'You know staff are forbidden to use the residents' bathrooms. You have your own downstairs.'

Olive opened the door and resisted the urge to spit in his snooty French face. 'I'm not staff any more,' she said in her coldest and haughtiest voice. 'I'm a professional actress and I'm on my way to Hollywood.'

Mollie had arrived in Duneathly just in time for tea. 'I'd like to go to Kildare tomorrow or the next day to get some more Christmas presents for the children,' she said to Hazel, who was washing the dishes while she dried. 'I've already got a few bits and pieces, but there's not much of anything to be had in Liverpool – I've got a list of make-up as long as my arm I promised to buy for people.' Lipstick and face powder had virtually disappeared from the shops, as had decent stockings, hairclips, and elastic.

'I'll come with you,' Hazel declared. 'I've bought most of me presents, but it'd be nice to have a day out and I wouldn't mind buying a couple of brassieres. You can't buy anything with a bit of uplift in Duneathly and me breasts have dropped down as far as me waist.' She put a thoughtful finger to her chin. 'I wonder if they could fit me in at Quinlan's for a shampoo and set?'

'Give them a ring first thing in the morning and see,' Mollie suggested.

Hazel finished the dishes, untied her apron and folded it neatly, then placed it on the back of a chair. 'Aren't men lucky?' she remarked, smoothing her hands over her broad hips. 'No one looks at Finn and thinks to themselves, "That boyo's lost his figure, I wonder how many kids he's had?"' Apart from me drooping breasts, I've enough pleats on me belly you could make a skirt from, and me right leg's so full of swollen veins it looks like a map of Ireland.'

'I think you're exaggerating, Hazel.' She was as beautiful as ever, if a bit larger than on the day she'd married Finn.

'Whatever.' Hazel shrugged. 'I'll buy some slap too while we're in Kildare, otherwise people'll start taking me for Finn's mother. There's no need to grin, Mollie. Your Finn's always had an eye for a pretty face. I've never minded him looking, but I don't want him touching.'

Mollie went to bed that night feeling totally at peace with the world. She was home for Christmas as she'd promised: Megan and Brodie were asleep in the bedroom on one side of her, and Joe and Tommy in the other. Tommy, of all people, had asked her to read him a bedtime story. She hoped he wasn't missing her.

The festivities here would be very different to those in Liverpool. Garston Electrics were having a dance in the canteen on the day before Christmas Eve, she'd been invited to loads of parties, and virtually everyone she knew had asked her to Christmas dinner, but the only place where she'd wanted to be was with her family.

Tonight, the children had put on a little concert for their parents in the parlour. Eoin had juggled three of his mother's old plates, Sean had played the spoons, Kieran had sung 'Show Me the Way to Go Home' wearing a top hat he'd found in the loft, and Finola and Bernadette had recited a nursery rhyme each. Patrick must have decided he was too old to play a part and acted as master of ceremonies. At that point, he came in to announce there was now an interval and refreshments were available in the kitchen. After a jam tart and a glass of lemonade, the audience had returned to hear Joe tell a very creepy ghost story while Tom supplied sound effects by banging the dustbin lid on the floor several times. Noreen played *Minuet in G* on the piano for Brodie and Kerianne to dance to.

Finally, Megan had sung 'Danny Boy' in a light, sweet voice, and Mollie and Finn had glanced at each other because it had been Annemarie's favourite song and she'd sung it to Mammy when she became ill. 'Well, if that didn't made me feel a whole world better, I don't know what would,' Mammy would say when the song had finished.

It had all been very innocent and charming, particularly when you considered the horrors taking place in other parts of the world.

Finn had opened an office in Kildare where he spent most of his time nowadays. He asked if Hazel and Mollie wanted a lift in to do their Christmas shopping.

'It depends if Hazel can get an appointment at the hairdresser's,' Mollie told him. 'It's possible we might go tomorrow. Anyway, she'd sooner see the children off to school before we leave.' Even Bernadette, who was only four, attended the nursery class at the convent.

'Give us a ring if it's today and we'll meet for lunch,' Finn said, and Mollie promised that she would.

Quinlan's had had a cancellation at midday and could fit Hazel in then, so the women hurriedly caught the little bus that trundled merrily along the narrow lanes and up and down the hills on its way to Kildare. It was a sunny, icy-cold day and the fields and the bare trees glittered with frost.

After Hazel had bought two well-boned brassieres and Mollie a bagful of cosmetics, Hazel disappeared into the hairdresser's and Mollie made her way to her brother's office to arrange meeting for lunch. She hadn't phoned as promised, but couldn't see that it mattered.

So far, she hadn't seen the new office. It was situated over a smart dress shop in Silken Street. Finn must be doing well, she thought, when she entered the reception area with its white walls, thick grey carpet, and comfortable black chairs. A low table held an assortment of magazines, an ashtray, and a little gold bell. Typewriters clattered in the neighbouring room. Mollie jingled the bell and a girl emerged.

'I'd like to see Finn Kenny, please,' Mollie said. 'Say it's his sister.'

'He's gone to lunch, I'm afraid. You'll find him in The Moon and Sixpence or Jock's Place. They're just around the corner from here.'

Mollie thanked her and the girl returned to her office. Before she left she heard a voice, not that of the girl she'd just spoken to, say, 'You eejit, you shouldn't have told her that. You should've said you had no idea where Finn had gone.'

'I didn't think.'

She was still puzzling over the words when she arrived at The Moon and Sixpence, a creaky old pub with the menu written in chalk on a board outside. She went in, did a quick inspection, but there was no sign of her brother. She remembered eating in Jock's Place with Mammy and Annemarie once when they'd come to Kildare to do their Christmas shopping. She was twelve and Annemarie ten, and it had seemed desperately exciting. They'd sat at the back in a booth only big enough for four people. Annemarie had remarked how private it was. 'We could get up to all sorts here and no one would know,' she'd said.

And now, twenty years later, her brother, Finn was getting up to something or other in the same place, possibly in the very same booth, where he was sitting opposite a dark-haired woman, holding both her hands across the table. What worried Mollie more than anything was that the woman wasn't young or more than averagely good-looking, and was modestly dressed in a plain black frock. This wasn't just an office fling, a moment of madness, with Finn, who was going on for forty and more handsome than ever, having his head turned by some young girl. From the way the pair were looking at each other, she could tell that this was serious.

'Hello,' she said loudly to Finn. Then to the woman, even more loudly, 'Hello, I'm Mollie, Finn's sister. I'm in Kildare with Hazel, she's Finn's *wife*, but she's just gone to get her hair done. We're meeting up in about an hour for lunch and I came to ask Finn if he'd like to have his with us.'

The woman immediately got to her feet. 'I'll be seeing you, Finn.' She gave Mollie a little nod and hurried away. Mollie sat in the seat she'd just vacated. 'What's her name?' she asked.

'Yvonne.' Finn licked his lips. The expression on his face was a mixture of shame and annoyance. 'I thought I asked you to telephone if you were coming today?'

'I forgot. We left the house in a rush to catch the bus. I didn't think it was all that important. Where did you meet her?'

'She manages the dress shop below the office,' he replied sullenly.

'How convenient. Is she married? Has she got children?'

'She had a husband once, but they didn't have children.' He had the nerve to glare at her, as if *she* was in the wrong! 'Are you going to tell Hazel?'

The question irritated her. 'Do you really think I would?'

'I suppose not.' He refused to meet her eyes.

Mollie had never had a reason to be so cross with her brother before and the situation felt very odd. 'And I suppose you're going to tell me it's not serious and that Hazel doesn't understand you?'

His reply shocked her. 'It *is* serious and Hazel is the best wife in the world. I love her dearly, but not as much as I love Yvonne.'

A waiter came with steak and chips for Finn and chicken salad for Yvonne. Mollie absentmindedly picked up a piece of chicken and began to eat. Finn didn't touch his food.

'What's brought this on, Finn?' Mollie asked. 'You and Hazel always seemed the happiest couple in the world. You've got eight children, for God's sake.'

'We *are* happy, we were . . . ' He stumbled over the words. 'I didn't mean for this to happen, Moll. I wasn't looking for an affair, but it just did – happen, that is.'

An affair! She took it for granted they'd slept together. The idea of her prim and proper brother having a mistress made her feel funny inside. She did her best to dismiss images of him and Yvonne in bed together. 'Do you realize everyone in your office knows what's going on?' Finn groaned and hid his head in his hands. 'Let's hope none of them sees fit to pass on the news to Hazel because it would kill her.'

'Nothing would kill Hazel. She's as strong as an ox.'

This was said so flippantly that she lost her temper. 'Don't you dare say things like that, Finn Kenny. Hazel's had eight kids and she had to be strong for that, but that doesn't mean she won't crumble to pieces if she finds out you're having an affair.'

'I'm *not* having an affair,' Finn said flatly.

'But you just said—'

'From this moment on, I'm not having an affair. I'll tell Yvonne I can't see her any more. It's over. I've been meaning to finish it for months and now I will.' As he and Yvonne worked in the same building, there was little chance of them not seeing each other again, but Mollie sensed he'd meant what he said and felt relieved.

'That's the best way, Finn,' she said. 'You owe it to Hazel.'

'I know.' He appeared close to tears.

Because he was her brother and she loved him, Mollie wanted to cry, too. She couldn't bear anyone she loved to be unhappy. She leaned across the table and took his face in her hands. 'You'll soon get over her, darlin'. Hazel and the children are the only ones that matter, never forget that.'

She'd collect her sister-in-law from the hairdresser's and tell her Finn was lunching with a client.

Mollie left. Minutes later, Yvonne returned to the table. 'I saw her leave,' she said. 'She seems very nice.'

'She is nice,' Finn mumbled. 'Hazel's nice, my children are nice. The only person who isn't nice is me.'

'And me,' Yvonne said sadly. 'We're sinners, Finn, the worst sort. I wish we had the will to give each other up, but I'll never do it. The only way I'll leave you is if you tell me to go.'

'That I'll never do, my darling girl.' He almost choked on the words. She was older than Hazel, plainer, but there weren't the words in the dictionary to describe how much he loved her. He'd just lied through his teeth to his sister. Yvonne hadn't carried his seed inside her for nine whole months to produce his child, but if she went away he'd die.

Chapter 16

1942

On Christmas Day, the Japanese captured Hong Kong. Esme's husband was taken prisoner. It was a terrible and unexpected defeat for the British. Horrific rumours were beginning to circulate about the cruel and inhuman way the Japanese treated their prisoners of war.

Mollie had no idea what to say to Esme. 'He'll be all right, darlin',' didn't seem enough, and was unlikely to be the truth. She just hugged the girl and didn't say a word.

'We had a gear Christmas,' Esme said tearfully; she lived in Wavertree with her parents and two brothers. 'None of us realized what was going on in Hong Kong. I felt dead ashamed afterwards that I hadn't sensed Peter was in danger.'

'You'd need second sight for that, darlin'. I felt nothing when my own husband was killed.' She'd walked into the house in Allerton expecting Tom to be there, yet he'd been dead for hours.

Esme sniffed. 'Did you have a nice Christmas, Mollie?' she asked politely.

'Lovely,' Mollie replied automatically. But watching Finn being the jovial father and loving husband, wondering if it was nothing but an act, had spoiled what should have been a wonderful holiday. She had genuinely believed her brother when he promised to end his affair with Yvonne, but on the day of the shopping trip to Kildare, she'd come out of Jock's Place and discovered she had mislaid a glove. When she went back to retrieve it, Yvonne was at the table again with Finn. They didn't notice her and she could tell from the expressions on their faces that they only had eyes for each other.

Her glove was lying under the table. It was only an old woollen one. Mollie had left it there.

On New Year's Eve, she stayed in to look after the children while Agatha and Phil went to a party. At first, Agatha wouldn't hear of it. Mollie could come to the party with them and she'd find someone else to babysit the children, but Mollie had insisted she didn't want to go. 'I honestly don't feel like a party,' she said wanly.

'Are you still worried about your brother?' She'd told Agatha about Finn.

'I'll probably never stop worrying.' It wasn't just that: she couldn't stop thinking about Esme and all the other wives whose husbands had been killed or taken prisoner, not just in Hong Kong, but in many other places. It brought back the memory of Tom's death and the anguish and emptiness she'd felt afterwards, and still felt on occasions like New Year's Eve.

Agatha put Pamela to bed before she left, but Donnie, who was ten, stayed up, and he and Mollie played cards, followed by Snakes and Ladders and Ludo. He was a lovely little boy, very smart: Mollie lost more games than she won.

The games over, she made tea for herself and a cup of warm milk for Donnie, who was beginning to look tired. He was almost asleep by the time the milk was finished, so she took him to bed.

'I won't see Mam and Dad until next year,' he chuckled when she tucked him in.

'I know, darlin'. It'll be nineteen forty-two by the time you wake up.' She'd be relieved when the festivities were over and life returned to normal.

The world seemed exceptionally quiet when she returned downstairs. She lifted the curtain a fraction. It was snowing quite heavily. A car passed the house, travelling so slowly it hardly made a sound, the headlights barely showing. The roofs of the houses opposite already had a coating of snow. Shuddering, she let the curtain fall and switched on the wireless. Vera Lynn was singing 'We'll Meet Again'. She hurriedly switched it off, knowing the song would only make her cry.

Impulsively, she went into the hall and was put through to the house in Duneathly. She'd spoken to the children earlier and had promised to telephone after midnight to wish everyone who was awake a Happy New Year.

'It's me,' she said when Hazel answered. 'It sounds like bedlam there. What's going on?'

'Aidan found a fiddler in the pub and brought him home: your Joe and Tommy are playing "Chopsticks" on the piano. There's a game of hide and seek going on upstairs. Not one of the children is in bed, not even Bernadette.' Despite this, Hazel sounded happy. 'Oh, and you know what happened, Moll? Finn took the office staff for a drink in Kildare and was awful late home – he's hardly been back a minute – but he'd bought me a lovely brooch. It's a gold bird with a diamond for an eye. Isn't your brother a marvellous husband?'

'Marvellous,' Mollie agreed. And also one with a guilty conscience. She'd like to bet it was Yvonne he'd been with, not the staff from his office. She rang off, wishing she hadn't rung in the first place. It had only made her feel worse.

She put the light off in the hall and opened the front door. The snow was falling steadily, the flakes as big as golf balls. Someone was trudging along the road towards her. She was about to close the door, when a voice called, 'Is that you, Agatha?' The figure had stopped and was opening the little garden gate. It was a man, she saw when he came closer, a soldier, his khaki uniform made white with snow.

'Agatha and Phil are at a party,' she told him. 'I'm babysitting the children.'

'Ah, it doesn't matter, then. I just thought I'd wish them a Happy New Year.' He turned and walked back towards the gate.

'Where are you going?' she called when he opened the gate to leave.

'Don't know,' he said, shrugging. 'A pub, I suppose. At least it'll be warm.'

'It's warm here and I'll make you some tea, if you like.' She couldn't turn a soldier away on a night like this, particularly not on New Year's Eve. 'Have you come far?' she asked when he entered the house and stamped his boots on the doormat. The snow came off in clumps. 'Take your greatcoat off.'

'It'll make a mess on the floor,' he warned.

'It doesn't matter, it's only lino.' She took the coat into the kitchen and hung it beside the boiler. It had two stripes on the arms meaning he was a corporal. Only the outside felt damp, inside was dry. She put the kettle on and returned to the hall where he was shaking his cap. 'Hang it on that empty hook,' she advised, 'then come and sit by the fire. The kettle won't be long boiling.'

He went into the sitting room and held his hands in front of the fire. 'This looks cosy,' he remarked. He was a tall man, very slim, with dark-blue eyes and brown hair. His lean face had a hungry look and she wondered if it was always like that or because he hadn't had a decent meal in days.

'Agatha and Phil had a delivery of coal just over a week ago and we've had big fires all over Christmas. As from tomorrow, they'll be little ones again.' Fuel was in very short supply. 'How come you know Agatha?' she enquired.

'Phil and I have been friends since we were at school together. My name is Mike Bradley.' His blue eyes narrowed. 'I was best man at their wedding and I'm pretty certain you were there. Your name is Mollie, but I can't remember your surname.'

'Ryan, Mollie Ryan. Agatha wanted me to be matron-of-honour, but I refused. I was eight months pregnant at the time and would have looked ridiculous. I'm afraid I can't remember you. I didn't feel very well that day, but Phil often talks about his friend Mike – you were the first person at his school to go to university.' She could hear the kettle boiling and went to make the tea. 'Have you come far?' she asked again when she brought his tea in the giant mug that Phil used.

342

'The north of Scotland. We were allowed five days and, like a fool, I decided to come home and see my wife.' He rolled his eyes as if to emphasize how foolish he'd been. 'It's taken two days to get here. I've travelled by train and bus, hitched lifts in lorries and cars, walked a bit. Last night I slept in a station waiting room, but when I arrived home, my wife was out.' There was a pause and he continued in a bleak voice, 'I knocked next door in case they knew where she'd gone. There's new people living there and the woman who answered said my wife was out with her husband.'

'I'm so sorry,' Mollie said gently. 'You should have let her know you were coming.'

'I thought about that, but decided not to.' He smiled and the smile was as bleak as his voice. 'You see, I don't trust my wife – she's been unfaithful before – and I was setting her a test: I was a teacher in civvy life, so I suppose I'm used to setting tests. I didn't expect her to be waiting patiently for me to turn up, not on New Year's Eve. I thought she might be at her mother's or with a friend, in which case I intended going to bed and seeing her in the morning.' He paused again and drank some tea. 'I also thought it quite likely she'd be out with another man, though not for him to be actually living there. After I'd spoken to the neighbour, I went upstairs and his clothes were all over the place.'

'What are you going to do?'

He stared into the fire. 'I've asked myself that same question quite a few times since I married Gillian and the answer is always the same – I have no idea.'

'It depends on how much you love her,' Mollie said awkwardly.

He must have been aware of the awkwardness in her voice, because he rolled his eyes again and said, 'I'm sorry. I expect you were having a nice, quiet evening, and I've come bursting in and laid my sad life bare. The truth is, I had a couple of whiskies on the way. I'm usually regarded as taciturn rather than talkative – ask Phil, he'll tell you.'

Mollie laughed. 'I'm actually glad you're here, though for your sake I wish it were for a different reason. Since Donnie went to

343

bed, it's been much too quiet. I was beginning to wish I'd gone to the party with Agatha and Phil.'

'Why didn't you?'

'I wasn't in the mood to have a good time. I'm still not. I'd've gone to the party and made everyone cry with my miserable face.' She made a miserable face and he smiled, a genuine smile this time. 'Are you hungry?' she enquired. 'You *look* hungry. If so, I can put together a meal. There's bits of chicken, half a tin of baked beans, some sprouts already cooked and cold roast potatoes – I've no idea what Agatha was keeping them for. If I put everything in the frying pan we can call it something foreign that you've never had before.'

'My mouth's already watering.' He seemed much less fraught than he'd done at first. 'As my old dad used to say, "Me stomach thinks me throat's been cut." I've had nothing but the odd sandwich since I left Scotland yesterday morning.'

'I won't be long. Put the wireless on, if you want, but keep it low in case it wakes the children.'

'I'd sooner listen to the fire hiss and crackle; it's very soothing.'

In the kitchen, Mollie put a lump of lard in the frying pan and was slicing the potatoes when Mike Bradley appeared in the doorway. 'I've just remembered something: your husband was a policeman and he was murdered. I take it you didn't get married again, otherwise you wouldn't be on your own on New Year's Eve?'

'You're right, I didn't. There's no need for me to be on my own: I have four lovely children who are having a wonderful time in Ireland where I've just spent Christmas, but I decided I wanted to do war work.' The potatoes went in the pan and began to sizzle. She wondered if Brussels sprouts had ever been fried before. 'I came to live with Agatha last September and work in the same factory as she does.'

'Good for you,' he said admiringly. He looked at the food. 'I'm starting to drool. I'd better go away before I embarrass myself.'

Ten minutes later, she gave him the meal along with a bottle of brown sauce, a piece of bread, 'to wipe the plate with', and a slice of Christmas cake for afters. 'It's the oddest Christmas cake you'll ever eat. It's made with marmalade because dried fruit has virtually disappeared from the shops, and it isn't iced. Did you know there is a government order restricting "the placing of sugar on the exterior of any cake after baking"?'

'I didn't know that, no.' He began to tuck into the food. It reminded her of another time she'd watched a man attack a meal with such enthusiasm, but couldn't quite bring the incident to mind, until she recalled it was Zeke Penn in Charlie's – he'd called it a 'diner'. She'd never heard of him again. Each night, Harry Benedict had taken him back to the Adelphi, worried someone would steal his coat. She didn't think about Harry nearly as much as she did Tom, she realized; he'd played a much smaller part in her life.

'Penny for them?' She looked up. Mike had finished eating and the plate had been wiped clean. 'I think I can say without fear of contradiction that that was the best meal I've ever had. My congratulations to the chef.'

She fluttered her eyelashes. 'Thank you.'

He enquired about her children and she told him all about them, then asked what he did in the Army.

'I'm a translator. Why I have to do that in the wilds of Scotland is a mystery to me. I expected to work in London, but the Army have a language section up there. I keep applying for active service, but they keep turning me down. I was a language teacher before the war and can speak French, German, and Spanish, so I suppose I'm more useful to them that way.'

They took turns answering each other's questions. It kept their minds off their own problems. Mollie liked him and guessed he liked her, but there was a distance between them. They'd been thrown together by circumstance and the likelihood was that they would never see each other again after tonight when he was there for her and she for him.

Just before twelve, she turned on the wireless and they listened to Big Ben herald the arrival of the New Year. She hoped he wouldn't feel obliged to kiss her and was relieved when he just nodded and said, 'Happy New Year, Mollie.'

'And the same to you.' She nodded back.

Not long afterwards, Agatha and Phil came home. Phil was delighted to see his old friend and the two men staying up talking after the women had gone to bed – they were due at Garston Electrics that morning.

When Mollie went into the kitchen ready for work, Phil had gone and Agatha was making porridge for the children's breakfast. 'Don't go in the living room,' she whispered. 'Mike's fast asleep on the settee.'

When they returned that night, Mike had left. 'Back to Scotland,' Agatha surmised.

Mollie's life resumed its normal, regular pattern: work, a visit to the pictures at least once a week, and a trip to Duneathly once a month. Every other Saturday afternoon, she met her sisters-in-law in the Kardomah for coffee. Sundays, she took Agatha and Blanche's children to the park while Agatha made the dinner. She had trouble thinking up things to tell the children in her weekly letters, which were beginning to get very repetitive, until one day something happened in the office that enabled her to fill three whole pages.

It was Friday, the busiest day, and Dolly had accompanied Mr Parrish to the bank to collect the wages. Half an hour later, she returned without him.

'I only turned me back a minute,' she said tearfully, 'but when I looked he'd disappeared.'

'With the wages?' an alarmed Mollie enquired.

'Oh, yes, he'd already collected them.'

Mollie had visions of Mr Parrish on his way to the Scilly Isles to buy the cottage he and his late wife had always wanted.

Mrs Havelock was told the news and immediately called the police. When she was questioned, Mollie didn't mention the Scilly Isles and neither did Esme, even if it meant they were protecting a criminal.

Two hours later, Mr Parrish's black attaché case containing the wages was brought into the office by a different policeman. Apparently, the old man had had a dizzy spell outside the bank. Someone had called an ambulance and he'd been taken to hospital.

'He was dead anxious that you should get this,' the policeman said.

'How did Mr Parrish manage to collapse and be taken off in an ambulance when all you did was turn your back a minute?' a furious Mrs Havelock demanded of Dolly, whereupon Dolly confessed she'd been talking to her friend who worked in a sweet shop a few doors away.

'But Mr Parrish knew where I was,' she wept.

'Anyway,' Mollie wrote at the end of her letter, 'I won't be bringing Dolly home to see you because she's been given the sack. Mrs Havelock would have sacked Mr Parrish, too, but he's needed in the office, dizzy spells or no dizzy spells, and from now on, me and Esme are to collect the wages.'

She finished with loads of kisses and a reminder that it would soon be Easter and she would be home for four days.

It was Ash Wednesday, and they'd hardly been in the office an hour when the telephone rang. Esme answered and handed the receiver to Mollie. 'It's for you.'

Mollie took it, expecting the call to be an internal one, someone with a query about their wages. 'Mollie Ryan speaking,' she said crisply. It sounded much friendlier than 'Mrs Ryan'.

'Mammy, it's Brodie.'

It was the first time she'd had a call from Duneathly at work. 'What's wrong, darlin',' she asked fearfully.

'Mammy,' her daughter said breathlessly, 'Uncle Finn's run away and Auntie Hazel's lying on the bed, all still and quiet like. I think she might be dead.'

'Finn's *run* away?'

'Gone away, then.' The young voice shook. 'He told Auntie Hazel he was going this morning before he went to work. He said

347

he was never coming back again. As soon as he closed the door, she screamed and ran upstairs.'

'Dear God!' She felt her blood run cold. 'Is Megan there, darlin'?' Megan would be more capable of dealing with the situation.

'She's gone to school. Everyone's gone. I only came back because I forgot my needlework and it was then I heard Auntie Hazel and Uncle Finn shouting at each other. I didn't like leaving Auntie Hazel on her own, but I don't know what to do,' she finished helplessly.

'Make Auntie Hazel a cup of tea,' Mollie told her, 'and put loads of sugar in it. She's not dead, darlin', I promise. Does anyone come today to help with the cleaning?'

'Not on Wednesday, no.'

Mollie thought hard. 'In that case,' she said eventually, 'telephone one of the women from Hazel's sewing circle – there's a Madge and a Carmel and a Theresa – and ask one of them to come over. You'll find the numbers in the blue book on Finn's desk in his office. I'll be there as soon as I can.'

'All right, Mammy. Shall I go to school or not?'

'It'd be best if you stayed at home today, Brodie, so you'll be there for Auntie Hazel if she needs you.'

She put the telephone down. 'You bastard, Finn,' she whispered. 'How you could have brought yourself to do something like that to Hazel, I shall never know.'

For a while, she sat staring into space, thinking about her sister-in-law, wishing now she'd told her about Yvonne so that Finn's leaving wouldn't have come as such a shock. But if Finn had stopped seeing the woman as he'd promised, it would have only upset her when there'd been no need.

How was this going to affect her own life? Drastically, she supposed. She couldn't just go to Duneathly and stay with Hazel a couple of days. Finn walking out of her life was worse than him dying. It was impossible to imagine how devastated her sister-in-law must be.

She went into Mrs Havelock's office. 'I'm sorry,' she said, 'but there's a family crisis and I have to go away.'

'Will it be for long, Mollie?'

'I'm not really sure.' She had a feeling it was likely to be for ever. Hazel had looked after her own and Mollie's children for long enough. It was time she had a bit of looking after herself.

At first, Hazel appeared to be coping marvellously until Easter Sunday when they all went to Mass and she looked as if she were about to fall apart. It was something she'd expected to do with Finn until one of them died but, from now on, Finn would go to Mass, not just on Easter Sunday, but every other Sunday, with an entirely different woman.

It was on that day that something inside her sister-in-law died: not just her heart, but her spirit. She was incapable of making decisions, she couldn't remember things, and found it hard to use the telephone. There were occasions when she forgot the children's names.

'Why are you still here?' she asked when Mollie had been in Duneathly a week.

'I'm back for good, aren't I, darlin'? I only said I'd be away six months.'

'I can't remember you saying that.'

That was because it wasn't true. Mollie hadn't gone away for any specific length of time, but she knew Hazel would be upset if she thought she'd come back because of her. 'I was getting a bit fed up with Liverpool,' she lied.

'Honest?'

'Honest.' She'd already written to Mrs Havelock to say she wasn't coming back and had asked Agatha if she would please send the clothes she'd left behind.

In the summer Megan turned sixteen. She left the convent and transferred to the Misses O'Mara's Commercial College in Kildare. Both Mollie and Hazel were relieved when it appeared she'd fallen out of love with Patrick. Joe decided he would like to be a farmer when he grew up. He started to work weekends on a farm owned by Matthew Collins, an old friend of Finn's, earning himself quite a bit of pocket money as a result. Brodie wanted to be a ballet dancer and Tommy prayed the war would last until he was eighteen so he could join the Navy.

'I want to drive a submarine,' he told his mother.

'Hi, Bobby? Bobby, this is John. Anne's had a boy. Congratulations – Dad!' He chuckled. For some reason he found it highly amusing that Bobby had become his stepfather.

Thousands of miles away in London, Bobby Gifford's heart gave a huge lurch. Now he was a *real* father. 'Can I speak to her?' he asked.

'She's asleep. The doctor gave her something. She'll call you when she wakes up.'

'Is she all right?'

'She's fine,' John said heartily. 'I don't know why women make such a fuss about having babies. It seemed real easy to me. Oh, here's Christina with Franklin. Hold on a minute. Let's see if he says something. He was screaming fit to bust earlier.' They'd decided to call the baby after the President if it was a boy, and Eleanor after his wife had it been a girl.

Bobby listened intently. A voice said, 'Congratulations, Bobby,' but he took that to be Christina, not Franklin. He thanked Christina, and said, 'He didn't utter a word,' when John came back on the line.

'He's asleep, that's why. Just went out like a light.'

'Is someone playing the piano?'

'Yeah, it's Herbie. He's here with Ollie. They came to be with Anne when she had the baby.'

The Blinkers weren't just a family; they were a tribe. Once you'd joined, you became a member for life. Just because Anne and Herbie were divorced it didn't mean she'd stopped being a Blinker; and by marrying Anne Bobby had become Blinker, too. Franklin was now the youngest member of the tribe.

'What does he weigh?' he enquired. He didn't know why size

should be so important, but people always seemed to quote weights when a baby was born.

John said he had no idea. 'Anne will tell you. Oh, and by the way, she said next time she wants a girl. Will you be in this afternoon?'

It wasn't afternoon in London, but evening. Bobby said nothing on earth would persuade him to move outside the four walls of his apartment until his wife had phoned. 'Give her my love,' he said, 'and kiss Frankie for me.' It would be another three months before he would kiss his son for himself. He was flying to New York for Christmas and had never looked forward to anything quite so much in his entire life.

In November, Mollie was the only one who stayed up to hear the special announcement promised from the BBC. It was midnight by the time Bruce Belfrage, the newsreader, came on to announce triumphantly that British troops had attacked the Germans at El Alamein and the enemy were in full retreat. It was more than two years since the war had started and this was Britain's first victory.

A few days later, Agatha telephoned. 'Listen, Moll,' she said. Mollie listened and could hear church bells ringing in the distance in celebration of the Army's success. After so much time spent in the darkness, a sliver of light had at last appeared on the horizon.

Early in December, Agatha wrote, enclosing a letter addressed to Mollie. 'It's from Mike Bradley,' she wrote. 'Phil recognized his writing.'

Mollie examined the envelope. The writing was large and firm, businesslike, without any of the whirls and curls she was inclined to use herself. She wondered what he had to say to her. His address was written on the back, a place in Scotland she'd never heard of.

She'd thought about him quite a lot in the months – almost twelve – since they'd met, though hadn't expected to. The time they'd spent together had been very pleasant. They'd found a lot to say to each other and she'd begun to wonder – no, hope – that

351

one day she'd see him again. He had a wife, but she'd got the impression the marriage was over.

It appeared, when she opened the letter, that Mike thought more or less the same as she did:

Another New Year's Eve is almost upon us, and I wondered if I came to Liverpool if we could meet: go to a dinner dance, or perhaps a party with Agatha and Phil? I would very much like to meet you again, Mollie. In case you are bothered at the idea of going out with a married man, Gillian and I have agreed to divorce. I understand she would like the 'husband' she was living with to become permanent. Like you, I am Catholic and divorce is strictly forbidden, but I have no idea how I am supposed to stick by Gillian till 'death do us part', when she has found someone else.

The letter went on to describe where he was billeted, the surrounding countryside, which was 'desolate and forbidding', and his longing to play a more active part in the war. He found his present role very boring. 'I don't exactly want to kill a German,' he wrote, 'but so far I haven't even set eyes on one.'

He finished by saying he hadn't forgotten the meal she'd made him: 'I still drool when I think about it. Nor have I forgotten you, Mollie, and I sincerely hope I will see you again very soon. Your friend, Mike.'

Mollie wrote straight away so he would get the letter in good time. She said she hadn't forgotten him, either, and also looked forward to them meeting again, though it couldn't be on New Year's Eve as she was in Ireland. She told him about Hazel and Finn, what her children were up to, what Duneathly was like, and how sometimes she longed to be in Liverpool where everything seemed to be happening.

She went out to post it and hoped it wouldn't be too long before she got a letter back.

Christmas came and went, but it wasn't quite as merry as usual; it was the first the Kenny children had known without their father.

Hazel put on a brave face, but went to bed early on New Year's Eve, unable to stand the thought of seeing in the New Year without a kiss from Finn.

Finn wrote and asked if the children would like to come and see him and Yvonne in Kildare. It was left to Mollie to phone and tell him that every single one had refused. 'Perhaps next Christmas, Finn,' she said. 'By then, they might have got used to the idea of their father walking out on their mother.'

Nineteen forty-three brought more good news. The mighty German Army appeared to be losing ground in Russia. In North Africa, it had retreated as far as Tunisia and the Americans were making advances in the Pacific. As the months passed, it became increasingly obvious that Germany and Japan would lose the war, but that the Allies would take a long time in winning it. It was going to be a slow, agonizing process and millions more lives would inevitably be lost.

At Easter, Megan left commercial college and went to work for a solicitor in Kildare where she made loads of friends. Brodie, fifteen, said she'd also like to go to the same college when she finished school.

'But I thought you wanted to be a ballet dancer?' said a disappointed Mollie.

'I'm not good enough to take it up as a career; the teacher said.'

'Perhaps you'd like to become an actress. There's bound to be an acting school in Dublin.'

'I'd sooner work in an office, Mammy.'

Mollie had thought it was the other way around: that it was children who wanted to do adventurous things and the parents who preferred them to have good, safe jobs.

She saw little of Joe, who spent more time on Matthew Collins's farm than he did at home. Tommy was the only one who didn't want to stay in Duneathly when he left school and was still bent on joining the Navy, even if the war was over by the time he reached eighteen. This was a bit *too* adventurous for

353

his mother, who knew she'd worry herself sick every minute he was away. He was growing more and more like his father, and sometimes she felt he was the only child she had left.

She told this to Mike Bradley in her next letter. She wrote to him every other Monday and he wrote back the Monday in between. Their letters were getting more and more affectionate. She was beginning to wonder if you could fall in love with someone by post. He wrote to say he'd had lots of experience with children, 'but only teaching them. I'd always wanted some of my own. Maybe one day you'll marry again and have more. Think about it, Mollie, and let me know how you feel.'

To please Hazel, she'd joined the sewing circle, a group of ten women who met fortnightly in each other's houses. She'd always liked making things and quite enjoyed the meetings. It was amazing how quickly you became involved in other people's lives. She was soon eager to know if Carmel's daughter was still going out with the disreputable young man from the garage who had tattoos on his arms, or how on earth Theresa's mother-in-law could be persuaded to keep her nose out of the family's business without Theresa killing her in cold blood.

No one talked about the war. A few young men from the poorer families had gone to England to join up, but the war was rarely a topic of conversation in Duneathly. Mollie gleaned most of the news from the BBC. She ordered the *Sunday Times* from the post office, though it often arrived days late. It didn't seem to have crossed anyone's mind that, if Britain lost the war, Ireland wouldn't be left to continue on its own, that it would become as much a part of Hitler's empire as the rest of Europe.

Summer came and went, and once again autumn was upon them. The nights got darker and the air colder. Thaddy married Ellen and they went to live in Dublin. Megan brought home a young man called Richard for Sunday tea. Hazel's second son, Kieran, who was seventeen, very quiet, and had never done anything remarkable in his entire life, announced his intention of joining the British Army on his next birthday. Finn wrote again to ask if he could see the children at Christmas. This time, Kerianne condescended to see her father, but only on a day when there was not much happening at home.

She went the day after Boxing Day and came back to report that Yvonne was very ill: 'She collapsed in the middle of our dinner and Dad had to call the doctor.'

Hazel worked herself up in a dither. In the New Year, she telephoned Finn to ask if there was anything she could do. Finn burst into tears and said all anyone could do was pray because Yvonne had an incurable brain tumour.

May 1945

It was a beautiful morning. The last of the children had just left for school and the sun poured through the windows of the Doctor's house, making the roses on the parlour carpet look almost real. In the kitchen, the wireless was on very loud and a woman was singing. She had a lovely voice: soft and whispery. '*Oh, Danny boy, the pipes the pipes are calling, from glen to glen and down the mountain side . . .* ' she sang. Her voice drifted throughout the house. There was something comforting about it. Mollie imagined it floating up the stairs like a whiff of smoke, curling against the walls and the ceilings.

She was shaking the cushions on the settee in the parlour. It was used by so many courting couples that Hazel had had to draw up a rota. Last night had been Megan and Richard's turn. They were engaged and getting married next year on Megan's nineteenth birthday.

' . . . *the summer's gone and all the flowers are dying, 'tis you 'tis you must go and I must bide . . .* '

Glancing in the mirror over the fireplace, she wished she'd washed her hair before leaving for Liverpool in an hour's time to stay with Agatha, but it was too late now.

' . . . *But come ye back when summer's in the meadow . . .* '

The door squeaked when Finn came out of his office and she

wondered how many times he'd have to be reminded before he oiled it. Yvonne had died in his arms a year ago and he'd returned to live with his family a few months later. Hazel's heart was the biggest and kindest in the world. Mollie wasn't sure if she would have had him back.

'*Or when the valley's hushed and white with snow . . .* '

She sat on the settee clutching a cushion to her chest. The other day, Hitler had killed himself. The day after, Berlin had fallen. Any minute now, an official announcement was expected to say the war was over at last. It was the reason the wireless was on so loud, so they wouldn't miss it. Finn and Hazel were anxious to know because Kieran was serving in Burma. Mollie would celebrate Victory in Europe in Liverpool with Agatha and the Ryans. She wouldn't have missed it for the world.

In her pocket was the latest letter from Mike Bradley. He'd managed to persuade 'the top brass', as he called them, to send him to Italy where he'd fought with the Army all the way to Berlin. Pretty soon, they would see each other again and decide if they wanted to marry. Mollie wasn't sure how she felt.

' . . . *'tis I'll be here in sunshine or in shadow . . .* '

She went into the kitchen. Hazel was sitting at the table looking thoughtful. Finn leaned against the sink, his chin sunk into his chest. No one spoke or looked at each other.

'*Oh Danny boy, oh Danny boy, I love you so.*'

The song finished and the announcer said, 'That delightful voice belonged to the great American Broadway star, Anne Murray, who has just arrived in London from Berlin where she has been entertaining the troops. The next record . . . '

Finn turned the wireless off. He'd gone very pale and his voice shook slightly. 'That was Annemarie. I recognized her voice straight away.'

'So did I.' Mollie put her hands to her cheeks as if that would somehow lessen the beating of her heart. So, it hadn't just been her imagination.

Hazel nodded. 'Anne Murray – Annemarie; they're very similar. "The great American Broadway star," the man said.'

They looked at each other. Could it really be *their* Annemarie?

Finn said, 'How can we get in touch with her? Where will she be staying, I wonder?'

'At one of the best hotels, I expect,' said Hazel. '"The great American Broadway star", if you please! You could ring them, one by one, and ask if she's there, except we don't know the names and we haven't got an English directory.'

'There's the Ritz, the Savoy, the Dorchester.' Mollie ticked them off on her fingers – the names were sometimes mentioned in the *Sunday Times*. They were the only ones she knew. All three went into Finn's office where the cats lay fast asleep on the window-sill; they did little else but sleep nowadays. 'Nona in the post office will have an English directory. I'll ask her to find the number of the Ritz first. If Annemarie's not there, we'll try the others. As a last resort, we could always ask the BBC if they know where she is.'

Nona promised to look for the number and call them back when she got through, leaving them to sit around the desk staring at the telephone and willing it to ring. No one spoke. Dandelion woke and lazily stretched his front legs, purring briefly, before going to sleep again. The sounds outside – the occasional car, a bicycle bell, people talking – seemed exceptionally loud and the sun exceptionally hot. Finn tapped his fingers impatiently on the desk, Hazel twiddled her thumbs. Mollie listened to the beating of her heart.

The telephone rang, making them jump: it was the Ritz. Mollie's voice shook as she explained what she wanted to a woman who said she was only on the switchboard and would transfer the call to the desk. Mollie explained again.

'We are not allowed to give out information concerning our guests,' she was coldly informed. Did that mean that Annemarie was actually there?

'But I'm Anne Murray's sister and I'm calling from Ireland,' she protested. 'I only want to know if she's staying with you.'

'Not until Thursday.' The owner of the voice must have relented and his voice was less cold. 'Until then, she's entertaining

357

at American bases, I've no idea where. Her family are already staying with us: her husband and children and an older woman we take to be her mother or mother-in-law.'

Mollie thanked him fulsomely. She put down the phone. 'First time lucky,' she said before giving Finn and Hazel the gist of the conversation.

'Her family! *We're* her family,' Finn spluttered. 'What day is it today?'

'Tuesday.'

'Will she come and see us, do you think?' Hazel asked.

'I doubt it, not if she thinks the Doctor will be here,' Mollie said. 'I think *we* should go and see *her*. I'm off to Liverpool any minute. I can get a train to London first thing on Thursday morning.'

'I'll go to Liverpool tomorrow and stay in a hotel and we'll go to London together,' Finn said. 'She must have realized the worry she caused us, yet all she had to do was write and say she was safe. The first thing I'll do when we meet is give her a piece of my mind.'

Hazel's eyes blazed. 'You will do no such thing, Finn Kenny,' she shouted – it was rare for Hazel to shout. 'We haven't the faintest idea what happened to Annemarie when she got to New York. She was ill, we already knew that: she might not have known who or where she was, the poor wee girl. She might have been worried the Doctor would come searching for her. She doesn't know the bastard's dead, does she? If you are thick enough and stupid enough to give her a piece of your mind, Finn, then I shall never speak to you again for as long as I live.'

At this, a shocked Finn mumbled something about it being a mad idea and he was surprised he'd ever thought of it.

Mollie would far sooner have met Annemarie on her own – after all, she'd lost her and she'd have liked to be the first to find her – but Annemarie was as much Finn's sister as she was hers.

The boat docked in Liverpool at three o'clock and she went straight to Agatha's house. 'Has there been an announcement that the war is officially over?' she asked as she embraced her friend. Although Agatha was, like Mollie, approaching thirty-seven, her frizzy hair was already beginning to turn grey at the front.

'Not yet.' She grimaced. 'I don't know why. After all, we *know* it's over, but it won't *feel* over until the government confirms it.'

The children, Donnie, now thirteen, and Pamela, eleven, came home from school, both wanting to know if the war had ended. 'Our teacher said it has,' Donnie claimed.

'It *has*.' Agatha grimaced again. 'We're just waiting to hear it from the horse's mouth.'

After they'd had their tea, Mollie asked Agatha if she would mind if she went for a walk. 'I feel restless,' she explained. 'It's because of Annemarie.' She'd already told Agatha of hearing her sister sing on the wireless that morning and going with Finn to London on Thursday to meet her face to face. 'It's over twenty years since we last saw her. The man on the wireless said she was a great Broadway star.' She was half dreading the meeting. What would Annemarie be like after all this time? She might not want anything to do with her old family again.

Agatha said she didn't mind at all, so Mollie walked a little way along West Derby Road, still feeling restless. Impulsively, she jumped on a tram and returned to the Pier Head, where she sat on a bench staring at the waters of the Mersey that shone like polished pewter under the warm May sun. It made her feel a little calmer, though didn't stop her re-living, as she had done a thousand times before, the sight of the *Queen Maia* sailing away with her sister on board.

'Whereabouts on this map are we?' Anne enquired.

'Here.' Major Murphy, the entertainments officer, pointed to a red dot on the left of the map. He was a handsome man, thirtyish, with a thick thatch of red hair. 'Burtonwood. I must say,' he added in an awed voice, 'I really appreciate you coming all this way to entertain us. We've had stars come before, but none as famous as you, Miss Murray. The big stars usually visit the American bases on the east coast.' He indicated the area on the right of the map that was littered with red dots. 'They're not too far from London. As you can see, we're what the English call "out in the sticks".'

Anne gave him a dazzling smile. 'I have an ulterior motive, Major. My son is stationed at this base, Lieutenant John Zarian. He's a pilot. I would very much like to see him.'

The Major's draw dropped. 'If you don't mind my saying, you don't look old enough to have a son in the forces, Miss Murray.'

'I must be older than I look, Major – oh, and please call me Anne.'

'Only if you call me Sean.'

'Agreed. Sean Murphy is a good old Irish name.'

'My late grandparents emigrated from Ireland towards the end of the last century. Since I've been here, I've gone to Liverpool a few times to see where they sailed from. It's a funny feeling, treading the same ground as they did half a century ago.' He picked up the telephone. 'Pardon me, while I get someone to fetch your son. Does he know you're here?'

'We spoke on the telephone last night.' Anne studied the map while he barked out an order.

'Liverpool isn't far from here?' she asked when he'd finished.

'Hardly any distance at all.'

'*I* sailed from Liverpool,' she said, 'but it was only twenty years ago.'

'Are you English?' She'd surprised him again.

'Irish. My name then was Annemarie Kenny. Would it be possible for John to take me to Liverpool today?'

'Of course. There's plenty of time. He can borrow a jeep. Tonight's concert doesn't start until eight, you're on last.' He studied his watch. 'It's only four o'clock. There's a party afterwards. All the top brass will be there. General Glazer is anxious to meet you; apparently he saw you dance on Broadway once when he visited New York.'

'I won't be dancing tonight, just singing,' she warned him. 'I've had two children and I'm not exactly in tip-top condition.'

'You look in tip-top condition to me,' he said, blushing slightly.

'Well, I'm not,' Anne said bluntly.

There was a knock on the door and a soldier in urgent need of a shave entered. 'Lieutenant Zarian to see you, Major.'

'Send him in, Petrov. Oh, and arrange for a jeep outside my office pronto, please.'

'Yes, Major.'

Anne watched, smiling, as John marched in, looking incredibly smart in his khaki uniform, and saluted the Major, who said, 'You've got a visitor, Zarian. I don't suppose it's a surprise.'

'No, sir.' He grinned. 'Hiya, Mom.'

'Hello, John.' Her eyes twinkled. 'You're going to drive me to Liverpool. Major Murphy has given us permission.'

'Do you know which dock you sailed from, ma'am?' the Major enquired.

'I've no idea. I was seasick on the ferry from Ireland and the time I spent in Liverpool is a complete blur, as is the journey to New York.'

'Take your mom to the Pier Head, son, let her see the River Mersey. It's the next best thing.'

'Yes, sir.'

There was a knock and Petrov came in to announce there was a jeep on its way.

'Thank you. Have you shaved today, Petrov?'

'Yes, Major, but I've told you before, I need to shave two or three times a day. I have a very heavy growth, sir.'

'You have my permission to desert your post, return to your billet, and shave again. That's a disgraceful way to present yourself in front of a lady.'

'I'm deeply apologetic, Major.' Petrov saluted.

'I don't mind a bit,' Anne said when the door closed.

'I didn't think you would. It's just a joke Petrov and I have between us. Ah, I think I hear a jeep outside.'

Minutes later, the Major watched through the window and saw Anne Murray laugh and fling her arms around her son. He picked her up and swung her around a few times, before setting her down and kissing her on both cheeks. Jeez! She sure was a looker. Those eyes! He'd never seen eyes like them before or such creamy skin and luscious hair. She wore a pale lemon frock that really showed off her neatly curvaceous figure. He tried to imagine having a mom like that, but found it was impossible.

'Less of the "Mom", if you don't mind,' Anne said when they set off.

'I didn't like calling you Anne in front of the Major.'

'I didn't like calling him Sean in front of you. Has peace broken out yet?' she asked.

'Not officially, but the guys have been celebrating all day. The Brits have what's called a Ministry of Information, but it prefers to keep all the information to itself.' He ruffled her hair. 'I've missed you.'

'And I've missed you – terribly, awfully, horribly.' As if words weren't enough, she put her hands over her heart to emphasize them.

'How's my baby brother and sister?'

'Frankie and Eleanor are fine. Bobby and I think we'll start calling her Ellie.'

'Ellie's swell,' John said with a happy sigh. Anne could tell he was as pleased to see her as she was him.

'Are you likely to get time off to come to London?' she asked. 'Bobby's moved into the hotel with the children and Lizzie. Everyone's aching to see you. Lizzie's going to visit her relatives in Manchester at the weekend.' She still looked upon Lizzie as her mother-in-law.

'Ask the Major for me if I can have leave. If the soppy look on his face is anything to go by, I reckon you charmed his socks off and he'll let me have a whole week.'

'I'll ask him tonight.' Anne stared at the rather featureless countryside. 'Where are we? Do you know the way to Liverpool?'

'No, I'll just follow the road signs,' he said confidently.

'I've been looking and there aren't any.'

'Damn!' He slapped the steering wheel. 'I've just remembered, the Brits took them down for some reason. I'll just have to stop and ask people.'

They lapsed into a companionable silence. She'd been devastated, yet very proud, when, two years ago, he'd volunteered to join the Army-Air Force without waiting to be called up. It was a big relief when he was posted to Britain rather than the Far East where the war had yet to end and where thousands of young Americans had died at the hands of the Japanese, one of them her very dear friend, Zeke Penn, who'd returned to defend his country as soon as the war had started.

John stopped and asked a man wearing a flat cap and overalls the way to Liverpool. 'It sounds quite straightforward,' he said when he got back in the jeep.

It seemed no time before they were entering the outskirts of the city where the houses were mainly new. They passed tramcars gliding along the middle of the road, which Anne found quite fascinating. 'I'd love to go for a ride on one of those,' she said excitedly.

'There won't be time, I'm afraid,' John told her.

'Spoil-sport,' she said, sticking out her tongue, though she knew he was right. 'What happened there?' she cried. 'Has there been an accident?' They'd reached the old part of the city, where a row of houses was little more than a heap of rubble.

'It must be where a bomb dropped. Liverpool was one of the most heavily bombed cities in the country.'

'Look, there's more. Oh, John, that's terrible.' She felt deeply distressed and suddenly wished she hadn't come.

'Would you like us to turn back?'

'No, no, of course not.' That would be cowardly. The people of Liverpool had had to put up with the bombs: all she had to do was witness the result.

In the centre of the city, there were whole tracts that were nothing but wasteland. It was a relief when they arrived at a wide open space where a vast expanse of water glittered at the far side.

John said, 'This is the Pier Head and that's the River Mersey behind it. I'll find a place to park the jeep and we can go for a walk.'

'Can I get out?' she asked.

'Yes, but don't move from the spot,' he said sternly. 'I don't want to lose you.'

She promised faithfully to stay put. John drove away and she stood on the pavement in front of a large, elegant building, looking around her, taking everything in. A group of young women walked by singing at the top of their voices, 'When the lights go on again, all over the world.' The celebrations in Liverpool had begun.

There were quite a few people about and they all looked so happy. She sang with the girls under her breath. A man came up smelling strongly of beer. 'Congratulations, luv,' he said, shaking her hand.

She smiled. 'The same to you.' She had no idea what they were congratulating each other about. Tramcars whizzed by. The driver of one had a garland of silver tinsel around his neck. He waved at her and grinned. Anne waved back.

The atmosphere was getting to her. She could feel herself glowing inside, just as she did when she was about to go on stage. She wanted to fling out her arms and dance up and down the pavement, and had actually taken a few steps when she noticed the woman sitting on a bench far away across the wide road. She was sitting very still facing the silvery river. Anne stopped dancing and stared at the back of the woman's head. She had no idea who she was, but felt as if an invisible cord had been thrown around her, drawing her towards this strange woman.

She stepped off the pavement, regardless of the traffic and began to walk, began to run, between the tramcars and the cars that careered busily to and fro. Brakes screeched, people shouted, but Anne ignored them. She was being pulled by the invisible cord and felt perfectly safe.

Then she was on the other side of the road, where the river shone even more brightly. A large ship was sailing across the water and people on board were waving flags. The woman was only ten feet away, five feet, and now Anne was standing in front of her. She looked terribly sad, the woman, and Anne knew straight away why she'd felt so drawn to her.

'Mollie,' she said quietly, and the woman raised her eyes, stared at her blankly for a minute until recognition dawned, and her face was transformed by a smile so sweet and lovely that Anne burst into tears.

'Annemarie! Oh, Annemarie, I thought I was seeing things. Is it you? Is it really you?' And now Mollie was crying and holding her lost sister in her arms. 'Did you just drop down from heaven or something?'

'No, no. Were you here waiting for me?' Annemarie sobbed.

'I must have been, darlin', mustn't I?' She broke away and gave Annemarie a little shake as if to reassure herself she was really there. 'We were all so worried about you. I wanted to die when Aunt Maggie wrote and said you hadn't turned up in New York. Our Finn actually went all the way there to search for you. Have you been all right, darlin'? What happened? I've never stopped wondering what happened when you arrived there all on your own.'

'I didn't know who I was, Moll,' Annemarried explained. 'Lev found me and took me to his heart.' It was only now, twenty years later, that she wondered why Lev hadn't tried to find out where she really belonged. Perhaps he'd loved her straight away and didn't want them to be parted.

'Lev?'

'Levon Zarian. He's dead now, but he was the dearest and most wonderful man who ever lived.' Annemarie shed more tears for Lev. '*I had a daughter very like you,*' he'd said when she got into his cab.

'Yours till the stars lose their glory,' the passengers on the boat sang as they waved their flags.

'You're so beautiful, darlin'.' Mollie stroked her face. 'More beautiful than ever.'

'And so are you, Moll.' Mollie's beauty wasn't showy like hers, but quiet and gentle. Goodness shone from her steady brown eyes.

'We knew you were in England, the man on the wireless said so this morning. On Thursday, me and Finn were coming to see you at your hotel in London. Oh, but fancy finding you here, darlin',' Mollie cried joyfully. 'If that's not a miracle, I don't know what is. Will you have the time to come back to Duneathly and meet everyone? Hazel and Finn have eight children and I have four, Thaddy and Aidan will be longing to see you.'

Annemarie felt the hairs go stiff on her neck. 'But what about the Doctor?'

'He passed away,' Mollie said soberly, and a shadow fell over her eyes. 'He died a long time ago.'

'Then I'll come back: we all will.' She caught her breath at the idea of going back to Duneathly with Bobby and her children – and Lizzie, if she wanted to come. She couldn't think of anything that would make her happier.

'I thought I'd lost you,' said a voice. They both turned and there was John, flushed and concerned. He managed to smile at them both. 'Who's this, Anne?' he asked.

'This is Mollie; she's your aunt.' She was also his sister, but this was neither the time nor place to reveal something like that. 'Oh, Moll,' she cried. 'I've so much to tell you.'

Epilogue

On her thirty-fifth birthday, Olive had vowed that if she'd got nowhere by the time she was forty she'd give up show business, though would stay in Hollywood. She loved everything about the place: the heat, the outsize flowers, the unnaturally green grass and the fact that no matter what time of day or night it was there were always people about. She had another seventeen and a half months to go. In January 1947 she would reach the big four-O.

Hollywood hadn't turned out to be a total failure. However, if the scales were weighted with the successes at one end and the failures at the other, the latter would outweigh the former with a loud clunk.

These thoughts passed through her head, as they so often did, while she waited in line for yet another audition.

'Next!' the secretary shouted from behind her desk at the far end of the room.

The spectacularly lovely blonde next to Olive rose to her feet and swayed out of the room into the studio beyond. Olive was old enough to be her mother – she was becoming obsessed with people's ages. But what chance did she stand against a girl like that?

The secretary singled Olive out for a dazzling smile. *She* was old enough to be Olive's mother. Was it a smile of pity? Did she realize Olive didn't stand a chance in hell of getting the part and the smile was just her way of softening the blow?

She was auditioning for a film called *Smiles Apart*. Her agent had phoned early that morning. 'RKO want someone who can do an English accent,' Jonesy had said. 'It's a musical. You have to be able to sing and dance.'

Olive had called the restaurant where she worked and told the manager she wasn't coming in. He didn't mind. He'd gotten used to it. Virtually every waitress in Hollywood had ambitions to become a movie star. Trouble was, most were half Olive's age, as were the girls she shared the house with in Burbank, all budding actresses. She'd lived there since coming from New York and had lost count of the women who'd come and gone since then. They'd left to get married, go back home, or do something different with their lives. Only three had got anywhere in the film industry and then not very far.

A few times a year Olive managed to get a small part in a movie. Twice she'd even had a few lines to speak. The longest time she'd spent on screen was just over two minutes. But nowhere in Hollywood had a producer or director spotted Rosalind Raines and shouted, '*I must have that girl for my next movie!*'

The blonde returned. She looked disappointed. The secretary shouted, 'Next,' and another woman left the room. She was a spectacularly lovely brunette even younger than the blonde. It struck Olive that the auditions were taking a very short time. There'd been about twenty girls there when she'd arrived. She'd hardly been there thirty minutes and half had gone. Another five had come since.

The secretary flashed Olive another smile. She smiled back. It was prudent to keep in people's good books. The woman might do her a favour one day. She was tall and silver-haired, smartly dressed in trousers and a white blouse. Olive wouldn't be surprised if she hadn't had acting aspirations herself at one time.

Perhaps it was getting old, but these days Olive yearned for a place of her own. The smallest apartment would do, as long as it had a balcony so she could sit outside in the sun. Mind you, a garden – a yard – would be even better. She was fed up sharing a kitchen and bathroom with six other women. They even had a communal lounge. There'd be a fight over what to watch on television almost every night. The idea of having a bathroom to herself was sheer bliss.

To achieve this, she'd need more than the occasional movie part with temporary jobs in between. She'd need regular work. She might take a course and become a beautician or a hairdresser. It would be a big disappointment, but there was a limit to how long and how hard she could aim for the top – or even halfway there.

The brunette returned and another blonde went in her place. Yet again, the secretary smiled at Olive. The blonde came back and it was the turn of a beautiful, willowy redhead. The girls seemed to be going in and out like figures on one of those foreign clocks. When it came to Olive's turn, the secretary went with her to the door.

'What this movie's about, honey,' she said in a low voice, 'is the male lead discovers he has a twin sister in England. They were separated at birth. As he'd going on for forty, the audience would have a big laugh if his twin turned out to be half his age. I told the agencies we wanted older women, but they insist on sending us the kids in the hope we'll be so impressed we'll change our minds.' She gave Olive another smile; an encouraging one this time. 'It's a really important part and you'd be perfect for it, though you'll probably have to dye your hair blonde same as your twin.'

'I wouldn't mind.' She'd dye her hair blue if it meant getting an important part. Excitement began to course through her veins. It was a long time since that had happened. Neverending rejections, snubs, insults, and indifference had worn her down. Without her realizing, a streak of hopelessness had set in.

The secretary squeezed her hand and murmured, 'Good luck, honey.'

Olive entered the vast studio. The remains of what had been a Roman temple covered half the space. Three guys were sitting by one of the plaster pillars. They were chatting together and didn't look up. A bored-looking woman wearing a man's white trilby sat at an ancient grand piano.

Olive handed over her music. 'Play it once slow, and once again fast,' she instructed. 'Thank you,' she added, remembering to smile. An uncooperative pianist could kill an audition if the mood took them.

She coughed and, in her best English accent, gave her name and announced she was about to sing and dance to 'I'm Old Fashioned' from the movie *You Were Never Lovelier*. The men looked up and one, a little tubby guy, nodded for her to begin.

So Olive began to sing. After a few notes, she just knew that she didn't want to become a beautician or a hairdresser. She'd wanted to make it in show business for as long as she could remember. The thought had given her heart when she was still a kid and already selling herself on the London streets. The same thought spurred her on now, giving strength to her voice and possibly a touch of desperation.

It was the same when she danced. She'd kept herself fit and still attended dance practice once a fortnight. She found herself smiling as she twirled to a halt after a couple of perfect cartwheels. After twenty years in the business she didn't think she'd ever danced so well.

She bowed, only slightly out of breath, and said, 'Thank you.' It was odd, but right then she didn't care whether she got the part or not. There'd be plenty of others she could try for. One of these days she'd make it, she could feel it in her bones.

The little tubby guy said, 'Thank *you*, Miss Raines. Wait there just a minute.' He turned to the other men. Olive hadn't looked at them properly before. The blond-haired handsome guy looked familiar. She'd seen him before a long time ago – it must have been in New York. Then the tubby one stood up and came towards, his face bearing a wide grin and his hand extended to shake hers.

She'd got it! And of course she cared. She cared more than she'd cared about anything before. Her head swam and she had a horrible feeling she was going to faint.

'Welcome aboard, Miss Raines.' They shook hands. The other two guys strolled towards her. One introduced himself as Abe

Collins and said he would be directing *Smiles Apart*. The blonde-haired one looked even more handsome close up: like Olive, he had a few crinkles around his eyes. She remembered then who he was.

'Hi, Rosalind.' He shook her hand. Olive had read about people going weak at the knees, but it had never happened to her. As she told him much, much later, she'd fallen in love with him there and then. 'I'm Herbie Blinker,' he said, 'and I'm sure we're going to get along just fine.'